D1044286

MORE MYSTERIES FROM THE
BERKLEY PUBLISHING GROUP . . .

CHINA BAYLES MYSTERIES: She left the big city to run an herb shop in Pecan Springs, Texas. But murder can happen anywhere . . . "A wonderful character!"
—*Mostly Murder*

by Susan Wittig Albert

THYME OF DEATH	WITCHES' BANE
HANGMAN'S ROOT	ROSEMARY REMEMBERED

KATE JASPER MYSTERIES: Even in sunny California, there are cold-blooded killers . . . "This series is a treasure!"   —Carolyn G. Hart

by Jaqueline Girdner

ADJUSTED TO DEATH	MURDER MOST MELLOW
THE LAST RESORT	FAT-FREE AND FATAL
TEA-TOTALLY DEAD	A STIFF CRITIQUE
MOST LIKELY TO DIE	

LIZ WAREHAM MYSTERIES: In the world of public relations, crime can be a real career-killer . . . "Readers will enjoy feisty Liz!"—*Publishers Weekly*

by Carol Brennan

HEADHUNT	FULL COMMISSION

also by the author

IN THE DARK	CHILL OF SUMMER

BONNIE INDERMILL MYSTERIES: Temp work can be murder, but solving crime is a full-time job . . . "One of detective fiction's most appealing protagonists!"
—*Publishers Weekly*

by Carole Berry

THE DEATH OF A DIFFICULT WOMAN	GOOD NIGHT, SWEET PRINCE
THE LETTER OF THE LAW	THE DEATH OF A DANCING FOOL
THE YEAR OF THE MONKEY	

MARGO SIMON MYSTERIES: She's a reporter for San Diego's public radio station. But her penchant for crime solving means she has to dig up the most private of secrets . . .

by Janice Steinberg

DEATH OF A POSTMODERNIST	DEATH CROSSES THE BORDER
DEATH-FIRES DANCE	

HUNTING GAME

Nancy Herndon

BERKLEY PRIME CRIME, NEW YORK

HUNTING GAME

A Berkley Prime Crime Book / published by arrangement with the author

PRINTING HISTORY
Berkley Prime Crime edition / December 1996

The Putnam Berkley World Wide Web site address is http://www.berkley.com/berkley

ISBN: 0-425-15579-X

Berkley Prime Crime Books are published by The Berkley Publishing Group, 200 Madison Avenue, New York, NY 10016.
The name BERKLEY PRIME CRIME and the BERKLEY PRIME CRIME design are trademarks belonging to Berkley Publishing Corporation.

PRINTED IN THE UNITED STATES OF AMERICA

10 9 8 7 6 5 4 3 2 1

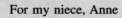

For my niece, Anne

Acknowledgments

I would like to thank my agent, Richard Curtis, my editor, Laura Anne Gilman, the members of my critique group, Elizabeth Fackler, Terry Irvin, Jean Miculka, and especially Joan Coleman, who was so generous with her time and suggestions. For information I used in writing *Hunting Game*, I owe thanks and appreciation to retired garment manufacturer Sam Ellowitz; members of La Mujer Obrera, an advocacy group for women workers in El Paso; and from the El Paso Zoo: Dr. Lea Hutchinson, Director; Dr. Anthony Smith, Assistant Director and Veterinarian; Hector Montes, public and media relations; Robert Nava, the zoo's snake expert; from the elephant staff George Howard, Randy Rakes, and Mando Alarcon; and security guard Jesus Neviz. All were very generous with time and information. At the El Paso Public Library, Librarian Wayne Daniel very kindly ran newspaper index searches for me that provided invaluable references. And as always special thanks to law enforcement officials in El Paso.

N.R.H.

Prologue

Monday, March 27, 5:54 A.M.

In the hour before dawn the night guards at the Los Santos Zoo were stemming a flood in the Reptile House—sealing off the offending pipe, mopping up. At the same time an interloper, black clad, slipped down the path to the elephant enclosure and whistled. Behind him the macaws and parrots stirred and squawked sleepily. The elephant, who welcomed any variation in her routine, appeared in the door of her house and ambled toward the guardrail, puffs of dust rising with each step.

In the darkness the visitor's arm drew back, and a gloved hand hurled a missile over the fence and the dry moat onto the dirt at her feet. Pansy investigated the object with the sensitive tip of her trunk. Then, pleased, she picked it up and stuffed it into her mouth. The interloper smiled and lobbed another pear.

Showing her appreciation, Pansy raised her right foreleg and waggled a thick foot. Then she investigated the second pear and ate it with relish. Four more gifts, two melons and two apples, flew through the air. The melons she crushed daintily before eating. But in each instance Pansy devoured the fruit eagerly and expressed her gratitude with a little trick—a coy crossing of the front legs, the airy extension of the left foreleg and right hind leg.

The visitor bowed to Pansy, then disappeared down the

1

path, keeping to the deep shadow. Past the enclosures of the black bear, the jaguar, and the Mexican wolf, cutting between the wolf den and the administration building to the gazebo. Skirting the parking lot in the shadows. Then down Boone Street on foot, past small houses with iron-grated windows, houses protected by elaborate stone and iron fences, to a pickup truck, which started quietly and sped away toward Alameda, Copia, and Interstate 10, on all of which there was little traffic and no one to remember the passage of a lone pickup.

1
..

Monday, March 27, 9:17 A.M.

Girls were flying in every direction when the first insistent peal of the telephone plucked Elena Jarvis from an exhilarating dream. She had been protecting Michael from a mob of garishly dressed Gypsy pickpockets in front of the Coliseum in Rome while he and three handsome Italian policemen applauded and kissed their fingertips. Because there were still female thieves to be dealt with, Elena opened one eye and stared resentfully at the ringing telephone. Admittedly, it was a silly dream: she'd never been to Italy, had never seen a Gypsy girl, criminal or otherwise, and Michael wasn't the finger-kissing type. Still, she'd been enjoying herself immensely—American Karate Queen abroad in French braid and jeans. She looked at the clock: 9:17 A.M.

The telephone rang again, and Michael stirred beside her. He had returned from Rome the day before, various members of the Herbert Hobart University faculty having taken a spring-break trip to Italy. Michael had invited her, but Elena hadn't had the vacation time, the money, or the inclination to let him pay her way. The mobbed-by-Gypsy-girls story, part of his adventures in Rome, she'd heard secondhand last night.

"You gonna get that?" he mumbled, endearingly sleepy-eyed with tousled brown hair. He hadn't even shaved between the airport, his apartment, and her house, which wasn't as endearing. Stubbled chins reminded her of her ex, Frank the Narc.

3

"Mmmm," she replied. Michael needn't have asked. Police detectives answered their telephones. "Jarvis," she said into the receiver.

"Elena, it's Manny."

She groaned and protested, "I worked the weekend shift, Manny. I'm *off* today."

"I know, but I've got a favor to ask," said her sergeant. "It shouldn't take long, but the zoo director insists there's foul play involved."

"The *zoo* director?" Elena echoed.

"Right," said Sergeant Manny Escobedo. "Pansy went nuts this morning and trampled one of the keepers. In front of a kindergarten class. It's a real mess from the kiddie point of view. Actually, it's a mess from the victim's point of view too. He's dead. Elephant mush."

"I don't think I want to hear about this before breakfast," said Elena.

"'Course, elephants sometimes do that," Manny continued. "It's called running amok."

"Right," said Elena. "Like the ones who stampeded into that mall parking lot in Pennsylvania and sat on a bunch of cars. Some jerk in a pickup truck had honked at them." She was awake now. "Maybe someone honked at Pansy. So what am I supposed to do? Arrest the elephant for involuntary manslaughter?"

"Nobody mentioned honking, but you could look into it. The thing is, Elena, the zoo director insists that Pansy is the world's sweetest elephant and wouldn't hurt anyone. So if you could just go over there, put in an appearance, you know? Calm him down. This is kind of the last straw for the poor guy."

"I take it that Burglary hasn't found his mountain lion or his snake?" Elena asked, grinning. She had a friend on the Burglary Squad who had been assigned that case—the disappearance, on the same night the previous week, of Leopold the mountain lion, and a big albino Mohave rattle-snake named White Fang. Detective Lina Peralta didn't even *want* to find the missing zoo animals; she claimed it wasn't burglary anyway, just carelessness on the part of the keepers.

There had been no sign of forced entry, and no reports of intruders from the security company that patrolled the zoo.

For four days the newspapers had been full of the story, until it was displaced on the front pages by the disappearance of more than sixty 75-pound manhole covers. Cars and kids were falling into the holes, sewer district administrators bemoaning the cost of replacement. That case had been solved quickly. Snakes and mountain lions knew how to hide out—if they had escaped on their own; manhole covers were big, heavy, and immobile, harder to sneak over the border and sell in Mexico, although why anyone would want to buy either a manhole cover or a mountain lion was beyond Elena.

"If the escapees had turned up, I think we'd have heard about it," said Manny dryly. "So will you go see the man?"

"Why me?" Elena muttered.

"Because you're the most diplomatic detective on the squad, hon."

And the detective who was quickest to take offense when called "honey" or "babe," she thought grumpily. In fact, she was the only detective in Crimes Against Persons that anyone called "honey" or "babe." "Oh, Sergeant, sweetie," she drawled in saccharine tones, "you're just sayin' that because Ah'm yo' one an' only li'l lady detective."

Manny laughed. "Pardon me, Detective Jarvis, but I was saying it because anyone who can handle the administrators and cases at H.H.U. ought to find an up-tight zoo director no big deal at all."

Elena thought about her cases at H.H.U.: the exploding snail, the skeleton in the bathtub, the gay poet and his murdered homophobic father, the killer statues. No wonder Manny thought of her when an elephant went nuts.

"Anyway, everyone else is on the street," said Manny. "So be a doll. It's overtime," he added coaxingly.

"Yeah, yeah, overtime." If she'd put in more overtime the last year, like twice as many hours, she'd have had enough money to go to Rome with Michael. "I'll take it," she agreed. "But I hope you're not in any big hurry—like you want me to head straight over there in my nightie without breakfast."

Manny laughed. "I think you got time to change out of your nightgown."

"Thanks." Actually, she wasn't wearing a nightie or any-thing else. She hung up and tossed back the covers.

"Don't tell me you're leaving," said Michael, awake and sounding miffed. "This is your day off. And I just got back."

"Sorry," she replied. "I have to go investigate a death by elephant." Michael tended to get pissed when her job inter-fered with their relationship—one of his few faults.

"Someone killed an elephant?" He propped his head on one hand and watched as she combed out her long black hair.

"No, an elephant killed someone," Elena replied.

"And that's murder?"

"I wouldn't think so," she replied. "Though I don't know what you'd call it exactly. An act of God?"

"Anyone ever tell you that you have a very sexy body?"

Elena grinned, turning from the mirror. "Just about every lech in the department," she replied, "but I've managed to convince most of them to keep their mouths shut."

Elena pulled on underwear, jeans, and a sweatshirt. She'd be damned if she'd get dressed up to go to the zoo. Michael was looking disconcerted, so she added, "You, however, are welcome to say sweet things to me any time you want, Professor Futrell."

The telephone rang again, and she grabbed it, expecting an elephant update from her sergeant.

"Are you in bed with Michael?"

Mark, thought Elena, scowling. He was Michael's twin, an assistant professor of kinesiology at Herbert Hobart, where Michael taught criminology. "Not at the moment," she snapped, resenting his words and his intrusion on their relationship. It wasn't the first time by any means.

"Don't be coy, Detective," said Mark. "Michael isn't at his apartment, and I happen to know he went straight over to your place once he dumped his bags."

"Is this Mark, by any chance?" she asked sarcastically. The jerk couldn't even be bothered to identify himself. As if, because he came on to her every time he got a chance, she'd be sure to recognize his voice.

"Did he give you a good time last night, Detective? You'd have had more fun with me."

"It's your brother," she said to Michael and thrust the

phone at him. "He just said I'd have had more fun in bed with him." She scowled at her lover. "I don't appreciate that kind of crap, Michael."

Michael put his hand over the receiver. "Hey," he said to Elena, "lighten up. The man's a jock. He doesn't mean anything. He's just used to locker-room talk."

"Well, I'm not," said Elena and turned away. Of course, she admitted to herself, that was only partially true. She doubted that squad-room talk was much better than locker-room talk, and she managed to fend off would-be lechers and ignore foul mouths among her fellow officers. Maybe she did need to lighten up where Mark was concerned. Or toughen up. When he said something she didn't like, she'd just forget he was Michael's brother and be rude. Satisfied with that idea, she turned her attention to Michael's conversation as she continued to get ready for her trip to the zoo.

"What's up?" Michael was asking. He listened for a minute, then laughed. As she worked her hair into a French braid, Elena wondered sourly what Mark had said to cause laughter so early in the morning—well actually, not so early. After another minute, Michael exclaimed, "You're kidding!" The voice at the other end of the line continued. "I'll get right over there," said Michael. Muttering "Damn," he reached across the bed to replace the telephone. Then he sat up and swung his legs over the side, saying to Elena, "You want to investigate a burglary on your way to the elephant attack?"

"I don't do burglaries," said Elena, but curious, she couldn't resist asking, "What burglary?"

"Mark says four apartments were broken into last night at the faculty unit, mine among them."

Elena patted his arm consolingly. However, she really didn't do burglaries; she was a Crimes Against Persons detective, and the detectives assigned to Michael's case wouldn't appreciate her butting in. She had no doubt that officers would be assigned. Any crime at Herbert Hobart University got a quick and thorough reaction from the Los Santos Police Department because the university brought so much money into the border community.

"I guess I'd better get over there," said Michael. Reaching

for the shirt he'd dropped on the rug the night before, he began to dress.

Elena tied a thong at the end of her braid and brushed on a little lipstick. Then, as she highlighted her dark eyes with shadow and mascara, her thoughts returned compulsively to her lover's brother. Mark, with his snide remarks and surreptitious come-ons, gave her a pain, and tough intentions toward him didn't smooth over her dislike. Not good, she thought uneasily, not when things were going so well between her and Michael. He was sweet and considerate, both as a man and a lover, although he tended to be somewhat possessive.

Which made her wonder why he didn't warn his brother off. Surely Michael could see that more was going on than jock talk. Unless he blamed *her* but hesitated to say so. She glanced over in time to see him putting things in his pockets—keys, pen, wallet, his lucky seashell, which he'd found at age seven just before a big wave knocked him over on some New England beach—he considered the shell lucky because he hadn't drowned—and last but not least, his honorary deputy sheriff's badge. He'd got that for teaching a class to jailhouse deputies on how to defuse inmate problems before they got out of hand.

What a sweetie he was. He hadn't even charged the county, which had little money and lots of jail problems. She brushed a kiss on his cheek and headed for the kitchen, calling over her shoulder, "Want some juice and a tortilla before you go?"

"A tortilla?" he echoed. "For breakfast?"

"Well, I don't have time to make *huevos rancheros*," she replied gaily. "Got an elephant to bust."

2
..

"Someone has tampered with my elephant," said Los
Santos Zoo Director C. Darwin Mandel. He was fiftyish with
gray-black hair—thin on top, long at the sides, accompanied
by a matching beard and mustache and round, rimless glasses,
tinted pink. "I promise you, this is not Pansy's fault," he said
earnestly. "God never made a sweeter-tempered creature. I
daresay Pansy is the most charming elephant in America—
playful, but never, never vicious." Elena was sitting in
Mandel's office, the walls of which were covered with
drawings, paintings, and photographs of animals, occasionally taken with government officials—mayors, councilmen
and women, county commissioners. She spotted a photo of
Police Chief Armando Gaitan, looking dapper beside the cage
of the resident gorilla, Cholo, so-named for certain rebellious
tendencies.

"Well, the fact remains, Dr. Mandel," Elena replied, "that
your keeper, Mr.—"

"Zubarate. Virgilio Zubarate."

"Right. Mr. Zubarate is dead. That being the case, I'd like
to see the scene of the—ah—attack."

"If you insist. But I must warn you that Pansy is still—
troubled." Dr. Mandel rose and escorted her out, keeping up
a running commentary on the histories and personalities of
various animals they passed. He seemed quite unfazed by the

9

dust storm in progress, more intent on telling her about an unforeseen public mating of two spider monkeys.

"We have them on birth control," he said defensively. "We are not a breeding zoo."

Elena wondered what kind of birth control—the pill? Diaphragms? It would probably be pretty hard to teach a monkey to use a diaphragm. Or a condom, for that matter.

"They're not supposed to come into season, but of course the implants don't last forever." He sighed. "So the female went into heat—without our realizing it. Some Eastside woman was outraged because her aged mother witnessed the—ah—coupling."

A snort of laughter broke loose from Elena.

Dr. Mandel eyed her reprovingly. "People who don't realize that animals are less circumspect about sexual matters than humans should stay home," the director snapped.

Much he knew, Elena reflected. Her first few years on the force, when she'd been on patrol in a squad car, she'd caught lots of humans being less than circumspect about their sex lives.

Unlike the zoo director, Elena was distracted by the wind, which had worsened since she got out of her car in the parking lot. Blowing dust had now turned the sun orange and curtained the mountains in a brown haze. Elena wore large sunglasses to protect her eyes, but the wind tore strands loose from her braid, whipping them into her face, while the sand abraded her skin and stuck to her lips. She was wiping her front teeth with a Kleenex when a huge blast of sound echoed through the park. "What was that?" she gasped.

"Pansy," said Dr. Mandel. "She's trumpeting. As I said, she's upset."

Squinting into the gritty wind, which was now trying to edge in under her glasses, Elena spotted a group of men. "The keepers," said Dr. Mandel. Elena headed in their direction, only to find that they were huddled in front of the Amazon parrot and toucan enclosure, which featured a tree, but no birds.

"We keep the birds inside on windy days," said the director. "Can't have them blowing off their perches. Pansy's—" Before he could tell Elena where Pansy was, the elephant did it for him with another blast of sound. Elena jumped and whirled. Across the way, on the other side of a fence and a dry moat that looked like minor protection, the elephant picked up a barkless tree trunk and hurled it in their direction. It tipped over the iron fence and came close to landing among the keepers, who scattered.

"Good lord!" said Elena. "Can't you tranquilize her or something?" Ears flapping wildly, Pansy headed for the entrance to her house and butted the side of it. Bits of adobe crumbled off.

"We can, but we'd rather not," said an earnest young man. "Surely you read about the Los Angeles elephant who died from tranquilizers."

Elena hadn't, but the sight of Pansy, now bashing a huge tractor tire against the elephant door, made her very nervous. She'd have taken the chance and drugged the animal.

"This is Dr. Richard Tockler, our resident veterinarian," said the director. "John Lark, elephant supervisor, Jesus Amado and Larry Fortly, trainers."

Elena nodded to the men while the elephant, having failed to destroy the tire, flung it in their direction. They all dodged, Mr. Lark not quite fast enough. The tire caught him on the shoulder. "That's her favorite toy," he said, rubbing the bruise. "She'd never have let it out of the enclosure if she weren't in an abnormal frame of mind."

"Just as I said," Dr. Mandel agreed. "She's been tampered with. Someone has mounted a vendetta against the zoo. Gentlemen, this is Detective Jarvis, whom the police department sent to solve the crime."

"Well, that says a lot about how much they care about the zoo and Virgilio," said Jesus Amado bitterly. "Sending a woman."

Elena would have jumped on him for the remark, but she had just spotted the elephant nudging a bloody heap ten or twelve feet out from the back wall. "That's not— Is that Mr. Zubarate? You haven't got the poor guy out of there?" She swallowed hard, sick at the thought of what had happened to the man.

"Couldn't," said Amado. "*You* wanna go in there and drag him out, lady?"

"We're waiting till she calms down," said John Lark. "And

Virgilio's dead. When an elephant does a headstand on you, you've had it."

"A headstand?"

"Means the elephant presses that flat part of the head above the eyes on the victim, full weight. No one survives it."

"How did it happen?" Elena took out her notebook. "Wasn't there any sign that she——"

"If we'd seen somethin' was wrong, we wouldn't a gone in," said Larry Fortly. "We're trained. We know what to do. Some things though——" He shook his head. "Virgilio an' me had the exercise session this mornin'. He had the ankus."

"It's the tool we use to guide the elephant and enforce commands," Dr. Mandel explained.

"I was in the doorway watchin'," said Fortly. "Jus' like the rules say. Virgilio called to her an' she come over like always. Then she grabbed him an' whacked him against the wall. No warnin'. Nothin'. Slammed him on the ground an' squashed him. Not a damn thing I could do but run." Fortly sounded defensive.

"We know that, Larry," said the director soothingly.

"Sounds like Mr. Zubarate didn't have much of a chance," Elena murmured, staring at the bloody heap that had once been a man. The elephant, having gotten no response from nudging the body, trumpeted and headed for the far wall, scooping up dust with her trunk and flinging it over her head and back. Elena clamped errant strands of hair back with both hands. "How long do you figure it will take her to calm down?" she asked.

"Since we don't know what caused this, we have no way of predicting," said Dr. Tockler. "Of course, once we can get the chains on her, I'll run tests."

"I thought elephants sometimes just—just went crazy," said Elena.

"That's not what happened here," Dr. Mandel assured her. "Malice is at work."

Pansy had dragged a second tree trunk loose from a chain and was hoisting it. "Maybe we should—ah—back off," Elena suggested quickly. She didn't want to get brained with a log flung by a crazy elephant.

"I want an investigation," said Dr. Mandel. "I want Pansy

exonerated." He took Elena's arm and turned her toward the administration building.

How was she supposed to exonerate an elephant who had trampled her keeper? Elena wondered. With a shudder, she looked over her shoulder at the mangled remains of the late Mr. Zubarate. Poor man. What a way to die! Then she considered trying to investigate the case. Another hour of this wind, and the site would be obscured by dust, the evidence, if any, buried.

"I'm afraid the witnesses, other than Fortly, have gone," said Dr. Mandel. "Some of the children were hysterical; others seemed to think the incident was an entertainment provided by the zoo for visiting school groups, some kind of bizarre educational experience." He frowned, then absently brushed dust out of his thinning hair. They were passing the enclosure of the American black bear. "If the little ones spent less time in front of television sets, they'd have a sharper grasp of reality."

"Uh-huh," said Elena, thinking this was one reality that twenty-three kindergartners from Vista Valle Elementary School might better have been spared.

"Their teacher, Miss—actually, I don't know the woman's last name; they called her Miss Anne—at any rate, Miss Anne insisted that she be allowed to take them back to their bus." Dr. Mandel was now shouting into the wind as they passed the jaguar area. "I understand that the school administrators are calling in psychologists and counselors to reassure the children. Nobody, however, seems to be worried about how this is going to affect poor Pansy. When she realizes what she's done, she'll be stricken." He wiped a veil of dust off his round lenses. "Elephants," he bellowed, "are very sensitive creatures with long memories. This incident could affect her for years."

"Uh-huh." Elena could feel the itch of grit working its way into her scalp. Ah, spring! Thank God it didn't last long. Was Mandel talking about elephant neuroses? Were there psychiatrists for elephants? She'd heard about psychiatry for dogs. "Did Pansy have anything against Mr. Zubarate?" Elena asked. She couldn't believe that she was pursuing an elephant's motives. Manny owed her for this one.

"Pansy was very fond of Virgilio. Not, of course, as fond as she is of me. In fact, if I hadn't been meeting with the city council about funding, this would never have happened." The director had given up shouting and was now talking directly into Elena's ear as they passed the elaborately landscaped enclosure of the Mexican wolf, who evidently had more sense than to be out on a day like this. "I usually take the first exercise session—a little indulgence I allow myself."

"You mean you get in there with Pansy?" Elena asked, astonished, thinking that obviously wasn't something the director *had* to do, in which case, why would he?

"As I said, Pansy and I have a rapport. Maybe we should step into my office, Detective. The storm seems to be worsening."

Elena agreed with alacrity, and the two of them, bent into the wind, staggered the last few yards to the administration building.

"This kind of weather is hard on animals," said Dr. Mandel.

"Not to mention people," Elena agreed. "Has it occurred to you, sir, that you might have been the person trampled by Pansy?"

"Absolutely not," said Darwin Mandel. "Pansy would never harm me. We've been close for years. Ever since she arrived in Los Santos." They reached shelter, and the director ushered Elena into his office. "And I warn you, Detective," he said, holding her chair with old-fashioned courtesy, "I shall fight tooth and nail to see that Pansy isn't put down."

Elena herself thought that it might be a good idea, although she wasn't sure what means of execution would work on an elephant. A police automatic wouldn't do the job. And Pansy would never fit in the pound's gas chamber. Lethal injection, perhaps?

"My brother Arnold, for instance, heard the news on his way to work and offered to come over with his elephant gun. I told him I thought that a very spiteful thing to say. Very spiteful indeed. I was astounded to hear him make such a suggestion." Dr. Mandel took off his round glasses and polished them with a paper he tore from an optometrist's folder in his pocket.

"Your brother owns an elephant gun?" Elena was surprised

that any of Los Santos' half million plus citizens had such a thing.

"My brother collects hunting weapons. He considered the elephant gun a great find, although elephants can no longer be hunted in their countries of origin. The Indian elephant—Pansy is an Indian elephant, as are most of those in zoos—is a great worker. No one would hunt an Indian elephant. Except my brother." The director's lips tightened. "African elephants, on the other hand, roam free, and are less amenable to domestication. This is an African elephant." He showed her a picture. "Notice how different the ears are from Pansy's. Unhappily, African elephants are still hunted for their ivory by poachers, although it's against the law."

Elena gritted her teeth—literally. What she needed was a glass of water, or maybe a gallon, and a chance to swish and spit; her teeth were coated with sand. She'd have been grateful, too, for a respite from elephant information. If she didn't dispose of this case quickly, she was going to hear more about elephants than she ever wanted to know.

"A male elephant will go into *musth*," explained the director, warming to his topic. "And become dangerous—ill-tempered and aggressive—which is why the more amiable female elephants are preferred in zoos. Pansy is, of course, female, so there is absolutely no natural reason for this to have happened."

Maybe Pansy had been suffering from PMS when she attacked Mr. Zubarate, thought Elena. "Since the elephant attacked the victim in front of twenty-four witnesses, plus the other keeper, I don't see how she can be exonerated, Dr. Mandel."

"I think she was drugged," said the zoo director. "Or tormented surreptitiously."

"Drugged?" It would take a hell of a lot of—whatever—to affect an elephant; or so Elena imagined.

"Naturally, Dr. Tockler will take a blood sample for analysis," said the director.

"And do what with it? Send it to us? The Department of Public Safety does most of our blood work." Did the DPS have someone who'd understand the ins and outs of elephant blood? Would anything show up when Pansy finally calmed down enough to be tested? Elena would hate to be the person sticking needles into an elephant, even a good-tempered one.

"We have our own labs. Also the local hospitals accommodate us. Shall we send our findings to the police department?"

"I suppose so," Elena replied.

"Poor Pansy," said Dr. Mandel. "Falsely accused. Not that I don't feel for Virgilio. And his family."

"Big family?" asked Elena with a sinking heart.

"Wife. Seven children. Although by Los Santos standards that might not be considered unduly large."

Elena nodded. All those good Catholics kept having kids, running her property taxes up to provide more schools. A Roman Catholic herself, Elena sometimes wished that Pope John Paul II would catch up with modern thinking on the dangers of population explosion. Los Santos was exploding faster than Mexico, which lay just across the border.

The elephant trumpeted again, as if to recall Elena's attention. "She doesn't seem to be calming down."

"Don't worry, Detective. We're watching her carefully. Which reminds me. Have you found my mountain lion? Or my Mohave rattler?"

"That's a burglary case," said Elena. "I'm from Crimes Against Persons."

"Quite so. Then please find the person who tampered with my elephant."

3
..

Tuesday, March 28, 2:45 P.M.

I think they should do something for that poor elephant. It's obviously in pain. All that noise, that trumpeting. It shakes the house. Don't they have elephant aspirin?

Sylvia Morano, Grandmother

Shoot her, I say. Pansy killed a man, didn't she? And she's making life in the neighborhood unbearable. How are we supposed to sleep at night?

Bruce Metterlick, Retired Construction Foreman

"Elephant Update," Los Santos *Herald-Post*, Monday, March 27

Elena had been in court all day, testifying for the prosecution in the trial of a nightclub owner accused of shooting a topless dancer. The girl had lived thirty-six hours after the attack and denied that her boss was responsible, evidently under the impression that she would profit handsomely from protecting her attacker. Then she died before she could tell the truth. It had been a hard case to make, but Elena had hopes that the club owner, a cockroach with a nasty temper and a history of abusing women, would go to jail for a long time.

When she finally returned to Crimes Against Persons at Five Points, it was after two-thirty. During the drive from the county courthouse downtown, she had debated on what, if anything, she could or should do about the elephant attack. It would be several days before blood work on the elephant came in to prove or disprove C. Darwin Mandel's contention that his elephant had been "tampered with." In the meantime, maybe a few telephone calls would reassure the distraught zoo director that something was being done to "exonerate" Pansy. Elena shook her head at the thought, waved to Carmen, the receptionist in C.A.P., pushed through the door that led into the rabbit warren of cubicles—Sex Crimes in front, Homicide Row at the very back—moved down the long aisle past the interrogation rooms and Manny Escobedo's office, which was empty, turned right, and dropped into her own gray tweed chair in her own gray tweed cubicle with its telephone, computer terminal, and file drawers.

Opening her bag to fish her notebook out from under her 9-millimeter, she thumbed through for the telephone number of Border Security, which provided patrols for the zoo. Before calling, she listened to her messages, then read a scrawl from her sometime partner, Leo Weizell. Lucky Leo. He hadn't got stuck with the crazed elephant case. Leo's note said, "I'm out buying another crib." That meant the obstetrician had decided that Leo's wife, Concepcion, was carrying at least three babies—not a happy situation for an ill-paid homicide detective. As he shopped for secondhand baby furniture, Leo would be worrying about where he'd find the money to support these kids, who were the result of his low sperm count and Concepcion's fertility pills.

Elena tapped out the number of Border Security and got the duty officer, who agreed to find the reports of the midnight-to-eight guards. "They got a big area to cover, you know," said the company representative defensively. "Not just the zoo but the old baseball stadium, the VFW hall, and the parking lot. They gotta check every door and lock, respond to any animal or human disturbances. Takes the night guys two or three hours to make one round."

As he talked, he was evidently scanning the report because he said, "Only thing happened that night, they caught some teenagers screwing in a car in the parking lot at twelve-thirty. Chased them off. And at five forty-five in the morning they both responded to a water leak in the Reptile House. Had a hell of a time getting it shut down and cleaned up. For my money they could have left it. Who cares if a bunch of snakes drown?" There was a pause, then, "Hey, don't tell the zoo people I said that."

"What time did they get back to their rounds?" asked Elena.

"Six-thirty," said the duty officer.

"Any sign that anyone broke into the Reptile House and sabotaged the water system?"

"Nah. Says here the place was all locked up."

"Then how did they know about the leak?"

"They check the locks inside and out," said the officer. "That's what I'm telling you. Takes two or three hours to make a nighttime round. We don't have to do all that during the day, when the zoo employees are around. They keep an eye on things themselves while our guys watch the customers. In case anyone gets in a fight or tries to feed the animals. Stuff like that."

Elena asked for the names and home telephone numbers of the two midnight-to-eight guards. One was picking his daughter up at school and taking her to soccer practice on a team for which he was the assistant coach. He wasn't expected back home until six.

The remaining guard had nothing to add to the report they'd made when they finished their shift and returned to the tower, which was really the second floor of the octagonal building at the zoo entrance. Tickets were sold on the first floor.

"So you think it was just a naturally occurring leak in the snake house?" Elena asked.

"Sure," said the guard. "It happens. The piping's old, and money's short. If they had more money, they'd have three of us on at night. We really need another guy."

Elena hung up doubting that the flood had been a diversion so that someone could "tamper with" the elephant, not when there was no sign of a break-in. Her next call would be to Lina in Burglary to check on the previous zoo case.

Before she could punch in the number, Leo showed up and dropped wearily into his chair across the aisle. "Find a crib?" Elena asked.

"Yeah, fifteen bucks. Some lady in the Lower Valley sold it to me."

"Good price," said Elena, who had enough nieces and nephews back in Chimayo, New Mexico, to have heard numerous discussions about the price of baby cribs.

"Hey, I paid for that crib in blood. She told me the whole medical history of the kid she bought it for. Childhood-onset diabetes."

Elena nodded. "Lots of diabetes in the Hispanic population."

"Yeah," said Leo glumly. "Scared the shit out of me. What if we get three kids with diabetes? Bad enough to have that many without having to give them shots all the time. And the medical expenses—"

"Leo," said Elena soothingly, "Concepcion doesn't have diabetes. No one in her family has it."

"How do I know that? She's got hundreds of relatives here and in Mexico. Some of them are bound to."

"Has she ever said so?"

He shook his head. "Anyway, I had to listen to all this, and I've still got to buy a mattress for the crib."

"Well, sure," said Elena. "You don't want your kid sleeping on a mattress that another kid peed on for a couple of years."

Leo agreed and turned his chair around to read his messages. Elena called Lina in Burglary.

When the detective had listened to Elena's first question, she said, "Let me guess. You got called in on that elephant thing yesterday."

"You got it," Elena agreed. "So how's your wild-animal case coming?"

"How's *your* wild-animal case coming?" Lina retorted. "Mine's dead in the water. No sightings of a big white rattlesnake or a big mean mountain lion. No evidence at the crime scene. No break-in. No suspicious fingerprints on locks, doors, cages, or the lock boxes where they keep the keys."

"What about the security guards?" Elena asked.

"They didn't see anyone creeping around or dragging animals out. According to their logs, the patrols were routine, but they only did two each, which makes me think they might have taken some time off. Of course, they won't admit it, and I can't prove it."

"So what do you think happened?"

"Beats me. I'd say the keeper just got careless and left the cage unlocked, except that two animals disappeared in one night and from different areas. That's too much of a coincidence. But why the hell would anyone want a snake and a mountain lion?"

"To sell, I guess," Elena suggested. "I know people buy snakes."

"But a mountain lion?" protested the burglary detective. "Jesus, what would you do with a mountain lion? It wasn't any cute little mountain kitty, or whatever they're called. The sucker weighed a hundred and twenty-five pounds. Cat like that could kill someone and probably would. That's what the keeper told me. She also said if the cat got free, it would head for the mountains. Wouldn't hang around town."

"When was the last time anyone actually saw either of the animals?" Elena asked.

"Well, the keepers checked them before going off duty, at four and four-thirty. That was a week ago Sunday. After that the guards can't say. I guess they don't expect the animals to disappear, so they just check the locks. I got nowhere to go with it," said Lina resentfully. "But hey, I did bust the guys who stole all those manhole covers and sewer grates."

Elena laughed. "Good for you!"

"Tell my sergeant. I'd never have got stuck with the zoo caper if he didn't hate me."

"Since when?" asked Elena.

"Since I filed a sexual harassment complaint against Ricardo Backus. I got sick of him patting me on the fanny. I personally don't consider that a sign of platonic admiration."

"I wouldn't either," Elena agreed. "So file a charge against your sergeant too."

"For what? For assigning me all the crap cases? He'll just say I'm there when they come in."

"Maybe you are."

"So are other people," said Lina. "See that column in the paper last night?"

"Yes," said Elena, laughing. The evening paper had insti-

tuted a column called "Elephant Update and Other Zoo
News." The first one included a bunch of man-in-the-street
interviews conducted in the neighborhood and in the zoo
parking lot, where visitors were being turned away because
Pansy was still tearing around her enclosure, throwing things
at worried members of the staff. Elena had enjoyed the
comments of the public, remarks such as, "So what if a few
animals got out? My cat's always running off. He comes
home." Elena had imagined the mountain lion showing up at
the ticket window, chastened and hungry but very satisfied
with himself after a week of catting around town.

Another member of the public, quite irate, had said, "I
brought my kids all the way from Canutillo to see the
elephant, and now they tell me the elephant's dangerous. If
it's dangerous, they ought to shoot it."

A third had said, regarding the death of Virgilio Zubarate,
"Are they sure Pansy did it? I don't believe it. She's so cute.
When I was a little girl, my dad held me up over the fence,
and I offered her a bite of my Sno-Cone. She ate the whole
thing, paper and all."

It occurred to Elena as she said goodbye to Lina that even
if they never solved their respective cases, the zoo was
getting lots of publicity. Would that increase attendance and
help with the financial problems caused by a stingy city
council? Or would the coverage scare visitors away? She
thought back to Pansy charging around her enclosure, trumpeting, butting the door to her elephant house, flinging tractor
tires and tree trunks. And poor Virgilio Zubarate, a big messy
lump in the dust.

If someone had set the elephant off deliberately, it was a
vicious act. Murder. But on the other hand, as Manny had
pointed out during the initial call to her house, elephants did
stuff like that occasionally. Several of the trainers had
delighted in telling her about how dangerous it was being in
proximity to an elephant, no matter how friendly. More
dangerous than being a cop, less dangerous than being a
coal-miner—that's what Larry Fortly had said. Proud—as if
she, the cop, was a wimp, and he, the elephant trainer, wasn't.

4
..

"You haven't read 'Elephant Update'?" Elena asked Leo as they passed the Porfirio Diaz exit on the interstate. They were answering a suspicious-death call in the country club district on the Westside.

"Don't get the evening paper," said Leo. He tried to change positions in the passenger seat and rapped his knee on the dashboard. "Damn little cars," he muttered.

"It's not the car; it's your legs," Elena retorted. "They're too long." Dust was rolling across the highway in brown clouds that gave the other cars a ghostly, mirage-like appearance. Elena slowed down, since visibility further decreased once they made the curve around the end of the mountain by the state university.

"I'll save you tonight's column. I'll bet their circulation jumps twenty thousand; 'Elephant Update' is something else. 'Should the killer elephant be done away with?' 'Will a decomposing elephant endanger public health?' No one seems to know what the city'd do with the body if Arnold Mandel—that's the zoo director's brother—is allowed to shoot the elephant."

"A decomposing elephant? Now there's a sickening thought," said Leo.

"Yeah. The EPA would probably want to get in on the act. 'Rotting Elephant Contributes to Border Air Pollution.' And

23

say, you'll like this one, Leo. They've announced the Pansy Contest—Pansy anecdotes from readers."

"You mean like the time she drenched the mayor and the city council with a snootful of water during a photo op? Now that I think about it, I'm on the Save-Pansy side."

"And I'm the detective of record," sighed Elena. "I'm supposed to find out why Pansy squashed the keeper."

"So what are you doing to solve the case?"

"Today? Nothing." Elena pulled onto Sunland Park Drive and passed the mall, which in the last few years had sprayed retail seeds in every direction, producing dozens of smaller malls, restaurants, and discount stores. "I'm waiting for the blood tests," she added.

"On who? Someone think the dead guy was stoned and provoked the elephant? Justifiable homicide?"

"The zoo director thinks an evil elephant-hater slipped Pansy something that made her crazy." Elena zigzagged to Thunderbird from North Mesa and headed toward the high-rent district—big houses, a golf course with lush grass. The only other enclave in the city with that much greenery was Herbert Hobart University—same side of the mountain, further north. Elena figured any case would be better than another of H.H.U.'s weird murders. She was wrong.

Their destination proved to be a stucco castle with turrets. It lacked only crenelated walls and a moat. An elaborately designed circular driveway with squares of multicolored stones held a Lincoln Continental and three blue-and-whites, one with its lights still revolving.

"Big-shot victim," Leo guessed as they got out and mounted broad steps bordered by handsome pots blooming with flowering shrubs. The massive double doors were bolt-studded, each decorated with a carved coat of arms.

"What would you call this?" Elena wondered. "Neo–Mediterranean Medieval?"

"Ostentatious?" Leo suggested. A weeping maid let them in, pointed to an open door down the wide center hall, and ran off, sniveling into a feather duster.

"Flagstones!" said Leo, studying the artfully arranged slabs of gray-green stone as they walked toward the room that presumably held the body. "I'd like to tap dance on them."

"You'd like to try tap dancing on anything that would hold you up," Elena retorted. Her partner was an avid terpsichorean, winner of the police talent show, founder of Los Santos Tap Night, an extravaganza held downtown on San Jacinto Plaza. The only reprimand in Leo's personnel jacket was for having used the surveillance cameras in the interrogation room at headquarters to film a tap-dancing routine.

They passed through a dark wood door, with recessed moldings, into a paneled room decorated with stuffed animal heads, multiple gun racks, and single weapons. Maroon leather furniture, brass-studded, rested on Persian carpets. Elena took in the decor quickly, her attention caught by two particulars that sent a shiver up her spine. A large composition bow hung on the wall, so arranged that a steel-tipped arrow seemed to be nocked on the string. The arrow head, wickedly sharp, looked rusty. Oxidation? Or blood? Not far from the bow, perched on a great spread of antlers, was a falcon, eyeing them with a fierce impassivity. It almost looked alive.

"Here's the victim, Detectives," said a sergeant from the Westside substation. Elena had gone through the police academy with Vincent de la Rosa. His uncle was a captain, the head of the Traffic Division; his cousin, Sergio, was a narc who sometimes partnered Elena's ex, Frank. She knew Vincent to be a smart cop. Following his direction, she saw the body of a middle-aged man, tall and husky, silver hair on the sides of his head, none on top, casually expensive clothing, a great red patch of coagulated blood on his shirt over the heart, and—she gagged when she saw it—his eyes were gone, only torn, empty sockets remaining.

"The way it looks," said Sergeant de la Rosa, "someone shot him with his own bow—that's a deer-hunting bow." He pointed to the wall. "Then they musta pulled the arrow out. His gut looks like someone put a foot on it." The sergeant pointed to a smudge on the victim's shirt near the belt area, and Elena pictured the murderer planting a boot on the victim's stomach to hold the body down while he dragged the arrow free.

"Then he—the killer—put the bow and arrow back up on the wall there. You can see where some blood dripped off on the paneling under the arrow tip." Leo went over to look.

Elena was still dealing with those eye sockets. "Then the guy musta unhooded the bird and loosed those tethers. The hood's on the floor, and the tethers are hanging off the perch. Bird did the rest."

Shivering, Elena turned to look at the falcon again. "It's alive?" she asked.

"And you're just letting it sit there?" demanded Leo. "After what it did to—"

The sergeant shrugged. "Hey, that's what falcons do. And the guy was dead before the bird had its snack. They like eyes, you know."

"Jesus!" said Leo.

"It's a beautiful specimen," said the sergeant. "Name's Ahab, according to one of the maids. No use to kill it unless it gives us trouble. Gomez over there is keeping his eye on it."

Unappeased, Elena and Leo looked nervously toward the falcon, who stared back, a feathered death's-head.

"Wife found the victim," the sergeant continued. "Come in on a private plane from Dallas; that's what she says. No one meets her at the airport. She can't get her husband at work or at home, so she hires a cab, mad as hell according to the other maid, walks in here to try him again at work, finds the body, and has hysterics." He closed his notebook. "She's upstairs popping Valium. One maid, Gabriella, is a daily. Doesn't live here. Other one, Anita, lives over the garage. Doesn't go in his study unless he says to, and then he watches her while she cleans. Last time the live-in saw him alive was when he come home last night. She put his dinner out and headed for her room."

"Don't know why you needed us, de la Rosa," said Leo sarcastically. "Seems like you got it all scoped out."

De la Rosa nodded, humorless.

"What's the guy's name, Vincent?" Elena asked.

"Mandel. Arnold Mandel. Owns a big pants factory."

"Owns an elephant gun too," muttered Elena, her eyes resting on a huge gun that hung over the fireplace in solitary splendor.

5
··

Wednesday, March 29, 2:15 P.M.

"Mrs. Mandel isn't asleep, is she?" Elena asked as she climbed a curving staircase with the live-in maid. The hysterical daily who answered the door had been sent home after a brief, unproductive interrogation.

Dark eyes slanting at Elena from a brown face, the young live-in said, "She lookin' out window. Señora take many pills before margaritas."

"Oh?" The sergeant had said that the victim's wife was upstairs zonked out on Valium. Alcohol combined with Valium could leave her comatose. Elena climbed faster. "Did you see or hear anything last night?"

"I put dinner out—*seis y media*—when he get home."

Six-thirty. Elena nodded.

"Then I go to my room an' turn on TV. Garage away from house. My room look on mountain."

"You didn't hear any cars?"

"Nothin'."

"Did Mr. Mandel have any enemies that you know of?" Elena asked. They had reached the second floor and turned down the hall.

"Prolly," was the reply. "Workers for sure."

"Which workers?" Elena stopped.

The maid took several more steps before she realized that Elena wasn't following. Then she turned back. "Garment workers an' La Mujer Obrera—workin' woman. *Comprende?*"

Elena nodded. It was a labor advocacy group.

"They—ah—walk around main plant an' many sweat-shops. Don' you watch TV?"

"Yeah. I just didn't make the connection. He owns Los Santos Apparel?"

"His papa owns. An' rest of family. Don' know who got what. Now TV say he got many small places. Sweatshops where sewin' is."

"I thought those guys were independents," Elena murmured.

"Everybody think that," said the maid. "Now Apache *abogado* say the Señor Mandel, he got many, maybe *ocho, nueve*. Kind they hire some poor *mujer*, fill—*como se dice*?—orders, then"— she snapped her fingers—"gone. No pay workers. My cousin, she don' get pay *tres semanas*. She—*como se dice*?—picket. Her an' her *niña*—in the dust, walkin' aroun'. *La niña's* got a—*como se*?" The maid demonstrated her meaning by coughing. "I tell my cousin she *loco* bringin' Anitessa along; my cousin say, wha's she gonna do? She got nobody to take *la niña*."

Elena nodded. It was a familiar story in Los Santos, a city of half a million or so, bordered on the Mexican side of the river by a city of a million and a half. The women—many of whom spoke no English—had to take whatever work they could get—jobs with no benefits; lousy, dangerous working conditions; sometimes no overtime or less than minimum wage; worst case scenario, no paycheck at all when the owners locked the doors and disappeared. "So Mandel was mixed up with all that," she mused, then glanced at the maid. "He pay you regularly?"

"Sure. His *esposa* woun' let him cheat me. Who clean toilets an' wax—ah—*muebles* an' make margaritas *por la* señora? Gabriella—she no worth much. Señora Mandel, she *necessita* train someone new—woun' like that."

"Ummm," said Elena. They paused at a pair of double doors. The maid knocked, but there was no answer. Frowning, Elena worried that the wife, who had discovered the body, might have O.D.'d.

"We go in," said the maid. "She prolly din' hear nothin'."

"What's your name?" Elena murmured as the girl turned the knob.

"Anita."

"Well, Anita, I may want to talk to you again."

Anita shrugged. "You fin' me here. 'Cept *Domingo*. Got—*como se*?—Sundays off." She entered and announced, "*La mujer policia*, Señora," then murmured to Elena, "No lettin' her think *mi inglés es muy bueno*. She expect me to understan' what she say." With a cocky grin the young woman turned and went back down the hall.

Elena studied the room, looking for Mrs. Mandel, who wasn't in sight but was evidently into the color green—pale green carpeting, pale green bedspread, green sheers at the great windows that looked out on the garden and the mountain beyond, darker green drapes held back with gold-fringed loops. Underwater-with-interior-decoration, Elena thought. "Mrs. Mandel?" Was she in the bathroom, or what?

Elena crossed the room and knocked at a white door, then opened it. She had found the bathroom—all green tile with a big tub that had gold-rimmed holes in the sides, out of which gushed, no doubt, swirling hot water to soothe Mrs. Mandel's aching muscles, should she ever have that problem—say, after a game of tennis on an indoor, air-conditioned court. The bathroom was mirror-walled on one side with double sinks, plants leafing out everywhere, an etched glass shower stall, a makeup counter and mirror surrounded with bulbs like an actress's dressing table, a door partially open on an auditorium of a closet, filled with clothes—and shoes. Elena peered in. The shoes had to be custom-made, since one of each pair was oddly shaped. Lots of shoes, but no Mrs. Mandel.

Elena left the bathroom and spotted a woman on a gold-fringed white chaise longue by the window. She had been blocked from Elena's view by the upholstered back of the chair. "Excuse me, ma'am," Elena said loudly, walked over, and drew up a brocaded armchair. "I'm Detective Elena Jarvis." No answer. "I'd like to ask you some questions about your husband's death."

In slow motion Mrs. Mandel's head turned. The victim's wife wasn't crying, but she certainly did look spaced out, eyes unfocused. The hair was a pale red-blond, the shade of a woman gone gray who had a good hairdresser. Her face was relatively unlined, except around the eyes and mouth, from which Elena judged her to be in her middle to late fifties. "You are Mrs. Mandel?"

"Ummm, Patricia Mandel," said the woman, plucking idly at her cream silk robe. Her feet peeked beneath the hem, a bunion on her right foot, which explained the custom-made shoes. "Would you care for a drink?" she murmured, as if Elena were a party guest.

"Of what?" Elena asked.

"I'm drinking—mmmm—margaritas. They go well with the room, don't you think?"

"I wouldn't think they go very well with Valium. I understand you took some after discovering your husband's body."

"Did I?" said Mrs. Mandel. She smiled dreamily. "It was a shock."

"I'm sure," Elena agreed. The sight of his eyeless face had been a shock to her, and she didn't even know the man. "Do you have any idea who might have killed him?"

"The Indian," Mrs. Mandel replied.

"What Indian would that be, ma'am?"

"The lawyer Indian. She threatened him."

"Alope Randall?"

Mrs. Mandel nodded solemnly, several too many times. "She said—what did she say? My husband had just gotten out of his car at the factory. It was the—the Lincoln Continental. He'd driven himself. I was with him. And she said, 'You son of a bitch. Someone ought to kill you. I ought to do it myself.' "

Elena was taking notes. Alope Randall was a Mescalero Apache but headed a Los Santos legal clinic that protected workers' rights. Elena admired the lawyer's dedication and would have hated to think her guilty of that grisly murder downstairs.

"The bow and arrow," said Mrs. Mandel. "That's the clue."

"Was it your husband's bow?"

"Arnold did love killing things. Anything that moved and was in season. He hunted deer with that bow. In the Sandia Mountains. They're outside Albuquerque."

Elena knew the Sandias. She was from New Mexico herself, although her hometown, Chimayo, was in the Sangre de Cristos, farther north.

"He and Oliver Formalee." Mrs. Mandel licked the rim of her empty glass, dredged it in salt from a crystal plate, and poured herself another drink.

Formalee. Elena recognized the name as that of the lawyer who had defended her friend Sarah Tolland in the acid bath case. A gray man—skin, clothes, hair—all gray.

Mrs. Mandel smiled. "They almost died up there one winter. Snowstorm. But the killer would have to be someone who knew how to use a bow and arrow, don't you think?"

"Are you suggesting Mr. Formalee as another suspect?"

"Oh, no." More sipping. "Oliver wouldn't kill Arnold. Where would he ever find anyone else silly enough to tramp around in a snowstorm trying to shoot Bambi's mother? I think it was the Indian. Utilizing her Native American talents. The Indian or one of the picketers. Vicious women. The things they said about Arnold! Poor Arnold wasn't well liked, but he did a good job of pulling his father's factory back from the brink."

"The brink of what?" asked Elena.

"Of his brother's idiocy."

"His brother Darwin?"

"Darwin?" Mrs. Mandel looked confused. "Darwin never had anything to do with the company. He was like his mother. Only interested in animals. J.J., the youngest brother, is the same. Out there on his silly llama ranch. His mother named him John James Audubon. Poor little cretin. A name like that would screw up your life, don't you think?"

Elena wondered if the regal-looking Mrs. Mandel used the phrase "screw up" when she wasn't wallowing in tequila and tranquilizers.

"Where would that be, ma'am? The llama ranch?"

"Oh, up the valley. On one of those farm roads. Their mother left the place to J.J. in her will when Jacob—he's their father—disowned J.J. So there you are. Two faunaphiles—my word for animal freaks—and two fashionophiles." Sipping from her flared crystal margarita glass, she hiccupped delicately.

"Rosalba's the second clothing lover. But she buys the clothing; Arnold makes it. Made it."

"Rosalba?"

"The only daughter. Owns three mink coats. In Los Santos—can you imagine? They must spend ten months a year in storage. Of course, it could have been his mistress."

Elena stopped taking notes, confused at the jump from mink coats to mistresses.

"Arnold's mistress," said Mrs. Mandel impatiently. "My husband's mistress."

"Name?" asked Elena.

"Priego. Josephine Priego. And little Priego. Priegette." Mrs. Mandel took another swallow and leaned her head back against the white upholstery. "He dumped them."

"I see. So you think Ms Priego—"

"Ms? How politically correct of you, Detective. She was a bartacker before he set her up with a condo and a few charge accounts."

"How recently did Mr. Mandel terminate the relationship?"

"Sure you don't want one of these?" The lady of the house held up a crystal pitcher, which was emptying fast. "Last chance."

"No thanks."

"He terminated the relationship, as you so quaintly put it, Detective—what was your name?"

"Jarvis."

Mrs. Mandel squinted at Elena, eyes now completely unfocused. "You look Mexican to me."

"My maiden name was Portillo."

"Ah." Mrs. Mandel tapped her forehead knowingly. "Well, termination. Arnold dumped her just before I left for Dallas. Because I said if he didn't—if he didn't, I'd divorce him and take half his stock. And if you're Arnold Mandel, the company is more important than your mistress, or your wife, or your—whatever. Could you pull that cord by the armoire? I seem to be out of margaritas."

"Do you know Ms Priego's address?" Elena asked as she rose to give the green silk tape a yank.

"I certainly don't."

"Where did you say you were when Mr. Mandel was killed?"

"As in 'What is your alibi, my dear'?" Mrs. Mandel laughed merrily. "In Dallas with friends named Panderene. Flew there in their plane, shopped together, flew back. Maid can give you their address, but I don't do bows and arrows, Detective. And I'd never let that nasty falcon loose. Did you see what he did to Arnold?" The widow shuddered. "Besides that, Arnold is the only one left who can keep the business afloat, and I, Detective, am an expensive woman to maintain. I appreciate his financial skills."

"He's dead," Elena reminded her.

"True. That may prove to be a problem. Ah, Gabriella, I'll have another pitcher."

"Anita," said the maid.

"Of course. Anything else, Detective? If not, maybe I'll have a little snooze." The lady's eyes were almost closed.

"I'd like to nail down the times. When you got in. When you found—"

"Oh, goodness, ask that sergeant. He wrote it down."

Before Elena could insist, Mrs. Mandel dropped her empty glass on the floor and keeled over sideways, her head tipped off the edge of the chaise longue. Damn, thought Elena. Passed out cold. Or worse. She took the woman's pulse and peeled back her eyelid. Satisfied that she was basically all right, Elena went to the end of the chaise and tugged at the woman's feet until she was lying flat on the white upholstery. When Anita arrived with the new pitcher of margaritas, Elena said she didn't think they'd be needed, then left the room, pausing in the hall to look over her notes.

She had lots of suspects—the labor lawyer, Alope Randall, who had threatened the victim; some disgruntled worker in one of Mandel's enterprises; the spurned mistress, Josephine Priego; Patricia Mandel herself, a spurned and threatening wife; C. Darwin Mandel, who probably preferred his elephant to his hot-to-kill-an-elephant brother; maybe even J.J. Audubon Mandel because he'd been cut out of his father's will. But that had evidently been a long time ago, and he'd landed on his feet—thanks to mama.

At the bottom of the stairs she met Leo, who had been

canvassing the neighborhood. "Find anything interesting?"
she asked.

"Got his address book. Otherwise, not a damn thing.
Houses are too far apart. How about you?"

"Got the names of a whole raft of suspects from the wife."

"Oh, great! Why couldn't there be just one—with a
clear-cut motive, no alibi, and bloodstains on his shirt?"

"We should be so lucky. What's all that racket?" Elena
turned toward the door to the study.

Leo shrugged. "Crime scene team, medical examiner. They
should be finishing up."

"So why are they shouting?" Elena entered the study and
was stopped by a voice she recognized as Onofre Calderon's
yelling, "Close the damn door!"

She closed it behind her. Fingerprint powder speckled
every surface in the room, but the fingerprint men and the
photographers were not doing their usual thing. They'd
formed a wide circle beneath the chandelier, for on one of its
arms perched the falcon, wings flapping in agitation, eyes
huge, cold, and mean.

The crime scene tech closest to Elena muttered, "Next time
you find an eyeball-eating bird, don't call me."

"You got a problem?" she asked.

"Yes, we got a problem. We can't catch the damn bird."

One of the men held what looked like a monster butterfly
net, but he didn't seem to know what to do with it. "What's
that thing?" Elena asked. She had chased Monarch butterflies
with a more modest net when she was a little girl, but this one
looked very high-tech.

"Hell if I know," said the officer. "Animal Rescue dropped
it off, but they were on their way to corral a pit bull who
won't leave the Western Hills schoolyard, so they said we're
on our own."

"How does it work?"

"You plop it over the bird—fat chance!—then you pull
this lever, and the ring that holds the net closes."

"O.K." Elena took the gadget from him. The bird had
turned to stare at her. "Distract him," she called across the
circle to Onofre Calderon as she examined the apparatus at
the end of the handle.

"I don't want him landing on me," the medical examiner protested. "Look what he did to the deceased."

"Come on, Onofre. Get his attention." The bird looked as if he was about to pounce on Elena. Calderon sighed, put two fingers between his teeth, and whistled loudly. The bird whipped its head toward Onofre, and Elena swung the net in a wide arc. It swished overhead, almost brushing the ceiling, and landed perfectly on the distracted falcon. Then Elena pulled back the lever that closed the net, catching both bird and chandelier arm.

"There you go, guys," she said and passed the handle to the man from whom she'd taken it. The falcon was bating frantically inside the net.

"What the hell am I supposed to do now?" the officer asked.

"Beats me," said Elena. "I caught him. The rest is up to you." She left to rejoin Leo in the hall, where she found him doing a soft-shoe routine.

"What was that about?" he asked, pausing for breath. Los Santos' champion tap dancer had been trying out the flag-stones.

"You don't want to know," she replied. "And quit dancing. We ought to be able to get in a couple of interviews before the shift's over."

"Nag, nag, nag," said Leo.

She'd have laughed except that he actually sounded pissed off.

6
..

Wednesday, March 29, 3:00 P.M.

With airborne dust streaming past the car, Leo drove away
from the Mandel house while Elena jotted down the name
Cyclops Security. "I noticed their signs and stickers on other
houses in the neighborhood," Leo said.

She nodded. "They probably have a regular patrol going
through. We'll check their logs to find out if they saw
anything last night." While they were driving around the
mountain to the Eastside to check out Mandel's mistress,
whose address they had garnered from his address book,
Elena filled her partner in on what she had learned from Anita
and from Patricia Mandel.

She had exhausted her notes by the time they stopped at the
secured gate of Atlantis East, the condominium community in
which Josephine Priego lived. Leo showed identification to
the guard and told her which apartment they wanted to visit.
"About time," said the guard and gave them directions.

"What's that mean?" Leo wondered aloud.

Looming up behind quantities of leafy non-desert shrub-
bery and cylindrical cedar trees, the units were made of gray
cement, precast to resemble stone and decorated with an-
tiqued blue shutters and doors. "Bet they've got a hell of a
water bill," Elena muttered as they walked up the sidewalk to
Josephine Priego's blue door.

"You've got a water fixation, Jarvis," said Leo.

"Comes of having to spend so much time at H.H.U., where they waste it like they don't know we're running out," Elena retorted and rang the doorbell.

A young woman answered, twenty-five or so, with shining black hair blunt cut at her shoulders, pale brown skin with a rosy glow, dark eyes, a generous mouth, and an even more generous figure. If this was Josephine Priego, it was no wonder rich old Arnold had been willing to risk his marriage for her, Elena thought. A little girl, maybe two years old, clung to the woman's hand. Mother and daughter wore matching caftans, gaily splashed with giant red geraniums. "Ms Priego?" asked Elena.

"Yeah. Who are you?" The detectives identified themselves. Echoing the security guard, Josephine Priego said in an irritated tone, "It's about time. Come on in." She slammed the door behind them. "He's at it again. Hear that?" She ushered them into a living room with a white rug and furniture upholstered in geranium-red rough weave with red-and white-flowered throw pillows. Through sliding glass doors, Elena could see pots of geraniums on a small patio. Josephine Priego's "Hear that?" evidently referred to the noisy, jarring sounds issuing from a pump organ in the apartment above.

The organ was producing what Elena immediately identified as roller-skating music. Although she'd only been to one roller-skating rink in her life, it had been a memorable experience—a family trip to Albuquerque in an old pickup and a visit for all the kids to the rink while her dad attended a sheriffs' conference. Harmony, Elena's mother, had had to teach her five offspring how to skate. They'd gone home to Chimayo with happy memories and multiple bruises on elbows and knees.

Josephine Priego picked up the little girl and gave her a hug. "She can't take a nap 'cause of that racket."

"Have you filed a complaint?" asked Leo.

"I've done nothin' *but* file complaints," the woman said indignantly. "The old fart moved in a week ago, an' this has been goin' on ever since. First, I pounded on the ceilin' with a broomstick. Then I went up there an' gave him hell. Then I went to the manager. Jesus Christ, I own this apartment, an'

now he owns the place above me. You think I want to spend
the rest of my life listenin' to that crap? It's not even rock. I
don't know what the hell it is, but I hate it, so last night I
stopped bein' nice. I called him; I called 911; I called the
manager. Isn't that what you're here for?"

"'Fraid not," said Elena. She had to admit that the sounds
coming from the apartment above were God-awful. During
certain passages the knickknacks trembled on Josephine
Priego's end tables. "Leo, why don't you go upstairs and get
that guy to knock it off? I'll talk to Ms Priego about our
business."

"Yeah. O.K.," said Leo. He unfolded his long thin body
from the couch, which he had occupied uninvited, and
ambled out.

"Well, at last." The furious young woman flounced down
with the child in her lap. "So what are you here for?" she
asked Elena. "You want a soda or somethin'? I really
appreciate your gettin' on that old bastard's case. Every time
I go up there, he says, 'Music's my life,' an' slams the door
in my face."

"Frustrating," said Elena. "I'm afraid I have some bad
news for you, Ms Priego."

"You mean you can't keep him from playin'?"

"No, it's about Mr. Mandel."

"Arnold?" The young woman's eyes went wide while the
little girl chanted, "Daddy, Daddy, Daddy, Daddy." "Hush,
sweetheart," said Ms Priego.

"Daddy coming?" asked the toddler.

Josephine clutched her child. "What about Arnold?" she
asked. "Somethin's happened to him? Is that what you're
comin' to tell me? My God, he's gonna be all right, isn't he?"

"I'm afraid he's—ah—" Elena looked at the child, wondering how much of the conversation the little girl understood. "—gone," Elena finished gently.

"As in *dead*?" Josephine shook her head energetically. "No
way. Arnold's as healthy as a horse. Healthier. You'd never
know he's fifty-seven. He's a tiger in bed. He can't—" The
flow of denial stopped abruptly, Josephine Priego's eyes
narrowed, and she said, "*She* killed him, didn't she?"

"Who, Ms Priego?"

The young woman glanced down at her daughter, whose face was screwing up into tears. Lifting the baby and crooning reassuring nonsense in her ear, the mother carried her to a playpen across the room and sat her down, handing her a floppy red- and green-plaid puppy, which the child grasped eagerly, popping a plaid ear in her mouth. Josephine returned to Elena, face flushed with anger.

"Who do you think killed him?" Elena repeated in an undertone.

"That bitch, Patricia." Josephine spat out the name. "I hope she gets the chair. I hope—"

"Ms Priego—"

"Yeah, what? You sure he's dead?"

"I'm sure. I saw the body."

"What did she do to him? Did she hurt him?"

"He was killed by a bow and arrow."

"*What*?" The woman looked dumbfounded.

"His own bow and arrow, actually."

"A deer-huntin' bow?"

Elena nodded.

"I gave him that for Christmas," said Josephine. "Shit, I had to look through a hundred catalogues full of guns an' bows an' stuff like that to get just the right one. She killed him with *my* bow? That bitch! Where'd she learn to use it?"

"Good question," said Elena. "I don't suppose you know how?"

"You're kiddin'? What would I do with a bow an' arrow?" The organ music suddenly increased in volume, and Josephine leapt up, grabbed a broom from behind the sofa and pounded on the ceiling, scowling ferociously.

"You never went hunting with Mr. Mandel?"

"Hell, no. But Arnold never told me he took *her*. If I'd a known that, I'd a gone."

"Well, we don't know that Mrs. Mandel killed him. She says she was in Dallas."

"Yeah, right. Spendin' his money. She was always off somewhere throwin' his money around. Bitch. I'll bet he spent four times as much on her as he did on me an' Ceci, an' *we* loved him." She brushed a hand across tear-filled eyes, long, blunt-tipped red fingernails curling against her palm.

"Now what are we supposed to do? I'm not goin' back to bartackin', no way. They'll just have to support us."

"Who, Ms Priego?"

"I don't know. The Mandels. The old man. Whoever has the money. Ceci is Arnold's kid." The music stopped abruptly. "Well, hallelujah," said Josephine Priego. "A minute's peace, an' now it's too late to enjoy it."

"Mrs. Mandel suggested, Ms Priego, that you might have killed her husband because he was terminating his relationship with you."

"What are you talkin' about? Arnold wasn't terminatin' anythin'. He spent Sunday with us, just like he always did. Arnold comes three times a week. Came. What's this terminatin' business? He was going to terminate her. Promised me he'd get a divorce."

Elena's eyebrows rose skeptically.

"You don't believe it, huh? Well, I'm not sure I did either. She'd get too much in the settlement. Part of the company or somethin', an' Arnold loved that company. But still, he wasn't gonna dump me an' Ceci. We were his happiness, you know?"

When Leo came back into the condo without knocking, Elena filled him in on what Josephine had just told her.

"Ms Priego says that Mr. Mandel never mentioned breaking up with her and that he had, in fact, suggested that he might get a divorce from his wife."

"Ah-huh," said Leo.

"Yeah," said Josephine. "Well, like I just told Detective Jarvis here, I didn't believe it either, but that was O.K. I knew he loved us."

"Ms Priego, can you account for your time yesterday evening?" Elena asked.

"Hell yes, I can. I already told you what I was doin'. I was callin' people. Every fifteen minutes that music went on, I called someone. The manager. That asshole upstairs. And 911. You think that stopped the racket? Hell, no. He was thumpin' away up there until two in the mornin'. If I'd a had a gun, I'd a gone up an' shot the son of a bitch. You think he'll quit for good now that you told him to?" she asked Leo.

"I can't guarantee it, ma'am," said Leo. "He's kind of a strange old bird."

"Tell me about it. Christ, he *looks* like a bird. That white hair looks like feathers. Some damn white pigeon, makin' my life miserable.

"So you think I was out of the apartment, killin' Arnold, huh?" When she said "Arnold," little Ceci, who had been looking from one adult to the other through the webbed side of her playpen, beamed and caroled, "Daddy, Daddy, Daddy," again. Josephine went to pick her up, to hug the child in one arm while she wiped her own eyes with the other hand. "Hey, call the 911 people. Call the manager. Ask that—that guy upstairs. Be my guest." She waved toward a telephone. Her tears were falling quickly, and the little girl took her thumb from her mouth and said, "Mama?" in an uncertain voice.

"Yeah, Mama's sad, honey. It's O.K. Mama's just sad."

Elena bit her lip. Even without evidence to support the alibi, she believed the young woman. But that didn't mean she wouldn't check it out. Given a second nod from Josephine Priego, she picked up the telephone to call the Communications Supervisor at headquarters. "Why don't you go upstairs and talk to that guy again," she suggested to Leo. "And check with the manager."

"Sure. Send *me* out in the dust storm," Leo grumbled.

He left the apartment, and Elena told the Communications Supervisor what she wanted. Then she hung up after giving Priego's number. "They'll call me back once they've looked at the logs. Guess you've kind of got a real feud going with the guy upstairs," said Elena, trying to take the young woman's mind off her shock and grief, which seemed to be catching up with her more each minute.

"Oh, yeah," said Josephine. "Bad enough I have to listen to it, but Ceci, she can't take a nap. Can't get to sleep at a decent hour. It's disgustin'. Isn't it, honeybun?" She hugged her little girl.

"Mama sad?" Ceci asked.

Josephine nodded. "Mama sure is sad. You want a soda or somethin'?" she asked Elena.

"Yeah, thanks. That would be great," Elena agreed. "You want me to hold the baby?"

"You know anything about kids?"

"Got tons of nieces and nephews up in Chimayo, New Mexico."

"Oh yeah? You're from Chimayo? That's one of those old Spanish towns, huh?"

Elena nodded. "Founded in the seventeenth century."

"I had a teacher at Bowie who told us about that stuff, the Spanish settlers, the Indians rebellin' an' drivin' 'em out. You know who your ancestors were that far back?"

"On my father's side," said Elena. "The Portillos have been there the whole time."

"So you're Hispanic too, huh? I thought so, but I didn't want to ask."

"My dad's Hispanic. My mother was this California hippie he met while he was raiding her—ah—herb patch."

"Why would he—hey, you mean herb like pot? Like marijuana?" Josephine Priego started to grin through her tears.

Elena grinned back. "Mom claims she never grew anything but herbs. Dad disagrees. He was a deputy sheriff back then. Anyway, they both say it was love at first sight."

"Hey, that's sweet," said Josephine. "Yeah, I like that. It's real romantic. Same for Arnold an' me. He saw me at a sewin' machine an' turned up after work in this big car an' asked me out. I was blown away, I can tell you." She plopped the baby into Elena's lap, saying, "You can hold Ceci. She's real friendly." Then Josephine headed for the kitchen.

The little girl looked up at Elena with large, dark eyes, not sure she wanted to sit on some strange woman's lap. Elena smiled at her. "You're a pretty little thing," she said. "Want to play with my handcuffs?" Ceci popped her thumb into her mouth. Elena reached down to her handbag, grabbed the cuffs, and gave them to the toddler. "See?" she said. She stuck her hand through one. Ceci grinned and stuck her own tiny hand through the other one and giggled.

"You bustin' my kid?" asked Josephine Priego, returning with two tall iced-tea glasses filled with Coke.

Elena laughed. "Just entertaining her," she said.

"I'd offer you some rum with this, but I don't guess you're s'posed to drink while you're investigatin', huh?"

"That's right," Elena agreed. "But if you want a rum and Coke, go ahead and have one, Ms Priego."

"Hey, why don't you call me Jo, huh? That's what Arnold called me." Her lips trembled. "Think I will have some rum." She blinked back tears and returned to the kitchen.

Leo popped in and said, "The guy upstairs says he never saw or heard from her last night."

"You get his phone number?" asked Elena.

"Think he's lying?"

"Won't hurt to check the phone company records. What about the manager?"

"I'm heading for there now. How come you get a Coke and I don't?"

"I'm holding the baby, but you can have a sip of mine." Leo took her glass and bolted half of it. "Hey," Elena protested, but he was already out the door.

"You must have been real thirsty," said Jo Priego when she returned.

"The guy upstairs said you didn't call him or go up there."

"Yeah? Well, he's a big fat liar, but then what's he gonna say? He probably figured I sicced your partner on him."

Elena nodded and bounced the child on her knee. "You've got better eyelashes than a giraffe," she said to Ceci. The little girl stared at her.

"What's that supposed to mean?" demanded Jo Priego.

"I was at the zoo Monday. Giraffes have the longest eyelashes you ever saw. Just like this little beauty."

"She is pretty, isn't she?" Josephine beamed at her daughter. "An' now she hasn't got a daddy, all because that bitch killed him."

"We don't know that, Ms Priego."

"Jo."

"How old is Ceci?"

"Two. Next year I was gonna put her in play school. Now I don't know if I'll have the money."

"He didn't make any provision for you?"

"Well, I own this place free an' clear, but other than that, nothin'. It wasn't like Arnold figured he was gonna die. He was in great shape."

"He looked to be in good shape," Elena agreed. Except for the eyes, but she didn't tell Jo about that.

Leo returned to say, "The manager backed up your story, ma'am."

"'Course, she did. It's the truth."

"She says you called her about every fifteen minutes from seven to two in the morning." Leo grinned. "She wasn't exactly happy about it."

"Yeah, well, if she didn't want me callin' her, she should have stopped that old bastard upstairs from playin' that damn organ."

Elena winced at Jo's language. When Ceci really started talking, the child would sound like a stevedore.

The telephone rang and Jo gestured toward it. "Prob'ly for you."

Elena shifted the baby and picked the receiver up. "Jarvis," she said.

"Got twenty-two 911 calls from that number from seven forty-five to two in the morning," said the supervisor.

"Then why didn't anyone come out here?"

"If you were working last night, you'd know why. We had trouble all over the city. The wind makes people crazy."

"Tell me about it," said Elena. Although she'd spent the morning following up on her existing workload, just before she should have left at the end of her four-o'clock shift, she had to go out on a freeway assault—a pile-up caused by no visibility, followed by one driver, whose car was totaled, crawling out of the wreckage and shooting another driver. After that she worked straight through until ten-thirty. One assault after another— domestic, gangs, even an attack on a policeman in the Lower Valley.

"Loud music wasn't high on the priority list," said the supervisor.

"Looks like you're in the clear," Elena told Jo as she put the receiver back into the cradle.

"Hell yes, I'm in the clear. I loved Arnold. You oughta go find out where the bitch was. Just because she said she was outa town—"

"We'll follow it up, ma'am," said Leo.

"Yeah well, you find out who killed Arnold. I'll attend the execution. Maybe she hired someone to do him."

"Can you think of anyone besides his wife who might have wanted him dead?" Leo asked.

Ceci scrambled out of Elena's lap and toddled to the sofa to nestle in the curve of her mother's arm. She fell asleep almost instantly.

Elena asked, "Do you think the labor troubles he's been having—?"

"If you're sayin' one of the garment workers killed him, that's a dumb idea. Most of those women couldn't afford a gun." Jo paused. "I forgot. You said it was the bow an' arrow. God, *my* bow an' arrow."

Leo's eyebrows went up. "Christmas gift," Elena explained.

"Ah," he said.

"How about Alope Randall?" Elena asked.

"You mean the lawyer? Why the hell would she? I don't believe the stuff she's sayin' about him, but if it was true, she could get him in court. She don' need to kill him. Who suggested that? Arnold's old lady? She *would* finger someone who wasn't white. That's what the cops always think too, isn't it?"

"Not me," said Elena dryly.

"Well, yeah, you. Sorry about that. No, I don' think Alope Randall's who you're lookin' for."

"How'd he get along with his family?"

"His papa thought he hung the moon 'cause he did so good with the company, you know?"

"And his brothers and sister?"

"Hell, I don't know why any of *them* would kill him. He was makin' money for 'em, wasn't he? They all got along O.K. He even got along with the fruity one who's raisin' llamas up on the New Mexico border. Llamas! Who ever heard of a llama ranch?"

"You've met J.J. Audubon?" Elena asked.

"Yeah, once. Nutty little wimp. Guess he's like his mother. Arnold said their mama was kinda strange. Cared more about animals than people. She was always runnin' around tryin' to make people be nice to animals. Not that I think people should be mean to 'em. Ceci's got a kitty, an' I make sure she treats it good. But Arnold's mama, she was always goin' out—I never knew her—but she was tryin' to keep scientists an' guys like that from usin' animals to find out ways to cure disease. Go figure. The way I look at it, I'd rather some monkey got the disease than my kid. That makes sense, don' it?"

"Makes sense to me," said Elena, glancing at her partner, who was looking jittery, tapping his foot as if he might leap up and break into a tension-releasing tap routine. But then the mention of children seemed to do that to him lately. Now that Concepcion was pregnant. "So you don't think anyone in the family, other than Patricia Mandel, would have had any reason to kill him?"

"Well, it wasn't like I got invited to family dinners. But hell, why would anyone murder Arnold? He was a real sweetheart."

"Uh-huh." Elena had been taking notes. Probably a lot of people in town didn't think Arnold was a sweetheart, but that didn't mean they'd kill him. It was beginning to look like this might be a hard case to close. "Well, thank you for your time, Ms Priego, and if you think of anything, I'd really appreciate it if you'd call." Elena passed the woman one of her cards.

"Sure." Jo laid the child gently on the sofa and went with the two detectives toward the door, high-heeled sandals clacking on the tiles in the entry hall.

When Elena turned briefly to say goodbye, she saw that the tears were once again beginning to flow down Jo Priego's rosy brown cheeks.

"Think she did it?" asked Leo once they were outside.

"No," said Elena.

"Probably right," said Leo. "Except for the old guy upstairs, her alibi looks solid, and given the fact that she actually made all the other calls, why would she lie about phoning him?"

Elena nodded as they headed toward the car. "Damn dust," she muttered. "It's the one thing I hate about spring."

"Supposed to let up tomorrow," said Leo. "The wind's driving Concepcion nuts. That and pregnancy."

"How's she doing?" Elena asked.

"Bigger than a beer barrel. Can't get out of a chair without help. We're gonna hit the damn rush hour traffic." They ducked out of the wind, into the car, and headed back toward headquarters to check in and write up reports, having already put in a half hour of overtime.

7
..

When Elena sat down in her gray-tweed chair on Homicide Row, she found several messages. One was from Oliver Formalee, the criminal attorney who had defended her friend Sarah Tolland last year—Formalee, the deer-hunting partner of the late Arnold Mandel. That call Elena returned immediately.

"Well, Detective," said Formalee when she had been put through by his secretary, "you're at it again, I see."

"At what?" Elena asked cautiously.

"You're harassing an innocent woman for a crime she did not commit."

"I'm not aware of having harassed anyone," said Elena.

"You don't think questioning Patricia Mandel when she was overcome with grief—"

"Actually, Mrs. Mandel didn't seem particularly grief-stricken. I'd say she was more interested in possible loss of income than in the loss of companionship."

"The woman was taking Valium," Formalee snapped. "How could you tell what she was feeling?"

"Valium and margaritas," Elena agreed.

"Exactly. Therefore, I hope you realize that nothing Patricia said can be used against her or taken as—"

"You mean," Elena interrupted, "I shouldn't follow up on the people she thinks might have murdered her husband? That's certainly going to screw up my case."

47

Formalee sighed. "I mean, Detective, that your snide remarks about her lack of feeling indicate that you are looking at Mrs. Mandel as a possible suspect in her husband's murder. But that's quite impossible. She was out of town and, believe me, had no motive to kill him, nor could she have drawn that bow."

"Aren't those fancy bows constructed so that you don't have to be muscular to use them?"

"They are," said Formalee, "but you do have to know what you're doing, and Patricia is not the sort of woman who has any interest in bows or hunting."

"While you, on the other hand," said Elena, "were his deer-hunting partner. You could have pulled the bow."

"Indeed, I could," Oliver Formalee conceded, "but if you're looking at me as a suspect, I was out of town as well, which you can easily confirm." He gave her the name of his hotel in Dallas and the length of his stay.

"I appreciate the information, Counselor," said Elena.

"I'm sure you do," he retorted dryly. "Please keep in mind that you interviewed the victim's wife while she was under the influence of alcohol and prescription drugs. You even provided her with more alcohol, and then when she passed out, you abandoned her."

"I did not," said Elena indignantly. "I took her pulse, I rolled back her eyelid, and then I told the maid to watch her. What did you want me to do? Call an ambulance? The papers would love that. 'Victim's Wife OD's on Tequila and Tranquilizers.' It would make a great story."

"Indeed, and I don't want to see it in the paper. Good evening, Detective." Formalee hung up before she could say anything else.

At the computer Elena wrote up her report on the afternoon's investigation and the conversation with Formalee.

"I'm finished," Leo called from across the aisle. "Goin' home to my wife and fetuses."

"Lucky you," said Elena and put in a call to the Dallas hotel, where Formalee said he'd been registered. According to the desk clerk, the lawyer had stayed there for four days and had not checked out until ten-thirty that morning. The clerk also told her that Formalee had ordered a room-service dinner for two the night before at eight-thirty and brandy at eleven-thirty. Elena asked to speak with the employee who had delivered the dinner and drinks. The waiter said he had not seen Formalee. He had knocked, and on both occasions left the tray outside the door. The food and brandy had, however, been consumed.

Elena pondered the information she'd garnered from the hotel. It was possible that someone else had stayed in Formalee's room and done the ordering while he came back to Los Santos and killed Arnold, but why would he want to do it? He'd been friends with the victim for years and had nothing apparent to gain from the death. She added the latest facts to her report, pressed *save*, turned off the computer, and went out to the parking lot to retrieve her Ford pickup.

While making the trip to her house on Sierra Negra, her mind wandered away from the case to a telephone call she'd had the evening before from Michael's brother. Why did Mark keep calling her? She'd been so upset last night that she'd hung up before he could say anything more than hello. She was going to have to tell Michael again that his brother was bugging her, and hope he paid attention this time. What a mess! She didn't want to cause trouble between them or, more important, between herself and Michael.

She pulled into the driveway and set the complicated alarm apparatus on the truck, a system she'd had installed to prevent her ex-husband, Frank, from moving the truck so she couldn't find it. Getting out, she recalled smugly that Frank no longer played those tricks on her, not since Elena's mother had come to town and sicced a local *curandera* on him.

"Elena. Yoo-hoo, Elena."

Elena turned from putting her key in the lock and saw her neighbor Dimitra Potemkin trotting down the walk holding a vase full of flowers. "You weren't home," said the old lady, every silver curl bobbing, "so the florist left these with me."

"My goodness, Dimitra, the physical therapy's done wonders. That hip's as good as new."

"It certainly is," Dimitra agreed. "Since God killed Boris, I'm a new woman."

Elena sighed. It did no good to point out that God hadn't

put that bullet in the forehead of Dimitra's late, unlamented husband.

"I like a young man who gives a girl flowers," said Dimitra, thrusting the vase into Elena's hands. "Enjoy them, dear. And now I have to hurry home. Omar and I are going to the movies this evening. That is if he wakes up in time." She scowled across the street toward the house of Omar Ashkenazi, the retired rug salesman who slept odd hours, practiced yoga, and courted Dimitra assiduously.

Elena smiled and went inside with the vase in one arm, spring flowers tickling her nose and obscuring her vision. How sweet of Michael to send them, she thought. She set the vase on the kitchen table, locked her gun away in a drawer, and plucked the card out. It said, "Sorry about the Monday morning call. Want to get together for an apologetic drink? Mark."

Mark had sent these flowers? She shoved the card, message facing outward, into the top of the bouquet where Michael couldn't miss it when he came over. Then she carried the vase into the living room and plunked it down on the coffee table. If he ignored the damn bouquet, she'd shove his nose into it and see whether he thought his brother inviting her out for a drink was just "jock talk."

Disgruntled, she studied the flowers, wishing that Michael had sent them. If he had, she could call to thank him, and he'd come over, and—well, he hadn't sent them! Mr. Jock Talk had. "Bastard!" she muttered under her breath and moved the vase to an end table beside the section of the sofa where Michael always sat. If it weren't so late and she weren't so tired, she'd call him right now. Let *him* read the note and warn his brother off.

8
..

They ought to shoot that Bruce Metterlick for his racist remarks he made in your column. Pansy is a Hispanic elephant. She likes burritos. And nachos. I shared my lunch with her in 1981. So what would you expect an Anglo to say? Shoot her, right? No way. She's Los Santos' elephant.

Carlos Terrazos, Newspaper Distribution Manager

"Elephant Update," Los Santos *Herald-Post*, Wednesday, March 29

"Phone company says Priego did call the guy upstairs a whole bunch of times," said Leo. "She was on the phone till two in the morning."

Elena nodded and made a note. She was trying to track down the Pandarenes, with whom Patricia Mandel claimed to have spent the days before her husband's death. The Pandarene maid at their Los Santos home had just given Elena a number in Mexico.

"I'll see what I can find out from Cyclops Security," Leo said, and turned back to his telephone.

Elena called a hotel in Cozumel. In neither English nor Spanish did the desk clerk wish to connect her with Ernest or Marianna Pandarene. Elena got the impression that she had made a mistake by identifying herself as a policewoman.

51

"Look," she said urgently, "their niece just got run down in Juarez, Mexico, by a Tecate truck."

The clerk changed his mind and put her through to the room after a short conversation with the occupants. "Ernest Pandarene speaking," said a rather high-pitched male voice. "Or if you prefer," said another voice, low and husky, "Marianna Pandarene, and we don't have a niece."

"Sorry," said Elena. "It was the only way I could get through to you. I'm a Crimes Against Persons detective in Los Santos, Texas, trying to verify Patricia Mandel's whereabouts this past Monday, Tuesday, and Wednesday morning."

"How delicious," said Marianna. "What's Patricia done? Killed her maid?"

"Would you say that Mrs. Mandel is the type to kill someone?"

"Well, that depends," said Ernest. "If the girl ruined a favorite dress or dropped a bottle of expensive perfume. What do you think, Marianna? Is Patricia murderess material?"

"I'd say it depends on the murderee," Marianna replied cheerfully. "Is there one, Detective?"

"Her husband, Arnold," Elena said.

"Oh well, she'd never kill Arnold," said Marianna with absolute certainty.

"Definitely not," Ernest agreed. "Where do you think the designer wardrobe and the Jaguar came from if not Arnold? And now you say someone killed him? How dreadful! Patricia must be beside herself."

"No doubt," said Elena. "Now, in regard to her whereabouts—"

"Oh, well, her whereabouts," said Ernest. "Patricia flew into Dallas with us on Monday morning. We dropped her back in Los Santos Wednesday morning. Does that help?"

"How much did you see of her in between?" Elena asked.

"We had lunch with her," said Ernest. "Which day was that, Marianna?"

"Monday. And I believe we passed her in the lobby several times, didn't we?"

"I believe we did."

"Were you by any chance with her on Tuesday night?"

"Goodness, no," said Marianna. "I had better things to do than spend my evenings with Patricia."

"And I," said Ernest, "was attending a delightful theater production of one of the late Preston Jones's plays. Patricia wouldn't go to a play if you paid her."

"Was she aware that you were on your way to Mexico when you dropped her off in Los Santos?" Elena asked.

"Of course. We invited her along, but she said she had to attend some dinner with Arnold. She did, after all, have to put in a wifely appearance from time to time."

"Are you saying they didn't have a close marriage?"

"They had a very satisfactory arrangement," said Ernest, "and believe me, dear girl, Patricia would never have killed Arnold. Her father lost most of his money in the Texas S & L debacle."

"Ernest," Marianna broke in, "I think the boy's here to take us sightseeing. We don't want to miss the boat."

"Absolutely," said Ernest. "I hope we've been helpful, Detective."

He hung up. Had they been helpful? Elena wondered. And where were they from originally? They didn't sound like Los Santoans. Or any kind of Texans.

"Here's something interesting," said Leo as soon as Elena put the receiver down. "The Cyclops Security log notes a brown pickup truck with a logo painted on the door in the Mandel driveway at ten, again at twelve, but gone by two. They took it for a Los Santos Apparel vehicle, but the company doesn't use brown trucks. I just checked."

"I gather the security guys didn't see what the logo said."

"Nope."

"And I don't suppose they got a license number?"

"Nope. I told you those private security patrols aren't worth—"

"Still, it might be useful information," Elena mused. "Especially if it turns out that someone who hated him owns a brown pickup with a logo. Somehow, I can't see his wife, Patricia, in one." Elena picked her purse up off the floor. "Let's go visit Alope Randall," she suggested.

"How did Mrs. Mandel's alibi pan out?" Leo asked as they

left through the side door to pick up an unmarked police car for the trip to the legal clinic.

"Not at all," said Elena. "They took her to Dallas on Monday, and they brought her home on Wednesday, had lunch with her on Monday, but that's about it. Neither one of them saw her on the night he was killed."

"Now, that's interesting."

"Another odd thing is that she gave me their names and home number, but she didn't bother to tell me they were on their way to Mexico. Maybe she thought I wouldn't follow up."

"Dumb," said Leo.

Alope Randall's offices were downtown in an old building on Magoffin. The waiting room was crowded with poor women and wailing children, but Elena and Leo, having presented their identification to the receptionist, were given preferential treatment, precipitating a number of infuriated comments in Spanish as they went through the battered door into the lawyer's office.

Elena had seen pictures of Alope Randall in the newspapers, hassling garment manufacturers on picket lines and in court, but the pictures didn't do her justice. She was a stocky woman, shapely but big-boned, standing less than medium height. Her hair was the same dead black as Elena's, but her skin was a rich, glowing brown, with two deep pockmarks to the left side of her mouth. Otherwise, her complexion was perfect, completely unlined, although she had to be in her late thirties. She had sharp, dark eyes that seemed to look right into your soul. Her hair had been whipped into a casual knot at the nape of her neck and skewered with a wooden pin thrust through a leather holder. She wore hose and white sneakers with a tailored khaki suit over a T-shirt that said "Female Empowerment."

"Crimes Against Persons," she mused once the detectives had introduced themselves. "I suppose you're here about Arnold Mandel. Fourteen poverty-stricken women could die at their sewing machines, but if one rich manufacturer is murdered, the whole police force gets right on it."

"Actually," said Elena, with a brief smile, "Leo and I don't constitute the whole police force. Your name has been mentioned as someone who didn't like Mr. Mandel."

"Well, you've got that right," said Alope Randall and dropped into an old wooden swivel chair. "Take a seat. He was a first-class bastard, but I'm sorry he's dead. I was looking forward to sticking it to him in court. We were about ready to sue him for sexual harassment at the family factory, not to mention all the unpaid wages and labor-law violations in the sweatshops he owned."

"Is it for sure he owned those?" Elena asked.

"Damn right. He used their product to feed the parent factory so he didn't have to pay as much out in wages and benefits. Bought through a middleman. Then he financed a bunch of them through a twisted little lawyer who fronted for him. You don't believe me, ask the feds. They're on his tail too." She grinned. "Because I put them there. If you want to get the feds to do anything, you got to give them a kick in the posterior. But the late Arnold was looking at a lot of trouble, maybe some jail time. There won't be many tears shed for him, not among my clients. I'm surprised you're interested in his business dealings."

"We're interested in finding his murderer," said Leo.

"Right. And you think I killed him? Why? Because anyone with Indian blood would know how to use a bow and arrow? Well, I do know how, but I'm not your perpetrator."

"Could you tell us where you were Tuesday night, ma'am?" asked Leo.

"Sure, I was at home, working on briefs."

"Can anyone vouch for that?"

"Not a soul," said Alope Randall, "but you're going to have a hard time pinning it on me, since I didn't do it. And if you give me too much trouble, I'll sue."

"Maybe you received or made telephone calls that evening," Elena suggested. She wouldn't mind crossing Alope Randall off the suspect list. She liked the woman.

"No phone calls. Just sat home working. Didn't even have the blinds up, so the neighbors won't be able to tell you anything."

"Where do you live?" asked Leo.

"Sunset Heights," she answered promptly. "Why don't you

check some of his front men. Maybe there was a falling out among thieves."

"Could you give us some names?" asked Elena.

"Sure. Carlos Aguilar. Everyone calls him Chuck. He was the middleman between the Mandel factory and the sweat-shops. Office on Lee Trevino. The lawyer who fronted for Mandel is Bascomb Pope. His office is down near the courthouse." Randall's telephone rang. She picked up, listened for a moment, swore, slammed down the receiver, and rose from her squeaking chair. "There's a lint fire in a sweatshop on El Paso Street. Know what that is? Lint from the piece goods collects all over the place. Then some bare wire that should have been fixed sparks, and the whole place goes up. No sprinkler systems, of course. No fire extinguishers. Anyone dies, it will be murder. Only the murderer's dead. Your victim. Arnold Mandel owned that place, or part of it." She grabbed a battered briefcase and circled her desk, Leo and Elena following behind.

Lamentations rose among the clientele when they saw that Alope was leaving. "Back as soon as I can," she called over her shoulder in Spanish.

Outside they ran into three reporters. "Is Ms Randall a suspect in the Mandel murder?" asked the first.

"No comment," answered Leo.

"If you want a good story," said Alope Randall, "follow me. There's a lint fire on El Paso Street at one of the sweatshops." They could all hear the sirens. "Even dead Arnold Mandel is still preying on poor women, and by God, we won't let him get away with it. We'll go after the estate."

She climbed into a pickup truck and drove off, reporters scrambling to follow. "Did you see that truck?" asked Leo.

"Yeah. Brown with a white logo on the side." The logo said "Border Legal Clinic." Given the information from Cyclops Security, Alope Randall was looking like a definite suspect.

9
··

Thursday, March 30, 12:35 P.M.

Leo and Elena ate chiliburgers from a fast-food place on Lee Trevino Drive, then went in search of Aguilar Apparel. They found the building, a two-story office complex fronted by dusty oleander bushes, but according to the insurance agent next door, Aguilar Apparel had moved to Copia Street about ten days earlier.

As Leo headed back toward the interstate, Elena mused aloud: "With Mandel dead, the middleman's pretty much cut out, but Aguilar moved to cheaper quarters *before* Arnold died."

"Maybe Mandel fired him," Leo suggested. "Then Aguilar, looking at a big drop in income, seeing his business going down the tubes, went over to the victim's house to try to make a deal, they quarreled, and Aguilar killed him."

"Or," Elena speculated, "maybe they had one of those partnership deals where the surviving partner gets everything. I wonder if Aguilar has a brown pickup."

They found the company in a peeling adobe on Copia near the freeway, sharing quarters with a dealer in rebuilt auto parts. In back there were two vans with logos on the doors. Neither vehicle was brown. In front, two kids who looked about ten years old shared a cigarette and leaning space against a bus-stop sign. "Got lung cancer yet?" Elena asked them.

"Fuck you, lady," said the smaller, skinnier kid.

"Ah, the joys of childhood," Elena murmured, "skipping school, smoking, foul language."

"Any of my kids start smoking," said Leo, "I'll make 'em eat the cigarettes." They entered the two-room office and stopped at the desk of Juanita, who had acne and killer fingernails. "Detectives Jarvis and Weizell to see Mr. Aguilar," said Leo.

The girl tapped the intercom and said, "Hey, Chuck, two cops out here."

Instead of answering, Carlos Aguilar opened his door. He was a barrel-chested man of forty-five or so, thick black hair and mustache, navy blue blazer with large brass buttons, embroidered shirt with a string tie, knife-edged crease on gray trousers, and polished boots. Very spiffy, Elena thought. He looked more prosperous than his office.

"What can I do for you, Officers?" he asked.

"We're investigating the murder of Arnold Mandel," said Leo.

"Come on in." Aguilar preceded them and dropped into a high-backed oxblood leather executive chair.

"Were you and Mr. Mandel still doing business at the time of his death?" asked Elena.

"Sure," said Aguilar. "Sit down."

"Maybe you could tell us the nature of that business," said Leo.

"You mean you haven't read about us in the papers?" said Aguilar, looking sour. "Damn nosy reporters. And that lawyer; she probably killed him."

"Your arrangement with Mr. Mandel," Elena prompted.

"I was Arnold's middleman, and I'll tell you, his death is going to shoot my business all to hell."

"You didn't act as middleman for anyone else?" Elena asked.

"Nobody else needed one. You have the cash flow, you buy from the contractors and sell to the retailers. I don't have the cash. Arnold did. He just couldn't let his father know he was using places like that, so I did the subcontracting." Hands on the padded arms, Aguilar swung his chair from side to side as he talked. "I supplied the piece goods to the washing operations, shipped from there to the sewing shops, from there to the finishers. Bird-dogged production. Then I picked up the product and delivered it to Los Santos Apparel."

"And your cut was?"

"Generally speaking, fifty cents a garment."

"That doesn't sound like much," said Elena.

"Don't kid yourself. I've cleared as much as a hundred and twenty-five thou a year." Aguilar swung the chair completely around. "So Arnold's death is a flat-out disaster for me," he said. "I gotta get a new angle."

"Well, if you were still doing business with Mr. Mandel when he died, how come you moved from that nice office on Lee Trevino to this dump?" Leo asked.

"Because I got one kid in college and another one going in next year. You know what that costs? Jesus Christ! So I figure I don't need a fancy office. Arnold and I did business by telephone. The sweatshop guys might show up, but they don't need any plush waiting room." Aguilar gave himself another twirl.

"And don't listen to those garment workers who are always bitching about the small contractors. Contracting's how people get started in this business. There's nothing illegal in what I was doing, and there's nothing illegal in the way my contractors deal with their workers."

Elena gave him a dry look, and he said defensively, "These women aren't pros. They're the ragtag, no experience, too young or too old—"

"Why did Mr. Mandel have to do business through you if there's nothing illegal going on?" asked Leo. "Tell us more about that."

"Because ten, fifteen years ago Los Santos Apparel was about to go under. Some big contract got all screwed up, trouble with the IRS, stuff like that." Aguilar stopped swinging and tipped his chair back. "Then the old man had a stroke, a couple of strokes, so Arnold took over, and he had to get things going again. There was no way he could do it with Jacob, his dad, insisting on health benefits and great working conditions and all that stuff for the employees." Having tipped as far back as he could, Aguilar let the chair spring down with a thump. "So Arnold expanded, only he didn't expand in the home factory. He expanded into subcontracting." Chuck Aguilar grinned and twirled the chair completely around again. "Hey, this is one great chair, don't you think?"

"Great," Elena agreed wryly.

"Got it wholesale from my brother-in-law. Came this morning."

"Were you also partners with Mr. Mandel in any of the sweatshops?" Elena asked.

"I didn't know he owned any. I still don't know it. That's just newspaper crap. Labor lawyer talk. Arnold wouldn't cut me out if he had a sweet deal going." Chuck Aguilar's face had turned red, and he stopped bouncing around in his new chair.

If Aguilar had known he'd been left out of a lucrative setup, would he have been angry enough to kill Arnold? It seemed to Elena that the contractor was less worried about his financial situation than he claimed. Either he had been partners in some of the sweatshops, or he'd skimmed off enough from his deal with Arnold that he was now sitting pretty. In fact, maybe Arnold had caught him lining his pockets and threatened prosecution, and Aguilar had murdered him. There were all sorts of possibilities here. "We'll need to know where you were the night of the murder."

"Sure. Tuesday, right? Well, I had a four o'clock appointment in Juarez to play handball at Los Baños Roma with a buddy. After the game we showered and had a couple of beers. Then we went out to the dog track for the evening. Placed a few bets. I even won some money." Aguilar had begun opening the drawers of his desk as he talked, peering inside, closing them. "After that we drove back to the main drag, had dinner at Martino's and hit the mariachi bars, picked up a couple of girls. Working girls. I'd appreciate it if you didn't mention that to the wife."

Elena's eyebrows went up. "Anybody ever tell you what percentage of those girls have AIDS?"

"Hey, you think I'm stupid? I used a condom," said Aguilar.

He'd finished with the drawers on one side and started on the other. Hyperactive, Elena thought.

"Anyway, I was over there till—I don't know—three in the morning. Somewhere like that. Then I came home and went to bed. Woke the wife up. She asked me what I was doing coming in that late, and I told her I'd been out drinking with Chato."

"This is the name of your friend in Mexico?" asked Leo.

"Right. Chato Rivas-Estrada."

"You got a phone number for him?"

"Help yourself." Aguilar flipped through a Rolodex, turned it around, and Elena copied down the address and telephone number in Juarez.

"Did your partnership with Mandel include insurance on his life or a clause that leaves the business to you?" she asked.

"We didn't have a partnership," said Aguilar, looking surprised. "We operated on a handshake." He sat still for a moment staring at the detectives. "You thinking I killed Arnold? Now that would be stupid. I'm gonna have to start hustling again to keep the wife in all those expensive aerobics classes and the kids in college. Don't know why anyone ever gets married. Man can have a lot more fun running around with his *compadres*. You detectives got any kids?"

"I don't," said Elena. "Leo's got some on the way."

"Some?" Aguilar looked surprised. "How many?"

Leo scowled. "Nobody knows for sure," he snapped. "The latest count is three."

"All that swinging and bouncing," said Elena once they'd left. "Could be a sign of guilt."

"Could be he just loves his new chair," said Leo. "But if he's really in financial trouble, why's he buying new furniture?"

10
..

Toward the end of their shift, Elena and Leo drove back around the mountain and called on Patricia Mandel, whose alibi had evaporated after Elena talked to the Pandarenes that morning.

"Steel drunk," Anita whispered as she opened the door and led them to a sunroom filled with cushiony chintz-covered furniture. Mrs. Mandel was settled in a chair, her feet on a huge ottoman, a nearly empty margarita glass in her hand.

"So," she said. "*Les gendarmes* arrive. I hope you've come to apologize for sending Ahab back to me."

"Who?" asked Leo.

"The falcon," said Elena. "I suppose the Crime Scene Unit returned it. And after all, since you're the widow, Ahab is now *your* falcon, Mrs. Mandel."

"That's one of Arnold's possessions I refuse to accept." She laughed into her margarita, causing a slosh of alcohol to cascade over the rim onto her green silk blouse. "I called Darwin and said I intended to set the bird free. Naturally, he fell all over himself to get over here and rescue poor Ahab, who, according to Darwin, couldn't survive in the wild after a lifetime of captivity. I suppose he means the bird would get run down by an airplane or something."

Patricia Mandell dabbed at the margarita stain on her blouse. "S-o-o, have you come to tell me that you've arrested Arnold's mistress?"

"No, ma'am," said Elena. "She has an alibi."

"Don't believe her," advised Patricia Mandel. "Would you care for a drink?" She waved toward the crystal pitcher, about a third full.

The detectives declined and sat down. Leo said, "Ms Priego's alibi is a lot better than yours, ma'am."

"What's wrong with mine? I was in Dallas. Correct me if I'm wrong, but I don't think you can draw a bow in Dallas and expect the arrow to hit someone in Los Santos." She smirked, visibly pleased with her own logic and wit.

"Except that no one saw you in Dallas the day or the night of your husband's murder," said Elena. "Not the Pandarenes, whose number you gave me, knowing that they wouldn't be there."

"Be where?"

"Be at the number you gave me. They've gone on to Mexico, which they said they told you."

The widow looked surprised. "And you called them in Mexico?" She poured herself another drink. "So you haven't arrested Priego? Well, even so, she's out of luck. No more money for Priego. And Priegette."

Elena thought of that beautiful little girl. "The child's name is Ceci."

"For Cecilia? I don't believe it!" exclaimed Patricia Mandel. "He named her after his *mother*? Hoping I'd find out, I suppose, and have some belated attack of guilt because I never presented him with a son and heir. I doubt that he was any too pleased to find himself the father of a bastard *daughter*." Draining her glass in one large swallow, she laughed bitterly and added, "Not that it *matters*. He could have named her Jacobette, and she wouldn't get a penny, because *I'm* the heir. That is if the banks ever unfreeze the accounts. Why would they do that? It's a community-property state. I'm the wife. I *own* half."

"Could we get back to your whereabouts the night of your husband's murder?" said Leo impatiently.

"No, we couldn't," retorted Mrs. Mandel. "On advice of counsel, I'm not supposed to be talking to you. If you want to talk to me, my lawyer has to be present."

"The honorable Oliver Formalee?" asked Elena. "He's a criminal attorney."

"Oh, for heaven's sake. I didn't kill my husband. And Oliver's a family friend. Gabriella, where are you?" Mrs. Mandel had raised her voice to a ladylike shriek.

Anita appeared in the doorway. "Gabriella take day off. Have hysterics."

"Silly twit," muttered the lady of the house. "Well, you'll do. You're the one who makes the margaritas, aren't you? I'll have a pitcher, and you can show these people out."

11
••

Elena and Leo had agreed that they needed to talk to Alope Randall again. Accordingly, when Elena returned to Five Points to do her supplemental reports for the day, she called the lawyer. Randall greeted her with the news that the lint fire on El Paso Street had sent four women to Thomason General, three suffering from smoke inhalation and one with burns on her hands and arms.

"How's she going to work if she can't use her hands?" demanded the lawyer, as if Elena herself had set a torch to the seamstress. "She's got two kids, no husband, lives in a shack in one of the *colonias* north of the freeway—no running water, no sewer connection, no health services, and if you think Arnold Mandel is going to—"

"He's dead," Elena reminded the lawyer.

"Right. I'll have to sue the estate. Damn, damn, damn," the woman muttered.

"I'm sorry about the seamstresses," said Elena honestly, feeling the horror of the burned woman's situation. "Could I make an appointment to talk to you tomorrow?"

"I don't have five minutes open tomorrow. I'll be in court all day."

"Look, Ms Randall, I'm investigating a homicide and—"

"I'm not trying to evade you, Detective. I plan to eat dinner at that Puerto Rican place on Montana about seven. You want to meet me, you can talk to me over chicken and plantains."

Elena glanced at her watch. Six-fifteen. She ought to be able to get there by seven. "How expensive is it?" she asked, thinking of her monthly budget.

"It's reasonable," said Alope Randall. "And don't expect me to pick up your tab just because cops are underpaid. I don't earn anything at all; I'm living on money my father left me. Seven o'clock." She hung up.

By six-thirty Elena had finished her report. She ducked into the ladies' room to comb out and rebraid her hair, ran a tissue beneath her left eye to take care of a mascara smudge she'd got because blowing dust caused tears, brushed on a little lipstick, and went out to her truck. Puerto Rican chicken, huh? She had no idea what it would taste like. Maybe like Aunt Josefina's Sunday dinners back in Chimayo. Tia Josefina could do things with chicken and chile that made you want to weep when the last bite had been eaten. The restaurant, when Elena finally found it, smelled of spices and garlic, and Alope Randall in her khaki suit was sitting on the left side of the room in serious discussion with the waiter.

"I'll order for you," said the lawyer as Elena sat down across the table.

"Not without telling me what the order's going to cost," Elena replied.

"Are you that hard up?" asked Randall.

Elena sighed. "I treated myself to three *ocotillos* last month, so I'm economizing."

"A cop-gardener? Very domestic."

"Would you say that if I were a *male* cop-gardener?" Elena snapped.

Alope Randall grinned. "Got me. I just don't like cops."

Elena shrugged. "Most cops don't like lawyers."

Randall seemed undisturbed by that information and pointed out the prices of the things she wanted to order. Elena agreed. The place *was* reasonable, and she could afford to splurge once this week. "I own a little adobe on Sierra Negra," she said after the waiter had departed. "I like to keep the yard looking good."

Randall grimaced and muttered, "My dad renovated a house in Sunset Heights and left it to me, but I pretend the yard's not there. Given the water shortage, I figure it's my civic duty to let the stuff fend for itself. I haven't put a drop of water on that yard in years."

And proud of it, thought Elena, who, because of rationing, had to rise early and stay up late to water. She rather envied Alope Randall's cavalier attitude toward gardening. The waiter deposited glasses of beer on the table and left again.

"Some of the really stubborn stuff survived," Randell went on, "but the roses all died. My dad would turn over in his grave. He really liked roses."

"I thought you were Mescalero Apache," said Elena. "What's an Apache guy doing renovating houses and planting roses in the historic district of Los Santos?"

"My dad was Anglo. An architect. He came to the reservation to ski and to design stuff for the tribe's tourist facilities, met my mother, and married her. Big mistake. He had to leave to make a living and she wouldn't go. So they split, and I stayed with her. Lived on the reservation till I was twelve and she died."

"And that's when you moved to Los Santos?"

"Well, my dad had to go to court to get custody—big Indian-kids-shouldn't-be-separated-from-their-cultural-heritage deal." Alope took a long, appreciative swallow of her beer. "The tribe lost, since he was the natural father, and off I went, madder than a coyote in a vegetable patch. I guess I didn't speak to my father for about eighteen months."

Elena grinned. "That must have been fun for both of you."

Alope shrugged. "He remembered my mother, who never had much to say, so he took it in stride. A patient man, my father. He put me in Loretto Academy, where I was about as out of place as jalapeños in flan, but I adjusted."

"What did you do when you graduated from Loretto?" Elena asked, thinking Alope had probably gone to some Ivy League school. The waiter put plates of food in front of them and trotted away.

"Went to U.T. Los Santos," Alope replied.

"Me too," said Elena, surprised. She took her first bite of chicken, which was delicious.

"I majored in political science. By that time I was interested in the labor situation here in town, so I went to law school at Texas Tech. My dad died while I was in Lubbock and left me his house and a small estate." Alope took a bite of plantain and chewed. "I'm living on the inheritance. Kind of ironic, isn't it? I do *pro bono* work for women who don't know where their next tortilla's coming from, and I'm a coupon clipper."

"The Mandels treat their workers well," Elena pointed out, sampling the plantains gingerly. Fried bananas? Well, they weren't bad.

"I've got no quarrel with Los Santos Apparel, except that Arnold and some of his execs sexually harass the women. You know— 'Put out or you won't get on the overtime list.' 'Put out or we'll doctor your quota sheets so you get fired.'"

Elena imagined herself listening day after day to the stories of women who had to trade sexual favors to keep their jobs and feed their children. Would it make someone angry enough to kill? Maybe.

"At his plant you meet your quota," said Alope Randall, "or you're history. But my main quarrel with Arnold Mandel was and still is what was going on behind the good-employer façade. You ever been to a sweatshop?"

Elena shook her head.

"Well, you should go some time. It's an education. In the first place, a lot of them are firetraps with no ventilation or sprinkler systems."

"I thought the fire department inspected once a year."

"They do, but those places come and go; the department doesn't always catch up with them." Alope cut up some chicken and forked a piece into her mouth. "Take that place today. Not only was it a fire hazard, but with no lint control the women develop respiratory problems. There's no air conditioning or heating. Half the time the toilets don't work, or they'll have one working toilet for thirty or more women. And there's no pay for toilet breaks. If the workers have to pee, they just hold it and end up with kidney problems. Imagine working under those conditions while you're pregnant." Alope took a sip of beer, and continued.

"They have to lift heavy bolts of material with no training and no lifting belts, so they hurt their backs. No health benefits, of course. No sick leave. The women say their benefits amount to 'Take two aspirin and get back to work.'

And of course they can't afford to take time off and lose the money or the job; they've got kids to support, most of them. And they can't even be sure of a full day's pay, much less a full week's pay; they're only employed for as long as it takes to fulfill the contract."

Alope waved her fork. "Half the time they don't get paid at all. The owner just skips, declares bankruptcy, and sets up down the street under another company name. I could spend the whole evening telling you what's wrong with those places."

Elena had watched the lawyer closely throughout the diatribe. Alope Randall was passionately angry. No question. If you were a labor lawyer, and you couldn't get the courts moving fast enough, how far would you go to accomplish your ends? Elena wondered. Randall might be angry, but what good would murdering one guy do? There would always be someone to set up another sweatshop.

"Laundries," Alope was saying, "where they wash and bleach the piece goods—they use chemicals that burn your skin and screw up your lungs." More fork stabs for emphasis. "Those outfits are hell on the workers—mostly men—and hell on the environment, not to mention using an ungodly amount of water when most of their employees don't have running water at home, when babies across the border are dying of dehydration. I suppose you know that our aquifer is—"

Elena finally cut her off. She knew all about the water problem. "I've read about the sweatshops. It's unconscionable, but my official concern is still the murder of Arnold Mandel."

"Right." Alope cut another piece of chicken.

"When was the last time you saw him?" Elena persevered.

"Last Friday. I've got sweatshop women picketing the family factory because the sweatshops are supplying Los Santos Apparel with finished product."

"Did you have any conversation with him?"

"Well, if you count calling him a son of a bitch, yeah. He and his wife in her fancy clothes! You look at Patricia Mandel; then you look at one of those poor women who buy their clothes secondhand. You know—*ropa usada*. Sold by the pound. They're plodding around in the blowing dust trying to get a living wage; she's sitting in her air-conditioned

Lincoln wearing an outfit that would feed a family of four for three months. Makes you wonder whether there's a God."

"Did you threaten him?"

"I don't know. Probably."

"And that's the last time you saw him?"

"Right."

"I notice you drive a brown pickup with a white logo on the door."

"Uh-huh."

"Is that your truck?"

"It's the clinic's truck, and I'm the clinic, plus whatever volunteer time I can get from other people."

"I also notice that it's out in front tonight."

"The truck's my transportation. You want to report me to the IRS? It won't fly as tax fraud."

"You take it home with you?" asked Elena. "Have it with you all the time?"

"Yes, sure. What's the problem with the pickup? You think it's unfeminine or something?"

Elena had to laugh. "I drive a truck myself. Where was yours on Tuesday night?"

Alope Randall hesitated, frowning. "Why do you ask?"

"Could you just answer the question, please?"

"In my driveway. Where's this going?"

"According to the security patrol in the Mandel neighborhood, a brown pickup with a logo on the door was seen at the Mandel house from ten P.M. to two in the morning the night he was murdered." Elena thought she saw something flicker in Alope Randall's eyes.

"Well, my truck was in my driveway at ten."

"And later?"

Alope Randall shrugged. "I didn't look out after that, but it was there the next morning. Any other questions?"

"Anyone else have a key to the truck?"

"No."

"Volunteers at the clinic?"

"No."

"Do you—"

"Look, I don't have an alibi. I hated the s.o.b., but I didn't kill him."

Elena sighed, and they finished their chicken with casual conversation, Elena thinking over Alope Randall's answers. The truck had been there at ten P.M. and in the morning. Was that some cleverly orchestrated response that saved the lawyer from telling a lie to a cop? Had Randall perhaps made several visits to the Mandel house that night, on one of which she killed Arnold? Elena hoped not. She kind of liked Alope. "Did you drive to his place that night?" she asked. If Alope's answer had been a lie by omission, Elena wasn't going to let her get away with it.

"I never left my house Tuesday night, or Wednesday morning before seven-thirty. I never drove to Mandel's house. Is that clear enough?"

It had to be. They said goodbye in the parking lot, and Elena returned home, where she found a message on her answering machine from Michael. He wanted her to attend a dinner party with him on Friday night, a party given by a woman whom he and the other professors had met on their spring break in Rome.

She returned his call, and they had what couldn't be considered an entirely friendly conversation. Michael opened by saying, "Where have you been?"

"Working the Mandel case," she replied, resenting his tone. "I had dinner with the labor lawyer, Alope Randall."

"How come you've been talking to my brother, Mark?"

That question took her by surprise. "The only time I talked to Mark, you were here. Don't tell me you've forgotten what you passed off as 'jock talk'?"

"He said he talked to you the next day."

"He called. I hung up on him," said Elena. "And tell him not to send me any more flowers."

"What flowers?"

"The flowers he sent with a suggestion that I meet him for a drink."

"You met him for a drink?"

"No, Michael, I didn't. I'm not interested in your brother. I don't even like him."

"Hey, if he sent you flowers, he was just trying to apologize for that call Monday."

Clearly there was no reasoning with Michael about his

brother. "What time are you going to pick me up, or have you changed your mind about inviting me to this dinner?"

"Of course I haven't." He sounded flustered. "How about quarter to seven? And it will be fairly formal. Our hostess is rich, so why don't you wear one of those hand-loomed outfits your mother sends you? The ones she sells in Santa Fe at exorbitant prices."

Great, Elena thought. *Now he's telling me how to dress.* "O.K.," she agreed. "Mom made me a pair of slacks and a serape to match the upholstery on my living room furniture. How about that?"

There was a stunned silence. Then Michael started to laugh. "In other words, don't tell you what to wear?" His tone was rueful.

Now that was the Michael she knew and loved, thought Elena, beginning to smile. Well, knew and *liked*. She wasn't absolutely sure she was in love with the man. "By the way, did you lose anything in the burglary at your place?"

"Yes," said Michael. "It's the strangest thing. The thief cleaned out my underwear drawer. Well, the boxer shorts. He left my socks."

"And that's it? Nothing else taken?"

"No, and the same thing happened to three other bachelor professors, my brother included."

"It must have been a panty-raid," said Elena. "My mother said her older cousins participated in them after World War Two." Grinning, she added, "I'll call Burglary and suggest that they check out female history students."

"No wonder you're such a great detective," said Michael, laughing. "I'd never have thought of that. I'll pick you up at six forty-five. O.K.?"

"Fine. I assume you'll have replaced your underwear by then. You can't go to a fancy dinner without any."

"Trust me," said Michael and hung up, still laughing.

Once off the line, Elena realized that he hadn't told her the name of the hostess, just that she was rich. That was going to be fun—a table full of rich people and professors, the males possibly shorts-less, and one poverty-stricken cop who'd blown her budget on three *ocotillo* bushes.

12
..

Friday, March 31, 8:30 A.M.

If Pansy's so crazy they can't even open the zoo,
someone ought to shoot the poor thing.
>   *Lupe Diaz, Sales Clerk*

"Elephant Update," Los Santos *Herald-Post*, Thursday,
March 30

The autopsy report on Arnold Mandel was waiting when
Elena arrived for her eight-to-four shift. It contained no
surprises. He'd died between ten and midnight, killed by the
arrow that pierced his heart. The damage to his eyes was
postmortem. He'd had for dinner just what the maid Anita
later said she served: steak, French fries, asparagus, green
salad, flan. He hadn't been drunk, although he had been
drinking. Toxicology showed no drugs in his system except
alcohol. Elena finished reading the report and passed it across
the aisle to Leo. "Notice how fast we got the results on this
one. Didn't even have to ask."

"That's what happens when the corpse is a big shot."

Elena picked up her ringing telephone, a call from Josephine Priego, demanding to know if they'd settled on who
killed Arnold. When Elena told her the case was still open,
Josephine said, "Well, let me know when you arrest her; I'm
going to sue his bitch of a wife for deprivation of support. My
lawyer says I can do it."

73

"Probably not until someone's found guilty," said Elena. "The civil cases usually wait on the criminal."

"Then I want the trial hurried up. In the meantime, I'm going to sue Arnold's estate for child support—for Ceci. Just because he's dead—" At that point Josephine Priego began to cry, and Elena, after murmuring a few comforting words and hanging up, wondered whether Patricia Mandel was weeping as well.

"I'm calling Aguilar's friend in Juarez to check out Chuck's alibi," said Leo.

Elena nodded. Patricia didn't really have an alibi. She could have returned to El Paso to kill Arnold, but why use that bow? Symbolic retaliation? His infidelity had wounded her heart—which was doubtful—so she wounded his? With Josephine Priego's Christmas arrow? Had Patricia known the bow was a gift from her husband's mistress?

The Pandarenes said Patricia didn't know how to use a bow. Of course, Patricia could have hired someone, but Elena had never heard of a bow-and-arrow hit man. Still, a hired gun—archer—would be pretty clever to make the hit that way, suggesting a personal motive, as opposed to professional.

Elena turned to Leo, who was saying, "*Abogado*? That means lawyer, doesn't it? You're not a suspect, Mr. Estrada . . . O.K., Rivas-Estrada." Elena signaled to Leo that she'd take over. "I'm transferring you to Detective Jarvis, who's fluent in Spanish," said Leo.

Elena picked up and said in Spanish, "Mr. Rivas-Estrada, were you with Carlos Aguilar on Tuesday night, the twenty-eighth of March?"

"I was," said Chato Rivas-Estrada.

"From what time to what time?" Elena asked. "And could you tell us what you were doing from hour to hour?"

Rivas-Estrada began with the handball game at Los Baños Roma, which he said he would have won if Aguilar hadn't objected every time Rivas-Estrada called a hinder.

"A what?" Elena asked.

"If he gets in the way when I'm trying to return the ball, I call a hinder, and the point's replayed. If we'd played those points over, I'd have won. An honorable man does not argue when a hinder is called against him."

Elena listened to it all, saying, "Uh-huh, uh-huh," sympathizing with the witness and his frustration over playing handball with Chuck Aguilar, who had no honor when it came to hinders. She was hoping that Chato Rivas-Estrada would become enraged enough over the hinder situation to slip up on his friend's alibi.

Rivas-Estrada went on to tell her that they'd had several beers at the club, then gone to the dog track, where one of the dogs he'd bet on had become distracted, jumped the fence, cut across the track, jumped the second fence, and pounced on the mechanical rabbit, causing havoc when the other dogs caught up and attacked the rabbit as well, not to mention each other. His conclusion was that greyhounds weren't too bright.

The man had been forthcoming about the handball game, the beers, and the dog track, accounting for Aguilar's presence in numbing detail. However, questions that Elena asked about later activities were met with a vagueness she found irritating until she reminded herself that Aguilar had mentioned hitting the mariachi bars and picking up girls. Because she was a woman, Rivas-Estrada evidently didn't want to tell her about the shank of the evening.

"Look, Mr. Rivas-Estrada, if you wouldn't mind, I'm going to put my partner, Leo Weizell, back on the phone. I've got a call on the other line." She reached across the aisle and tapped Leo, who was working at his computer while she talked to the witness.

With her hand over the receiver, she gave Leo a quick synopsis of the conversation and the problem that had developed. "I'll listen in while he tells you things too shocking for respectable female ears," she said dryly.

Leo nodded and picked up. "Weizell here, Mr. Rivas-Estrada. Sorry about my lousy Spanish, but we appreciate your cooperation."

Sounding relieved, Rivas-Estrada said, "*No problema, amigo*. I speak some *inglés*." And he explained that he could hardly tell a lady officer about the tail end of the evening. He went on to reveal to Leo that he himself was an accomplished mariachi singer and always paid the band in the mariachi bars to let him sing with them. "The señoritas, they love a man with a fine voice," he said in thickly accented English. "I sing and we got girls three deep, got our pick of the talent, *verdad*?"

Now Elena did have a call on the other line. Before she took it, she heard Rivas-Estrada say that he had taken two women to bed, compared to Aguilar's one, something that he could hardly tell the *mujer policia*, but these were hot girls, *"muy ardiente."*

Rolling her eyes, Elena pressed down the flashing button. It was Darwin Mandel. "Detective Jarvis," he said, "has Dr. Tockler contacted you?"

"Who?"

"Dick Tockler. My veterinarian."

"No," said Elena. "I haven't heard from him."

"Nor have I," said Dr. Mandel, sounding very upset. "He left town yesterday, something about his mother having been injured in a roller-coaster accident, and he failed to provide me with a number where he can be reached or the name of the lab where he sent Pansy's blood for analysis."

"I'm sorry to hear that, Dr. Mandel," said Elena, "but I'm sure he'll get in touch. He knows how anxious you are about the elephant."

"Of course I'm anxious. The poor dear is just now regaining her accustomed charm and amiability. Which, of course, proves that we handled the situation properly. Without tranquilizers. You may not realize it, but a much loved elephant in Los Angeles died from tranquilizers because they wanted to ship the poor beast to a zoo in Mexico and the elephant didn't want to go."

"What a tragedy," said Elena.

"Indeed. And here I have an elephant, still not quite herself—God knows what drug she was given—and my vet is out of town. It's not as if Los Santos has many veterinarians who are prepared to treat an elephant, especially one who has killed someone, no matter that the death is not her fault."

"I'm sure," said Elena. "Do I take it that the zoo is still closed?" she asked, remembering the complaint in "Elephant Update" the night before. That kind of reaction from the public had to be very upsetting to Dr. Mandel who, now that she thought about it, hadn't said a word about his brother's death.

"The mayor has insisted on keeping it closed," said Dr. Mandel angrily. "For the safety of the public. Although I assured him that his concern was unwarranted. It's not as if we invite visitors into the enclosure. We don't give elephant rides or—"

"Is she still hurling trees at the keepers?" Elena broke in.

"No, Detective, she isn't. And I want those blood results. They should be at a local hospital or lab, but they're not. I've called. What if they've been lost?"

"Oh, I'm sure—"

"This is a terrible situation. Our Public Relations director is working night and day to pacify the public, but there are those who blame Pansy—as opposed to the real culprit—for Virgilio's death. And why haven't I heard from *you*, Detective? Do you have any leads on who tampered with my elephant? What have you done to exonerate Pansy?"

"I'm afraid I haven't had time for Pansy's case," said Elena. "You do realize that your brother was killed Tuesday?"

"Of course. We are all distraught. Although I was not surprised to hear from Patricia that Ahab attacked him. I told Arnold that it was cruel to keep a falcon tied up. Unnatural."

Elena wondered why Darwin thought that it was all right for him to have a whole zoo full of imprisoned animals but unnatural for his brother to keep one falcon. "I'm the detective on your brother's murder, sir, which has been keeping me busy."

"Well, you mustn't neglect Pansy because Arnold was killed by one of those irate garment people."

"Do you know something I don't, sir? We haven't proved that the murder was connected with his business."

"Well, it stands to reason, doesn't it?"

She made a note that she'd have to interview Darwin Mandel about his brother's death. He had, after all, been angry with Arnold for wanting to shoot the elephant. Angry enough to do Arnold in before he could drum up more support for disposing of Pansy? It sounded like an odd motive, but then so was the crime itself. "Dr. Mandel, if I may, I'll call back later and make an appointment to see you."

"Well, I should hope so," said the zoo director. "I want Pansy's name cleared."

Elena said goodbye. "So what did Rivas-Estrada have to say? Anything else?" she asked Leo.

"He says he's got a bigger cock than Chuck Aguilar, and they were together from late Tuesday afternoon to three-thirty or four the next morning."

"Charming guy," muttered Elena. "Do all men run around measuring their genitalia?"

"Just those of us who have something worth measuring," Leo replied, grinning. "What do you say we canvass Alope Randall's neighborhood? See if we can find someone who knows whether her pickup was in the driveway like she says."

13
..

Elena stood on the sidewalk in Sunset Heights looking at Alope Randall's house, a solid, square brick building with porches fronting the first and second floors, and a slightly peaked roof. The house was situated at the crest of a hill overlooking Juarez to the south, with mountains to the south and west. Randall undoubtedly had spectacular views of sunsets and, after dark, the green glow of the sodium vapor lights in Mexico and the great black patches of the *colonias*, where there was no electricity.

The yard was as Alope had described it, bare except for a gnarled and hardy hedge lining the walk and fronting the long porch railing, one immense oleander not yet in bloom, and a straggle of piñon pines. The feature that most caught Elena's eye was the door, which was framed by narrow panels of clear leaded glass set in intricate geometric patterns reminiscent of a Frank Lloyd Wright design. Maybe it *was* a Frank Lloyd Wright design. His work was one of the few things she had enjoyed in a college course called Interior Decoration Through the Ages.

Elena had to view the yard and first floor of the house through a wrought-iron fence made of tall spear shafts with wickedly pointed heads. Those ought to deter would-be vandals and thieves, she thought. The gate was padlocked. Anyone who tried to climb the fence and made one little

mistake could end up impaled on a spear. A large Beware of
the Dog sign hung beside the gate. If the intruder was lucky
enough not to be impaled, he would have to face the dog on
the other side of the fence—a lean, slavering Doberman,
baring its teeth in the hope that Leo and Elena would be
foolish enough to enter his territory.

They canvassed the houses on Alope Randall's side of the
street, but no one had seen any activity at her place on the
night of the murder or noticed whether or not her pickup was
in the driveway. Crossing to the other side of the block, they
worked their way down the street, getting only one hit, an old
man, one George Venegas, whom they found sitting at his
window in a battered recliner, military binoculars in his lap.

"If we find out anything, it'll be from this guy," said Leo,
and he was right. Venegas was highly offended at the idea of
a female police officer and would talk only to Leo. But to
Leo, he said plenty: first, that he spent most of his time right
where he was, watching the street. He was a veteran of the
Pacific campaign against the "Yellow Peril" in World War
Two and would gladly have given Leo a detailed account of
every "Nip" he'd discovered in some island cave and killed
with a hand grenade, rifle, or machine gun. Now, after he'd
gone to the trouble of winning the war, he saw his country
being taken over by those same "Japs." Even Mexico, which
had once denied foreigners the right to buy in, now let the
Japanese build plants across the river. *Maquiladoras*. Leo
offended the old man by not being sufficiently upset about the
situation.

In addition to hating the Japanese, Mr. Venegas had no use
for Indians and pushy women: Indians because the Tiguas had
opened a casino on their reservation in Ysleta and were luring
hundreds of stupid Anglos and Hispanics in to squander their
money on gambling; pushy women because, in George
Venegas' opinion, a woman's place was at home looking after
the *niños*, not out trying to compete with men. After that
statement he glared at Elena, who had to resist the impulse to
throttle him.

Leo finally managed to get the old man onto the subject of
Alope Randall who, to Mr. Venegas' mind, was the worst of
both lots, an Indian *and* a pushy woman, who spent her time

representing other pushy women, who, since they insisted on working, ought to be glad they could get any job at all. At least sewing was a woman's task, although it didn't take talent and therefore didn't deserve much in the way of a salary, so why was Alope Randall always harassing the men who employed those women?

"Mr. Venegas," Leo interrupted politely, "what we need to know is if you saw any activity at Alope Randall's house on Tuesday night before or after midnight. Do you stay up that late?"

"Don't get no sleep atall," said Mr. Venegas. "Damn Japs shot up mah hip. Hurts worse ever' year."

"I'm sorry to hear it, sir," said Leo. "Would you know whether Miss Randall was home Tuesday night?"

"Early on," said the old man. "Later—ten-thirty or so—truck was gone. S'pose she was too. Stands to reason."

"You're sure?" asked Elena. She hadn't expected to hear anything implicating Alope.

"I said so, din' I?" snapped Venegas. "You deaf?"

"It would have been hard to see," said Elena, "because of the fence, and of course, it was nighttime."

"Woman's got security lights," snapped Venegas, "an' the fence don' cross the driveway. I can see if the truck's there." He waved his binoculars. "I can see what she's got in the back." He shifted uncomfortably in his chair, rubbing his hip. "Women drivin' pickups! It ain't proper."

"When did she leave?" asked Leo.

"Don' know. Most likely I was in the bathroom. Man my age spends a lot of time in the bathroom. When you gotta use a walker like I do, gettin' around's a problem. But her driveway was empty till way after midnight. Pickup's brown. Says 'Border Legal Clinic' on the side." He held up the binoculars, grinning slyly. "Got a dent in the front bumper. Prob'ly run someone down. That why you're askin' these here questions? Women is piss-poor drivers. You're lookin' for a hit-an'-run, she's prob'ly it."

"Did you see the vehicle come back?" asked Elena.

The old man ignored her.

"Sir," Leo prodded.

"'Twas back before the moon come up."

Elena made a note to call the weather bureau to find when moonrise had been that night. They thanked George Venegas for his time, and the old man departed for the bathroom, they for the street.

"Finally some information," said Leo. "She says she was home. He says she wasn't. She says her truck was there the last time she looked, at ten. He says it was gone by ten-thirty or so."

"He'll make a great witness," retorted Elena. "He spends most of his time in the john. He says the truck wasn't there, but he didn't see it leave, and he didn't see it come back, and he's not too clear on the times."

"Still, she lied."

Elena thought back over what Randall had said. Maybe she'd lied; maybe she hadn't. "Let's stop for lunch," she suggested, "then go see the Mandel patriarch. Murders are often family affairs."

"Let me guess," Leo retorted. "You liked Randall."

14
..

Friday, March 31, 1:30 P.M.

Jacob Mandel lived in a stone mansion on Montana Street, hemmed in by dwellings that had been converted to lawyers' and accountants' offices, and beyond those by deteriorating blocks of small businesses—printing firms, family restaurants, liquor stores, small discount clothing establishments.

Leo and Elena were admitted into a gloomy hall by a middle-aged nurse named Mrs. Maldonado, who was still lecturing them on the fragility of the old man's health when they entered a large room with front windows overlooking the bustle of the street.

"Stop gabbling and leave us alone," snapped Jacob Mandel.

"Mr. J., I am responsible for—"

"Don't call me Mr. J.!"

"Calm yourself," she replied.

"I hate being hovered over."

"I'd better take your blood pressure."

"Get *out*!"

"Bad-tempered old fool," she muttered and stamped from the room.

The old man had turned his wheelchair away from the window to stare at the two detectives, heavy white brows bristling over eyes that, although faded, were still shark-sharp and not at all friendly. His shoulders were wide and heavy, his hair thick and white. No male-pattern baldness in the father, although it was certainly evident in the sons, Elena thought. She introduced herself and Leo.

Mandel rolled toward a table, controlling the chair with one hand. The other hand and arm lay awkwardly in his lap, evidently paralyzed by one of his strokes.

Leo began by telling him that they were sorry for his loss, then progressed to questions about Arnold's involvement in the sweatshops.

"Lies," said Jacob in a rough, hoarse voice. "Lies thought up by that female labor lawyer. She probably wants to unionize my factory, but I treat my workers well. They'll never vote in the unions." His anger seemed to seep away, and he muttered, "My people have it all—benefits, wholesome lunches. And she knows it—that Randall woman. That's why she's been slandering Arnold."

"Do you think she could have had anything to do with his death?" Elena asked gently.

"Probably," he answered. "Who else?"

The old man was silent after Elena asked if he had any evidence of Alope Randall's culpability. Then he said, ignoring the question, "Why would Arnold have anything to do with sweatshops? He knows how bad they are; I told him."

"Told him what, sir?" asked Leo.

Jacob looked up, seemingly surprised by the question. "*I'm* the one who started as a contractor fifty years ago," he said. "The Army mustered me out at Fort Bliss after the war, and I liked it here. It was warm, warmer than New York City, where I'd have spent my life hawking fish in the streets with my father. I took the money I'd saved, bought six secondhand sewing machines, and went into business." He fell silent, staring into the past, then roused himself. "I worked fourteen hours a day, seven days a week, till I owned one of the biggest factories in town," he added brusquely.

"Arnold knew that. He knew how I felt about sweatshops. My mother worked in one. But *I* gave my workers a decent shake as soon as I could afford to, even when I couldn't afford to. Arnold wouldn't have gone against me."

Elena wondered if Jacob knew how much evidence the feds had against Arnold. However, she let that topic alone and said, "Could you tell us who would profit from your son's death, Mr. Mandel? How was the company owned?"

"By the family," said Jacob. "I've got fifty-five percent; Arnold had twenty-five; Darwin and Rosalba ten each because they're not active in the company, not even interested. My wife's dead. So I'm the one who'll profit by Arnold's death. Twenty percent of his stock will come back to me."

Not much there for Patricia, Elena thought, noticing that the father hadn't mentioned the younger son, J.J. Audubon.

"Maybe you think I killed him to get that twenty percent?" said the old man sardonically. "I don't even know who's going to run the company now. Doctors won't let me."

"You understand, don't you," said Elena, "that we have to cover every possibility in investigating your son's murder? Many killings are family affairs."

"I read the papers," he mumbled, chin sinking wearily to his chest. "You don't have to tell me that." Rousing himself again, he asked with heavy sarcasm, "Which of my children do you think murdered Arnold?"

"Well," said Elena, "there was the elephant controversy between Arnold and Darwin."

The old man laughed, a brief, gravelly sound. "You mean because Arnold thought the elephant should be shot? He was right. That elephant was queer before it ever trampled the keeper. Answering to Pansy. Having birthday parties. You'd think animals were sacred or something. They're not." He glowered at the two detectives as if they'd contradicted him. "Now the whole town thinks, just like Arnold did, that the elephant should be put down."

"But they *were* at odds over the elephant," Elena reminded him.

"Darwin wouldn't kill his brother over an elephant," Jacob replied. "If the profits from the company fail, Darwin loses money on his ten percent, and Arnold was the man making the money."

"What about your other son?" asked Leo.

"I've only got two sons, and one was just murdered," said Jacob, his voice cold.

"Detective Weizell is referring to John James Audu—"
Elena stopped because the old man's face flushed dark red,

and it occurred to her that he could suffer another stroke if they upset him. Mrs. Maldonado wouldn't be the only one who blamed them.

"J.J. wouldn't have killed his brother," said Jacob through gritted teeth. "The boy's a coward and a fool, spoiled rotten by his mother."

"What kind of relationship did he have with his brother Arnold?" asked Leo.

"He came into the business and nearly wrecked it before I fired him. My oldest boy had to take a cut in salary when he succeeded me as president. Only way he could get Los Santos Apparel back on its feet. Arnold was the injured party, not J.J."

"Don't you think J.J. resented—" Elena began.

Jacob interrupted her. "That fool hasn't succeeded in anything else; not likely he'd be able to pull off a murder." The old man slapped his good hand down on the arm of his wheelchair. "Who are you going to ask about next? Rosalba? She was out of the country. Me? I can't get out of this chair without help. Maybe you think the Maldonado woman's an accomplice."

This was hard going, thought Elena. And touchy. "Were there any hard feelings among your children because of the stock split or the younger son being cut off from the family money?" she asked.

"J.J.'s mother took care of him," snapped Jacob. "If he hasn't wasted it all, he doesn't lack for money. As for the other two, if they wanted more stock they should have come into the company." He paused. "Well, not Rosalba," he amended. "She's a woman. I see that she's taken care of."

"Perhaps the fact that your wife left her property to the youngest son caused hard feelings."

"My wife has nothing to do with any of this," said Jacob, his face turning red again.

"Sir, in a murder investigation," said Leo, "we have to—"

"We're not talking about my *wife!*" the old man roared.

Mrs. Maldonado, who must have been standing outside the door, burst in and said, "That's enough. I told you not to upset him. *Out!*" She flapped her hands at them as if they were chickens in her barnyard.

"For once I agree with this idiot woman," said Jacob. "Get out of my house. Those labor people are responsible for the death of my son. Go ask them questions." His hand went to the controls on the arm of the wheelchair, and he rolled toward the window, presenting the detectives with his back.

Elena glanced at Leo, and he shrugged as if to say, We're not going to get anything else here. So they left the old house and its brooding, crippled owner.

15
..

Pansy's my favorite elephant in all the world. I saw her eat a broom. Her pee pee is very big. Mrs. Cavalos helped me write this.

Ricardo Mota, 2nd grade
Rio Grande Elementary School

"Elephant Update," Los Santos *Herald-Post*, Friday, March 31

Elena stared sourly at the clothes laid out on her bed, a hand-woven navy shift and a long coat, beige with border designs in teal, rose, and navy, but particularly the pantyhose, which she hated. And she was running late. Michael was due to arrive in fifteen minutes. She had just wiggled the hose to her knees when the telephone rang.

"Great," she muttered. Trapped in the damn stockings and Michael was probably calling to say the dinner was canceled; the hostess had fallen ill from something she ate in Italy. Or maybe she'd drunk the water. Could you drink the water in Italy, or did you have to be careful like you did in Mexico? Leaving the hose bunched at her knees, she launched herself sideways on the bed, picked up the phone, tucked it under her chin, and said, "Jarvis."

"Elena, this is Lieutenant Beltran."

Not Michael. She breathed a sigh of relief and rolled onto

her back, legs in the air so that she could drag the nylon to her hips. "Yes, sir?" she said. Beltran was the head of Crimes Against Persons. Calls at home from him were bound to be bad news.

"I just had a call from the chief."

Lifting her bottom and maneuvering the panty portion to her waist, Elena thought, *Now what?* Either the chief had some complaint about her job performance or he wanted her mother's telephone number. When Harmony had visited Los Santos the previous fall, Chief Armando Gaitan had been seriously smitten, although Elena's mother was married to a New Mexico sheriff and had five children and four grandchildren. Of course, Harmony Portillo was also drop-dead gorgeous, but that didn't give the chief a right to pursue her, at least not in Elena's opinion.

"Jacob Mandel gave him a call," Lieutenant Beltran was saying.

Powerful Local Businessman Pressures Police Chief. Police Chief Harasses Hard-working Detective, Elena thought and wriggled into a half slip. "What's Mr. Mandel's problem?"

"His problem," said Beltran, "is what he calls your female illogic in thinking anyone but labor agitators killed his son. I've just been reading over the reports. Looks to me like Alope Randall is your prime suspect, not some member of the family."

Phone still tucked under her chin, Elena shrugged into her bra and hooked it. "Yeah, Randall's promising, except that I think she'd be more liable to take him to court than kill him."

"I want you to remember that Jacob Mandel is a power in this community," said Beltran, "and the man's seriously irritated about your visit."

"Hey, Leo was with me," said Elena. "Is he seriously irritated with Leo?" There was no way she could get into the dress and keep talking.

"You're the one he complained about," said Beltran. "Just your luck—you're a woman. The chief told him you were a crackerjack detective, and Mandel said you were too pretty to be a crackerjack anything but female."

"Sweet," muttered Elena, knowing that Beltran was delighted to pass that little gem on to her.

"Anyway, I want you to get this case closed as quickly as possible. The Mandels are important people. When one of them gets killed, we need to find out who did it and why."

"Well, we're working on it," said Elena. "It's not every day I get a corpse who's been skewered with his own arrow."

"Speaking of oddball cases," said Beltran, "the chief said to tell you you did a great job on that killer-statue case out at H.H.U."

"Hey, did he?" said Elena, all smiles. "Thanks for telling me, Lieutenant."

"No *problema*," said Beltran. "You did do a good job. That was a strange one."

"Yeah, well, everything out at H.H.U. is strange. Don't worry, I'll be in tomorrow to pick up the Mandel murder."

"What's wrong with tonight? You got a big date?"

"Uh-huh," said Elena. "With a criminologist. Honing my detective skills." She laughed. "And he's about to knock on my door."

"Be sure you look through the peephole before you open it," said Beltran, and hung up.

Elena shook her head. As usual, Beltran was either hassling her or treating her like a not-too-bright daughter. Look before she opened the door? As if she didn't know that.

16
..

Friday, March 31, 7:15 P.M.

"Rosalba, I'd like you to meet Elena Jarvis," said Michael.

Rosalba? Wasn't that the name of Jacob Mandel's daughter? Elena stared at the woman, who was tall with wide shoulders and a lean figure, hair black, eyes brown, face long. She wasn't a beauty, but she was beautifully dressed and made up—*chic* would be the word.

"Our hostess, Rosalba Mondragon," Michael was saying.

"Jarvis?" said Mrs. Mondragon. "You're not a policeman, are you?"

"Detective," said Elena, then hesitantly, "You're not Jacob Mandel's daughter, are you?"

Rosalba nodded. "And you're investigating my brother's death. My father mentioned you."

Elena could well imagine what he'd said.

"I suppose you're shocked to find me entertaining just two days after Arnold's murder."

Elena was but didn't say so. Michael looked astonished. He obviously hadn't known that the woman he met in Rome was also the sister of Elena's murder victim.

"We met for the first time and made the arrangements for this dinner party at a restaurant in Trastevere," said Rosalba. "I did consider canceling when I learned about Arnold, but decided it might be better to go ahead. The planning has been a distraction for me." She sighed, looking bleak.

"If you wouldn't mind," Elena murmured, "I'd like to talk to you later, Mrs. Mondragon."

"For just one evening could we get away from your job?" said Michael.

"My dear Michael," Rosalba chided, "my brother has been murdered. I'd like to see the killer caught."

Michael flushed.

"Stay when the others have left," Rosalba told Elena. "If you're in a hurry, Michael, I can see that Detective Jarvis has transportation."

They followed her into the two-story-high living room of the town house, Elena thinking that Michael was going to be pissed off about that last remark. The room had a glass roof, presumably so that the sun's rays could reach the luxuriant jungle plants set into a pit encircled by white sofas. The walls were hung with bright geometric paintings—Zifkovitz, thought Elena. Because the artist was the special friend of her own friend, Sarah Tolland, professor and chair of Electrical Engineering at H.H.U., Elena recognized his style. Then, even more surprising, she recognized him, standing a few feet away. And Sarah.

"Elena!" exclaimed Sarah and came toward her, every gray-blond hair in place. Smartly attired as always, she wore a short-jacketed, off-white suit with white embroidery on the lapels. Zifkovitz, tall and wild-haired, towered behind her.

His sister Rina was present as well, draped in red and blue ceramic jewelry of her own design. As Rosalba began introductions, Rina said, "We met at that coffeehouse jazz concert. Your mother's a weaver, right?" Elena nodded while Rina waved at the man behind her. "Remember Arkin, the potter?"

Arkin was a stocky, dark-skinned man, with graying hair. Rafer Martin, physicist and trombone player in a jazz group with which Elena occasionally sang Dixieland, smiled at her from across the room. Michael scowled. For no good reason he'd always been jealous of Rafer, even though the man was married. Rafer came over and introduced Elena to his wife, Helen, whose blond good looks were spoiled by the dissatisfied twist of her mouth.

"Don't forget me," said Mark Futrell, Michael's brother.

He came up and leaned forward to kiss Elena on the cheek. She dodged. So much for having a nice evening, she thought gloomily. Michael hadn't mentioned that his twin would be at the party.

Rosalba Mandel Mondragon led her guests into the dining room, which featured a long black table with white upholstered chairs and a centerpiece of colorful tropical flowers, each one of which looked as if it might eat the hand of anyone who tried to touch it. The chandelier, a great white frosted globe, was hung just above the flower arrangement and shone in the diners' eyes. Maybe if she watched closely, Elena mused, the flowers would devour the chandelier. Springing out at odd angles above the globe were black wires from which smaller globes of varying sizes were suspended. It must be a work of art, Elena decided. It certainly wasn't anything you'd find in a lighting fixture store, not in Los Santos.

Elena was seated between Mark and Rafer Martin. Michael and Mark sat to the left and right of Rosalba. Elena sighed. She didn't want to sit beside Mark. She wasn't even particularly pleased to be seated beside Rafer, although she liked him. His wife, across the table, glared as he held out Elena's chair. It was, however, nice to be directly across from Sarah. Since the divorced woman's support group had stopped meeting, Elena hadn't seen as much of Sarah. She smiled at her friend. "Did you enjoy Rome?" she asked.

"We all enjoyed Rome," Rosalba broke in. "I'm afraid you're the only one, Detective, who wasn't there."

Well, that puts me in my place, thought Elena.

"So we all owe a vote of thanks to Michael for bringing you this evening," Rosalba continued. "Now we can justify retelling our adventures because we have an audience." She smiled at Elena.

"Italy really isn't my favorite place," said Sarah, carefully placing her napkin in her lap.

"How could Italy not be anyone's favorite place?" demanded Rina. "It's heavenly."

"*You* weren't attacked by Gypsy girls," said Michael.

"That's because I look like one of them," Rina replied, candelabra earrings jingling as she leaned forward.

"I rescued you from the Gypsies," said Mark. Turning to Elena, he added, "I don't suppose he told you that?"

"No," she replied, thinking that the rescue could hardly have been as spectacular as her karate dream rescue. A thick soup with green and yellow swirls had just been set before her by a uniformed maid. Elena wasn't sure it looked edible; nonetheless, she dipped her spoon in once her hostess began to eat.

"The thing that bothers me about Italy," said Sarah, "is that nothing works properly there."

Zifkovitz laughed heartily. "Sarah's still put out because the ticket machine on a bus ate her ticket."

"I paid six thousand lire for that ticket!" Sarah retorted. "It should have lasted me all day. The machine was supposed to stamp it and give it back."

"Why didn't you take a cab?" asked Rosalba.

"Because Italian cab drivers are insane," Sarah replied. "They attempt to run down pedestrians; they run red lights; they—"

"Not only didn't the machine return her ticket," said Zifkovitz, "but two Italian guys were watching while the machine ate it and said, '*Buon appetito*,' to the machine."

"That was only funny after the fact," said Sarah severely. "At the time I knew I was going to have to get off, go into some tobacco shop, where the owner would be smoking and so would the customers, and spend another six thousand lire—"

"That's less than four dollars," Rafer pointed out.

"—not to mention the danger of having some transit authority person, who didn't speak English, come through asking to see the stamped ticket and arrest me for not having one," said Sarah indignantly. "The bus driver wouldn't do anything about my predicament."

Elena, who had been watching Rosalba Mondragon and noting that she seemed depressed, caught the end of Sarah's complaint and stifled a giggle.

"Stop grinning," Sarah said to Elena, but Elena couldn't help herself. She could just picture the non–English-speaking Italian bus driver getting a lecture from Sarah Tolland, who didn't tolerate inefficiency in people or machines.

"Sarah took down the number of the bus," said Zifkovitz. "Have you written to the transit authority to complain?" he asked fondly.

"We've only been home a few days, Paul, and I do intend to get my six thousand lire back. Even if I have to write to the prime minister."

"I think the prime minister is being tried for Mafia connections," said Arkin.

"The Mafia probably supplies the ticket-stamping machines," Sarah replied cynically.

Elena was sampling her nasty-tasting soup, wondering what it was. A nasturtium floated in the center, and while she knew they were edible, she didn't care to eat one.

They must have had a lot of fun in Rome, she thought wistfully. All of which, as Rosalba had pointed out, Elena had missed—as the result of being the only poverty-stricken person at the dinner table. She comforted herself with the thought that she had three really great *ocotillo* bushes, probably better than any *ocotillos* these people had.

Elena was relieved when the maid removed her soup bowl—until Mark put his hand on her knee. Damn him! She slipped her salad fork off the table and gave him a good jab. Turning pale, Mark snatched his hand to safety. The maid returned and served salads consisting of red leaves and orange sections.

"Very chic," Rafer Martin murmured to Elena. "Tastes awful."

She choked back laughter. Mark was rubbing his hand while Elena tried to decide whether she really wanted to eat her salad with a fork she'd just jabbed into a scumbag.

"So what do you do, Detective, when you're not detecting?" asked Rosalba.

What was that about? Elena wondered. Maybe Rosalba thought she should be out hunting Arnold's murderer instead of dining on exotic foods at his sister's ebony table. "Well, I—" Elena had decided to use her dinner fork to sample a red leaf in the salad.

"You're using the wrong fork," Mark whispered snidely.

"The salad fork's contaminated," she hissed and nudged it

off onto the floor. The maid, who was passing by, noticed, snatched it up, and returned with another.

"Elena sings with the H.H.U. jazz band," said Rafer Martin in answer to Rosalba's question. "The lady has a fantastic voice."

"I really can't understand the attraction of Dixieland," Helen Martin said. "I much prefer classical music myself. Do you sing lieder or opera at all, Miss Jarvis?"

"No," said Elena, "but I guess there's always a first time." What a bitch the woman was! Poor Rafer.

"A good many years of training are necessary for the singing of the finer types of music," Helen said condescendingly.

"Oh, I don't know," Zifkovitz objected. "Anyone who's a good screamer should do just fine with opera."

Arkin had scarfed down his salad, then turned over the plate to examine the mark on the back.

"It's Spode, Arkin," said his hostess, "and you're dripping salad dressing on the place mats."

Elena checked surreptitiously to see whether she'd dripped anything. She'd hate to be called down for place mat desecration.

"We saw an excellent performance of *Macbeth* at the Rome Opera," said Sarah.

"Great sets and costumes," Zifkovitz agreed. "They did the whole thing in black, white, and gray with just a few touches of red, and they used the lights to make it seem as if the people were fading in and out of the castle walls."

Elena, trying to picture it, decided that the production sounded eerie—like the play.

"It was the singers I remember," said Sarah. "A wonderful soprano—"

Elena was happy to see the salads removed, but then the maid served each guest a small piece of fish in a sauce topped with bananas. Now that looked unpromising.

"—and the baritone who sang Macbeth was excellent as well. Did you ever see it in Santa Fe?" Sarah asked Elena.

Elena shook her head. "I only went a couple of times."

"Elena's from Chimayo," Sarah said to Rosalba.

Elena nodded, taking a bite of her fish. To her surprise, it was delicious.

Rosalba brightened and replied, "I *love* Chimayo! Especially the weaving."

"Both my mother and aunt are weavers."

"I noticed your dress," said Rosalba. "Did it come from one of the boutiques in Santa Fe?"

"Came off my mother's loom, actually," said Elena, "but her clothing is sold in my brother-in-law's gallery on Canyon Road."

"Now this is edible," Rafer murmured in Elena's ear. "First thing I've liked."

She agreed, eyes twinkling. "Me too."

"You're supposed to talk to both your dinner partners," said Mark. "First, you chat with one; then you chat with the other. Maybe they didn't teach you that in Chimayo."

"Why would she want to talk to a jock?" asked Rafer and promptly engaged Elena in a conversation about the last session of the jazz band.

Rafer's wife, who had been looking bored as she listened to Arkin, said, "I hate this city. Spring is supposed to be beautiful. Flowers and gentle rain. Here all we have is wind and blowing dust."

"I suppose you'd rather have a winter with snow and ice," said Rosalba sharply, coming out of a moody silence.

"I'd rather have any kind of winter," said Helen Martin, "as long as it doesn't take place in Los Santos, Texas."

Elena bit back an angry retort. She knew herself to be prejudiced. In some ways she thought Los Santos was even better than Chimayo.

"Now in Rome," said Helen, "there's culture—great art, beautiful churches—"

"Ah, here's the veal Marsala," Rosalba interrupted. The maid had come in with plates of sliced veal in a thick brown gravy. "You remember? Some of us had it at Checco in Trastevere? Where we all met. In honor of the occasion, my cook has tried to duplicate some of their wonderful dishes."

Elena looked suspiciously at a bowl full of red stuff. What was it? Mashed potatoes colored with some carcinogenic red dye?

"For instance, we've tried to do the *Carciofi alla Romana*," said Rosalba. "Poor Manuela is having a nervous breakdown attempting dishes she's never tasted and only heard described."

A plate of artichokes had arrived—sort of blue-gray-green. Were they colored by the same fungus as blue corn tortillas? Elena wondered. Fearing that this was going to be a particularly difficult culinary experience, she tasted the veal Marsala and fell in love with the wine-flavored dish. Sarah smiled across the table at her and mouthed, Better than you thought?

Elena grinned and nodded. Mark put his hand back on her knee. Because she couldn't stab him with her fork again—she had Marsala sauce on it and didn't want to spot her good dress—she took a second to judge the position of their feet, then brought her high heel down on Mark's instep. This time he gasped.

Rosalba, who had been watching them, asked wryly, "What is it, Mark? Don't you like the Roman artichokes?"

"They have a kick," Mark mumbled.

Feeling smug, Elena cut another piece of the delicious veal. Michael was frowning at them while a basket of warm Italian bread was passed down the table.

Rafer Martin nodded to the bread and said, "This is for sopping up the Marsala sauce."

"You're kidding!" murmured Elena. "No one's mother would approve of that."

"European mamas do," he replied. "They figure if you're going to make a great sauce, you want to get every last drop." He illustrated his point by breaking off a piece of bread, dipping it in the wine sauce, and popping it into his mouth.

"Really, Rafe!" snapped Helen.

"It's perfectly acceptable," said Sarah knowledgeably. "Eating in the French style." Helen turned red. Elena happily followed Rafe's example. She might not like all that goose liver and snail stuff that Sarah tried to foist on her in French restaurants, but she approved of the sopping routine, although she noticed that Michael wasn't taking part. She hoped she wasn't going to get a lecture on the way home about the proper use of bread at a formal dinner given by the sister of a murder victim.

Rosalba had fallen silent again. Strange woman, Elena thought, giving a fancy dinner for a bunch of near strangers two days after her brother had been discovered with an arrow in his chest. From the expression on her face, Elena guessed that the party wasn't proving as much a distraction as Rosalba had hoped.

17
..

In the interest of professional discretion, Michael was banished to the terrace while Elena and Rosalba Mondragon sat on one of the white sofas, a leopard-skin rug beneath their feet. Elena couldn't help staring at it, and Rosalba, noticing, said defensively, "It's a fake, so don't even think about arresting me for having the skins of endangered species around the house." Elena turned a puzzled face to her hostess, and Rosalba chuckled. "Not your type of crime, right? Well, some bastard turned me in for some stuff I bought abroad and had shipped. Cost me a lot in fines and embarrassment."

Elena smiled. "I don't do illegal skins," she said. "Don't even know which ones they are."

Then facing the sunken tangle of jungle plants, they talked about Arnold's murder. Rosalba said that Patricia would not have killed her husband, since his death would cause her financial loss. Nor would Josephine Priego have killed him, because she loved him, and he her. Nor did Rosalba think either of her brothers would have done it. "They aren't the type," she said.

"Darwin and Arnold did have a controversy going," Elena pointed out. "Over the elephant. Arnold wanted to shoot it. Darwin—"

Rosalba laughed sadly. "You'll never find another family that has more squabbles over animals than ours," she said, "but that doesn't mean Darwin killed Arnold. Even to protect Miss Pansy. Darwin cries at funerals. He leaves town when they have to put down an animal at the zoo. He couldn't kill anyone. And I didn't do it; I was in a plane over the Atlantic. Check American Airlines. I flew first-class."

Elena nodded and made a note. "What about your youngest brother, J.J.? Maybe he was resentful—Arnold being president of the company while J.J. had been kicked out."

Rosalba shrugged. "Arnold wasn't to blame for that. J.J.'s just not the cutthroat business type, and the garment industry can be vicious. In case you haven't noticed, the jobs are moving across the border, more every year, especially since NAFTA, so it's hard, even at minimum wage, for American manufacturers to compete."

"What did J.J. do?" Elena didn't want another lecture on labor problems.

"My little brother's very arty, so he talked Papa into starting a new line—a high-fashion label with J.J. handling everything himself. Papa didn't like it, but he'd given Arnold some autonomy in the company, so he did the same for J.J." Rosalba reached for the brandy bottle and held it up questioningly to Elena. When Elena shook her head, Rosalba poured herself a tot.

"Well, J.J., who never did anything right in his life, subcontracted the line, but he didn't follow it up. The result was shoddy workmanship, but J.J. didn't know the difference. He had the stuff boxed up and sent to the retailers who'd ordered. Thousands of garments came back, which meant big losses." Rosalba set her snifter down.

"You see, J.J. had to pay his contractors, so that money was gone, but the retailers have thirty days to pay or return. Los Santos Apparel was left holding the bag. Then instead of admitting that he'd blown it—Papa was in the hospital at the time—J.J. covered the losses by keeping back employee-withholding taxes. Of course, the government caught him, and the company not only had to make up the taxes, but we were assessed big fines. By the time Papa got out, *sans* his prostate, we were close to losing our shirts. The banks wanted to call our loans and cancel our credit line."

"You seem very knowledgeable for someone who's not actively involved in the business," said Elena.

Rosalba shrugged. "I'm as smart as any of them, but I'm female, and Papa's old-fashioned. I didn't want to fight with him about it. He's always been very generous to me. Anyway, the accountant who helped my dumb little brother fudge the books was fired and J.J. disinherited. I've never seen my father so mad. I think that's what brought on his first stroke. The really bad one came after Mama died." Sighing, she picked up her brandy again.

"As it turned out, J.J. landed on his feet. He decided he didn't need Papa; he was going to be an artist, so he rented himself a decrepit cotton gin out in La Union and started painting. Since he was doing animal pictures, Mama slipped him money from time to time." Rosalba took another sip of brandy. "Then she died and left him her property in the Upper Valley, so, as I said, J.J. landed in clover. And I don't think he'd have killed Arnold over the company; that was a long time ago. And he's doing all right with his llamas and his paintings."

"Your mother's death seems to be something of a—"

"Mother's death isn't relevant," said Rosalba, "but if you want to know more about J.J., you can contact Bernie Golden. They're pretty good friends. Maybe one of the few J.J.'s got. Bernie's the sports coordinator out at the Oasis Country Club."

Elena wrote that down, wondering why no one wanted to talk about the death of Cecilia Mandel.

"Who do you think would profit from Arnold's death?"

"Money-wise? Well, I guess Darwin and I—eventually. Twenty percent of Arnold's stock will go back to Papa, and I suppose when he dies, he'll leave it to us."

"Who'll run the company now?" Elena asked.

Rosalba shrugged. "Papa will have to turn it over to the vice-presidents."

"Not to you?"

She laughed. "No, not to me. Aren't you going to ask who I think killed Arnold?"

"Yes. I'd be interested in your opinion."

Rosalba stared at a huge Zifkovitz painting on the far side

of the jungle pit, thinking over her answer. "Before I left for Rome, Arnold was getting threats."

Elena frowned. "Nobody else has mentioned that."

"Well, he was. Phone calls. Notes. He thought it was the labor people. They've been accusing him of all kinds of stuff. Unfairly. Arnold ran a clean shop. He had to. Papa wouldn't have let him do anything else."

"Did your brother report these threats to the police?"

"He didn't say, but I don't think he took them too seriously. Seems that he should have."

"Yes," Elena agreed. "I'll have to look into that. Thank you, Mrs. Mondragon."

"Rosalba," she corrected, studying Elena. "You probably have a lot of fun," she said wistfully. "Being a policewoman, doing something worthwhile with your life. I spend my time traveling and buying clothes. I guess that's what they'll put on my tombstone. 'Rosalba Mandel Mondragon. Well-dressed and well-traveled. Rest in Peace.'"

Elena smiled at her. "Nothing wrong with being well dressed. And I wouldn't mind being able to travel." But she felt a little sorry for the woman—intelligent, but living an aimless life—no children, evidently widowed or divorced, no career.

"You know what scares me?" said Rosalba. Elena looked at her inquiringly. "That it's not a labor thing. That it's something crazier."

"Why do you think that?" Elena asked.

"Because it seems to me that someone may have tried to kill Darwin too. He's always the one to take the elephant through her paces in the morning. He loves it. It could have been Darwin she trampled. I keep thinking maybe someone's after the family. Maybe Papa's next. Or J.J. Or he'll try for Darwin again. Does that sound paranoid?"

"Are you afraid for yourself?" Elena asked.

Rosalba looked surprised. "Why would anyone want to kill me?" She crossed her legs and held up the brandy snifter, studying the golden liquid. "I guess I *was* being paranoid. Forget I said anything. It must have been a labor agitator who killed Arnold."

Elena nodded, but she wouldn't dismiss Rosalba's idea.

She herself had thought there was a connection between the two deaths. "Thank you for talking to me."

"You're welcome," said Rosalba. "I hope you catch the person who did it. Arnold may have been obsessed with the company, but at least he found some happiness the last few years. He loved that little girl. Ceci. Even named her after Mama. Have you seen her?"

Elena nodded. "She's a beauty."

"She is that. Arnold brought her over to visit me a few times. Maybe I'd better call her mother, see if they need any help."

"Didn't Arnold have any children with his wife?"

"No," said Rosalba. "Kind of ironic. Papa always thought of himself as building a dynasty here in the desert, and the only grandchild he's got is illegitimate." Rosalba tossed back the last of her brandy and called out, "Michael, I'm giving you your girlfriend back."

When Elena and Michael reached his car, he was scowling. "What?" asked Elena as they climbed in. "I could hardly pass up the opportunity to interview her."

"I don't mind about that. Her brother's dead; she'd want to help. What I mind is how much attention you paid to Rafer Martin."

"He sat next to me. Was I supposed to pretend he wasn't there?"

"You paid more attention to Rafer than you did to Mark."

"You're right about that," said Elena sharply. "Mark's a—" She stopped herself. "Oh, what's the use? I didn't *want* to talk to your brother."

"Why? Because you didn't want to arouse my suspicions? He says you've been calling him."

"*I've* been calling *him*!" exclaimed Elena, incensed. "I already told you that he's been calling me, and you can just tell him to knock it off. I don't like it." She thought about the hand on her knee but couldn't bring herself to mention it. If Michael believed her, he'd probably say it was "jock behavior," which would make her twice as mad. She guessed that no man wanted to realize his twin brother was a sleaze. Then, grinning, she remembered how she'd taken care of that wandering jock hand.

"What are you smiling about?" demanded Michael, having glanced at her and caught the expression.

"I was thinking about Sarah's ticket getting eaten on the bus in Rome," Elena improvised quickly. "And the two Italian guys saying '*Bon appetit.*'"

"*Appetito*," Michael corrected.

"Whatever."

18
..

Saturday, April 1, 8:20 A.M.

In the interests of public safety, I think the zoo
director, not the elephant, should be dispensed with.
First, we hear that in one night a mountain lion and an
exceptionally poisonous rattlesnake have escaped from
our local zoo. Then a usually peaceable elephant turns
on her keeper. It took two days to calm the elephant
enough so that Virgilio Zubarate's body could be
retrieved. What next? A responsible zoo administration
would have prevented these unfortunate occurrences.

Professor Harold Matthews, Chair,

Department of Zoology, Herbert Hobart University

"Elephant Update," Los Santos *Herald-Post*, Friday,
March 31

Elena couldn't believe how grumpy Leo had been when
she called to tell him about her dinner with the victim's sister
and to suggest that they work on the Mandel case.

He snapped, "My wife's pregnant. I need to spend some
time with her."

Elena had snapped right back, "The overtime money
should come in handy when you start taking a diaper service
and buying baby clothes." Leo groaned and hung up on her.
Evidently she had said the wrong thing. So she'd gone to

headquarters by herself, dug out a telephone book, and begun the investigation anew by making calls.

Alope Randall had said she'd used a bow and arrow as a child, but a child's bow would be a lot different from that monster hanging in Arnold Mandel's study. Elena wanted to know if Alope had kept her skills honed. Accordingly, she began calling archery clubs. There were three, and on the second call she hit pay dirt. Alope was a member.

"Best woman I've ever seen with a bow," said Tommy Montes, who had answered the phone. "Better than most men. Alope got a deer in each of the last four seasons, and that's not easy." Elena thanked him. She hadn't wanted to hear that news, although she wasn't surprised. Elena had noticed the muscles in the lawyer's arms when she took off the jacket of her khaki suit at the Puerto Rican restaurant.

Shaking her head, she noted the information she'd just obtained, then went on to call various federal investigators whose names Alope had given her, men and women who had been tracking Arnold through the paper blizzard his front men put out. Because it was Saturday, she had to contact the feds at home. Many were unhappy to be interrupted on the weekend, but what she learned was significant. Arnold's father, sister, and mistress might not think him guilty, but government agents considered that they had good information against him.

She talked to an OSHA inspector named Gwen Merran, who said that she had evidence of unsafe working conditions in several local contracting establishments—inadequate air filters and toilet facilities, unsanitary eating areas, no sprinkler systems. OSHA believed that Arnold was an investor, albeit hidden, in these unsafe work places. The woman suggested that Elena check with the fire department, to whom Ms Merran had referred material. Elena did and got hold of a very defensive fire inspector, who hadn't got around to following up the OSHA tips. An INS investigator said they'd raided a place just yesterday that was employing illegal aliens and that was, according to Treasury, partially owned by Arnold Mandel. "We're about to bring suit," said Joseph Obregon. "We've got him."

"He's dead," said Elena.

Obregon was disappointed. "So, we'll get his partners," he grumbled.

An IRS accountant, who took her call on a cellular phone from a golf course, confirmed that one of Arnold's sweatshops had collected income and social security taxes and failed to turn them over to the government. He knew that Arnold was dead, and said, with relish, "We'll get it from the estate. Don't you worry, Detective." Elena believed it. Not many people won with the IRS.

Finally she talked to Benny Hope, a Labor Department investigator who had been making pancakes for two offspring staying with him on the weekend. He told her that Arnold owned a shop which closed without paying its workers and then tried to sell off the machinery. "Alope Randall got him, though," said Benny Hope. "Do you know her?"

"I do," said Elena. "She gave me your name."

"Yeah, well, she's a tiger. If we could lure her into our operation, we would, but she doesn't need an outside income. Some people have all the breaks. Me, child support takes half my salary."

Elena gave him a bit of sympathy and hung up. If Arnold hadn't been killed, the roof would have fallen in on him—courtesy of Alope Randall. So why would Alope want to kill him and miss all the fun?

Elena now had the names of the contractors with whom Arnold had been silent partners, and from Alope she had the name of the lawyer who had set up the deals. She called the lawyer and made an afternoon appointment. Then she called Darwin Mandel's home number, but he was, as she might have expected, at the zoo, so she checked out a car and headed for the Los Santos Zoological Gardens—home of Pansy, controversial elephant; empire of Darwin, brother of the deceased. Possible suspect.

19
..

Saturday, April 1, 10:45 A.M.

The dust storms having blown east, the newly reopened
zoo was crowded with parents, children, and miscellaneous
protestors carrying placards that said Save Pansy, Los Santos'
Sweetheart. Others said Protect our Children, Put Down the
Killer Elephant. There was a man with a sandwich board
listing the names of people killed in the United States by
elephants during the past five years. Elena was surprised at
the number. I Love Pansy buttons were being passed out by
a woman wearing an elephant head complete with papier-
mâché tusks. Vendors sold Pansy pennants, and in the midst
of the hubbub, Darwin Mandel was holding a press conference by the gazebo—TV cameras whirring, little children
waving with wide grins on their faces and ice cream on their
chins.

Darwin, who had been detailing for the press the more
delightful of Pansy's personality traits, spotted Elena and
said, "Here's the police person who will exonerate Pansy.
What have your investigations revealed, Detective?"

Elena smiled noncommittally at the TV reporters and
murmured to Darwin, "I'm here to talk to you about another
matter."

"It's been five days since the incident. Surely you've
discovered something."

"Is your vet back yet?" she asked.

"No, he isn't." Darwin looked distressed. "And he hasn't sent word. Fortunately, none of the animals has become ill. The techs have taken care of routine health maintenance, and Pansy seems to have recovered, but I am most upset with Dr. Tockler."

"Could you tell us about that, sir?" asked a TV reporter, thrusting a microphone at Darwin.

"My veterinarian is missing," said the director.

"As in kidnapped?" the reporter asked eagerly.

"As in going to visit his mother without leaving a telephone number where he can be reached," said Darwin. "The interview is over." He strode off to his office, Elena trailing.

"I've come about your brother's murder," said Elena once they were inside.

"Oh, yes," Darwin agreed. "We're hoping to bury him tomorrow. My father is, needless to say, extremely upset."

"And you, sir?" asked Elena. "Are you upset?"

"Well, he's my brother," said Darwin, "although we didn't see eye to eye on a number of matters. However, if you're thinking I killed him for Pansy's sake, you are mistaken. Just because Arnold wanted to shoot her, doesn't mean I'd allow it. Pansy's fate is and always has been my decision. *I* am the zoo director. Still, I have wept for Arnold. What brother would not?"

Elena doubted that Arnold had been a weeper. "Could you tell me where you were the night he died?"

"Right here until eleven-thirty. As a matter of fact, I was writing an editorial explaining why Arnold couldn't be allowed to shoot Pansy."

"Did anyone see you?"

"I doubt it. I don't remember seeing either of the night guards."

"And after eleven-thirty?"

"I went home to bed, of course."

"So your wife—"

"—was asleep when I got home."

Darwin had no alibi. "Do you drive a brown truck?" she asked.

"No," he replied, surprised. "I drive a blue Cadillac Seville."

"Does the zoo have brown trucks?"

"Our trucks are white with the blue and orange city logo on the side. But as I said, I didn't kill Arnold. I am my mother's son. I couldn't kill anything—human or animal."

"Do you know how to use a bow and arrow?" Elena asked.

"We all do. Our grandfather—Mother's father—taught us when we were children, although I haven't handled one in years."

"Could you offer any suggestions as to who might have killed your brother?"

Darwin tented his fingers, looking thoughtful. "Perhaps an animal rights activist. Arnold was, after all, fond of killing animals. Our mother was an animal rights activist; she'd turn over in her grave if she knew Arnold wanted to kill Pansy."

"Do animal rights activists generally kill people?" Elena asked.

"Well—" The director looked embarrassed. "My mother wouldn't have, but there's always the—ah—lunatic fringe. Not that I think of the movement as lunatic."

He cleared his throat. "Another possibility is a person from the labor movement. I'm sure you know that my brother was a power in the garment industry. I've had people picket the zoo because *I* own stock in the family company. One of the picketers even threatened me for profiting off what she called the 'misery of the workers.'"

Darwin shook his head sadly. "I thought that quite unfair. Los Santos Apparel treats its employees very well. She was evidently talking about some sweatshop, which I, needless to say, have nothing to do with, although there have been stories in the papers recently indicating that Arnold might have been involved in such enterprises."

"What about your younger brother and sister? Would Rosalba or J.J. Audubon have—"

"What a bizarre idea!" cried Darwin. "My sister, Rosalba, wasn't even in the country when Arnold died, and as for J.J., he's more our mother's son than I; he would never kill a living being. J.J. is an animal artist. He does pictures for our gift shop here at the zoo. Would you like to see a portrait of Pansy done by J.J.?"

Before Elena could protest that it was unnecessary, Darwin

went to a stand that held large prints, thumbed through them and triumphantly whipped out a watercolor of Pansy the Elephant, looking remarkably human given the fact that she had a long trunk. In the corner were the letters JJAM. John James Audubon Mandel, Elena presumed.

"Very nice," she said. "It looks just like her."

"I do believe it's more than realistic," said Darwin. "J.J. has caught the essence of Pansy. The playful delight she takes in life, the *joie de vivre*, if I may say so." He was staring fondly at the painting. "You can buy a copy in our gift shop."

"I'll certainly consider it," said Elena, thinking that what she didn't need on her living-room wall was a picture of an elephant, especially a killer elephant. She said goodbye to Darwin and went back to her car.

Outside she counted placards and decided that Darwin was winning the Pansy controversy, even if opinion in "Elephant Update" seemed to be going against him. More people here wanted to save the elephant than kill her. That didn't make Darwin as viable a suspect in his brother's murder. Granted he had no alibi, but the motive was weak.

20

Saturday, April 1, 1:00 P.M.

In order to interview Bascomb Pope, Elena had to drive to a racquetball club on Yarborough where she met the lawyer in the health bar. It featured various types of vegetable juice with celery sticks rising like badly pruned trees from the glasses. Pope was wearing crisp white shorts and a white knit shirt with the club insignia embroidered on the pocket. He stood about five feet five, all wiry muscle and an even, salon tan. From his muscled calves to his bald pate, he seemed completely hairless, except for a black fringe on the sides of his head.

"I recognized your name from the papers," he said, sipping an eggplant-and-carrot concoction he recommended. Elena opted for water. "That was an amazing piece of detective work you did on that killer-statue case." He had the look of a man on the make, leaning forward, giving Elena an appraising smile that signaled sexual interest.

"Thanks," she said, carefully noncommittal.

"I suppose you're investigating my client's murder."

"I am. First, I'll ask you where you were the night of his death."

Abruptly the sexual-awareness quotient dropped, and he said with solemn propriety, "My wife and I attended a banquet supporting Insights, the children's science museum. That began at seven-thirty and ended three hours later. Then we went home to bed. Will that cover the estimated time of the murder?"

"I imagine so," said Elena and took down his home number so she could check with his wife. "My second question is why Arnold Mandel would want to buy into sweatshops when he was president of Los Santos Apparel."

"That's easy enough to explain," said Bascomb Pope.

Elena noticed that he didn't deny Arnold's involvement.

"Fifteen years ago when Arnold's brother was associated with Los Santos Apparel, the business lost an appalling amount of money. In a bid to raise confidence in the company's viability with the banks, Arnold took a substantial cut in salary. Unfortunately, he couldn't also cut his personal expenses."

"Why not?" asked Elena. She'd have thought selling that huge house up by the country club would have saved him a mint.

"Because his wife, Patricia, was accustomed to a lavish lifestyle and unwilling to economize."

"I got the impression that he wasn't that fond of her. Why didn't he divorce her if she wouldn't go along?"

"At that time you'd have been mistaken about Arnold's feelings for Patricia. He considered himself very fortunate to have won her. She's from a wealthy, socially prominent family, and Arnold liked to travel in prestigious circles. Although as his life became more complicated because of his extracurricular business dealings, I believe he came to resent her."

"Evidently," said Elena dryly, "since he took a mistress and had an illegitimate child."

Pope nodded, eyes gleaming, the overhead lights flashing off his head like signals. "Exactly, my dear."

Elena gave him a repressive look, and the lawyer cleared his throat. "At first, Arnold just used the sweatshops to increase the profit margin of the family company. However, he soon saw the benefit of buying into such operations. That's when he contacted me and became a silent partner in a number of small firms, using the profits to cover his personal expenses.

"I, of course, kept his name out of all this because of his

father's prejudice against such establishments. Unfortunately, Alope Randall has publicized the secret. But then Arnold's dead, so it can't hurt him. And Patricia has already contacted me. She's discovered that, instead of twenty-five percent of the family stock, she'll only be getting five. She wants me to act for her in the acquisition of partnerships with these small contractors, not to mention continuing to handle the holdings Arnold acquired prior to his death."

"That ought to infuriate Jacob," said Elena.

Pope shrugged. "Patricia has nothing further to gain from her father-in-law."

"Isn't she afraid of being sued? I understand that a number of cases are pending against Arnold."

"Ah, but there's the beauty of the arrangements I made," the lawyer bragged. "Arnold will not be liable. He's a money investor. The shops are run by others, and the original owners are answerable for any infractions." Pope gave her what he evidently considered an inviting smile. "I have a talent for law—and other things."

Yeah, right, Elena thought. "And none of the flak will hit you?"

"I'm just the go-between, although I must say that, in most cases, there's nothing wrong with the way the shops are run."

Elena raised her eyebrows. That's not what Alope Randall claimed, or the feds either. "I'd like to check them out. Do any of them operate on Saturdays?"

"Some," said Pope. "When they have work, they do whatever it takes to fulfill the contract. Nights, weekends. I'd be happy to give you names and addresses."

"I'd be happier if you came with me," said Elena.

"Really?" Pope looked delighted.

"Since a police detective isn't likely to be welcome."

"I do have a game in ten minutes."

"Cancel it."

"What do you hope to learn, Detective?" The swarmy smile was back.

"Whether any of the partners or any of their workers had reason to kill Arnold," Elena replied.

"The partners are businessmen," said Pope, surprised. "Seeing them as murderers would be a stretch of the imagination. As for the workers, they're busy trying to survive."

"I still want to go."

"How can I refuse such a pretty lady?" Pope rose and tried to take her arm. Elena managed to give him an accidental elbow to the ribs.

Then, taking her car—she refused to let herself be maneuvered into his—they went from one sweatshop to another, where the owners were as nervous over a visit from the police as Elena had expected—and even more nervous when they realized the reason for her visit. All claimed to have been unaware that Arnold was the source of their financing. They'd dealt only with Pope. They all had alibis for the time of Arnold's death. Elena wrote down every one.

Although they were anxious to keep her in their shabby little offices and away from the working areas, she insisted on talking to workers as well. The owners protested: their employees spoke only Spanish; her presence would disrupt production; did she plan to pay for product lost during the interviews? And so forth.

Still, Elena insisted and, interviewing workers in Spanish, found them as reluctant to talk as the owners, but not because they knew anything about Arnold Mandel. They were either afraid of losing money by taking time off or just generally afraid of the police. She learned very little, except that their working conditions were appalling. Because of the smell in one place, she asked to use the bathroom, and the owner, turning pale, tried to steer her to his own facilities while the women laughed bitterly and called out to her that she could pee in the alley if she didn't want to use the boss's toilet.

By the end of the depressing afternoon, once she'd dropped the disappointed lawyer off at his club, amorous hopes unfulfilled, she'd formed a new hypothesis about the murder. If one of the sweatshop owners had known that Arnold Mandel was the silent partner, that would have made Arnold a prime target for blackmail, and blackmail sometimes ended in murder, either of the victim or the blackmailer. Arnold could have threatened the would-be extortionist and been killed to keep him from carrying out the threat.

It was five forty-five before Elena got back to headquarters, determined to check out all the alibis she'd been given that afternoon, including Bascomb Pope's, not to mention calling all the sweatshop owners she hadn't visited. It didn't really matter how late she worked. After their quarrel last night, she didn't expect Michael to call.

21

Sunday, April 2, 1:15 P.M.

Who Will Come To Pansy's
Birthday Party This Year?

For many years Pansy, our beloved elephant, has been
a source of delight to the children of Los Santos. How can
we now explain to our sons and daughters that she has
killed a man who thought himself her friend and, in the
language of elephant keepers, a dominant member of her
herd? Elephants are enormous creatures and only to be
approached with the greatest care. Elephants are also
easily upset; so we are told by experts. Was Pansy's
keeper so ill-trained that he lost his life because of some
carelessness on his own part? Not according to the
testimony of his partner. Pansy's actions are considered
inexplicable by the elephant staff. That response is not
good enough. Pansy's attack is causing angry divisions in
the community, divisions exacerbated by sensationalist
journalism on the part of our competitor. Reasonable
explanations of this tragic event, not hysteria, are needed
if the present zoo administration is to retain public support
and Pansy is to remain a local favorite. Otherwise, Los
Santoans may refuse to attend the festivities when Pansy
celebrates the big 30 in May.

Editorial, Los Santos *Times*, Sunday, April 2.

"Welcome, welcome," said John James Audubon Mandel as Elena drove into the dirt yard in front of his sprawling adobe house and got out of the unmarked police car. He had been walking toward an outbuilding when he spotted her approach. "Which newspaper are you from?"

"I'm a Los Santos Crimes Against Persons detective," she replied.

"Oh." He looked disappointed. "I thought you were coming to interview me about my llama-raising program."

"'Fraid not," said Elena, looking around, noting the cottonwoods down by the Rio Grande, the outbuildings, fields, and pastures spreading toward the river to the west and the mountains to the east. Then she studied him. He was a thin man of medium height, rather dressed up for a rancher, but then he'd been expecting to be interviewed, perhaps to have his picture taken. He had a lush head of brown-blond hair and a very thin face—something peculiar about it. What? He certainly didn't look like the other Mandels. Was it possible that Jacob hadn't been his father? J.J. had the dark eyes, but not the height or the male-pattern baldness of his brothers.

"Ah, well," said J.J. "Welcome anyway. Would you like to see my llamas? Why don't I give you a tour? I'm very proud of my *rancho*."

Elena agreed, deciding that she could ask her questions while staring at a llama. They passed a block of stables, which J.J. gestured to indifferently. "For the horses. There's a long tradition of horse-breeding in my mother's family, but horses aren't as profitable as they used to be. The Indian casinos are taking gamblers away from race tracks. In fact, every track in New Mexico lost money last year."

Elena thought that surely horses were also sold to buyers unconnected with racing.

"Now, llamas—they're the wave of the future," said J.J. They had reached a pasture where ten of the furry, long-necked beasts stood nibbling at the grass. "Come along," urged J.J. "You needn't worry about stepping in llama droppings. They're very tidy in their toilet habits and use only one section of the field. Which is fortunate. It's easier to collect the droppings that way. Llama manure makes an excellent fertilizer for flower beds. I'm starting up a nice little business selling it to nurseries and local gardeners."

"Is it very expensive?" asked Elena, who was always on the lookout for new garden products.

"Well, I'm making a tidy profit," said J.J., "considering that I have to feed the llamas anyway."

She supposed that a tidy profit meant she couldn't afford to feed her tulips and daffodils llama manure.

"And of course, their wool is much sought after. But my primary reason for raising llamas is golf."

"As in putters and golf balls and country clubs?" Elena asked.

"Exactly," said J.J. "Llamas *love* to pull golf carts."

"They do?" That was news to Elena.

"They're basically stubborn creatures, but if a llama enjoys an activity, it will learn quickly and participate over and over again with great enthusiasm. My llamas will be featured in the upcoming golf tournament at the Oasis Country Club. Pulling the carts. I hope to get national coverage and increase my business tremendously.

"Don't hang back, Detective." He tugged Elena into the field. "They like humans. Although they don't want to be petted. Don't pet them. But they do like to stand close." He walked away from her into the general vicinity of an idle llama, and the beast edged up to him, then proceeded to stare, unblinking, at Elena. The stare made her uneasy. What did the creature find so interesting about her?

"Go stand by one yourself," J.J. invited.

Elena edged toward another llama. The first one continued to stare at her. Much to her surprise, when she got close, the second llama turned around and spat. Elena jumped back. Too late. It had left a glob on the lapel of her car coat, and if she wasn't mistaken, its spit was bleaching the color out right in front of her eyes.

"Oh, I'm so sorry." J.J. dashed over and pulled her away from the ill-mannered llama, brushing vigorously at the spot with his handkerchief. "I'm afraid she perceived you as invading her space. Or perhaps she thought you wanted to eat her food. Female llamas will spit bile if—"

"Bile?" Elena looked at her lapel, horrified.

"—you invade their space or eat their food."

"Believe me," grumbled Elena, "I wasn't planning to sample her grass."

"Of course not, but she didn't know that, did she? Well, enough of my llamas. Would you like to see my *hacienda*?"

Elena decided that she'd be happy to see anything that didn't have a live llama in it. She glanced down at her coat several times on the way to the house. Each time she looked, the llama bile had turned the spot on her lapel a lighter blue. By the time J.J. pushed open the wooden gates to the patio, the spot was almost white, and J.J. hadn't even apologized for his llama's bad manners or the damage to Elena's clothing.

"I imagine you'd like to see my animal paintings," he said, leading her through a courtyard partially overhung by the red tile roof. "Everyone who comes here does."

"Actually, I saw them when I visited your brother Darwin at the zoo."

"Did he show you my Pansy painting? Darwin's particularly fond of that one."

"Yes, he did," said Elena.

"Do sit down." He ushered her into a huge rectangular room broken up by various furniture groupings situated around Navajo rugs. There were Indian weapons and religious objects on the walls and, on shelves and tables, wonderful pottery which Elena recognized as having come from famous potters in the pueblos of New Mexico. Delighted with the room, she allowed J.J. to take her damaged jacket and usher her to a deep, comfortable leather chair.

"Will you have some lemonade?" he asked.

"I'm afraid this isn't a social visit, Mr. Mandel," she said. "I'm here about your brother's death."

"J.J.," he corrected. "Do call me J.J." He picked up a wooden stick with a knob on the end and clanged it against an old ranch bell. Then he sat down. "Poor Arnold. A great tragedy. I imagine if he'd given more thought to the happiness and well-being of his workers, it would never have happened. Still, it's a tragedy." He turned to a squat, dark-skinned woman who had entered the room. "Manuela, will you bring us some lemonade, please?" Without speaking, she turned and left.

"Your father's quite upset," said Elena, "but I'm sure you know that."

"I could have guessed," said J.J., his eyes darting away from hers.

"What kind of relationship did you have with your brother Arnold?"

"Oh, pleasant enough," said J.J. "We didn't see a lot of one another. Our interests are quite different, you understand."

"I'm sure," Elena agreed. "I've heard that you disapproved of Arnold's passion for hunting."

"Yes, certainly," said J.J. "I thought it very disloyal to our mother, who was a lovely woman and adored animals. She gave her life for animals."

"Literally?" Elena asked.

J.J. shifted uncomfortably. "I meant she devoted her life to their protection."

"Just how did your mother die?" Elena asked.

"Natural causes," he mumbled. "Nothing unusual. Have you met my sister, Rosalba?"

"Yes, I have," said Elena.

"A dear girl. Of course, she *will* wear furs and leather. Mother wouldn't have cared for that at all. Sometimes I feel that everyone has ignored Mother's principles except me."

"And your brother Darwin," Elena suggested.

"Of course. His zoo does try to take in endangered species. That's a fine thing to do, I suppose. Ah, here's our lemonade."

As he was pouring, Elena studied the interesting array of objects hung on the walls until she came, with a shock, to a large bow. It was big enough to be a match for the one that had killed Arnold, but constructed differently. "I notice that you have a bow and arrows."

"A gift from my grandfather," he said. "I keep it for sentiment's sake. Of course, I'd never use it. It's for deer hunting, and I don't believe in hunting animals."

"Mr. Mandel—"

"Oh, please, J.J. Everyone calls me J.J."

"O.K. I have to ask you what I've asked your brother and sister. Where you were and what you were doing on the night of your brother's murder."

"Let me see. That was last Tuesday?"

"Between ten and midnight, give or take an hour," said Elena.

J.J. jumped up and went to a large desk in one corner of the room, opened the middle drawer, and took out a leather-bound desk calendar, which he thumbed through earnestly. "Ah. I spent the evening making telephone calls," he said. "Till quite late, actually. I was calling golfers who will be here to participate in the tournament. Which will be featuring my llamas, you understand. And I called tournament organizers in other parts of the country to suggest that they attend so that they can see my llamas in action. With an eye to their using llamas themselves. Very exciting, don't you think? The idea of making so many llamas happy? You'd be astounded at how much delight they take in pulling two-wheeled golf carts."

No accounting for taste, Elena thought. She'd played golf once and hadn't enjoyed dragging around a golf cart at all. "Can you give me a list of the people you called and their phone numbers?"

J.J. wrinkled his forehead in surprise, and Elena realized what was strange about his face. He had no eyebrows, just bare ridges. Did he shave them? Maybe he'd lost them to eyebrow disease.

"I could certainly do that," he said in response to her request. "I'll just photocopy the pages of my calendar." Which he proceeded to do, all the while telling her about a one-man art show he would be having in a Los Santos gallery. "I do hope you'll come," he said. "I'll have the gallery owner send you an invitation. These pictures are a departure for me. I think of them as my paleolithic period—my way of extending thanks to our distant ancestors for the lovely animal drawings they left us in caves."

Had he done the paintings on stones?

As Elena drove home she mulled over her interview with J. J. Audubon Mandel. He'd refused to talk about his father, which was understandable. But what was it about the mother? No one would discuss her death. He seemed to feel friendly enough toward his sister and brothers. Elena hadn't detected any anger at Arnold, just mild disapproval. On the whole, J.J. seemed innocuous, if eccentric. Llamas! She glanced at her car coat with its white llama-bile spot. Elena really didn't appreciate being spat on by a touchy llama. How was she to know she'd invaded the stupid creature's territory? It didn't seem fair, not when she'd been standing by the llama because J.J. told her to. And he hadn't even offered to pay for the damage. Probably too rich to realize that the loss of a coat would matter to her.

22

There was a message on the answering machine when Elena got home, but not, as she'd hoped, from Michael. The lawyer, Oliver Formalee, wanted her to call him at home, which she did. Was he going to confess to killing Arnold himself? Or turn Patricia in for the thousand dollars from Crime Stoppers? Not likely. He probably charged a thousand dollars an hour for his time. "Mr. Formalee," she said when he answered, "this is Elena Jarvis returning your call."

"Ah, Detective, it seems that you bothered my client again Thursday. I do not want you to talk to Patricia Mandel unless I'm present."

"Then perhaps we should set up an appointment, since your client did have cause to kill her husband, and she does not have an alibi."

"Just because Patricia wasn't with the Pandarenes on Tuesday night does not mean that she was by herself."

"Well, if she had a companion, she didn't tell me who."

"Patricia was with me. If you'll remember, I mentioned that I was in Dallas when Arnold died. Patricia spent the night with me before she flew home. I stayed another day."

"I see."

"And may I point out to you," he continued, "there are a good many people with more cause to kill Arnold than either Patricia or I."

125

"Maybe you're alibiing each other because one of you killed him so that you could be together."

"We *were* together. Patricia's marriage didn't interfere with that. I doubt that Arnold would have been interested had he known."

"You couldn't marry her while he was alive."

Formalee chuckled. "I have *been* married, Detective Jarvis, and when I was married, I kept my wife on an allowance. I doubt that anyone could control Patricia's spending. As fond as I am of the lady, I would not care to marry her, and I rather imagine that if she remarries, she would prefer someone richer than I. Our relationship was not a motive for murder."

"I see. Well, thank you for the information, Mr. Formalee." Elena hung up, still considering them good suspects since they were alibiing each other. She had already verified Formalee's alibi—he had ordered dinner for two from room service. No one, however, had seen his companion, or him for that matter.

With those thoughts, she decided to give up for the night. She'd worked the entire weekend on the case and wasn't much further along than she'd been on Friday. Fixing herself a plate of *huevos rancheros*, getting out a cold bottle of beer, putting a Ray Lee Ribbon jazz tape on her tape deck, she settled down for a pleasant evening.

She'd just finished her dinner and was singing along with "St. Louis Blues" when her telephone rang. She picked up and said, "Jarvis."

"I think Michael's mad at you," said the voice at the other end.

Mark, she thought, fuming.

"But I'm not. Want to go out for a drink? We could talk about it. Maybe I could help."

Yeah right, thought Elena. Half the problem was Mark. "No thanks," she replied.

"Maybe another time," he said, seemingly unfazed by her refusal. "See you."

Elena shook her head. His calls were starting to give her the creeps.

23
..

Monday, April 3, 12:15 P.M.

It had been a long morning checking Arnold's bank and tax
records, much good it did her. Even with the help of Detective
Jean Moreno from Fraud and Forgery, Elena could find no
evidence that the victim was being blackmailed.

Returning to her desk with lunch in mind, Elena found a
telephone message from Josephine Priego. She returned the call.

"I wanted you to know that my lawyer filed suit today
against Arnold's estate," Josephine told her. "An' you'll never
guess who got me the lawyer."

"Who?" asked Elena. It was probably someone with a
grudge against the Mandels.

"His sister, Rosalba. She came over to visit, an' she was real
nice to us. She said the only way I'd get child support was to go
to court; then she gave me the lawyer's name. An' she's crazy
about Ceci. Here I thought Arnold's whole family was a bunch
of snobs, an' his sister turns out to be a real nice person."

Elena detected the sound of suppressed tears in Josephine
Priego's voice.

"So anyway I filed suit this morning, an' guess what
happened? Arnold's daddy's lawyer called me about twenty
minutes ago an' said there'll have to be blood tests on Ceci.
Like Ceci isn't Arnold's kid. Why would we name her after
Arnold's mother if she wasn't—" Josephine began to sniffle.
"It's really the last straw, don't you think?"

"I wouldn't get upset," Elena replied soothingly. "If they do DNA tests, there'll be no question, and you'll get support."

"I know that. My lawyer told me, but I'm still insulted. I just wanted you to know that if someone kills that old man, it's me."

"Come on, Jo," said Elena. "You don't want to kill Ceci's grandfather. Anyway, it wouldn't be sporting. He's in a wheelchair."

"Yeah, I guess you're right," said Jo. "I guess I just wanted to talk to someone. You mad?"

"Not at all," said Elena. "Good luck with your suit."

"Thanks. His sister even offered me money to tide me over until I can get some from Arnold's estate. Pretty nice, huh?"

"Yes, it is," Elena agreed and found herself liking Rosalba Mondragon even more than she had during the post-dinner-party interview.

After lunch she spent a slow afternoon getting a record of telephone calls placed from J.J.'s number the night of the murder. The calls had been made but were very brief; evidently there wasn't much interest in the upcoming llama demonstration. When she got back to headquarters and tried to contact the people he'd called, she had no luck at all. Either they didn't want to talk to a Los Santos detective—these were the people who weren't planning to go to the tournament—or they were on the road doing golf-type things. Still, he had made the calls. Elena gave up for the day and went home at four.

The highlight of her evening was a call from Michael, apologizing for his jealousy. She felt somewhat relieved. Evidently Mark hadn't stirred up any trouble between last night and tonight. To show that she accepted Michael's apology, Elena invited him to J.J. Mandel's animal art show. The invitation had been in the mailbox when she got home.

"I suppose he's a suspect," Michael grumbled.

"Not so you'd notice," said Elena. "He says this show is inspired by prehistoric cave art."

"Really." Michael sounded more interested than he had initially, and suggested they go to dinner first.

Elena agreed, guessing that their quarrel was mended. If she could think of some way to get rid of Mark, like finding him a job he couldn't refuse at the University of Alaska, things would be even better.

24
∴

Tuesday, April 4, 6:30 A.M.

This columnist resents the charges of divisive and sensationalist journalism leveled by the competing newspaper. "Elephant Update" addresses a controversy of great interest to the community and gives our readers a forum for their opinions. To that end, we publish the following letter:

"Maybe that snake that escaped from the zoo bit Pansy and got her all upset so she killed my uncle, Virgilio Zubarate. I don't think Uncle Virgilio would want anyone to shoot Pansy. I was named after her."

Pansy Zubarate, Sophomore
University of Texas at Los Santos

"Elephant Update," Los Santos *Herald-Post*, Monday, April 3

Elena had risen early because it was Tuesday, a watering day. She set the sprinklers to drench her spring flower beds, then went in to eat breakfast, turning to the editorial page of the *Times* see if there would be another fusillade in the new war of the newspapers. Nothing. What a disappointment.

On the front page, the first thing to meet her eye was a large picture of Rosalba Mandel Mondragon, draped in furs and striding into the family factory with picketers shouting at her. The accompanying story opened with the announcement that Rosalba was to be the new president of Los Santos Apparel. Well, good for her, thought Elena. That ought to give her life some direction. And Rosalba hadn't killed Arnold to get the position; she'd been on a plane. Elena had confirmed that.

The second paragraph said that Rosalba had refused to talk to a delegation of non-company workers or to address any of their complaints or the complaints of company workers relating to her late brother's extracurricular business affairs.

In the third paragraph Rosalba was quoted as saying, "Our employees couldn't be better treated if they were the blood children of Jacob Mandel. So if they aren't satisfied with their health benefits, their burial insurance, and their company cafeteria, we can always move the whole operation to Guatemala."

Elena shook her head, her admiration fading a little. That threat would *not* make a favorable impression on the work force.

When she got to headquarters at eight, Leo informed her that they had been summoned by Jacob Mandel. "Maybe he's going to confess," said Leo. "He probably had the chauffeur drive him over to Arnold's house and wheel him in. He talked Arnold into taking the bow and arrow off the wall. Then the old man shot him."

"Who let the bird loose?" Elena asked. "I don't think Jacob could have reached the bird from the wheelchair."

"Well, that's a problem," Leo agreed. They were in an unmarked car heading for Jacob's Montana Street mansion. "Maybe he's not really crippled. He's just pretending to need that wheelchair so that he can go around murdering people."

"Neat idea. You ask him about it."

"I think you should. Manny's always saying you're our detective-with-tact."

"I don't think there's any tactful way to bring that theory up, Leo," said Elena. She was driving in bumper-to-bumper traffic, averaging about five miles an hour.

For the rest of the trip Leo regaled her with Concepcion's pregnancy symptoms. The one that bothered him most was the waking up at night with a shriek when she was hit by leg cramps. "Every time it happens, I leap out of bed, reaching for my gun. If she doesn't knock it off, I'll probably shoot *her* some night."

"Maybe you ought to lock the gun up," said Elena dryly. "Once the kids arrive, you'll have to, anyway."

She pulled into Jacob Mandel's driveway. "Maybe you should just push him out of his wheelchair," Elena murmured to Leo as they entered. "If he can walk, he's our murderer. If he can't, he'll sue."

"I like it," said Leo. "Especially if you do the honors."

The Mandel patriarch had called them to demand that they arrest the labor agitators who had killed his son.

"We don't know who did it," said Elena.

"Then find out," said Jacob. "Immediately. If you don't make an arrest, they'll go after Rosalba next. I've made her the new CEO of the company."

"I saw it in the paper," said Elena. "Congratulations. Your daughter seems to be quite knowledgeable about the garment industry."

"How would you know?" Jacob demanded.

"I had dinner at her house Friday. She's a charming and intelligent woman."

"She is," he agreed grudgingly.

The man must be mellowing in his old age, Elena decided. Or desperate to keep the reins in the family.

"There's something I want you to see," he said and shouted for the nurse. "Get me those notes," he ordered. "I went down to the office and grilled all the vice-presidents, found out that my son was getting threats, both by mail and phone. He didn't tell me. Afraid I'd have another stroke, I suppose. Look at these." He took photocopies from the nurse and passed them to Leo. "And there was a police tap on Arnold's line. If you knew he was in danger, why didn't you protect him?"

"There's not a whole lot we can do," said Leo, "unless a crime is actually committed."

The old man looked infuriated. "Calm down, calm down," the nurse murmured until he shouted at her to shut up.

"You may not know who did it," snarled Jacob, "but I do. That Alope Randall. I want her arrested."

"She's a suspect," said Leo.

"But we don't have enough evidence against her," Elena added.

"Well, for God's sake, arrest her and then get the evidence."

"I'm afraid it doesn't work that way."

"What are you going to do? Delay until she kills my daughter too? Fine, I'll take care of it myself."

Outside in the car, they looked over the photocopies. In awkward printing, one said, "Our children are starving while you eat steak." Another said, "Sweatshop bastard, you'll get yours." Nothing specific. No wonder the department hadn't acted, Elena thought. They drove back to headquarters to find the officer who had been in charge of Arnold's problem.

"Why the hell didn't you contact us about these notes?" Leo demanded. "We looked like fools, being told by the vic's father what our own department was doing."

"We weren't doin' anything else," snapped Bill Colioso, who had caught the complaint. "Those notes were sent a couple of months ago, an' nothin' came in on the phone tap except his wife gossipin' and orderin' expensive stuff an' him talkin' to his girlfriend. Big waste of manpower listenin' to that shit."

"That doesn't mean you couldn't have told us about it," said Elena. "The man is dead—murdered."

"Hey, I just got back from vacation. Didn't know till late yesterday that someone had done him. I'd a called you today. Anyway, there aren't any fingerprints on the notes."

"Asshole," muttered Leo.

"Who you callin'—"

"Cool it, guys," said Elena. Leo looked as if he was ready to punch Colioso. And of course, Leo was right that the information was important, but that didn't mean it was worth getting into a fight over. With the two men glaring at each other like fighting cocks, Elena took back the photocopies of the notes and dragged her partner away.

Was Rosalba in danger? she wondered. And how did Jacob plan to protect her? Not by hiring a hit man to take out Alope Randall, Elena hoped. One murder and one possible—if you counted the elephant and the fact that Darwin usually worked her in the morning—those were enough. They didn't need another Mandel getting killed.

25
..

Michael handed Elena a flute of champagne and took one for himself. They had been wandering along a gallery wall looking at J.J. Mandel's pictures—abstract, dreamlike herds of bison, prides of lions, flocks of birds, who seemed to emerge from gray mists with exploding, muscular energy, jostling one another for the light. Surprisingly, Elena found that she liked them. They had a primitive power she wouldn't have expected from J.J. with his sentimental, anthropomorphic Pansy pictures and his llama fetish.

"Rosalba, how *could* you?"

Elena turned at the sound of the artist's voice. J.J. was staring reproachfully at his sister, who was bedecked in furs, looking flushed and happy.

"Now don't pout, little brother," said Rosalba, giving him a hug. "These little minks would never have lived at all if they weren't raised for coats."

"Mink farms are an abomination," said J.J. He turned to look at his sister-in-law Patricia, who had come to the one-man show with Oliver Formalee and Rosalba. "You two did this just to spite me." Patricia was wearing furs as well.

Arnold's widow hadn't wasted any time in starting to date openly, Elena thought. Did Rosalba know that Patricia had been seeing Formalee before Arnold's death?

"Nonsense," Rosalba told her brother. "We're celebrating

133

my presidency, and I love your pictures, J.J. They're scrumptious. I've bought two already."

J.J.'s anger waned a little, and he said, "Are you going to hang them?"

"Absolutely. In the dining room. And J.J., sweetie, as soon as this is over, I'm going to take you out for a night on the town. We'll both celebrate."

"I appreciate the offer, Rosalba," said J.J. stiffly, "but I couldn't be seen with a woman in furs."

Rosalba laughed, kissed him on the cheek, and whirled away to talk to friends. J.J. was approached by the gallery owner, who looked both arty and worried.

"My dear J.J.," he said, "the show is going wonderfully, but a crowd of appallingly dressed people carrying signs about their wages just arrived. Could they be your farm hands? Most of them are female. And they're blocking access to the gallery."

Fearing trouble, Elena followed J.J. to the door, where he confronted a horde of angry garment workers. "My good people," he said, once he'd read their signs, "you have mistaken your target. Not only do I have no investment in the garment industry, having been exiled by my father, but you have my deepest sympathies for your plight."

Someone threw an egg at him. A shower of overaged long green chiles and rancid refried beans followed the egg, while J.J. stood paralyzed in the doorway. Elena dragged him inside and shut the door. Through the large, tastefully arranged display windows, she could see globs dripping down the glass.

"My opening is ruined," said J.J. wretchedly.

"Nonsense," Elena told him. "No one out there could afford one of your pictures. And everyone in here likes them."

"Do you, Detective?" He turned to look at her.

"Absolutely," Elena replied, but she wasn't sure, given his expression, that he considered her opinion a compliment.

"Then maybe you'll call someone to disperse those poor people. I imagine it was Rosalba they meant to attack."

26
..

Remember when Pansy squirted water all over the mayor and the city council and when she flung dust on the Sun Bowl Queen and her court and when she broke wind on TV during her birthday party after stamping out all her birthday candles and getting pieces of her birthday watermelon all over her trunk and knees? There's an elephant after my own heart. Yea, Pansy! Keep up the good work.

Ramon McGill, Iconoclast

"Elephant Update," El Paso *Herald-Post*, Tuesday, April 4

Elena was at the jail, interviewing a beautician who had attacked a female customer. The customer had called the owner's daughter "a cheap bimbo." In reprisal, the owner had shaved two paths from the customer's forehead to her ears before the woman escaped, screaming, into the street. The charge was assault, and the perpetrator was not in the least repentant. A sheriff's deputy cut the interrogation short by motioning Elena out of the interview booth and informing her that she had an urgent call from the zoo.

Now what? Had Pansy attacked someone else? Darwin this time? Elena went downstairs, picked up her gun from the locker, got her car, and headed for Darwin Mandel's preserve.

She found him in his office with redheaded, freckled-faced Dr. Richard Tockler. The vet beamed at Elena and insisted that she call him Dick.

Elena swallowed down a giggle. Doc Dick? Doc Dick Tockler? She got hold of herself and shook his hand.

"Dr. Tockler has important information, Detective. Just what I suspected has turned out to be true."

"Really?" said Elena.

"Yes, tell her, Dick."

The vet shrugged modestly. "Lab tests show amphetamines in Pansy's blood, and believe me, we do not feed elephants amphetamines. My theory is that someone got her hooked, then stopped the administration of the drug, and Pansy went into withdrawal, causing her unfortunate attack on Mr. Zubarate."

"Wouldn't it take an awful lot of amphetamines to get an elephant hooked?" Elena asked.

"Given the size of an elephant, yes, it would," said Dr. Tockler.

"And how would this person have given her the pills?"

"I have no idea, Detective. That's your province, not mine."

"Maybe there was a medication mistake."

"Pansy was not on medication, and none of our animals are taking amphetamines."

"Well, you'll have to admit that it's a bizarre theory," Elena pointed out.

"Not at all," said Dr. Tockler. "I see it as a copycat crime. There was a case in India where work elephants were fed amphetamines to increase their productivity. Then when the drug was cut off, they went crazy and killed a number of people."

"A copycat elephant drugger?" muttered Elena.

"Murderer," corrected Dr. Dick. "The person administering the drugs, then cutting them off, if that's what happened, wanted Pansy to kill someone."

Elena reminded herself that Darwin was usually the first person to greet Pansy in the morning. If Darwin had been the victim instead of Mr. Zubarate, it would tie in with the Arnold Mandel case, given that Arnold had also died under strange circumstances in which an animal was involved, although the animal wasn't the cause of death, just of postmortem mutilation.

Elena had called Leo before she left the jail. He arrived just as she came to the conclusion that neither M.O. seemed like the sort of thing a labor advocate would do in retaliation for bad working conditions and lost wages. When Leo heard the doctor's theory, he said, "How would the guy give her the amphetamines? In her water, or what?"

"That's possible," said Dr. Tockler.

"How does she get her water?"

"There's a tap in her enclosure," said Darwin Mandel.

"O.K.," said Leo. "Let's go look at it," and the four of them set off, Leo walking with Dr. Mandel, asking questions; Dick Tockler walking with Elena and staring at her so fixedly that he tripped twice.

"I hope, Detective Jarvis," he said, "that I haven't made your work more difficult by leaving town as I did."

Elena shrugged. "To tell you the truth, I wasn't taking the Pansy thing very seriously up to now."

"Even so, you must accept my apologies. I had to rush to my mother's side. She suffered serious injury on a roller coaster."

"Really?" said Elena. "I thought they were supposed to be pretty safe."

"Oh, they are," Dick Tockler assured her, "but my mother is a roller-coaster reviewer."

Elena cocked an eyebrow at him.

"She writes articles and books about roller coasters. Her *History of the Roller Coaster on the North American Continent* is a classic."

"You must be very proud." Was he *serious*?

"Yes, and this particular roller coaster was a rebuilt early model. Naturally, she felt she had to ride it. Unfortunately, she leaned out of the car to take a picture and hit her head on a strut. If it weren't that her significant other dragged her back into the car, I fear she would have died."

His mom had a significant other? Elena took that to mean "lover." "How terrible," she murmured sympathetically. "How is she?"

"Recovering. Mother is very hardy. She suffered a skull

fracture, a broken collarbone, and several compressed vertebrae, but the doctor assures me that she'll be her own active
self again in three to six months."

"I guess that's good news," said Elena doubtfully. Six months
sounded like a long time, but it was better than dying.

"Indeed," said the veterinarian, "and in the meantime, she
plans to write a children's book about her experience on the
roller coaster."

Well, that sounded like a winner, thought Elena. Parents all
over the country would certainly want to read their kids a book
about how you could get a skull fracture, a broken collarbone,
and several compressed vertebrae by riding roller coasters.

"Would you care to have dinner with me tonight?" Dr. Dick
asked suddenly.

Elena hastened to tell him that she was already in a serious
relationship.

"What a shame," said Dr. Dick. "I'm sure Mother would
have liked you. If you ever find yourself free, give me a call.
My offer is open-ended."

"Nothing wrong with the plumbing out here," said Leo when
they caught up. Leo had looked at the system outside the
enclosure. Two keepers, coming down a path to the entrance
gate beside the elephant's quarters, listened to the problem and
offered to take him inside.

"With Pansy?" he asked, horrified.

"She's chained," said Dr. Tockler. "That was accomplished
once she'd calmed down. Of course, she's not happy about it."

"Right," said Leo.

"There's nothing wrong with the pipes," said Jesus Amado.
"I'd a noticed."

"I'll go," Elena offered. "We don't want the expectant
father here running any risks." Still, the idea of getting
anywhere near that crazy elephant gave her the creeps.

"You know anythin' about plumbin'?" asked the keeper.

"Sure," said Elena. "I do my own." She followed him in,
and they both examined the water system.

"See," said Amado. "No one's been messin' with it. No
changes, no wrench marks. And that idea about her bein' in
withdrawal's a crock."

"She tested positive for amphetamines," said Elena, glancing over her shoulder. She could hear the elephant shifting position, the rattle of the chains.

"Someone probably came along the path an' pitched her some poisoned food. She'll eat anythin'. Ate my ankus once—except for the hook."

"It could be that simple? Someone put the drug in—what?"

"Fruit. Give her a melon, she'd probably scarf down arsenic. Ain't like our security's that terrific. Someone made off with the lion an' that snake. All they'd need to do was jump the fence when the guards was somewhere else—"

"Did you see any sign in the enclosure of food that wasn't part of her usual diet?"

Amado shrugged and led Elena back to the gate. "Couldn't even get Virgilio out till nightfall the second day. By then so much dust had blew through, we couldn't tell nothin'."

"The pipes don't show any evidence of tampering," Elena announced. "Mr. Amado says someone could have thrown Pansy doctored fruit."

"However it happened, it won't happen again," said Darwin Mandel. "I intend to go straight to the city council and get another night guard."

"Maybe you ought to consider getting some protection for yourself," Elena suggested. "This may have been a plot against *your* life. You did tell me that you're usually the first person to see Pansy each day. Perhaps this was part of a vendetta against your family."

"Nonsense," Darwin objected. "Why would anyone want to kill me? It must have been some cruel person who hates animals and wanted to make poor Pansy's life miserable. I call that unconscionable."

As Elena and Leo left, she suggested that they interview the kindergarten teacher and pupils who had witnessed Mr. Zubarate's death. "Maybe the elephant drugger was hanging around to watch."

"I'm off this afternoon," said Leo. "Concepcion and I are going to the obstetrician. He's supposed to make another try at figuring out how many babies she's carrying."

"You mean there's a chance of more than three!" Elena exclaimed.

"For all I know, we've got ten kids in there," Leo muttered.

"How does the doctor find out for sure?"

"Ultrasound," said Leo. "But it's no guarantee."

"Gee, Leo, good luck. If he doesn't know it's three, maybe it's only two."

"Fat chance," her partner replied.

Elena headed back to headquarters by herself, since they'd come in separate cars. When she got to her desk, she made an appointment with the kindergarten teacher, Ms Anne Klempt, who said that she could arrange to talk to Elena, but that Elena could not speak to the students, who were much too traumatized by the event to be questioned by strangers. Ms Klempt did offer to run videotapes of the children talking to counselors. Elena had to be satisfied with that; when it came to children, the law was very protective.

Then Elena called Rosalba Mondragon to explain the elephant situation and suggest that she might want police protection. Rosalba said her father had already arranged a bodyguard for her, which Elena was relieved to hear, although it surely was a stretch to imagine that the drugging of Pansy had been a plot to kill Darwin and in some way connected with his brother's death. Still, Elena didn't want another dead Mandel turning up, especially Rosalba, whose life seemed to have taken a turn for the better.

Next she returned a call from Michael, who invited her out to lunch. She accepted after ascertaining that Mark would not join them, and they met in the Kern Place area on North Mesa to eat ribs. Much amused by Dick Tockler and his offbeat mother, Elena passed the story on to Michael. "I was invited to dinner by a vet whose mother reviews roller coasters. He said he was asking me out because his mother would like me. Isn't that hilarious?"

Michael didn't seem particularly amused, so she said teasingly, "I guess the question is, Would *your* mother like me?" to which Michael replied, "Not if she knew you're causing trouble between Mark and me."

"What's that supposed to mean?" Elena snapped. "I haven't caused any trouble. In case you didn't notice, *he* put his arm around *me* last night." Mark had shown up unexpectedly at J.J.'s show.

"He was just being friendly," said Michael.

"He was just being a pain in the ass," Elena retorted. "And he knows I don't like him touching me. I'd think you wouldn't want him doing it either."

"Maybe he feels that you're sending him signals."

"I am *not*," she snapped, gnawing the last bit of meat off her rib and adding, "I've got to go. I have an interview with a kindergarten teacher who saw the elephant murder."

"Since when is it murder?" asked Michael.

"Since we discovered that someone was slipping the elephant amphetamines."

"You're kidding." Michael looked intrigued.

"I wish I were," said Elena. "What a week! Elephants strung out on speed and going into withdrawal, garment tycoons shot with a deer-hunting bow, eyeball-eating falcons. What next?"

Seemingly over his pique, Michael had listened with interest. "A fascinating case. If I can help, let me know."

"If you've got any theories, I'd love to hear them. I suppose you could want to kill someone over a labor squabble, but these deaths are so bizarre that they seem more personal."

Michael agreed. "Labor disputes, if they become violent, are usually settled with guns or baseball bats."

"You want to come over tonight?" Elena asked.

"Can't," said Michael. "That's why I asked you to lunch. The Sociology Club is meeting at seven. Our discussion topic is parenting among the homeless."

"That sounds like a real downer," said Elena, thinking she'd rather work on an elephant murder.

27

The school was a cheerful place with paneled siding in primary colors between the windows, and gaily colored playground equipment on a wide expanse of asphalt. Elena wondered whether they'd had grass before water rationing. She parked in a visitor's space and went inside to ask for Anne Klempt at the main desk. Ms Klempt proved to be a tall, slender young woman with swinging brown hair and blue eyes, solemn-faced with a smile that burst out unexpectedly when she was speaking of her students.

"It's such a sweet age," she said. "They're a pleasure to be with."

Thinking of her nieces and nephews, Elena agreed and allowed herself to be led down the hall to the teachers' lounge, which was labeled Smoke-Free. Were there elementary teachers these days who smoked? And if so, did they have to sneak out to light up behind the dumpsters, desperate to get their ration of nicotine? "I'm here about the elephant attack," said Elena, "the one witnessed by you and your class."

Anne Klempt nodded sadly. "It was a terrible thing. I still have nightmares, and I do worry about the children. We've provided counseling, and most of them seem to be doing well. In fact, there are a number who are less traumatized than I am," said the young teacher, "but it was horrible. The

142

elephant trumpeted, wrapped its trunk around the poor man, and then slammed him against the stone wall. After that" —Ms Klempt shuddered—"the elephant dropped him and ground him into the dirt with her head. It was—" she looked a little green—"very violent, and I saw the man's face just before it happened. He looked astounded. Obviously he couldn't believe the elephant was attacking him. When the elephant first picked him up, he patted her trunk, as if he thought she was making a gesture of affection."

"Until that incident," Elena pointed out, "Pansy had a pretty good reputation."

Ms Klempt shook her head. "I can't understand why she wasn't put down immediately."

"There seem to be a number of people who agree with you—not, of course, the zoo director."

"Yes, I've seen the articles in the paper, the letters to the editor, and that column 'Elephant Update.' People have such a taste for blood and violence these days. It's no wonder sweet little children turn into criminals."

"I wonder, Ms Klempt, did you notice anyone else in the vicinity, either before or after the attack?"

"There weren't many people at the zoo that morning," said Anne Klempt. "Actually, I had thought of canceling because a dust storm was predicted. It hit when we were on our way back. But no, I didn't notice anyone. We got there at nine-thirty, when the zoo first opened."

"What about the children? Did they mention seeing anyone?"

"Not that I remember. I have the tapes of the counseling sessions if you'd like to see them now."

Sighing, Elena agreed. It was going to be a long afternoon, she thought, if all twenty-three children had been taped. And so it was, as she and Ms Klempt viewed videos that showed children drawing with crayons and talking about their visit to the zoo. One said, "He wrapped his tail around the man and spanked him against the wall." Another said, "When the elephant pushed her head on the man, he went squish, and all this red and pink stuff came squishing out, and it was really yucky." The little boy seemed quite taken with the experience.

One little girl said, "I was watching the birdie. He was hopping down the path, pecking at the dirt, and I thought he was eating the dirt, but Maria said he was looking for worms, only he never found any. Poor birdie, he must have been really hungry, because he never found anything to eat, so I didn't see the elephant until he tried to do a headstand on the man in the zoo suit, and by that time the man was all floppy like my sister's rag doll. I can do a headstand. Do you think he was dead?" The counselor didn't answer.

One child thought it probably hurt to be stepped on by an elephant. "I'll bet a big fat elephant like that would weigh a lot, like fifty pounds or something, don't you think?" Another child had been watching a squirrel running up and down a tree and missed the whole elephant incident. However, she had a lot to say about squirrels because she had a book about a lady squirrel whose pretty house got all messed up by mean red squirrels. The little girl had been watching the squirrel in the zoo to see if any mean red squirrels came around to mess up her house.

"Aren't they amazing?" murmured Ms Klempt. "They're so resilient, and so fascinated with every little thing. Imagine watching a squirrel when you could see an elephant."

One boy said, "I just wished the elephant would stop 'cause I had to pee pee, and I kept pulling on Miss Anne's hand, and she didn't pay any attention." Anne Klempt shook her head. "I don't even remember his speaking to me. Poor child. He must have held it all the way back to the school."

Another kindergartner told the counselor that the elephant wasn't at the zoo anymore because it was in her closet, and it stayed there all night trying to get out and put its head on her, so she had to sleep in Mommy's bed so the elephant couldn't get her. And Mommy's boyfriend didn't like that.

In none of the interviews was there any mention of the children having seen a stranger watching the elephant attack. "I really don't think anyone saw it but us," said Ms Klempt. "And the second keeper, who was in the doorway of the elephant house until Pansy went wild. Several zoo attendants arrived while she was—" The teacher shuddered. "That poor man! As soon as I could, I herded the children together and rushed them away. Some were crying; some were giggling. They didn't know quite what had happened."

Ms Klempt removed the last cassette and turned to Elena. "Many of my students think violence is something that occurs on TV, and when the program's over, no harm has been done. It's no wonder society's such a mess. How can their parents let them watch that garbage? Some of the parents have complained, you know. As if I knew what was going to happen when I took the children to the zoo."

It was four-thirty by the time they'd seen the last of the tapes and Elena could get away. She'd learned something about children, but nothing about the person who drugged the elephant. As she thought about him on the way home, she decided that he had to be very disturbed and very violent. But was he the same person who had killed Arnold? The M.O.'s were so vicious. And strange. A madman? These couldn't be labor-relations hits. It all felt too personal.

28

I don't believe that elephant was drugged. She's just
mean. Typical female. The zoo ought to get rid of her.
Brian Motty, Welder

What about, *Just say no*? I'm shocked that our own
zoo is using drugs on its animals.
Cora Medrano, President, Mothers Against Drugs

"Elephant Update," El Paso, *Herald-Post*, Wednesday,
April 5

"You're late," said Leo.
"Check the schedule," Elena snapped, still short-tempered
because of yesterday's quarrel with Michael. "I'm on twelve
to eight today." She dropped into her chair on Homicide Row.
"Well, then you're early," said Leo and grinned at her.
"What are you trying to do? Impress Manny with your—"
"Oh, shut up," said Elena, but she had started to laugh, glad
that Leo was in a good mood for a change.
"How'd the papers get hold of the elephant-drugging
story?" Leo asked.
"Dr. Mandel thinks one of the keepers must have talked,
but no one's admitting anything, and the director claims that
he would have made the announcement himself at a more—
these are his exact words—'propitious time.' Anyway, it was

a big coup for the 'Elephant Update' columnist. He got to break the story."

"And how did the kiddie interview go yesterday afternoon?" Leo asked.

"I didn't talk to any kiddies. I watched video cassettes of them talking about the elephant attack. Nobody saw anything except squirrels and birdies and Pansy squashing Mr. Zubarate. No dangerous spectator in the area." She started to boot up her computer.

"Forget that," said Leo. "We just got a call from Jacob Mandel. Says his daughter didn't report for work this morning, she doesn't answer her telephone at home, and her new bodyguard can't get into her residence."

Elena swung her chair around and stared at her partner. "Oh God," she said. "Not Rosalba too."

"Hey," Leo replied. "You don't know anything's happened. She's probably shacked up with a boyfriend and forgot all about her new presidential duties."

"I don't think so," said Elena.

They checked out a car and headed for Rosalba's condo. There the bodyguard, a husky young man with a stubbled head and huge shoulders—he told them that he had been a swimming instructor before becoming a bodyguard—stood dithering at the front door. "I didn't know what to do," he said. "I called her father. I called my boss. Am I supposed to knock the door down?"

They calmed the bodyguard, pounded on the door, rang the bell. No answer. "So what do you think?" asked Leo.

"Kick it in," Elena suggested.

"If there's no problem, she'll sue us."

"No, she won't," said Elena. "Kick it in."

Leo backed up and planted one long, tap-dancing foot against the door, which flew open with little resistance. "You'd think they'd have better locks on a place this expensive," he said, and they began to search. Rosalba's purse had been dropped on the white sofa in front of the jungle pit. To Elena that meant she was at home.

"This place is weird," said Leo.

"But kind of neat," Elena replied. Rosalba wasn't on the first floor.

"I guess you're wondering about my head," said the bodyguard.

"Not really," Leo replied.

"I shaved it," said the young man. "More aerodynamic. For competitive swimming. I know it looks bad, but—"

Elena patted his shoulder. "Stubble is in," she said.

"Not on your head," said the young man. "My girlfriend hates it."

"Let's hit the next floor," said Leo. They climbed the stairs, the husky bodyguard trailing behind, looking very young and very nervous.

"Much good he'd have done her," Leo murmured to Elena.

Rosalba wasn't on the second floor either, but the bathroom door in the master suite was locked. They rattled the knob and pounded. Elena called, "Rosalba?"

"Maybe she fell in the shower and knocked herself out," said Leo.

"Do you hear water running?" Elena asked. "Kick the door in."

"You do it this time. What if I break a bone in my foot?"

"Yeah, right," said Elena. "You'd never tap dance again." She backed up and gave the door a good thump. It opened partway, then stopped, caught against an obstacle. Again Elena felt a wave of foreboding.

Leo stuck his head through the opening. "Tall, dark-haired woman?" he asked.

"That's right."

"She's here. On the—oh my God!" He backed out hurriedly and closed the door.

"What are you doing?"

"There's a rattler in there. I heard it."

"Did you see it?"

"I think it's on the far side of the bathroom, maybe behind the clothes hamper."

"If you didn't see it—"

"Listen, I know a rattlesnake when I hear one."

"Well, we can't just leave her in there," said Elena. She poked her head around the door. Rosalba was naked, sprawled face down, arm outstretched, fingers clawed, her neck, face, and shoulder—what could be seen of them—puffed and discolored.

"I'm not going back in there," said Leo from behind Elena. "An enclosed place with a rattlesnake. No way."

"What if she's still alive?" Elena tried to discern breathing. "Snakebites don't always kill you," she muttered. Then she saw the snake—big, white, slithering from behind a lavender wicker laundry hamper beside a shower stall with stalks of iris inset in the glass door. As Elena ducked out, she took another quick look at Rosalba.

"We'll call Animal Control," said Leo. "Unless you know anything about snake catching." He looked from Elena to the kid, who turned pale and backed up.

"I just got here a half hour ago," stammered the bodyguard. "It isn't my fault something happened to her. I gotta report to my boss."

Elena rolled her eyes and hurried to the guest bedroom, where she had seen a long, gaily painted stick hanging on the wall, some purchase from Rosalba's travels, she assumed. When she lifted it from the curved wall braces, it rattled. Great! Maybe the snake would think it was a lady snake. The stick was surprisingly light. Not too light to hold the rattler, she hoped.

When she returned to the master suite, Leo said, "God, Elena, you're not going in there, are you?"

"It's just a snake," she said. "I've been around them all my life."

"What are you going to do? Beat it to death?"

"Just stand back," she said and pushed past him, opening the door to the bathroom cautiously, grabbing a laundry bag off the hook on the door, edging around Rosalba's body. The snake, all the way out of its lavender corner, reared back. Elena extended the stick and put the end down on the middle coil. As she had hoped, the white rattler wrapped itself around the stick. So far, so good.

She snapped the laundry bag open, shortened up on the stick, thrust the snake into the opening, and shook the stick hard. When she felt the weight release, she yanked the stick out and pulled the cord, her heart pounding frantically. With her brothers, sisters, and friends, she had caught snakes this way in the Sangre de Cristos. It was a game, a contest. Of course, her parents hadn't known about the game, but the kids had kept score and considered it great fun. She must have been crazy, she thought now. Working with a snake the size of this one was crazy! The bag rested on the floor, thrashing, Elena holding the strings high. She thrust the stick through the loops and lifted the stick to keep the mouth of the laundry bag tight.

"Are you O.K.?" Leo called from the bedroom.

"I think we've found that albino rattler that escaped from the zoo a couple of weeks ago." She was edging away from the sack, hand over hand on the stick, not an easy task with the heavy, woven-cotton bag wiggling and rattling vigorously. "Get in here and see if Rosalba's still alive," Elena called to Leo. "I can't let go of the stick."

"Jesus, Elena."

"You're not going to get bitten," said Elena. And neither was she. She hoped.

Gingerly Leo edged around the door and goggled at the wriggling bag. "Couldn't you get it further away from me?" he asked. "I really hate snakes."

"Good thing you didn't grow up in my family," she snapped and extended the end of the stick to push open the door to the shower stall. The bag swung from side to side. If it slipped down toward her, she was in trouble. But that wasn't going to happen. She dumped the bag into the shower stall, yanked the stick back, dropping it, and sprang forward to slide the door closed. She was shaking hard—but she'd done it.

As Elena leaned against a lavender pedestal sink and took a deep breath, Leo knelt beside the body. "Her neck's so swollen I can't find the artery," he said.

"Try the wrist," said Elena, studying the bathroom, trying to figure out how this happened. "She must have got out of the shower, dropped her towel"—there was a towel lying on the carpeting—"bent to pick it up, and the snake got her in the neck. If it's the one from the zoo, it's a Mohave rattler. Very venomous."

"She's dead," Leo murmured. "The body's cold. You sure that snake can't get loose?" He rose and looked toward the shower. They could hear the snake still thumping in the bag behind the glass door.

The bodyguard called to them from the bedroom, "Is she all right?"

"She's dead," Leo called back.

The young man groaned. "I gotta report to my supervisor." They could hear his footsteps pounding down the stairs.

"Why didn't she leave the bathroom?" Elena asked. "A rattlesnake's bite isn't immediately lethal, even in the neck. At least, I didn't think so." As she examined the body, she saw fang marks on one ankle and both calves.

Leo rose and studied the lock on the door. It had been damaged when Elena kicked it in. "I think the lock's been tampered with. I think once she got in, she couldn't get out."

Elena shivered, imagining Rosalba—taking a shower while the snake lurked behind the laundry basket, stepping out, hearing the rattle and feeling the fangs strike her neck as she bent for her towel, finding she couldn't open the door to get away, taking more strikes, falling, bleeding internally as the hemotoxin dissolved her flesh and her blood vessels, dying. Elena shuddered, wondering if she could have prevented this. If she could have saved this woman, whose life so recently had taken a turn for the better.

"I never heard of a white rattlesnake," said Leo, eyeing the shower door, behind which the snake was still rattling in the laundry bag.

"They're rare," said Elena, "which means it's unlikely it came from anywhere but the zoo. At least, we'll be able to trace it." She looked down at Rosalba, wanted to put a towel over the woman's nakedness, but knew she couldn't disturb the crime scene. And this *was* a murder. Stolen snakes didn't just show up in people's bathrooms. Unable to take her eyes away from the swollen, discolored flesh around the fang marks, Elena thought, *God, what an awful thing to do to someone!*

"That's two hits and one miss on the Mandel family," said Leo, "all of them weird and unpleasant."

"I know it," said Elena, still staring at the woman who had been her hostess, whom she had liked, who had offered help to Arnold's illegitimate daughter. Had Patricia found out? Set this up? "I guess we'd better call Animal Control—and the zoo—and get the forensic team over here."

29
··

Downstairs in the Mondragon condo, Elena picked up the ringing telephone and said, "Jarvis."

"Why haven't you called about my daughter?" Jacob Mandel demanded. "Is she all right?"

Elena closed her eyes. She'd rather have gone over to tell the old man in person. "I'm afraid Mrs. Mondragon is dead, Mr. Mandel," she said.

"Dead?" There was a long, bleak silence. "God damn it, I told you to arrest Alope Randall." Although the words were strong, his voice sounded weak. "She's trying to kill everyone who can run the factory. If you'd arrested her, Rosalba would be alive." His voice had almost faded to a whisper. "What happened to her?"

There wasn't any gentle way of saying it. "She got locked in her bathroom with a rattlesnake."

Another long silence hummed over the line. "Rosalba was terrified of snakes," he said. "How could she have got locked in the bathroom?"

"My partner thinks someone tampered with the lock," said Elena. "Do you have protection for yourself?"

"I don't need protection. Who'd want to kill an old man who's half dead anyway?"

"It looks to me, sir, like the whole family's at risk. I think that elephant incident was an attempt on your son Darwin."

"It's an attack on the factory, not the family," said Jacob. "And if you won't arrest the Randall woman, by God, I'll go over your head."

He was working himself up. Taking charge. Elena wondered whether that was better or worse than his first, stunned reaction. "Do you know where Rosalba was last night or who she was with?" Elena asked gently.

"She went to a Chamber of Commerce dinner, gave a speech about the new goals of the company. I didn't agree with everything she wanted to do, but I agreed to let her try. The boys had their chance. I guess it was her turn. But now it's gone. She's gone." His voice broke.

"Did she go to the dinner with anyone?"

"Oliver Formalee was to pick her up and drive her home. Rosalba didn't care much for driving. But Formalee wouldn't have killed her. He was Arnold's lawyer."

And Patricia's lover, thought Elena. Patricia, who would have been furious if she knew Rosalba was befriending Josephine Priego and her child. But why, assuming the deaths were connected, would Patricia try to kill Darwin?

"Get that lawyer woman," said Jacob. "You hear me?" He hung up as Onofre Calderon came down the stairs shaking his head.

"Would it have been painful?" Elena asked. "Her death?"

Calderon grimaced. "It's not a pleasant way to go." To the morgue boys he said, "You can take her away now." Then turning back to Elena, he added, "I don't much like examining a corpse when I have to do it in a room with a rattlesnake, even if the snake is bagged. She had six bites. Poor woman didn't have a chance."

Elena shuddered and glanced up the stairs. They were bringing Rosalba down in a body bag.

"George Prettle, Animal Control," said a tall, gangly man in a brown uniform. He came in without knocking, carrying an armload of equipment. "Got a call about a snake."

"I've already put the snake in a bag," said Elena. "Then I threw it in a shower stall."

His eyebrows wiggled, Groucho Marx style. "I heard it was a rattler."

"Yes, a white one."

"Albino? Only one of those I've heard of was at the zoo."
Elena nodded.

"Better call and ask if they're missing one."

"They are," said Elena. She had called. Darwin was out
fundraising, but Dr. Tockler thought the snake must be the
one that had disappeared.

"Someone ought to tell you, lady," said the Animal Control
man, "that it's dangerous to fool around with snakes."

"I knew what I was doing."

"Well, it's your butt," said Prettle, "but I don't want to haul
your snake off if it belongs to the zoo."

"They're coming to check," she said, turning her thoughts
to Darwin Mandel, who knew how to shoot a bow and arrow,
whose brother had been killed with one, who insisted on
taking in his brother's falcon, and who had had an albino
rattlesnake, which had killed his sister Rosalba. The two
deaths left Darwin as the sole heir to Los Santos Apparel. He
might not be interested in running the company, but he might
be very interested in inheriting the whole thing. And he didn't
have an alibi for the night of Arnold's death.

Maybe the elephant attack was a red herring to make it
look as if Darwin was in danger too, although it had been Mr.
Zubarate who'd actually been killed. And who had more
access to zoo creatures like Pansy and the white snake than
Darwin? But why would he take the mountain lion? In case
his father reconciled with J.J.?

Then there was Oliver Formalee, who had escorted Rosalba last night. If all the children designated as Jacob's heirs
were dead, would Formalee's lover, Patricia, inherit the
company? Or would Jacob relent and leave it to his son J.J.?
That supposition left J.J. in danger. But if Jacob were the
relenting type, J.J. himself would have reason to kill them all.
Not that Jacob seemed likely to forgive his youngest son,
even if he had no other children left. Jacob seemed to be a
screw-up-and-you're-out sort of father. The damned case just
kept getting more terrible, more violent, more complicated.

Leo came downstairs, saw the Animal Control man, and
said, "I hope you're going to take that snake away. It's going
to shake its rattles off if someone doesn't do something."

"We're waiting on the zoo," said George Prettle. "Albino, huh? Think I'll go take a look."

"Don't, for God's sake, let it out," said Leo.

Giving the detective a condescending smile, Prettle headed for the stairs, calling over his shoulder, "Lady, could you call the zoo again? I haven't got all day."

Elena nodded. "Leo, why don't you get on the car phone and contact Oliver Formalee, the lawyer. Rosalba's father says he escorted Rosalba to dinner last night and brought her home. See what he has to say. I'll find out why no one has shown up from the zoo."

Leo nodded and left. Elena dialed, got hold of Darwin this time, and told him the bad news about his sister.

"Heaven help us!" cried Darwin. "Rosalba was terrified of snakes."

"So I hear," said Elena.

"I told her many a time that she should learn how to deal with reptiles since there are so many in the desert, but she wouldn't get near one. I can't believe she'd stay in a room long enough to be bitten more than once."

"She didn't have any choice," said Elena. "The door locked behind her, and she couldn't get out."

Darwin groaned. "That's horrible. Truly horrible."

"I called earlier, Dr. Mandel. The snake is an albino. Dr. Tockler—"

"You found White Fang?" He seemed to forget his sister on hearing that his snake had turned up. "I do hope so. He's very valuable."

"Have you ever heard of another albino rattlesnake in this area?" Elena asked.

"No, I haven't. It has to be White Fang."

"The snake that killed your sister."

There was a pause. "How would he get in her house?"

"That's what we'd like to know."

"Is the snake still alive?"

"Yes," said Elena.

"Well, bring it here, for heaven's sake."

"Dr. Tockler is supposed to send someone to identify it."

"Of course. Even if it isn't White Fang, bring it here. This may sound unfeeling, but the snake was probably as terrified as my sister. We need to put it in a reassuring environment. What have you done with it?"

"I tied it up in a laundry bag and threw it in a shower stall."

"*Threw it*? You may have injured it!"

Jesus, thought Elena after she'd hung up. The man's sister had just died a horrible death, and he was worried about the snake.

Leo returned and said, "Formalee says he dropped Rosalba off at her front door, didn't go in with her, then took several other people home and went over to see Patricia Mandel. The people he dropped off after Rosalba verify his story. So does Mrs. Mandel."

"I guess that lets him off." Or maybe not. When had the snake been put in the bathroom? If it was after Rosalba left for the Chamber of Commerce dinner, Patricia was unaccounted for. She hadn't gone. But then Elena couldn't imagine Patricia handling a snake. Or stealing one. However, Arnold's wife could have hired someone to do it. Although hiring someone to shoot Rosalba would have been easier.

"If the snake does belong to the zoo," Elena said to Leo, "I think we need to start questioning zoo employees. Not to mention the director. The person who could most easily steal a snake from the Reptile House is someone who works at the zoo."

"You think Mandel put the snake in his sister's bathroom?"

"Could be," said Elena.

30
⋮⋮

Thursday, April 6, 1:00 P.M.

"I don't know how you can wolf down tacos when you know there's a snake in the car," said Leo. Driving to the zoo, they had stopped for Mexican take-out. George Prettle from Animal Control had received a rabid-bat call and left Rosalba's house before anyone arrived from the zoo. Then Darwin Mandel called to say their chief snake handler had been in an automobile accident while on his way to make the identification. Anxious to get on with it, Elena insisted on taking the snake over herself. Darwin agreed reluctantly, but offered all sorts of snake-handling instructions—more, Elena thought, for the safety of White Fang than because he was worried about her.

"And who's going to carry the snake in?" Leo demanded before biting into his third taco. "He can probably sink his fangs into you through the laundry bag."

"Dr. Mandel thinks he ought to be out of venom by now," said Elena, spooning hot sauce onto her taco from a white plastic container. They finished eating and drove on toward the zoo. "We loved snakes when I was a kid," said Elena.

"Poisonous snakes?" asked Leo, horrified. "What's with you? Did you belong to one of those snake-handling sects?"

"No, Leo. We were just your ordinary, run-of-the-mill Roman Catholics. We went to church at the Sanctuario, took home a little dirt from the sacred corner; then when a thunderstorm hit, we threw it up the chimney."

Leo grinned at her. "You're just full of weird folk tales, aren't you?"

"You bet. For instance, I had this *santo* one of my uncles carved. You could pray to it for luck in love. About two months after I got it for my birthday, I fell for this guy at my high school, but he didn't pay any attention to me, even though I prayed to the *santo*."

"The guy must have been blind," said Leo.

"Thanks," said Elena. "So anyway, I told the saint, 'I'm going to put you in the closet under my brother's smelly socks, and I won't let you out till I get a date with Rafael.' So I put the *santo* in the closet, and guess what? Two days later Rafael asked me to his sister's *quinceanera*."

"So did you let the saint out from under the dirty socks?"

"Sure," said Elena. "I put him back up in his saint niche and gave him a plate of chiles stuffed with piñon nuts. Rafael and I went together for six months."

"Did that really happen?" asked Leo, pulling into the zoo parking lot.

"Yeah."

"Listen, I remember a story like that. In a newspaper column."

"Uh-huh. Just goes to prove the columnist knows what goes on up in the Sangre de Cristos."

Leo shook his head as they got out. "Mom made us give up snakes when she caught us with a bag full," Elena admitted. "What's that mob doing over there?"

"Demonstrators," said Leo. He eyed the signs. "Looks like they're mad at Darwin now. Couple of the signs say Fire Darwin Mandel, Elephant Drugger."

A TV crew moved toward Elena and Leo. The reporter, a young guy Elena had never seen before, thrust a microphone in her face. "Are you with the animal activist group that's protesting cruelty to animals at the zoo?" he asked.

"No, I'm with the Los Santos Police Department," said Elena, "and I'm about to deliver a dangerous rattlesnake. Maybe you'd better—"

The whole crew leapt backward before she could finish her sentence. "Leo, why don't you go warn those protesters off," she suggested.

"I'd rather face them than the snake," he agreed and strode toward the milling crowd. Darwin was evidently being blamed because Pansy had been drugged under his administration. The question was, Had Darwin done the drugging? Elena fished the snake bag gingerly out of the trunk. Its occupant was still rambunctious, so the ride evidently hadn't injured it. Meanwhile, she could see that the activists had given the entrance to the zoo a wide berth, so she walked through, snake bag held at arm's length, waving to the demonstrators and smiling, Leo ahead of her clearing the path.

"Be careful how you handle that snake," one of the activists called out. "We're watching for cruelty to all creatures."

"Hey, you haven't bought tickets," yelled the ticket seller, bolting out of the gazebo and chasing them down the walk. When she heard the rattling in the bag, she scurried back to safety. Leo and Elena turned left and left again into the administration building, passing through the reception area, Elena with the bag still held at arm's length, Leo keeping out of her way. The snake handler, having returned from the hospital with bandages on the left side of his face, awaited them. He and Darwin Mandel, using pilstrung tongs clamped behind the snake's head for safety and, for control, farther down the body, fished the rattler out and pinned it to the director's conference table. "That's White Fang," said the keeper. "I'll take him back to his cage." He and the director transferred the angry reptile to a box, clapped on a lid, and the keeper went off with the box under his arm.

Darwin sighed and motioned the two detectives to sit at the conference table. Leo looked very reluctant, staring at the tabletop as if the snake were still there. Elena, tired after her exertions, fell into a chair.

"What a disaster," said the director. "Our public relations person is beside himself. He says there's no way to put a positive spin on any of this."

Elena gaped at him. His sister was dead, killed by his snake, and he was worried about "positive spins"!

"We're already experiencing a wave of public indignation since 'Elephant Update' revealed that Pansy was drugged,

and I can't even find out who leaked the story. Not that I
didn't plan to issue a press release myself, as I told you in our
telephone conversation, Detective Jarvis. And now—" He
looked close to tears. "—the snake attack on Rosalba!
Someone is trying to destroy the zoo."

"Or your family," Elena suggested.

"Either way, it's terrible for the zoo. Has my father been
told about Rosalba?"

"I told him," said Elena.

Darwin shook his head. "Papa must be distraught. Rosalba
and Arnold were his favorites. He hardly needs shocks like
this at his time of life and in his precarious health."

Sibling jealousy of the favored brother and sister? Elena
wondered. Greed? Was Darwin her murderer? Her creepy,
animal-exploiting murderer? He seemed genuinely upset. But
then he'd seemed just as upset about the reputation of the zoo.
Was he hoping to inherit all the money and spend it on the
zoo?

Well, the snake hadn't escaped on its own. Not when White
Fang showed up in Rosalba's bathroom with the lock rigged.
"How would someone go about stealing your snake?" she
asked.

"I can't imagine," said Darwin miserably. "The snake was
in a locked glass cage, in a locked Reptile House, the keys in
a lock box, with two guards patrolling. I just don't know what
to think."

"Maybe you were the one who took the snake and left it in
your sister's bathroom," suggested Leo. "That would leave
you heir to the whole Los Santos Apparel shebang, wouldn't
it, now that Arnold and your sister are dead?" Elena had
discussed her thoughts on Darwin as the killer while they
were driving over, but she hadn't expected Leo to come right
out with their suspicions.

Darwin looked horrified. "I would never do such a thing. I
was very fond of Rosalba. I would have been delighted to
have her volunteer at the zoo. Our mother would have been
delighted as well. I always thought of my sister as a sort of
lost soul who didn't seem to have any direction in her life."

Well, the man knew something about Rosalba.

"I was so pleased to hear that my father had appointed

her president of the company. Rosalba was very intelligent, very practical, very knowledgeable. She'd have done a fine job. I imagine she always wanted to be associated with the family business. More's the pity. Father wouldn't let her, yet he was angry with me because I was uninterested."

"Tell us about the snake disappearance," Elena requested.

"That would be Sunday, the—ah—nineteenth of March—but White Fang was there when the keeper left that evening, gone when he returned Monday morning. This would never have happened if we'd had the extra security I asked the city council for. They'll have to agree now."

"We'll want to talk to anyone who had anything to do with the reptile section of the zoo."

"Of course."

"Are you going to kill the snake?" asked Leo.

"Certainly not," said Darwin.

"It killed your sister."

"The snake perceived Rosalba as a threat and attacked her, which is natural for a rattlesnake."

"And you've taken in that falcon that ate your brother's eyes, haven't you?" Leo scowled at Darwin.

"As soon as I received word that it was homeless. What happened wasn't Ahab's fault either," said Darwin defensively, "any more than it was Pansy's fault that she attacked Mr. Zubarate. Someone is using animals as weapons. I can't imagine who would be so cruel. These incidents are terrible for the animals as well as the victims, you know. But there'll be no more incidents, not connected with this zoo. That I can promise you."

Elena stared at him thoughtfully, remembering that there was a missing mountain lion as well. What did the murderer mean to do with it? Get Darwin? Get J.J.? Or Jacob? Darwin seemed earnest, but he also seemed uneasy, and he didn't really need any more deaths if he was the killer. The brother and sister who would have inherited were gone. "We'll also want to talk to your night guards," she said.

"They're not here now, but I'm sure Border Security can give you their home numbers." Darwin wrote out the number for the security company. His hands were shaking. Was he upset? Or guilty?

31
..

Traffic was picking up on Alameda when Elena finally got away from the zoo. She and Leo had interviewed every zoo employee they could find, although Leo had left before her, riding back in a patrol car because his shift ended at four and he wanted to get home to Concepcion. Elena, who was on until eight, continued the interviews, talking the last half hour to volunteers. No one could shed any light on the snakenapping of White Fang, the albino Mohave rattler. Not a very creative name, she thought, slamming on her brakes as some idiot pulled out of a tacky auto-repair shop straight into her path.

The rattlesnake's keeper, Jesus Chavez, was practically in tears when interviewed, and said over and over that he had nothing to do with the death of the director's sister; that when he left work on the evening White Fang disappeared, the snake had been curled up in its glass case. The next morning the snake was gone. How that happened he didn't know. And his face hurt from the auto accident. Couldn't he go home?

Elena said no and questioned him further. Confirming what Darwin had said, Jesus explained that the glass cages were all locked, the keys kept in lock boxes. The Reptile House was locked. Only the night guards should have been inside at night. Elena considered the possibility that one of the night guards had a connection to the Mandel family. Were their wives or sisters or girlfriends garment workers?

162

The guards swore that they hadn't seen a soul on the grounds when they made their rounds that Sunday night, or any other night in months. One admitted that he might have dozed off between his rounds when he came into the tower to write up his report. What else was he supposed to do? Nothing ever happened in a zoo, except animal noises, which he was used to. He denied any knowledge of or connection to the garment industry and looked so bewildered by that series of questions that Elena believed him.

The second guard insisted that he had been alert and on the lookout for prowlers the whole shift. There had been none. He had a sister who worked for Los Santos Apparel. The director had got her the job, which was a terrific one— benefits, $7.50 an hour. He was scared to death the factory might close, what with two Mandel executives dead. Then his sister wouldn't be able to afford to marry her fiancé, and he wouldn't get his sister's room when she left home.

The night guards insisted that all the keys had been on their racks. They checked that as part of each tour. Not that she trusted them. They might have failed to notice missing keys or been afraid to admit it. Darwin Mandel had his own set. And it was possible that some unknown person had copies. Elena, unable to see that she'd made any progress after all those interviews, shook her head and hit the gas pedal to get through a yellow light.

She'd called Lina Peralta about fingerprints on the cage, but there had been no prints unconnected with the staff, not even Darwin's. Whoever stole the snake worked with the snakes or wore gloves. No help there.

When she got to headquarters, she found a message on her desk instructing her to check in with Lieutenant Beltran. Elena groaned, remembering that Jacob Mandel had threatened to go over her head. She trudged over to let the lieutenant lecture her about Alope Randall, thinking that if they'd found Alope Randall's prints on the snake cage, she'd have arrested the woman. But they hadn't.

"I had a long and not very pleasant conversation this afternoon," said Beltran, her stocky, middle-aged, grizzled superior. "With Jacob Mandel."

"It figures," said Elena.

"Of course it does. He's now got two dead children, and he's sure the second could have been saved if you'd arrested—"

"—Alope Randall," Elena finished for him. "We don't have enough evidence. She wasn't seen near either crime scene. No fingerprints—"

"She had a motive."

"She's a lawyer. She doesn't like someone, she takes them to court. She doesn't kill them."

"Jarvis, you're letting your feminist sentiments blind you to how dangerous that woman is."

"I had dinner with her—"

"Are you making friends with another suspect?"

"No, sir. It was the only time I could get an appointment to question her."

He grunted skeptically.

"She didn't strike me as a violent type," Elena added.

"Well, you're wrong. Let me tell you a story about Alope Randall. It must have been—I don't know—ten years ago. There was this guy owned a sweatshop over on Texas Street, lived in Juarez. He closed up shop and locked the workers out without paying them, but he came back to get—well, people figured he wanted to move the machines out. Probably planned to sell them. Somehow or other, Randall, who was representing his workers, got word of it. She caught him in the parking lot and yelled at him, but he wouldn't talk to her, started to drive off. So she rammed his car with her truck. Guy ended up in the hospital.

"The next day five hundred garment workers showed up, broke into the place, confiscated his sewing machines, which is, in case you don't know it, against the law, even though he did owe the women money. No one ever found the machines. The women threatened to close down every factory in town if he pressed charges against Randall. Soon as he got out of the hospital, he left Los Santos. No one's heard from him since."

Elena thought about it. "Maybe she just meant to keep him from leaving, not to hurt him."

"You run your truck into the driver's side of a car, you mean to do more than stop the car," said Beltran.

"I guess so," Elena conceded. "But the animals, you know. That's what doesn't figure. Why would she do it that way? If she goes in for smashing cars with her truck, the animal part doesn't seem like her kind of thing."

"I want you and Weizell to go after Randall. Find the evidence to arrest her," said Beltran. "Oh, and I've got another piece of news for you." He scowled. "Your buddy Sarah Tolland is suing the city. For false arrest and imprisonment last year when we thought she'd dissolved her husband in the bathtub."

"Ex-husband," said Elena, "and you can't blame me for that. I never thought she was guilty." What she didn't say was that it had been Beltran who insisted on Sarah's arrest. "Is that all, sir?" she asked. She hoped Sarah got a pot full of money from the city. It would serve the lieutenant right. Too bad he didn't have to pay it himself.

"That's it. Call Weizell. Tell him tomorrow the two of you are going after Randall."

"Yes, sir." She left the office and, from her own desk, made the call to Leo, who grumbled that he was cooking dinner for a wife who was so big she could hardly move, much less get near enough to the stove to cook.

"Well, Leo, it won't go on forever. She'll give birth sooner or later, and then things will get back to normal."

"Normal? We still don't know how many kids we're going to have. And how can things be normal if you've got a bunch of kids the same age?" He paused to address his wife. "No, I'm not complaining, Concepcion," he said to her. "I do want to be a father. I just hadn't figured on being a father so many times at once." Coming back to Elena, he asked, "So what did you call about?"

"Jacob Mandel is after Lieutenant Beltran, who wants us to find some reason to arrest Alope Randall."

"Did you have another quarrel with Beltran?"

"I wouldn't exactly call it a quarrel."

"No? What did he say? He said he wanted you and me to wise up, right? You drag me into your quarrels with the lieutenant, and when I come up for promotion, he'll remember and say, 'Don't give Weizell sergeant's stripes. He and Jarvis are always screwing up some case.'"

"Oh, cool it, Leo," said Elena. "It's me he's mad at, not you, and I won't be in until twelve tomorrow, so you can go after her yourself and get on Beltran's good side without me to screw things up for you."

"Fine. So it'll be my bust," said Leo. "What are you going to do tomorrow morning? Follow up some peculiar idea of your own?"

"No. I think I'll stay in bed and eat bonbons and read romances."

Leo started to laugh. Then he yelled, "Shit, my squash is burning." He hung up on her, and Elena thought glumly that her usually jolly partner was getting to be a real pain in the ass. She understood why, but it still didn't make him much fun to be around.

32
..

Friday, April 7, 9:30 A.M.

The zoo should be closed for good. First their elephant kills a keeper. Then their snake kills some woman in her bathroom. And there's a mountain lion out there. Who's he going to kill? Close the zoo. Find the mountain lion. Because of the zoo, our streets aren't safe. Our children are at risk.

Charles Potter, Alarmed Citizen

"Elephant Update," Los Santos *Herald-Post*, Thursday, April 6

As Elena carted compost from the pile at the end of the yard to a flower bed reserved for summer annuals, she thought about the case. Animals. The whole Mandel family was involved with animals. The zoo director, the llama raiser, the fur wearer, the deer hunter, but it was those who used animals rather than protecting them who were dead. As if the mother, Cecilia, had come back to enforce her beliefs.

Of course, the dead Mandels were connected with the factory as well. Obviously Leo, Beltran, and Jacob Mandel thought that was the key, but Elena kept returning to the mother, the animal rights activist. About whom the husband wouldn't speak. The topic of whose death was evaded. Maybe she was way off base, but Elena wanted to know more about Cecilia. Accordingly, she put her wheelbarrow and shovel away, took a quick shower, and called her friend Paul Resendez at the Los Santos *Times* for permission to use their morgue. "I want to read about Cecilia Mandel. Does that name ring any bells with you?"

"Sure. Married to Jacob, mother of your two murder victims, plus a couple of other kids. Dead. I'll call the librarian and have her pull the files. And if there's a story there, it's mine. Agreed?"

"Agreed." Elena drove downtown, parked her truck in the visitors' lot, and walked across the street to Times Plaza, where a guard at the lobby counter gave her a visitor's tag. Then she went upstairs and pored over the newspaper clippings the librarian had gathered for her. She read for two hours.

Cecilia Mandel had organized boycotts of local pet shops and kennels that didn't treat their animals well. She'd had a New Mexico horse breeder thrown in jail because he wasn't taking proper care of horses who were past their prime. She had advocated raiding labs that experimented on animals. Organizations to which she belonged conducted such raids, although she herself had never been caught or arrested. She had gone into the forest during hunting season to protect deer from hunters, who gave irate interviews about her interference. She had been present when blood was thrown on the furs of wealthy women in New York City and at various Colorado ski resorts. She had made speeches and held offices in activist groups both locally and nationally, and she had died about ten years ago, in her early sixties.

The obituary, interestingly enough, said nothing about the great crusade of her life. The headline read "Spouse of Los Santos Apparel Owner Dies." The accomplishments of her husband were listed and the long-time importance of her family in the Rio Grande Valley. Jacob must have overseen the obit. No cause of death was given.

That wasn't unusual, but Elena was curious. She asked the librarian to make photocopies. Then, in the twenty minutes that remained before she had to leave for headquarters, Elena called a clerk who could look at Cecilia Mandel's death certificate. The cause of death was listed as "fever." Now that, thought Elena, was very strange. Who signed the death certificate? she asked and wrote down the doctor's name.

33
..

Elena grabbed a hamburger and ate it as she drove to headquarters, thinking about Cecilia Mandel, but also about what she'd wear that evening to a performance of *The Magic Flute* being given by the Los Santos Opera Company. She'd worn jeans the few times she'd gone to the Santa Fe Opera when she was a kid—jeans and a heavy, waterproof poncho because rain was predicted, but she doubted that jeans would do here, and she probably wouldn't need a poncho, even though the roof did sometimes leak at the Civic Center. Michael had said people would be dressed up; some of the men might be in tuxes. Elena decided she'd wear a black number that she'd bought for the H.H.U. Christmas ball.

She pulled into the police lot, parked her truck, stuffed the photocopies of the Cecilia Mandel stories into her large handbag, and took the side entrance to Crimes Against Persons, where she found Leo leaning on the reception counter talking to Carmen, the C.A.P. receptionist.

"You ever going to change your hairstyle?" Carmen asked Elena.

"Not likely," Elena replied. "It's easy and tidy. What more can you ask?"

Carmen groaned. She was into elaborate hairdos. Her own on that particular day was a mass of tiny braids with dangling beads. She must have paid a mint to have that done, and she wasn't even African-American.

"You should have listened to us when we said that Alope Randall was in on this," said Leo. "We finally have a good lead, as opposed to one of your off-the-wall theories."

Elena's heart sank. "What have you got?"

"Fingerprints. Found them on the falcon's perch and the French doors in Arnold's study, finally matched them."

"To Alope Randall? How come it took so long?"

"Because they were in the juvenile files, and you know how they are about giving out anything."

"Randall has a juvenile record?" It must have been from her period of silent rebellion when she first came to live with her father, Elena decided.

"Not Randall. This is some female gang member named Angela Lechuga, who grew up to be a garment worker at Los Santos Apparel."

"So how does that implicate Alope?"

"Randall's her lawyer."

"Being someone's lawyer doesn't make you guilty of anything." Fingerprints from the falcon's perch? Weird. But Lechuga must be the murderer. For whatever reason, after she killed Arnold she must have reached up, grabbed the perch, and released the falcon. That took nerve. The falcon had made Elena nervous, and she was carrying a gun. All this murderer had was a bow and arrow? Or maybe not. Who knew what weapon she'd been carrying—and just chose to use Arnold's bow and arrow. You had to wonder about her powers of reason. "Have you arrested her?"

"Beltran sent some uniforms last night. They caught her going into her apartment building and took her downtown for booking. She's at the jail now, so we're going over to interrogate her."

They left immediately. However, when Angela Lechuga was called down from the women's floor, she refused, on advice of counsel, to say one word. "So we find out more about her," grumbled Leo. "If she was innocent, she'd tell us something, wouldn't she? Like maybe she was there to deliver him a pair of jeans or something."

"Yeah, right," said Elena. "Where do you want to start?"

"How about the apartment house where she lives?"

They drove to a decaying, four-story structure perched

precariously on a ledge overlooking the freeway. "Great view," said Elena, staring down at cars buzzing along the interstate, the railroad tracks beyond, then the cement-encased Rio Grande with Mexico across the river. Beltran had provided a search warrant for Lechuga's apartment, so they climbed three stories on splintered wooden stairs, having obtained a key from a reluctant building manager wearing tight black jeans, a denim shirt missing all buttons but one, a three-day beard, and a Diablos baseball cap. The manager spoke little English and obviously distrusted the police. Elena had to translate the warrant for him and show him her badge twice before he would relinquish the key.

As they were about to let themselves into the apartment, a woman of indeterminate age poked her head out of the apartment one door down the hall and demanded to know what they thought they were doing. "That's Angela's place. Eef that *hijo de puta* Luis eez tryeeng to rent eet, he's gotta evict her first. I tell her that. I tell heem that. I—"

"We're the police, ma'am," said Leo.

"*Policia*?" She came out into the dim hall, which had windows at either end for light, and one hanging bulb. "Sometheeng happen to Angela? I wonder why she don' come home last night an' get the keed. She no pay me for las' night. She no pay me for other nights. I can' feed no keed when I don' get no money."

"What kid?" asked Elena, staring at the woman, whose chest was concave under a worn print dress that hung on her skinny frame like a dishrag. Stick legs extended from the uneven hem; veined feet were thrust into disintegrating sandals.

"Angela's *niña*. What happen to her?" The woman thrust a strand of gray-black hair into a lopsided bun on her scrawny neck.

"She's in jail," said Elena.

"*Madre de Dios*. What you put her een jail for? She don' do notheeng but lose her job."

"Do you baby-sit regularly for Ms Lechuga?" Elena asked. "Can we come in?"

"You gonna take the keed, you come een. You not gonna, you stay out een the hall."

"We'll call a social worker," said Elena. The woman nodded and opened her door. Leo and Elena followed her into a shabby two-room apartment where they could see beyond the open door to the second room a little girl of about four. She sat on the bare floor singing a lullaby in Spanish to a Barbie doll in a ski outfit.

"Maria," said the woman, nodding toward the child, who didn't look up. "Natividad Munoz." She tapped her own bony chest and dropped into a rocking chair. Leo and Elena sat on a couch with threadbare upholstery that might once have been purple but had faded over the decades to dun-mauve.

"Did you baby-sit for Ms Lechuga—"

"*Señora*. Angela married to Maria's *padre*. Divorced heem too, may the Holy Mother forgeeve her." Natividad Munoz crossed herself.

Elena nodded and got back to her question. "Did you baby-sit for Mrs. Lechuga—"

"Then she take back her own name, so *la niña*, she got a deefferent name from her *madre*. What kinda *estupido* woman do that?"

Elena took a deep breath and tried again. "A week ago Tuesday—did you baby-sit for her that night?"

"*Sí*, an' she no pay me."

"How long was she out?" Elena asked.

"Long time. Come over when I getteeng ready to sleep. Wants me to keep the baby. 'Jus' let her sleep on the couch,' she say. 'I pay you,' she say. She breeng Maria over; *la niña* eez already sleepeeng, an' off she goes. Mus' have a boy-friend. No?"

"What time did she bring Maria?" Elena asked.

Natividad shrugged. "*Nueve. Nueve y media*."

Nine or nine-thirty. "When did she get back?"

"I sleepeeng. I geeve her a key. Maria gone een the morneeng."

That meant Angela had no alibi for the night of Arnold's death.

"Why you arrest her?"

"Murder," said Leo.

Natividad Munoz' face went pale. Then she said, "Nah. She no keel someone. Her *esposo*, the one she divorce, he might keel someone. She say he beat her up. She say he go to prison. He might do a keeleeng. Who she suppose to keel?"

"Her employer. Arnold Mandel."

Natividad shook her head. "'Cause he fire her? Work eez hard to find. She no find a new job. All the jobs eez goeen' to Mexico. Lotsa women they get laid off, but they don't keel the bosses. She's a good mother—Angela. She woun' do notheeng to make her leave her baby."

"Does she drive a brown van?" Leo asked.

"She don' drive notheeng no more. She has an ole car, but the finance company take eet. She need a job to get eet back. To pay me. But she no gonna keel someone for a job or an' ole car."

They left Mrs. Munoz' apartment, promising to send someone for the child. As they searched Angela's place, Elena wondered why the jailed woman hadn't told the police she had a daughter at home. If Alope was her lawyer, why hadn't Alope made arrangements for the child? They found Angela's dismissal notice from Los Santos Apparel. It said she had failed to meet her quotas.

"That gives her a motive," said Leo. "They fire her. She loses her car, doesn't know how she's going to support her kid. She evidently was facing eviction from this rat hole."

Elena nodded. "But still, why Arnold? It's not likely the president of the company fired her personally. The dismissal notice was signed by someone else. Why didn't she do *him* if she was that angry?"

They found an old court order prohibiting her husband from getting near her or her child and a newspaper clipping saying that he had been convicted of armed robbery. They found her divorce papers. They found an application for welfare. Unpaid bills. Pitifully few possessions. No weapons.

34
..

"What now?" asked Leo. They were sitting outside Angela Lechuga's apartment house in an unmarked, faded green Toyota Corolla. Angela's neighbors, aside from Natividad, were either out or disclaimed knowledge of anything relevant to a police investigation.

"Call a social worker for the kid, then see what we can find out about the mother," Elena responded, and made the call on the car radio while Leo read over his notes.

"Let's go see Yvonne Lesoto in Gang Intervention," he suggested. "She arrested Lechuga the first time." They found Yvonne working out of a neighborhood storefront in Northeast. She was a moderately ugly woman with a big nose and heavy dark eyebrows, a lively smile and twinkling eyes. Elena wondered what the gang members thought of her.

"Sure, I remember Angela," she said. "She was in the female auxiliary of the Scorpions. Got arrested for assault. Her boyfriend was robbing a convenience store while Angela stood by eating Nacho Cheese Flavored Doritos and watching. She saw the clerk press an alarm button, so she picked up a big can of bean dip and threw it at the woman's head. Knocked her out cold. That was the assault."

The Juvenile officer took a long swig from a can of Diet Coke. "Let's see—what happened to her? Well, first they discovered she was preggers—this was during her jail

174

physical. She named the boyfriend. Then Alope Randall took an interest in her."

Leo and Elena exchanged glances.

"Got her off with probation. The boyfriend too. Angela married the guy, but he took off for California before his probation was up, before the kid was born. Alope got her into a GED program—Angela was a dropout when she got arrested. For a wonder, the girl graduated. That's as far as I can trace her. She in trouble again?"

"She may have killed Arnold Mandel," said Leo. "Her fingerprints were found at the crime scene."

"Damn kids," muttered the officer. "You think one of them's headed in the right direction, and look what happens." Her telephone rang, and she picked up. Leo and Elena nodded their thanks and left.

"Who did Angela list as next of kin?" Elena asked.

"A sister. Lives up in San Elizario."

Elena sighed. "Long way to go." They drove up the Mission Trail through Socorro until they came into the old plaza in front of the San Elizario Mission, where they had to ask directions to find the sister's rundown adobe. Nina Lechuga Cordova was probably twenty-five, looked thirty, had a grimy wash hanging on the line in back of her house, a battered car on blocks in the side yard, and a tired look in her eyes as she stood at the door with a baby limp against her shoulder and two toddlers playing on the floor inside.

"We'd like to ask you some questions about your sister Angela, Mrs. Cordova," said Elena after they had identified themselves.

"Don't tell me Angie's in trouble." The sister's face sagged into worry lines, and she waved the detectives in. The room they entered contained little furniture, just a table, some rickety chairs, and one battered recliner sitting in front of a television set. The house evidently wasn't connected to sewer or water lines; Elena had noticed an outhouse in back and could see, through the door to a lean-to addition, a dry sink and a barrel, probably containing water.

They sat down at the table with Nina, who said gloomily, "She's in trouble? Right?"

"'Fraid so, ma'am," said Leo. "You act like you expected it. Mind telling us why?"

"She use'ta live here. Her an' Maria. I watched after the kids. Angela an' Ernesto—that's my husband—they worked. Nacho, stop hittin' your *hermana*." The little boy responded by running a toy truck into his sister's knee. She shrieked. "We was doin' pretty good," said Nina, "till Ernesto got mad an' said Angie had a leave." Nina patted and jiggled the baby, who had begun to fuss.

"She din' hafta—Angie. I coulda calmed him down. Wasn't like it's his house. My papa built it, an' Mama left it to me. 'Cause she was mad at Angie. 'Cause Angie got pregnant an' got in trouble with the cops an' all. I guess you know that. But that was a long time ago. Five years."

"Why did she leave here?" asked Elena. Had Angela been another of Arnold's girlfriends? And her brother-in-law objected? Or maybe Angela had been mixed up with a rough crowd again. Maybe some new boyfriend helped her off Arnold.

"She said she wasn' stayin' nowhere she wasn' wanted. An' off she goes. Guess she was still mad about Mama leavin' me the house. Angela—she got herself some dump in Los Santos. Payin' some ole woman to take care of Maria like she was made of money or somethin'. Even when she still had a job, which paid good—she was makin' seven-fifty an' hour. At Los Santos Apparel. More'n I ever made."

"How long had your sister been working for Los Santos Apparel?" Leo asked.

"Oh, two years, I guess. They got benefits. Wish we had some. Kids get sick, I gotta find a ride, take 'em to the free clinic, an' wait two days for a doctor."

"You were telling us why you expected your sister to get in trouble?" Leo prompted.

"She lost her job. She din' have no money. What'd she do? Rob another Seven-Eleven?"

"No, Mrs. Cordova," said Elena.

"She coun' even get hired at a sweatshop after she got canned at her ole job. Both of us, Angie an' me, worked the sweatshops. I got her on after she had Maria. Then I married Ernesto. Now that's piss-poor work, sewin' for a sweatshop.

Better than nothin', but no job security, no air conditionin', not that I got any here."

Elena nodded. "I visited some of those shops."

"Yeah, well, then you know. Anyway, Angie got good with the machines. An' she's pretty. I used to be. It helps to get hired at the Mandel factory if you're pretty. An' then after workin' there two years, she gets fired."

"Why was she fired?" Elena asked.

"They said she wasn' meetin' her work quotas. She says it was a lie."

"Who fired her?"

"I don' know. Her boss, whoever that was."

"Did she ever mention Arnold Mandel?"

"That the guy got shot with a bow and arrow? I saw it on the TV." Nina looked horrified. "Listen, my sister woun' kill no one. I mean, she got in trouble when she was a kid, but she was just excitable, you know, but she woun' *kill* no one. Anyway, she don' know how to use a bow an' arrow. Who the hell does?"

Whirling, she yelled, "Lupe, don' you put that bug in your mouth. Kids!" said Nina. "They'll eat anythin'." She grabbed a cockroach from her daughter's hand, dropped it on the floor, and stepped on it.

Leo looked shocked.

"A lesson in parenting," Elena murmured to him. "Was Angela very upset about losing her job?"

"Upset don' half tell the story. She was afraid of losin' her car, for one thing. Hard to look for work when you got no car, an' a kid to take care of, an' no money to pay a babysitter— even if it is only some ole woman."

"When did you last hear from your sister?" Leo asked.

"I don' know. Mus' be a week, ten days. Come to think of it, I don' know why she ain't been to visit. She comes when Ernesto's at work. Least, her an' Maria get a good meal here. Maybe they repossessed her car. But I'm tellin' you, she woun' kill no one, no matter how mad she was about bein' fired."

"She was angry, then?" said Leo.

Nina gave him a contemptuous look. "Wad're you? Some

bachelor with no kids an' a job no one's gonna steal? You
Anglos gimme a pain."

They left Nina Lechuga Cordova to preside over her three
children and the cockroaches, and drove back to the county
jail. Angela Lechuga was still refusing to talk to anyone,
wouldn't even come down from the eleventh floor, where the
women were kept. They called Alope Randall's office and
were told that she was out but would get back to them.

By that time the four o'clock shift was over. Leo left,
muttering about kids and cockroaches. Elena drove home to
press her party dress and then take a nap. She'd traded the
second half of her shift in return for working Saturday in
another detective's place. Michael would pick her up at
six-thirty; they'd have dinner downtown at the San Francisco
Bar and Grill, then walk over to the Civic Center for the
opera. She was hoping the nap would keep her from embar-
rassing Michael by falling asleep during *The Magic Flute*.

35

As they crossed the pavilion, Elena gazed admiringly at the Civic Center with its swooping roof and tall, arched windows. Michael was holding the door for her when she tuned in the conversation around her. "You paid seventy dollars apiece for the tickets?" she whispered as they walked into the lobby, her black skirt swishing deliciously against her sheer black hose.

"If we're going to have an opera company in Los Santos, we have to support it," said Michael, "and this performance is supposed to be excellent."

"At seventy dollars a ticket it should be," said Elena, looking around the lobby. After all that seafood pasta, she was feeling sleepy, and the opera hadn't even begun.

They were with a crowd of Herbert Hobart University people, and Sarah Tolland murmured to her, "Actually, *The Magic Flute* is a rather silly opera. I've never been particularly fond of Mozart."

Even worse, thought Elena. She was sleepy and the opera silly; she'd never stay awake. And Michael would be upset because he'd spent seventy dollars on a ticket without managing to provide her any cultural exposure. They took their seats in the orchestra, and she looked appreciatively at the curtains of lights that hung from the ceiling, and at the warm blond curving walls of the auditorium. Unfortunately, the roof she liked so much had been leaking again, and there were stains on the paneling. Still, it was a neat place.

She slid her seat back and forth, testing, and decided she'd better sit up straight, not get too comfy. Then she opened her program to discover what Mozart's silly opera was about.

Before she could read the synopsis, Michael said, "Want to go nursery hopping tomorrow? I need to get my spring patio garden started."

Elena thought ruefully of the shift trade she had negotiated with Beto Sanchez and the appointment she'd made with the doctor who had signed Cecilia Mandel's death certificate. "I'd love to, Michael," she replied, "but I have to work."

"You've already worked one Saturday in the last couple of weeks."

"I know, but I've got an interview, and I had to—"

From the row in front, Mark turned around and, grinning wickedly, said to his brother, "Nobody thinks patio tomatoes are more interesting than murder detection."

Elena scowled at him. "I *like* patio tomatoes," she snapped, and with that the lights dimmed and the orchestra began the overture before she could explain to Michael how she'd managed to get off tonight. It might be a silly opera as Sarah had said, but the costumes proved to be lovely and whimsical and the voices excellent. Although Elena had no idea what was going on, she enjoyed the music and only dozed off occasionally.

Michael awakened her from one brief nap by whispering, "This is the Queen of the Night's aria, the most famous in the opera."

Elena nodded and set herself to listen. She would *not* fall asleep during the most famous aria, she promised herself, and she needn't have worried. While the Queen of the Night was trilling away on stage, Elena's pager went off. About two hundred people in the orchestra seats turned to glare at her, Michael foremost among them.

"I can't believe you didn't turn that off," he hissed.

Elena turned red with embarrassment but, nonetheless, fished the pager from her evening bag, trying to hide from Michael the fact that she was also carrying a gun. She looked at the number. Headquarters. "I've got to leave," she whispered.

"In the middle of the act?" he whispered back.

She stood up and excused herself all the way down the row. They had center seats, and the theater had no aisles except those on the outer edges. She figured she'd infuriated and stepped on the toes of about forty people before she finally got to the end, where a female usher awaited her. "Madam, we don't allow pagers during performances." She opened the door and followed Elena out, hissing, "And you're not supposed to leave in the middle of the act." Behind them the Queen of the Night was still warbling.

"I'm a police detective," said Elena. "I have an emergency call." And no car, she realized. "Do you think there'll be taxis out front?"

The usher seemed to be impressed to find herself involved in an emergency police situation. "I'll call one," she offered.

Elena called headquarters and was told by Beto Sanchez that Angela Lechuga had decided to talk to the police with her lawyer present. Elena was wanted immediately at the jail. She was sorely tempted to send the waiting taxi away and walk. It wasn't that far from the Civic Center to the jail, but in high heels she'd end up with blisters, if she didn't get mugged on the way over. So she took the cab, hoping the department would reimburse her, also hoping that Michael would forgive her. Seventy dollars, and she'd walked out in the middle of the performance. God knows what snotty thing Mark would say to make more trouble.

Within ten minutes, she, Leo, Lieutenant Beltran, Alope Randall, and Angela Lechuga were having a conference at the jail. "I din' kill him," said Angela. "I jus' went over to screw. He was already dead when I got there."

"*How* did you get there?" asked Leo. "Your sister says your car must have been repossessed."

"That's what I went there for. Gettin' back to work. I was gonna put out like he wanted if he'd give me my job back so I could get my car, an' feed my kid, an' keep from bein' evicted. He screwed around with my quota records an' got me fired 'cause I woun' put out. So I was gonna say I was willin'."

Alope Randall shook her head. "You should have let me sue him, Angela."

"Hey, that would take forever, an' I din' have forever. You think my ex is payin' me child support? He's in jail. Now I'm in jail. Whad'my gonna do? My sister calls me an' says Maria's gone. The babysitter says some social worker took her. I thought you was gonna see she got to Nina." The young woman looked accusingly at her lawyer.

"She was gone when I got out of court," Alope explained. "But she's in the system; I'll find her. The question is, will your brother-in-law—"

"Nina says jus' get Maria to San Eli, an' Ernesto won' have nothin' to say about if she stays."

During this exchange, Elena had been studying Angela, who was a reasonably good-looking woman with a spectacular figure. Arnold evidently liked his ladies voluptuous. Unlike Patricia. Maybe in his later years voluptuous was the only thing that turned him on. Poor Jo Priego. Had she known that he was chasing women at the factory?

Leo repeated his question. "So how did you get to his house?"

Angela glanced nervously at Alope. "I borrowed Alope's truck. Listen, I never tole her what happened. I jus' said I needed wheels, an' she said, 'Sure, take it.'"

"You told us," said Elena to the lawyer, "that the truck was in your driveway all evening."

"I told you the truck was in my driveway at ten and the next morning. That's all I could testify to."

"But you never said anything about lending it to anyone."

"You never asked," said Alope.

"Damned shifty lawyers," muttered Lieutenant Beltran. "We ought to charge you with obstructing justice."

"In your dreams," said Alope, giving him a fierce glance. "Go ahead, Angela. Tell them the rest."

"I'm sorry about gettin' you mixed up in this," said Angela.

"It's O.K." Alope patted her shoulder. "Maybe you people should know that Angela wasn't the only employee to be harassed by Arnold Mandel. He made a practice of it."

"I'll say," said Angela. "He was a real dirtball. I mean he had a wife an' a girl on the side. Why go after me? I din' wanna sleep with him."

"Ms Lechuga," Elena prompted. "The night of the murder."

"I called him," said Angela sullenly. "He tole me to come over aroun' one in the morning. I said what about his wife, an' he said she was out of town, so everything would be O.K., so I get there aroun' one, an' he don' answer the door. I'm really pissed off. I figure he's givin' me a hard time, so I turn the knob, see, an' it's open, an' I yell real loud, 'Mandel, you *hijo de puta*, where are you?' an' he don' answer, so I start down the hall openin' doors an' fin' one's ajar. I look in, an' there's this big blue-gray bird, all tied up on a bar an' flappin' its wings. Poor thing. An' there's Mandel on the floor, blood all over. I don' think I ever been so mad in my life. Or so scared. Here he's dead, an' I'm on the scene. I got nothin' to do with it, but I'm gonna get in trouble, an' there's no way I'm gonna get my job back. I coulda kicked him. But I din'," she hastened to add. "An' I swear I never killed him."

"You say the falcon was tied to the perch?" asked Elena.

"Yeah. It's got these straps aroun' its legs. Jus' like Mandel—tyin' some poor bird up. Oh, an' it's got this hood on its head. How'd you like to be tied to a stick with a hood on your head? So I look at Arnold, an' I say, 'Fuck you, Arnold.' So then I go over, an' I untie those strings on the bird an' drop 'em, an' I reach up an' take the hood off its head an' say, 'There you go,' an' I swear that bird smiled at me. There was these glass doors to the outside, so I sneak out that way an' leave the doors open, but I guess the bird din' leave."

Had the doors blown shut? Elena wondered. Or had someone else come on the scene and closed them? Or was Angela lying?

"What time was this?" asked Leo.

"I don' know. 'Bout one-fifteen."

"So you got there at one and left at one-fifteen?"

"Yeah."

"And he was dead when you got there?"

"Right."

"Then how come the brown truck was in the driveway from ten o'clock on?"

"It wasn'," said Angela. "I swear. I din' borrow it from Alope 'til after ten."

"That's right," said Alope Randall.

"What time did she return it?" Beltran asked.

"I don't know. She left it in the driveway, put the keys in the mailbox."

"The truck was seen at Mandel's at ten," said Leo.

"It wasn't mine," said Alope.

"An' there wasn' no brown truck when I got there," Angela protested.

"How did you get home from Ms Randall's?" Elena asked.

"I walked. I live in one of them apartments above the freeway. It's only three blocks. 'Course, they're gonna evict me. What the hell am I gonna do? I lost my job. I lost my car. I'm gonna lose my apartment. An' now you think I killed that son of a bitch."

"Where were you and Ms Randall's truck between the time you picked it up and one o'clock, when you arrived at Mandel's?" Elena asked.

Angela looked uneasy. "I stopped off to see my boyfriend."

"What's his name?"

"Jimmy."

"Jimmy what?"

"Jimmy Bets. He was supposed to be at this bar, but he wasn' there."

Alope frowned at her.

"I didn' kill him."

"What bar?" asked Elena.

"The—the Quick Coyote."

"Bartender or anyone else see you there?" Elena asked.

"How do I know? Anyway, I didn' kill Mandel."

"Of course you did," said Beltran. "Your fingerprints are there, on the perch, on the doors, the only ones except for the Mandels' and the maid's."

"But I din'—"

"Maybe your boyfriend came with you and killed him," said Elena.

"He din'. He—"

"The charge is first degree murder," Beltran said to the detectives.

"Hold on," said Alope Randall. "What did the coroner say? When did Mandel die?"

"Between ten and twelve," said Elena.

Alope frowned. "She'll take a lie detector test."

Angela looked alarmed.

"You're innocent, Angie. You'll take the test."

"O.K."

"They're no good in court," said Beltran.

"But when she passes, that ought to tell you something," said Alope. "You won't have an excuse to stop looking for the real murderer."

36
··

Saturday, April 8, 8:05 A.M.

Just like an Anglo. Close the zoo says Mr. Charles
Potter. He probably doesn't have any kids who want to
go see the monkeys on Sunday. Los Santoans of
Hispanic descent support the zoo, but they ought to quit
charging us to go. We pay taxes. Why do we have to
pay entrance fees? If you've got a bunch of kids, it's
expensive.

Virginia Zeno, Mother of Five

"Elephant Update," Los Santos *Herald-Post*, Friday,
April 7

There were no calls from Michael on her answering machine
when she got home from the jail. None this morning. She'd
thought of phoning him, but decided to give him a day to cool
off. In the meantime, she was scheduled to see Dr. Mortimer
Brawley, who had attributed Cecilia Mandel's death to "fever."
He was retired and living in Horizon City, according to the
County Medical Association. When Elena called, he hadn't
sounded happy at the prospect of giving up a morning of golf to
talk to her. Only fair, she wasn't happy with the prospect of
driving to Horizon City, which was well east of Los Santos.

She arrived about nine and was met at the door by a tall
man in his seventies, the only fat on him a little pot belly
distending his buttoned-up cardigan sweater. He ushered her

into his living room and looked around at the disorder, astonished. "Sorry about the mess," he said. "Lost my wife last year." He slid a pile of magazines from an easy chair and shoved them under the coffee table. "Maid quit last week." He waved to the newly cleared chair. "Sit down, Detective. I can't imagine what information a retired doctor could give you."

"I'm looking into the death of Cecilia Mandel."

Brawley shifted uncomfortably. "She wasn't murdered."

"Her son and daughter have been," said Elena.

"They have? Which son?"

"Arnold."

"Recently?"

"Yes, sir. Both within the last two weeks."

"That's terrible," said the doctor. "Hard to believe. You don't expect people with that much money to be murdered."

"According to the death certificate, she died of a fever. What kind?"

"I was never sure."

"Weren't any tests run?" Elena asked.

"Jacob wouldn't allow her to be hospitalized—or autopsied after she died. Poor woman. It was an unpleasant death; I'll say that."

"You must have had some idea what killed her."

The doctor stared at laced fingers. "A patient's relationship with her doctor is confidential."

"She's dead, sir, and the death certificate is surprisingly vague. I guess I can go to court and—"

Dr. Brawley looked alarmed. "Jacob would be very upset if you did that."

"I'm sure," Elena agreed. "So why don't you tell me what happened—or at least what you think happened?"

"I think she died of rabies," the doctor admitted.

"Rabies?" Elena tried to assimilate that idea. "Were there any rabid dogs in Los Santos at the time?"

"Not that I know of," said Dr. Brawley. "Nor were there any bites on her, which is why I hesitate to mention rabies. Jacob had a fit when I suggested it. Called me an addled old fool. I don't know; maybe I was. My own wife was sick at the time. I guess I've always wondered if I could have saved

Cecilia if I hadn't been so worried about June—that was my wife.

"And rabies?" he mused wonderingly. "Why would Cecilia have rabies?" He shook his head. "Of course, I'd never seen a case, but I've read the literature. She died hard, and there wasn't much I could do for her. I wanted to send her to the hospital. Told Jacob over and over we should, but he wouldn't have it. He said her best chance to recover was in her own home."

"There were *no* bite marks?"

"None."

"Could she have had rabies without being bitten?" asked Elena.

"It's possible," said Dr. Brawley. "If the saliva from a rabid animal gets into an open cut or sore, it can cause rabies. And Cecilia loved animals. She wasn't averse to being licked. Although surely she wouldn't have let a rabid dog lick her. I just don't know. It's bothered me for ten years."

"There's nothing else you can tell me? None of the family said anything?"

"They were all upset. Especially the youngest son. Jacob let him visit as long as Cecilia was rational, but later he kept the boy away. J.J. called me every day, twice a day, to find out how she was. The boy adored his mother, and I guess she felt the same about him. She left him everything she had, which was a considerable estate."

The doctor leaned down to pet a lean cat which brushed against his leg, then lifted the cat onto his lap before he continued. "Cecilia came from a wealthy family in the Upper Valley. Land in Texas and New Mexico. You think Cecilia's death has something to do with the murders of the children?"

"It seems like there might be some connection because— maybe this sounds silly, but Rosalba died of snakebite, and Arnold was killed with a hunting bow and had a falcon turned loose on him." Of course, she knew who turned the falcon loose. If Angela Lechuga was telling the truth, she hadn't done it to savage the body but out of sympathy for the bird.

"Strange," said Dr. Brawley, but could tell her nothing more.

Elena bade the doctor goodbye and made the long drive

back to the center of town, where she found the newspaper morgue closed and Paul Resendez out. She then tried the Los Santos Public Library, which indexed the local papers. The reference librarian ran a computer search for her on rabies during the year of Cecilia Mandel's death.

Once Elena had the list, she went downstairs to use one of the library's ancient microfilm machines. The blurry screen gave her a headache, and the squeaking crank caused a pain from wrist to shoulder. If another library bond issue came up, she'd not only vote for it, she'd go out to campaign for it. Then she found the story she was looking for, the story that explained the death of Cecilia Mandel.

In Lubbock, Texas, at the Texas Tech Med School, an animal activist group had broken into a lab at night and freed twenty-three dogs that were part of an experiment. The activists hadn't bothered to check the nature of the study. Twelve of the dogs had been infected with rabies. The whole pack had run loose through the city, biting a number of citizens. All the victims had to take rabies shots because no one could be sure whether the dog doing the biting had been a rabid or a control dog. One of the victims suffered permanent paralysis because of the shots. None of the activists had been arrested.

In Elena's mind was Dr. Brawley's voice saying, "Cecilia wasn't averse to being licked . . . If the saliva from a rabid animal gets in an open cut or sore, it can cause rabies." That, thought Elena, must have been what happened to Cecilia Mandel, and even when she saw in the newspaper that some of the dogs she'd released had been rabid, she hadn't believed that an animal could cause her death.

Had she confessed her involvement to Jacob? But too late to take the shots? Had Jacob seen himself sued by fifty-nine dog-bite victims from Lubbock, Texas, one of whom was paralyzed? That would explain why, knowing that his wife couldn't be cured, he had taken the financially safe road, never allowing the nature of her illness to be revealed. The reference librarian had said that Elena could photocopy from microfilm. The periodicals librarian showed her how.

The question was, Did Cecilia's death have anything to do with the murders of her children? On the way to headquarters

Elena asked herself whether someone from Lubbock had found out and taken revenge, maybe a relative of the paralysis victim. An avenger who had used animals to kill Cecilia's children because animals had caused so much havoc as a result of the mother's actions.

Elena decided to see what she could find out about the dog-bite victims via computer and telephone. Once she arrived at her desk, she discovered two reports waiting for her. The first told her that Angela Lechuga's lie detector test was over and some of her responses were indicative of lies. Leo came in while Elena was reading the report, and they went to the jail, where Angela was charged with first degree murder by the jail magistrate. When the judge heard a description of the crime, he refused bail.

"What part of the test did she fail?" Elena whispered to Leo.

"The part about what she was doing between ten-thirty and one. She wasn't lying about letting the bird loose, though."

Elena frowned. What did that mean? That Angela had killed Arnold? Or that she was covering for someone else? Like Alope Randall. Maybe Alope had gone with her to Arnold's house but had been smart enough not to leave fingerprints. Or the boyfriend. They hadn't found any other prints, nothing on the bow, but he could have been wearing gloves.

And what about Elena's rabies theory of the crime? She explained it to Leo as they left the jail, and he muttered, "You're nuts."

"Why? Even if Angela did kill Arnold, that doesn't explain Rosalba's death."

"She didn't kill Rosalba," Leo agreed. "This boyfriend she mentioned—he was with her the night Rosalba died. At least so he says."

"There, you see. And what about the elephant attack that was supposed to kill Darwin?"

"We don't know what the hell that was about."

"Yeah," said Elena morosely as she mentally pursued the rabies connection.

"Listen, Elena," said Leo, once they'd got in the car, "I don't want you saying one word to Beltran about this rabies business. He'll blow for sure. His idea is that Alope Randall put Lechuga up to killing Arnold and someone else up to killing Rosalba in a vendetta against the company."

"That's—crazy!"

"Any more crazy than your rabies theory?"

"I suppose not." She'd have to pursue the rabies connection on her own.

37
. .

Saturday, April 8, 12:15 P.M.

Leo was clearing his desk with the idea of going home to his wife and unnumbered incipient offspring. Elena sat down in front of her computer planning to finish a submarine sandwich she'd bought on the way back from the jail and begin a long-distance investigation of the rabies victims in Lubbock. While biting off a hunk of roll with multiple mysterious meat and vegetable ingredients, she noticed the second report on her desk. A friend working in the fingerprint department had just that morning discovered that Angela Lechuga's prints from the door and falcon perch at Arnold Mandel's house matched prints found on a hall table at Rosalba Mondragon's condo. "Hang on, Leo," Elena called urgently.

"What now? I gotta get home."

"Didn't you tell me Lechuga's boyfriend said he was with her the night of Rosalba's death?"

"Yeah. He told us he came over in the afternoon and spent the night there."

"Where?"

"Her apartment."

"Where was Maria?"

"In the apartment with them."

"In the lie detector test, did they ask Lechuga questions about Rosalba Mondragon?"

"Yeah, but Randall objected, so they laid off."

"Does the boyfriend work at the zoo?" Elena asked eagerly, her mind whirling with a half-formulated idea of the boyfriend stealing the snake, and the two of them killing Rosalba with it, having already killed Arnold. Maybe it *was* a labor-management killing.

"Nah. He works for the city parks department, plants trees, waters grass. Why are you asking me about this?"

Elena sighed. So much for the zoo-keeper accomplice theory. "Because Lechuga's prints were found at Rosalba's."

Leo whistled, then said, "We can look into it Monday. Lechuga's not going anywhere." And he left.

Elena stared at the fingerprint report. What had Angela Lechuga been doing at Rosalba's, and when had she been there? Was the boyfriend telling the truth when he alibied her for the day and evening of Rosalba's death? If he worked for the parks department, he should have been at work, not hanging out both afternoon and evening at Angela's. Muttering to herself, Elena left the building and drove back to Angela's apartment house, back to Natividad Munoz, who had heard on the radio that her neighbor had been charged with murder.

"Now I no get my money," she said.

Elena asked if Mrs. Munoz had seen Angela or the child on the day of Rosalba's murder. Natividad had. Maria had stayed with her for a couple of hours at the end of the afternoon— more money she'd never get paid.

So the boyfriend had lied, thought Elena. And just maybe Angela had been able to get the snake into Rosalba's house, although how she'd have done it was problematic. Her car had been repossessed. It would be hard to take a big snake on the bus. Or in a cab. But the lying boyfriend might have driven her.

"Even if she owe me money an' kill some rich Anglo, she was a good mother," said Natividad generously. "Always taking *la niña* places. Every Sunday the zoo, every Saturday the—"

"Hold on," said Elena. "They went to the zoo?"

"*Sí.* An' it costs. If she have money for the zoo, why she no pay me? Maybe she kill the Anglo for money."

Elena thanked Mrs. Munoz for her help and drove to the jail, where she called Alope Randall, knowing that Angela wouldn't say anything without her lawyer present.

Within forty-five minutes, the three women were together in an interview room, and Elena put her first question to Angela: "Were you ever in Rosalba Mondragon's house?"

Simultaneously Angela said, "No," and Alope said, "You don't have to answer that."

Elena stared grimly at the young woman. "We found your fingerprints in her house—"

"Don't say one word, Angela," warned the lawyer.

"And the alibi your boyfriend gave you for the time of Mrs. Mondragon's death was a lie," Elena continued. "He claims he, you, and your daughter were in your apartment the whole time. Mrs. Munoz says she baby-sat Maria for a couple of hours late that afternoon while you went out."

Angela burst into tears. "I jus' went to ask for my job."

"Angela, shut up," said Alope.

"She was the new boss. I heard it on the radio. I jus' wanted my job back. I tole her he said I could have it. He did. On the telephone."

Alope Randall threw up her hands.

"What did she say to you?" Elena asked.

"She said reapply an' she'd look at my application. I'm a good seamstress. I'd be workin' right now if someone had'na killed her. Someone's out to get me."

"You're doing a pretty good job of that yourself," Alope muttered.

Angela, sobbing hard, turned to her. "I din' kill no one, Alope. I jus' wanna support my kid."

Angela stuck to her story—her new story. Elena returned to headquarters, thinking that now she had to find out where the lying boyfriend was. The remains of her sub still lay on her desk, rewrapped in wax paper, now quite soggy. She accessed Leo's supplemental reports and got a name and number for the boyfriend. When she called, his mother said he was visiting relatives in Chihuahua City. Great, thought Elena and returned to the Lubbock connection that she'd abandoned when she saw the note on Lechuga's fingerprints. She spent the rest of the afternoon pursuing dog-bite victims and the people who had loosed the dogs. The Lubbock police hadn't a clue as to who broke into the lab ten years ago. The dog-bite victims claimed to have no idea either. The paralysis victim had died, and his only relative was his eighty-year-old mother, who was in a rest home and senile. The nurse thanked Elena for calling, saying it was the only call or visit the old woman had had in eighteen months, that she had no relatives left alive. So much for that.

Discouraged, Elena went home at the end of the afternoon, thinking that she needed to locate Angela Lechuga's lying boyfriend and to find out more about the dynamics of the Mandel family, talk to people who had known Cecilia and the children. Tomorrow was Sunday. She wasn't on shift. So Beltran couldn't complain if she pursued the investigation on her own time.

And the boyfriend. Maybe she could secure a warrant to bring him in as a material witness. Could she get him back from Mexico? Not if he didn't want to come. Not unless he was charged. Elena sighed, mentally waving her personal life goodbye. She considered the case so scary that she didn't want to let up, for even one day. What if someone tried to kill Darwin tomorrow?

38
..

Sunday, April 9, 9:15 A.M.

It has come to the attention of Los Santoans Against Rampant Immorality that the Los Santos Zoo is forcing its animals to use birth control. God did not mean for either animals or humans to interfere with the natural propagation of species. Next we will hear that the zoo is aborting animal fetuses. For shame. We hope that the city council will force the zoo to stop these immoral practices.

Father Conrad Bratslowski

"Elephant Update," Los Santos *Herald-Post*, Saturday, April 8

It was a mild day, no wind blowing, no dust, and Elena sat on her patio reading, first, the Saturday *Herald-Post*, then the Sunday *Times*, and finally some photocopies she hadn't had time to read in the newspaper morgue on Friday. She found a letter to the editor from a woman named Arleen Nevinell, who was very disappointed that the newspaper had not seen fit to mention the good works of the late Cecilia Mandel, a shining light in the movement to protect the rights of helpless animals.

Elena wrote the name down and went to look in her Los Santos telephone book. The only Nevinell was Claude, but she called the number and got his wife, Arleen. When Elena explained that she was investigating the deaths of the two Mandel children and trying to find people who had known their mother, Mrs. Nevinell said she would be delighted to help. "Come by the house around two," she suggested. "We'll be through with church and Sunday dinner by then."

The couple lived in an affluent neighborhood close to Los Santos High School in a two-story house distinguished by its size rather than any architectural elegance. The lady herself was tall and slender, with perfectly white hair and a face still pretty but very wrinkled. Her husband, who sat in on the interview, was just his wife's height, about five ten, but had an immense stomach that made a half circle from high on his chest to the tops of his thighs. He also had a large red nose and angry eyes, whereas Mrs. Nevinell had kindly, twinkling blue eyes and was delighted to see Elena.

"Cecilia Mandel was a wonderful woman," said Arleen Nevinell once they were seated in high, hard-seated armchairs. "An inspiration to us all."

"A crackpot," said Mr. Nevinell.

His wife patted his hand as if he were a rebellious grandchild. He scowled. "Many an animal had a better life because of Cecilia," said Mrs. Nevinell and proceeded to regale Elena with some of Cecilia Mandel's triumphs in the field of animal rights. Fifteen minutes later, as the maid served coffee, she was saying, ". . . and the poor little puppies. You can't imagine the dreadful conditions under which they were living. But Cecilia—"

"Oh, for God's sake," exclaimed Mr. Nevinell, "Cecilia may have saved the poor little puppies, but she never had any time for her own children."

"How can you say that, Claude? It was Jacob who had no time for the children. Look at the way he treated J.J. Never paid the poor boy the least attention."

"Why should he?" asked Claude Nevinell contemptuously. "All J.J. ever did was burst into tears, paint pictures of animals, and lose the company a pile of money."

"He is a dear, sensitive boy," said Arleen. "And he adored his mother."

"Because she treated him with tolerance, which is more

than the rest of the family did, but she still didn't have any time for him."

"Claude, you're irritating me," said Arleen, a steely glint coming into her eyes.

Before they could get into another squabble, Elena asked about relations between the Mandel brothers and sisters.

"They were very close," said Arleen. "Thought the world of each other."

"Oh, absolutely," said Claude sarcastically. "Let's see. J.J. turned his sister in for wearing sea turtle boots or some damn thing."

Now that was interesting, thought Elena. Rosalba hadn't known who turned her in for importing proscribed skins.

"Cost her about ten thousand dollars when they went through her closet and confiscated everything made of an endangered species. She wouldn't say where she was getting the stuff. Probably smuggled it into the country on one of her trips. But the point is that J.J.—"

"Well, Rosalba shouldn't have done that," said Arleen. "Her mother would have been horrified."

"And he financed a protest against the zoo for ill treatment of its animals," said Claude. "I'm sure Darwin thought that was a mark of brotherly affection."

"The condition of the monkey cages was atrocious," snapped Arleen. "If you'd been willing to put up the money, I'd have financed the protest myself. Fortunately J.J. was delighted to do it. The poor little monkeys. There was excrement piled in their living space."

"And they loved it," said Claude. "When you dragged me down there, they were hurling it at each other."

"It was their way of protesting," Arleen shot back.

"Bull," said Claude. "They just liked to throw shit around."

"I wish you wouldn't use that word."

"It's not as if they have that much fun. If you and J.J. hadn't interfered, they'd still be happily tossing turds."

Elena left shortly thereafter; the couple were still arguing. It had been a peculiar visit, but she had learned something. J.J.'s claim to be so fond of his siblings didn't look quite as believable now. She sat in the truck for a minute thinking, then decided that she'd pay an unannounced visit to Jacob

Mandel. She was admitted immediately, although she could hear an argument between nurse and patient as to whether he should forgo a nap to talk to a policewoman.

"I was glad to hear you finally arrested someone for Arnold's death. Now, what about Rosalba?" he demanded. "You have news for me there?"

"More like questions, sir," said Elena. "About your wife's death."

Jacob's face turned purple, which made Elena decidedly nervous. Maybe she shouldn't have— "I don't talk about my wife's death," he snarled.

"What if someone in Lubbock who was bitten by one of those dogs has come back to get revenge?"

"Get out of my house!" shouted Jacob. "If I ever hear you've said anything like that to anyone, I'll sue you and the city for slander. My wife had nothing to do with rabid dogs."

"I didn't mention rabies," Elena pointed out. "I'm investigating two murders, and you have two more children. If someone is—"

"The murders are labor-related. You think that fired seamstress had anything to do with my wife?"

"Maybe the seamstress isn't guilty."

"You arrested her."

Elena sighed. "We're not always right."

"You're right this time."

"And if we're not? As I said, you still have two children."

"No one would want to kill Darwin; he's the only child I have left."

"They may come after you next," said Elena.

"What difference would that make?" said Jacob bitterly. "I've spent my whole life building a garment empire here in Los Santos, and now I've got no one to run it, no one who cares about it." He pinned Elena with a furious glance. "Who told you about Cecilia?"

"According to you, sir, there's nothing to tell."

"Don't get smart with me, young woman. I want to know who told you that lie about Cecilia and the rabies thing."

Elena shrugged. "I figured it out for myself."

"The hell you did. Just remember what I say. You go

spreading that story around, and I'll take every penny you've got."

"I'm afraid that would turn out to be neither profitable nor satisfying," said Elena dryly.

39
..

Monday, April 10, 9:00 A.M.

Angela Lechuga's case was being taken to the grand jury.
Elena spent the morning in court testifying to what she found
at the crime scene. She didn't doubt that Angela would be
indicted for Arnold's murder, since hers were the only
fingerprints of significance at the scene and she admitted
being there. Beltran, Chief Gaitan, and the D.A. were pleased
with the case and talking about bringing charges for the
murder of Rosalba as well. Elena still doubted that Angela
had actually killed Arnold Mandel, or Rosalba for that matter,
although Angela's explanation of where she was between
ten-thirty and one on the night of Arnold's death couldn't be
backed up. No one had seen her at the Quick Coyote,
including her boyfriend, who was still missing.

Elena did not wait to see if the grand jury came in with a
true bill. Leaving the courthouse, she used her lunch hour to
head for the country club where J.J.'s llamas were making
their debut in the golf tournament. She had been sure he'd be
there; he wasn't, but disaster had struck in his absence.

Without J.J., the llamas had disgraced themselves by
spitting on golfers who came too close and by running off
with carts containing the clubs of the players, thereby
completely disrupting the tournament. Elena heard the details
of the llama debacle from a horrified out-of-town official as
they walked toward the clubhouse restaurant, whose broad

picture windows faced the eighteenth green. Golfers and invited guests were inside being served a sumptuous repast.

Elena and the tournament official arrived in front of the restaurant in time to see the final llama spectacular. Freed from their golf carts, two of the llamas had evidently fallen in love and were gamboling around the eighteenth green in a decidedly erotic fashion while people inside the restaurant watched through the plate-glass windows. Then the male llama mounted the female. Fascinated, diners stood up to get a better view. A short, stocky blond came racing across the grass screaming to the groundskeepers, "Turn the hoses on them." The hoses were directed at the young lovers, and the distraught man came to a halt beside Elena groaning, "For God's sake, why did I ever agree to this?"

Elena assumed that this was Bernie Golden, the club's sports coordinator. The llamas were separated and led away, spitting sullenly and nipping at the groundskeepers. Bernie Golden locked both hands into his blond curls, red-faced. "Excuse me," said Elena, "I'm Crimes Against Persons Detective Elena Jarvis." She flashed her badge.

"What now?" he demanded.

"I'm looking for J.J. Audubon Mandel."

"So am I," snarled Golden. "I let him talk me into using those damn llamas to pull the golf carts. He assured me they were reliable, that we'd get a lot of great publicity for the tournament, but he never showed up, and the llamas have been absolutely intractable. Did you see what just happened?"

Elena grinned. "Well, it is spring. I guess in spring a young llama's fancy turns to thoughts of—"

"—copulating on my eighteenth green," snapped a grounds keeper, who had just joined the group. "The male bit me. Has it had shots?" He pointed to a bloody place on his arm. "I'm filing suit."

"Now, Homer," murmured Bernie Golden soothingly. To Elena he said, "Homer is a magician with grass. God, I hope we can keep this quiet."

Elena didn't think so. She'd seen two reporters scurrying for their car phones as she stood with the tournament official.

One worked for a radio/TV station, so the affair of the lustful llamas would be reported shortly on at least one local radio station. TV stations might even break into the soap operas with news flashes.

"If J.J. ever gets here, I want you to arrest him," said Bernie Golden.

"Actually, I just wanted to talk to him," Elena replied.

"Isn't there some law about indecent public behavior?"

"Yes, there is," said Elena, grinning, "but it wasn't Mr. Mandel who wanted to copulate in front of your restaurant; it was his llamas."

"There he is," growled Bernie. He had spotted J.J. trotting through the crowd. "J.J.," he said when the llama rancher came up to them, "I will never, never listen to you again. Do you know what those damn beasts of yours have done?"

"Acquitted themselves admirably?" said J.J. Then he looked at Elena. "Are you here for the tournament, Detective?"

"No, I'm here to talk to you."

"Why weren't *you* here?" demanded Bernie. "They've been spitting on people; they've been running off with the golf carts. They tried to have sex right here on the eighteenth green. In front of the restaurant. It's a disaster. And where were you?"

J.J. shifted uneasily. "Something came up. I'm sure things will go better this afternoon, Bernie. Maybe they were just reacting nervously to the crowds."

"If they react nervously to crowds, you should have warned me. And there won't be any afternoon. You're taking them away. Right now. I've got someone rounding up caddies. Although my caddie group is probably incensed because I used the llamas."

J.J. had turned pale. "I promise you," he said, "they'll do just fine this afternoon. Bernie, if you pull them from the tournament, I'll—I'll sue you."

"You will not. I'll sue you," screamed the sports coordinator. "For misrepresenting your llamas and making a shambles of my tournament. And that's my final word." He stalked off.

"Mr. Mandel," said Elena, "I wonder if we might have a chat."

J.J. looked at her with narrow, angry eyes. "Yes, we can have a chat," he said. "I want you to go straight into the clubhouse and call my father. Tell him that I have not been talking about my mother's death."

"Your father said I told him that?"

"He called this morning. First time I've heard from him in years, and he was furious. I'm surprised he didn't have another stroke. And it would be your fault if he died." J.J. seemed distraught. "He can't die. Now, please make that call."

"I did talk to your father," said Elena, "but I never mentioned anything about you."

"I don't believe you. You must have said I'd been gossiping, and I haven't. I told you she died of natural causes."

"Yes, you did," said Elena, "but it wasn't quite true, was it?"

"I don't know what you mean. Now, call my father. Before you do anything else." He looked desperate.

Elena wondered whether his father's suspicions or the llama fiasco had set him off. Before she could reply to his demands, a white bus pulled into the club parking lot. The blue lettering on its side read "Catholic Diocese of Los Santos." From its doors streamed a crowd, mostly women, all carrying signs. "Oh boy," said Elena. She recognized them. Father Bratslowski of the Lower Valley church. Ora Mae Spotwood of the Anti-Fornication Brigade. Los Santoans Against Rampant Immorality had arrived. It hadn't taken them long to hear about llama copulation at the country club.

"Who are they?" cried J.J., appalled after he'd read the first sign, which said Down with Public Immorality. A second said Stop Public Fornication. Someone had painted a caret between "Public" and "Fornication" and inserted the word "Llama" above the line of text. J.J. looked close to tears.

"It's a group called Los Santoans Against Rampant Immorality."

"What does immorality have to do with my llamas?"

"As your friend Bernie said, two of the llamas were overcome by springtime lust out in front of the restaurant."

"They're animals!" cried J.J. "These people must be crazy."

Elena couldn't argue with that. She'd had to interview a number of LSARI members while investigating the deadly statues case. It wasn't one of her fonder memories. "Why don't you go talk to them," Elena suggested.

"I intend to." He headed toward the Anti-Fornication contingent from one direction. She saw Bernie racing toward them from another. Two TV vans arrived and started to unload. It was going to be an unusual golf tournament. Elena walked to her truck. She wouldn't be getting any information out of J.J. this afternoon, not when his project was in complete disarray and her lunch hour almost over. She might as well return to see if Angela had been indicted.

She had.

Elena went without lunch and spent part of the afternoon at her desk as she continued to make phone calls to Lubbock. Not with any noticeable success. By slipping away to visit the lying boyfriend's mother, Elena did manage to evade her sergeant, Manny Escobedo, when he came looking for detectives to send out on cases.

Mrs. Barranca insisted that her son, Jimmy Bets—his father was Mr. Bets, her first husband—was still visiting his grandmother in Chihuahua City.

"It's Monday," said Elena. "Isn't he supposed to be at work?"

"He's taken some vacation time," said Mrs. Barranca. "Hees *abuela* eez seeck."

I'll bet, thought Elena and left her card and the message that the police wanted to talk to him. At four, her shift over, she went grocery shopping. Having had no lunch, she'd fix herself a decent dinner for a change.

40
··

Monday, April 10, 6:30 P.M.

Elena had invested in a small filet of beef. She made a large
salad while she grilled the steak and played back a tape of the
evening news. For some reason her VCR hadn't recorded the
network news, but the local news was unusually lively,
featuring background film of the llamas grazing on country-
club grass while Bernie Golden tried to explain why his
tournament had turned into a fiasco, while J.J. insisted that,
handled correctly, llamas were the pets and workhorses of the
future, while Ora Mae Spotwood deplored llama copulation
and pointed out that there had been children in the restaurant
to witness the shocking event. As well as shots of grazing
llamas, there were shots of Los Santoans Against Rampant
Immorality, who had co-opted the eighteenth green once the
llamas were dragged away.

Elena forked up and savored her last bite of filet, ate the
last piece of tomato from her salad bowl, and mopped up the
dressing with a piece of French bread, that lovely European
custom she'd learned at Rosalba Mondragon's dinner. Now
that Beltran had someone for Arnold's death, not necessarily
the right someone in Elena's opinion, there wasn't as much
pressure to find out who had locked Rosalba in her bathroom
with a rattlesnake. Elena herself seemed to be the only person
really working that case.

Well, she deserved a night off, time away from the

Mandels. Hopefully no one would run into a deadly animal tonight. After rinsing her dishes and pans, she put them in the dishwasher and went into the living room, where she sprawled full length on her sofa with its desert-mountain design in maternal hand-woven fabric, and opened the evening paper to "Elephant Update," her favorite column. Tonight it featured a letter from Darwin Mandel.

> The Los Santos Zoo is not a breeding zoo. We do not have the capability of raising young animals or the room to house them. Therefore, where male and female animals of the same species inhabit the same enclosures, birth control measures must be initiated. Furthermore, when these measures fail, as they sometimes do, and the animals come into season, our visitors complain about the resulting copulations. As Zoo Director, I feel that the complaints of Father Bratslowski and the Los Santoans Against Rampant Immorality are unfair and misjudged. The handling of animals has everything to do with expediency and nothing to do with immorality.

The columnist had added his own comment on Darwin's letter:

> This writer has to agree with Dr. Mandel. You can't have it both ways, LSARI. This afternoon you were demonstrating against llama copulation at the country club. How would you like a zoo full of oversexed animals doing their thing?

Elena grinned. That ought to stir up controversy.

When the telephone rang, she sat up reluctantly and put the newspaper on the coffee table. It could be headquarters calling, but it could also be Michael. How did she feel about him? She hadn't heard a word from the man since she was forced to leave *The Magic Flute* Friday night, and she was tired of being made to feel guilty about doing her job. Michael was a criminologist, for Pete's sake. He ought to understand that when she was paged she had to go. She picked up the telephone, prepared to treat him coolly, and discovered that it wasn't Michael. It was tall, cute Rafer Martin, physicist and jazz trombonist.

"I know it's a little late," he said to Elena, "but I just ran into some of the band at Pizza Accademmia, and we decided to get the group together. You in?"

"Absolutely," said Elena. "Where are we meeting?"

"The rehearsal hall at the Fine Arts Center on campus. I'll call the guard and tell him you're coming."

"What time?"

"Seven-thirty if you can make it. If you can't, we'll do instrumental till you get here."

Just what she needed, Elena decided. An evening singing Dixieland would take her mind off her case and her problems with Michael. She hurried into the kitchen to start the dishwasher, then dashed to the bathroom to take a shower and change into jeans and a sweatshirt. Sniffing, she thought she detected a bad odor. Had a mouse died in a vent again? She'd just tied the laces on her sneakers when the telephone rang. She picked up and answered, "Jarvis."

"Elena?"

She didn't say anything.

"It's Michael."

"Hi."

"I—ah—" He sounded rather sulky. "I'm giving a lecture tonight at eight. I wonder if you'd like to go."

"Sorry," Elena replied. "I've made other plans."

"Still working on the Mandel case? I thought someone had been arrested."

"Not for Rosalba's death. Don't you care who killed her?" An uncomfortable silence followed. "Oh, never mind," she snapped. "The jazz band's getting together, so I'm going over there to sing." Then she relented a little. "If you want, you can pick me up at the rehearsal room in the Fine Arts Center after your lecture."

"Forget it," said Michael. "I wouldn't want to intrude. You'll be seeing Rafer, I suppose?"

"Well, he's in the band," she retorted sarcastically.

"Exactly." Michael hung up.

"The hell with you," she said to the dial tone, grabbed her handbag, and headed for her truck. It was ten minutes past seven. She'd barely make it.

41
..

Monday, April 10, 10:05 P.M.

The jazz session had broken up at ten. As the musicians were locking their instruments into cases, Elena put on her jacket.

"You did a great job on 'Saint James Infirmary,'" said the pianist, Bob Spanky.

"Thanks." She picked up her bag. "It's my favorite. Reminds me of the Ribbons."

"Yeah, that Ray Lee was some trumpet."

"And he could sing," said Elena.

"His kid played a mean sax too. I wouldn't mind having them sit in again."

"Any of you heard from them?" Elena asked.

"Not the musical ones. The brother who's a writer joined the Creative Writing Department second semester," said Spanky, who was himself an associate professor of Modern Languages. "They say the kids are flocking to his short-story classes."

Elena was pleased to hear that Langston Lee Ribbon was doing well. She'd liked his poetry, what she understood of it. His mother must be very proud now that he was an assistant professor, although she probably missed him. "I'll have to look him up," she said. "Has he got any readings scheduled?"

"Nobody in this group would know," said Rafer Martin, coming over, trombone case in hand. "You want to go get a beer, Elena?" People were starting to leave.

Elena glanced at him in surprise. "I don't know, Rafer. At Rosalba's dinner I got the impression your wife didn't like me. I don't want to cause you any trouble."

"It's my wife who makes trouble," he muttered. "That's why I need a beer—to fortify myself before I go home." One-handed, he buttoned his coat and added, "Come on. Be a pal."

Elena shrugged. She liked the tall physicist. He was good-looking and pleasant. "Where do you want to meet?"

"How about Triangles?"

Elena laughed. "The last time I was there, I had to arrest a robber. Michael didn't take it too well."

Grinning, Rafer said, "Sounds exciting to me. You see a robber, give me a nudge so I don't miss the action."

They agreed to meet in five minutes at the combination bar and Greek restaurant, which was close to the campus. Elena figured she was going to hear a sad tale about Rafe's marriage, and she did feel sympathy for him. She'd taken an instant dislike to Helen Martin the night of the dinner party. How could anyone hate living in Los Santos? Rafer had already ordered beers for both of them and a plate of spinach-and-cheese pastries when she slid into the booth.

"Thought you might be hungry," he said.

Elena nodded enthusiastically, poured her beer, and took a long drink, savoring the cold liquid as it slid down a throat dry from singing for over two hours. "Trouble at home, huh?" she said, picking up a pastry, thinking they might as well get the marital miseries over with.

"You know it," said Rafer. "I guess I shouldn't have taken a job out here. She hated it even when we came to interview, but the truth is, there aren't that many jobs for new physics professors. The money was good; they promised me the equipment I need, and an apartment. And besides the perks, *I* like it here. The desert and mountains are great."

"You'll get no argument from me," Elena agreed. "I've got so I feel kind of claustrophobic when I'm in a forest. I'm used to all that sky."

"You ever go hiking in the mountains?" Rafer asked.

"Sometimes."

"When there's been some rain, and all the cactus are

blooming, and those scraggly, prickly bushes cover over with flowers?"

Elena nodded. "Aguirre Springs is a good place."

"Yeah? That's east of Las Cruces, isn't it? I mostly just go up in the Franklins. Helen won't go, of course. She's sure she's going to get bitten by a rattlesnake. Since she read about Rosalba, all I ever hear about is snakes. You'd think our apartment was full of them. I don't know where she thought we were going to settle. I couldn't keep taking research fellowships forever."

"You like Herbert Hobart?" Elena asked curiously. The tart was wonderful, the pastry hot and flaky, the filling rich. She took a second one and bit in with gusto.

"Yeah, H.H.U.'s O.K. I've got a few good students. They even gave me money to hire my own post doc, and we've got a great research project going. I think it's going to get funded by NSF." He poured the rest of his beer into the stein. "Actually, I couldn't be happier. Except for Helen. It's kind of hard—going home at night to a woman who hates the place where your job is, who doesn't want to hear anything about physics, and who thinks jazz is the pits."

Poor guy, Elena thought. "Maybe Helen would be happier," she suggested, "if she got a job or had a baby—something to—"

"Well, a baby's out. Not that I don't like kids, but I'm not going to father a child to keep a marriage going that's as bad as this one. But a job's not a bad idea."

It sounded as if divorce wouldn't be a bad idea, but Elena couldn't very well make that suggestion.

"The thing is, I don't know what she'd do," Rafe went on. "She majored in Music Appreciation, but she can't sing or play an instrument, and she doesn't like anything but Mozart. What did you think of *The Magic Flute*? Michael said you two were going."

"Pretty neat, but I had to leave during the Queen of the Night's aria."

Rafer laughed. "That was you? I thought all the local opera buffs were going to stone you. We could see it from the first balcony, where we were sitting."

Elena flushed. "I know it wasn't the proper thing to do, but I'd been paged."

"It wouldn't have been so bad if it hadn't been during that particular aria," said Rafer, still laughing. "You should have heard Helen on the subject of someone leaving during that amazing piece of female twittering."

"Come on," said Elena. "I kind of liked it."

"It's O.K." Rafe didn't sound very enthusiastic. "Anyway, Helen never got beyond her B.A. She had to take a science course, put it off till her senior year, then made the mistake of taking physics, which of course she hated—although she claimed that I made it worthwhile; I ran her lab. Now I wonder if she ever really liked *me*."

"Sure she did, Rafe," Elena assured him. "You're a good guy."

"I wish you'd tell her that."

After they finished their beers and food, Rafe walked Elena to her truck. "Thanks for listening," he said. "You're good company, Elena, not to mention a terrific singer."

Elena laughed. "I'm an even better cop," she said and climbed into the driver's seat. Now, there was a nice man, she thought as she shifted into first. Of course, if she were dating him or married to him, he'd probably turn out to be a world-class nagger, or jealous, or abusive, or some damn thing.

Slotting a Ray Lee Ribbon tape into her cassette deck, she took the interstate home, singing "Saint James Infirmary" with Ray Lee. Maybe he and Lavender would come to Los Santos to visit their eldest son sometime. Then she could get together with them. On the other hand, their daughter had been killed here. By a statue. The town wouldn't have really great memories for them.

Well, she'd had a nice evening, and now she was going to get a good night's sleep. She'd worry about the Mandel case tomorrow. Having pulled into her driveway, Elena climbed out of the pickup, set the alarm system, and headed for her front door.

42
..

The temperature had dropped while she was at the university. Elena shivered and pulled her coat up around her chin with one hand as she walked toward her door, her lovely, round-topped door, set back into its adobe arch. If anything ever happened to the door, she'd never find another that would fit the space. She felt for the house key, which she slipped into the keyhole. It had been a pleasant evening, although she regretted refusing Michael's invitation. They'd never make up their latest tiff that way, and she was very fond of Michael.

She turned the key, pushed the door open, and stepped inside, then gasped and went still with shock. Her house reeked with the most ungodly feral odor and, underlying it, blood. That was the one component in the stench washing over her that she could identify. But the other—dear God! What was it?

She glanced from the arch that led to her living room on the right to the dining-room arch on the left. There she saw the eyes, glowing in the dark, and heard the snarl. It raised the hair on the back of her neck in an atavistic reaction to danger that must have been passed down in human brain cells for a thousand, thousand years.

The mountain lion, she thought. The big cat missing from the zoo. Her hand had been inside her sling bag, putting the keys back. As the snarl came again, she dropped the keys and clasped her revolver. She was sweating and cold, terrified. Although her eyes were caught by the glowing eyes across the room, in seconds she had the gun leveled in a two-handed grip. The snarl cut the stillness, and she fired. As the creature screamed in rage and pain, a savage ancestor who had been living undetected in Elena's brain smiled with satisfaction. Her finger tightened a second time, and the snarling scream died.

Shaking so hard that she could no longer hold the gun steady, she pried one hand away and fumbled for the light, missing the switch on the first try, succeeding on the second, leveling the gun again in the direction of those eyes, whose feral glow had diminished. When her own pupils had adjusted to the light, she saw the cat clearly, bleeding on the carpet she'd bought herself for Christmas last year at the Brass Shop. The creature wasn't moving. At this distance Elena couldn't tell if it still breathed, and she was afraid to cross through the arch and check. But it was a mountain lion; that she could tell—large, lean-muscled. What in God's name was it doing in her house?

She leaned against the living room archway, still shaking. Once her mind began to function again, she realized that it must have been left here by the person who put the albino snake in Rosalba's bathroom, who put the arrow through Arnold's chest, who had fed Pansy amphetamines to send her on a crazed rampage. But Elena wasn't a Mandel! She wasn't cruel to animals or to garment workers! This move against her had to mean—well, that she was getting close to the murderer.

Keeping her eye on the big cat, she backed toward the sofa in her living room and sank down. She kept the gun on the mountain lion, hoping that it was dead, picked the phone up with the other hand and laid it in her lap so that she could call headquarters. If she was so close to solving the case, who was it? This creature had to be the one taken from the zoo. Was Darwin, after all, the murderer? You'd have to know what you were doing to steal a mountain lion.

She got the detective on night duty and told him what had

happened. "God almighty, Elena," he muttered. "A mountain lion in your house?"

"That's right, Beto. I think it's dead."

"We'll be right out. Keep your gun trained on it. Don't get too close."

"You don't have to convince me," she agreed and hung up, thinking wryly that the police radio bands would start humming right about now. Attempts on the lives of officers got a lot of attention. She leaned her head against the sofa, not taking her eyes from the cat, and inhaled deeply. That was a mistake. The smell of cat mixed with the smell of blood turned her stomach. And then her heart sped up. The reek of blood had been there before she shot the cat, so where was it coming from? She had no pets. No one lived in the house but her. Shivering, she knew she had to search the rooms.

But she didn't want to. She was afraid of what she'd find. To look in the kitchen, she'd have to go through the dining room, past the mountain lion. What if it regained consciousness and sprang at her? And if she looked in either of the bedrooms, it would be out of sight. It might creep up on her and spring. Cold sweat began to dampen her skin again, making the gun feel slippery in her hand, making her teeth chatter.

Elena forced herself to walk slowly toward the animal, which showed no signs of life. The bleeding had slowed. Now that she was in the hallway again, looking through the arch into the dining room, she could see that she'd shot it in the head and shoulder.

She pulled an umbrella from a stand in the hall. She and Frank had bought the stand in Mexico when they were first married, when stores were still open at the Pronaf. The stand had been crafted by Indians in the south of Mexico for goodness knows what purpose, made of rough wood and carved with ugly gods. Holding the curved umbrella handle in her left hand and the gun in her right hand, trained on the cat, she gave it a poke.

No reaction. She nudged again. Then she circled it cautiously and opened the swinging door to the kitchen with the umbrella while keeping the pistol trained on the cat. When she took a quick glance into the kitchen, she saw a can of beer open on the table. Her shivering increased. She hadn't left a can there, which meant there was someone in the house.

Oh dear God, she thought. Let it be some burglar who had broken in to steal. Not Michael. Anyone but Michael. Swallowing hard, she drew the umbrella back and let the kitchen door close. Then she circled the cat again, and moved out to the hall, heading for her own bedroom. There was a light, the door half open. Had she left a light on? Glancing back toward the dining room archway, she pushed the door wide and looked in. A wave of dizziness swept over her. The bedroom was wrecked, splashed with blood. On the floor near the bathroom door was the body. Torn, gnawed, bloody. Elena leaned her head against the doorjamb, closed her eyes. She was quivering like an aspen in a high wind.

Without looking, she knew it was Michael. He was the only person who had a key. The body had his light brown hair, caked with blood. She forced herself away from the jamb, closed the door behind her in case the cat should be alive, and walked slowly forward. He must have been trying to get to the safety of the bathroom, whose door he could have locked behind him. But the cat had been too quick.

She knelt in blood, leaned over to look at the face, what was left of it. Pure terror. Terrible gashes on the throat and face. One hazel eye left to stare at her, blank in death. "Oh, Michael," she whispered. "If only I hadn't gone to the jam session. If only you hadn't forgiven me and come over." Elena felt as if her heart would break. He'd died in her stead, but if she'd been here, she wouldn't have died. She hadn't. She'd killed the cat. Had it been here when she came home for dinner? In the guest bedroom? Unconscious from tranquilizers? Or had the murderer come in with his living weapon after she left for the university?

Sirens screamed down the street, more than one, she thought. Forcing herself up from the floor, she was dimly aware that her hands, her knees, her shoes were covered with her lover's blood.

43
..

When Elena tried to leave the room where Michael lay torn and bloody, she couldn't open the door. The bastard had jimmied the lock again, just as he'd done with Rosalba. She thought back. Had she closed the bedroom door when she came home for dinner? No. And how had the catman got into the house? Her alarm system should have gone off, sending a signal to the nearest police station. Backing up, she braced herself and kicked the door open, meeting Beto Sanchez in the hall.

"You O.K.?" he asked.

Elena nodded.

"The cat's dead," said Beto.

"Not soon enough," she replied, trying to keep her voice steady, pointing toward the bedroom. Beto frowned and went through the door, which was hanging drunkenly off its hinges.

"You know who it is?" he asked.

"My lover, Michael Futrell."

"Oh, babe," said Beto. "I'm sorry."

On leaden feet Elena walked into the living room, where she sat down. Beto followed her. "I'll get a crime scene team." He made the call. "What do you think happened?"

"We'd had a quarrel," she said dully. "I decided to go to a jam session. Then Michael invited me to a lecture, and I said no. He must have come over to make up."

"He had a key?" asked Beto.

"Yeah. I got home about eleven, eleven-fifteen. When I opened the door, I smelled the—" She paused, shuddering.

"Me too," Beto agreed. "Smells like a damn zoo."

Elena nodded. "We'll need to check—be sure the cat came from the zoo."

"O.K." Beto had been taking notes. "But it's not likely it just wandered in, and it's the only mountain lion I've heard of that's missing."

"The lights were out in the front rooms. I smelled it." She took a deep breath. "Saw the eyes. It snarled. You know? An awful sound. So I shot at the eyes. I—ah—I shot it twice. Then I turned the lights on."

"And your boyfriend's body?" Beto prodded gently.

"He—ah—well, I went and sat down in the living room. I was shaking. You know? And then I thought—I remembered I'd smelled blood when I came in. Before I shot the cat. So I knew I had to look around. I checked the kitchen, went back to my bedroom. It was—what you saw. I didn't move anything. Touch anything."

Beto looked at her skeptically.

"Well, I guess I got some of his blood on me." She closed her eyes and swallowed again. "I had to kneel down. You know? To be sure it was—to be sure it was him."

"I know you did," said Beto. "And you can get cleaned up pretty soon."

"I'd have to go into that room," she said and started to shiver again.

"I'm going to get you a glass of water. O.K.? Or something stronger. You got any brandy?"

Elena shook her head. "I've got a liqueur. Something Sarah gave me."

"Where?"

"On the top pantry shelf."

"I'll get it," said Beto.

Elena huddled on the couch, thinking of the last time she'd poured that liqueur. Michael had come home with her; it was last December. They'd been to hear Ray Lee Ribbon, his son, and the H.H.U. jazz group she'd sung with tonight. First time she'd ever met those guys. And she and Michael had come home. She'd poured him some of the liqueur that Sarah had given her. They'd sat on the couch but hadn't drunk any. Instead they started making love, but it turned out that Michael didn't have a condom. They'd quarreled about it. How many dumb things they'd quarreled about. She'd only known him since— when? Last September. She met him at that bicycle race in Chimayo, when she and Leo were guarding Lance Potemkin, who was a suspect in the murder of his father. Michael had come up and introduced himself. The memories cut off when Beto handed her a water glass filled with Cointreau.

More cops were crowding into the house, and Beto joined them. The crime scene team. Onofre Calderon, the medical examiner. And she was sitting on the couch like a dummy, with tears running down her face. They glanced at her, looking uneasy, standing around the cat and muttering, going back to the bedroom where Michael lay all torn apart.

When they finally got together—she and Michael—it had been nice. Not all quarreling. Some really good times—in bed and out. And now he was dead. She brushed the sleeve of her sweatshirt across her eyes and thought she ought to go find a Kleenex. She ought to find out who brought that cat over here and left it to kill her, killing Michael instead. At least, *she'd* had a fighting chance. Michael might have been a criminologist, but he never carried a gun. He probably didn't know how to shoot one; she'd never asked. There were all kinds of things she'd never asked, and now she never could.

But where had the cat been? If the killer jimmied the bedroom lock, he must have put the cat in the bedroom. How did he know she usually closed the bedroom door when she went to bed? Had he put the cat under the bed? No, it wouldn't fit. Had he—

"Elena." Beto came in and sat down beside her. "Does he have any family we should call?"

She nodded, sniffed back tears, took another slug of the Cointreau. "He has a brother."

"You know his number?"

"I'll call," said Elena. She picked up the phone and realized that she didn't know Mark's number. And her hands were shaking. "Maybe you could look in the phone book. Mark Futrell."

Beto found Mark's number for her. "Why don't you let me make the call?" he suggested.

Elena wondered where Leo was. Why hadn't he come? He was being such a prick lately. Beto had written down the telephone number. She put her glass on the coffee table and, after two tries, managed to punch in the right digits. No one answered. He was probably out bar-hopping. She shivered and glanced toward the cat. "Are they going to take it away?" she asked.

"Yeah, sure," said Beto. "I guess we'll need to show it to someone at the zoo. You think this is connected to the murders you've been investigating?"

She nodded.

"I thought you nailed someone."

"Yeah. So it's not Lechuga who left the cat in my house," said Elena. However, it could have been Angela's missing boyfriend. Elena tried Mark's number again, just in case she hadn't dialed it right. It rang and rang; no answering machine picked up. What did that mean? And then she had the strangest thought. "I've got to look at the body again," she said, hanging up.

"Come on. You don't want to do that," said Beto.

"Yes, I have to. Maybe it's not Michael."

"Elena, you already said it was him."

"His twin brother looks just like him. Maybe it's Mark."

"Elena, don't kid yourself, huh? His brother didn't have a key, did he?"

She shook her head and went down the hall, Beto trailing her.

"Hon, don't get your hopes up," he said. "How would he have got in? You don't leave your house open. You got an alarm system."

"I don't know. He's a sneak. Maybe he did. Maybe it's not Michael." She went into the bedroom and, swallowing back a wave of nausea, approached the body. The team was at work, but the photographer backed off when she stepped up close. She looked at the clothes. It was hard to tell because they'd been ripped up badly. "I don't think it's Michael," she said.

The men exchanged glances.

"I don't think that's his shirt. I've never seen him wear that shirt."

"Elena, it doesn't figure that it would be his brother," said Beto, who had followed her in.

"It looks like a shirt Mark would wear. And the shoes. Look at the shoes. They look like Mark's. Don't you think?" They were loafers. She tried to remember whether Michael had loafers like that. "I'm going to call Michael," she said. "Maybe he's home. Maybe he didn't get killed." She hurried out of the room, away from the body. Back to the living room. She had to stop short because they'd put the mountain lion into a body bag and were hauling it away. "You've got to show it to the zoo director," she called after them. "See if it's his cat."

"Don't worry. We will," called one of the men.

She went into the living room and punched in Michael's number. No one had to look that up for her. Her hands were shaking so badly that the receiver bumped against her chin. The answering machine came on. "Michael," she said, "pick up." His message was playing. "Pick up, Michael," she said again. "It's Elena. Get on the line."

And then he did. "What is it?" he said, sounding angry and sleepy.

"You're alive?" She began to cry.

"Elena?" he asked. "Why wouldn't I be?"

"He's alive," she said to Beto, then into the phone. "This *is* Michael, isn't it?"

"Of course it's Michael. What are you talking about, Elena? You got me out of bed."

She choked on tears. Beto took the phone out of her hand and told Michael what had happened. She heard the detective say, "We don't know how he got in. She found his body after she got home from some jazz session." There was a pause while he listened. "First, she shot the cat. Then she found him." Another pause. "He was in the bedroom." Elena couldn't stop crying, couldn't stop thinking about how awful this must sound to Michael. His brother dead in her bedroom.

44
..

Tuesday, April 11, 12:15 A.M.

Michael came out of the bedroom, face gray-white and stricken. Elena, who was still sitting on the couch, looked up at him, believing at last that it was he who had survived. The clothes were right, more conservative, the walk less swaggering. "You really are all right," she said, almost to herself.

"Don't act as if you didn't know that," said Michael. "When I called tonight, you wouldn't see me. Now he's dead because you had to have both of us."

His accusation stabbed at her. If he really cared about her, he couldn't have thought that. "Mark was dead when I got home," she said, no longer expecting him to believe her, after this last shock, almost too numb to care.

Michael dropped heavily onto the love seat. "Why would he be here if you weren't?"

"I don't know that, Michael. I don't know how he got in."

"The detective said your back door had been tampered with, but Mark didn't do that. He wouldn't know how. Someone must have picked that lock and let the lion in while you two were in the bedroom. For God's sake, if you had to have him over here behind my back, you could at least have protected him."

"Michael, please!" What could she say to explain? "I found him after I killed the cat. I thought it was you. You're the only one with a key."

"He had one in his pocket. The detective showed it to me."

"I didn't give it to him." Elena felt as if she were caught in a nightmare that kept getting worse. "He must have had a copy made from yours."

"He didn't," snapped Michael. "Why are you doing this? My brother's dead, and you're making him out to be some sort of pervert! He wasn't like that."

Elena shook her head hopelessly. She didn't want to criticize Mark now that he was dead, but she hated being put in this position—as if she'd done something wrong. "I don't know what he was doing here or how he got in. The only thing I'm sure of is that the cat was left here to kill me and got him instead. And I thought it was you."

"He said you'd been calling him."

"*He* called *me*. He sent me flowers. I told you that. He was always coming on to me. And you ignored it."

"If it weren't for you, my brother wouldn't be dead."

"Just stop it right there!"

They both turned toward the voice. The other cops had been avoiding the living room. Lieutenant Beltran strode right in. "You're blaming Elena for your brother's death?" asked Beltran. "That's crap."

How long had he been listening? Elena wondered, humiliated.

"In the first place, she's not the kind of woman who'd play brothers off against each other. In the second place, if she says she didn't give him a key, she didn't."

"Who are you?" Michael asked resentfully. "I don't see that our discussion's any of your business."

"I'm her lieutenant," said Beltran, looking more like a father defending her against a boyfriend he disliked.

"You don't know anything about our relationship or my brother."

"I know something about my officers," said Beltran angrily. "You owe her an apology."

Michael turned to Elena and said, "I hope you realize that there's no way we can continue."

Elena just looked at him. She understood that he was distraught over his brother's death; she was too. Although not as upset as she'd been when she thought it was Michael who had died. Nonetheless, what he'd just said seemed to be the last straw, and she replied, "Do what you have to, Michael. I'm sorry about Mark, but it wasn't my fault. He had no business here."

Michael rose and said, "I'm leaving." He glared at Beltran and headed for the hall.

"Could he have laid a trap here for his brother?" asked Beltran when the door had slammed behind Michael. "Out of jealousy or something?"

Elena shook her head wearily. "Where would he have got a mountain lion? Michael doesn't know anything about animals, and he never believed that Mark was harassing me. In fact, I don't think Mark really has anything to do with this, except that he's dead by mistake. This is connected with the Mandel murders."

Beltran frowned. "We've got that garment worker in custody."

"Right. So she didn't set this up."

Two men came through with Mark's body, now zipped into a body bag. Dull-eyed, Elena watched the trolley pass down the hall. She thought of the bedroom and shuddered, then tried to pull herself together.

As Beltran studied her, she knew what he was seeing—a blood-stained, tear-stained, red-eyed woman. "It's been a rough night," he said. "Why don't you—" Before he could finish, the telephone rang.

Elena picked up automatically and said, "Jarvis." The lieutenant sat down beside her on the sofa, watching as she listened to the voice at the other end.

It was her ex-husband. "Ellie, it's Frank. I just heard on the police radio that someone put a mountain cat in your place and it killed some guy. Are you O.K.?"

"I am, Frank. Thanks," Elena replied. Not that she was, but what else could she say?

"Listen, babe, I thought you might not want to stay in the house after what happened. I mean to your boyfriend."

"Turns out it wasn't him," said Elena.

"Well, whatever," said Frank. "You can stay at my place."

"Oh, I don't—"

"Hey, it's O.K. I don't go off shift till tomorrow at eight, and then I'll bunk in with someone else. The place is yours for as long as you need it. I don't want you sleeping in a house that's covered with blood. O.K.?"

"It's really nice of you to offer, but I—I have a place to stay," said Elena. "So thanks anyway. O.K.?" She hung up.

Beltran looked at her with raised eyebrows. "You thick with Frank again?"

Elena shook her head. She hadn't seen or heard from her ex in months. "No, I guess he was just being nice." She laughed sadly. "There was a time when Frank was pretty nice. He offered to let me stay at his place."

"I don't think that would be a good idea," said Beltran.

"Oh, he wouldn't have been there, but I still didn't want to be obligated."

"You're welcome to come over to my house. My wife will find you a bed."

Everyone was so kind. Except Michael. Elena felt the tears starting again.

"I can see you don't think much of that idea," said Beltran. "You told him you had a place to go. Where?"

"I just said that," said Elena wearily. But she knew she couldn't stay here. If Leo had come, she'd have gone home with him. Concepcion would have taken her in, but Elena didn't want to wake them up.

"How about your friend Sarah Tolland?" said Beltran.

Elena looked at her lieutenant in dumbfounded surprise. He couldn't stand Sarah; she was suing the department—and him—for false arrest.

"I hate to call her in the middle of the—"

"Then I'll call her," said Beltran, and he did. Elena listened to him talking; he managed to give a horrifyingly vivid picture of her situation. Then he hung up and said to Elena, "She'll be over to get you—thirty minutes. You'll stay with her."

Elena nodded. Sarah was what she needed—calm, rational, well-organized Sarah, who probably wouldn't even have to put clean sheets on the bed in her spare room.

The team finished. Onofre Calderon and the forensic guys stopped to express their sympathies. "Wait," she said before they could leave. "What could you tell from the body and the room?"

"Well," said Rudolfo Chin of the crime-scene unit, "the guy had a key to your place."

"Not from me," she reiterated.

"He evidently came in and laid down right in the center of your bed. The cat must have been in the bathroom, probably drinking water out of the toilet. It came in and jumped him. He managed to get off the bed. From the spatter patterns, I'd say they struggled on the floor. Looked to me like he broke the cat's leg. The deceased must have been a hell of a strong guy to be able to mix it up with a mountain cat."

"He was a Phys Ed professor, a bicycle racer. I suppose he was in good shape," said Elena.

"Yeah, well, it looks like he was trying to get to the bathroom, maybe shut the door on the cat."

Elena nodded. "That's what I thought."

"But the cat slashed his throat before he ever got there, and that was the end of it for the victim. Later the cat must have dragged itself into the dining room and hid out under the table, but it wasn't up to jumping you when you got home, not with a broken leg."

"Anything else?" asked Elena.

"We picked up prints where we could. We'll run 'em."

"I might learn more after the autopsy," said Calderon. "But not much. It's pretty obvious what happened."

"Hell of a shot you made at the cat," said Rudy Chin.

"Yeah," said Elena. "In the dark. I had to shoot at the eyes."

"Some gutsy lady," said Calderon.

"Not me," Elena protested. "I was terrified. I still thought the cat was alive until Beto told me different."

"Hey, you're shivering," said Calderon. "Maybe we ought to get you a cup of coffee or something."

Elena shook her head and picked up the water glass on the table. Time for another gulp of Cointreau.

At that point Sarah walked in the front door and said, "No coffee. She's coming home with me." After getting a closer look at Elena, she winced. "I'll have to get you some clothes."

"You can't go in there, Sarah. It's—awful."

"I'm sure it is," Sarah replied. "One of you can go in with me and help me pack some things." She noticed Beltran, and the two glared at one another. Sarah held him completely responsible for her arrest the year before.

"I'll go with you," said Rudy Chin. "Just don't look around. It's pretty bloody."

Sarah and Rudy left the room. Elena swallowed another slug of Cointreau and turned to Beltran. "Lieutenant," she said, "I really appreciate your coming over."

"It's O.K., *niña*," said Beltran. "It's a hell of a thing to happen to you, and I guess you're right. There's something more to this than a garment worker shooting an arrow into her boss. But don't worry about it. In fact, maybe you'd better take some time off. You're not going to feel much like—"

"No!" said Elena sharply. "I'll be in tomorrow. I'm going to find out who did this. Mark is the fourth victim, but it was meant to be me."

"Well, I'll tell you, Elena, I think you're well rid of that Michael. That was a hell of a way to treat you."

Elena thought so too.

"And you need some time off."

She shook her head. "No, I intend to be the one who catches this killer."

"If he doesn't get you first," cautioned Beltran. "Watch your step."

"All right," said Sarah, coming out with a suitcase. "You're ready to go, Elena. What you need is a long, hot bath and a good night's sleep."

Elena looked up at her friend. For once, Sarah wasn't wearing a suit. She'd thrown a coat over her nightgown, which was completely unlike Sarah. But Elena had never been so glad to see anyone. "I don't know how to thank you for coming," she said in a wobbly voice.

"Anytime," Sarah replied, smiling at her. "Let's go."

45
··

Next we'll have those rampant immorality people sneaking in and ripping out the birth control implants. Well, Pansy doesn't have one, so leave her alone. Los Santos is full of nut cases. There's nothing dangerous about zoo animals if they're handled by professionals like me and not messed with by lunatics.

Jesus Amado, Elephant Keeper

"Elephant Update," Los Santos *Herald-Post*, Monday, April 10

At ten minutes before eight Elena walked into headquarters. She'd had three and a half hours in Sarah's guest bed, but she hadn't slept well. When she dozed off, there were nightmares; when she was awake, her memory called up the same scenes: her blood-soaked bedroom, the savaged body, Michael's unforgiving words, cat eyes in the dark, the smell, the snarl, the jump of the gun in her hand, the cat's scream, Michael's unforgiving words.

She was up and out of Sarah's by seven, her pickup having been delivered to the university parking lot by a patrolman at the same time that Sarah drove her to the apartment. Elena left a note for her hostess on the dining room table and stopped for an egg and *chorizo* burrito and a cup of coffee on her way to work. She knew she looked terrible. Her clothes

229

were wrinkled because she hadn't unpacked the night before. There were dark circles under her eyes. But she went into headquarters obsessed with the need to find out who had put that mountain lion in her house. It wasn't Angela Lechuga.

Maybe the cat would prove to be the pry bar that opened up this case. Mountain lions surely weren't that easy to kidnap. She'd start with the zoo, with Darwin Mandel. With the possibility that he'd killed his brother and sister for money. The Pansy incident, in that case, would have been a red herring, the cat attack an attempt to stop the investigation before it got to him. He must have found her questions threatening, so he'd tried to frighten her off or kill her. But why would he have taken the cat in the first place? Had it been meant for J.J.? Or his father? If Darwin was the killer. No matter who it was, if he thought he could get her off the case, he'd failed. She might be having nightmares; she might be jittery, but she'd be there when they arrested him.

Walking into C.A.P., she found Leo already there, her partner who hadn't bothered to come over last night. When she scowled, he looked surprised. "Hey, I just heard about it," he said.

"No one paged you?"

"We had everything turned off. Concepcion's having so much trouble sleeping that I wanted to give her one night without interruptions."

"Is something wrong?" asked Elena, feeling guilty that she'd been angry with Leo, who had so many problems.

"Just what you'd expect," he answered grumpily. "If it isn't leg cramps, she's getting kicked by God knows how many little feet. Jeez, Elena, I can see her stomach jumping. It makes me feel guilty. Like *I'm* in there kicking her."

"Come on, Leo," said Elena, "you know she wanted a baby."

"Yeah, but she never said she wanted three or four."

"You still don't know, huh?"

"The doctor's going to try for another count in a couple of days. But she's only six months along. She shouldn't be having trouble sleeping."

"Look, could you two knock off the obstetrics and pay attention."

They turned in surprise. Carmen, the department receptionist, was standing at the end of Homicide Row, fists on hips, her dark hair in huge rolls on top of her head. She'd got rid of the braids and beads. "The lieutenant wants to see you."

"When?" Elena asked.

"Right now. He's sitting in his office tapping his foot. Sergeant Escobedo's on his way in."

Leo and Elena exchanged glances and went off to Beltran's office.

"You look like hell, Elena," said Beltran when they entered. "Why don't you go back to Sarah's and get some sleep."

"I don't want to," said Elena.

"Then go see the police psychologist. Last night's bound to have an effect on you, and I don't want you off the job because of psychological trauma or whatever."

"Leo and I need to talk to Darwin Mandel," said Elena.

"First, we're gonna sit down and brainstorm the case," said Beltran. "How do you see it, Manny?" He turned to Sergeant Escobedo, who had come in and taken a seat.

"I've been reading over the reports," said Manny. "The labor angle still looks good to me."

"I don't know why you say that," Elena objected. "Angela Lechuga couldn't have had anything to do with that mountain lion in my house last night."

"Her boyfriend could have," Manny replied. "We've got a call in to the police in Chihuahua City, checking on him. But about the labor angle, we had trouble back in '90 or '91. Remember, Lieutenant?" said Manny. "L.A. union organizers came in. There was violence. They didn't get anywhere then, but if they could unionize Los Santos Apparel, that would be a big foot in the door."

"If this is the way they go about it," Elena muttered, "there won't be anything left to unionize."

"The way it looks to me," said Beltran, "is Lechuga was acting for Alope Randall. Lechuga definitely killed Arnold Mandel and probably killed Rosalba Mondragon. Last night, like Manny says, it could have been the boyfriend who's supposed to be in Chihuahua City. Or maybe Randall hired someone else to screw up the investigation by putting that cat

in your house, Elena. I'm sure she knows that you've closed
some pretty difficult cases."

"I don't see her as—"

"I'm not saying that Alope Randall's the one who's calling
the shots on all this. There's probably someone more powerful pulling her strings," Beltran theorized.

"She didn't strike me as the kind of person with strings on
her," Elena argued. "She's very independent."

"Yeah, well, she'd work with someone who had the same
goals as her," said Manny.

Elena had been shaking her head. "Manny, it's got the
marks of a personal vendetta. Admittedly, Lechuga had
reasons to hate them. She and the boyfriend are a possibility.
But we shouldn't rule out Darwin. He's got financial motive,
not to mention the opportunity and know-how to get the
animals. Leo can tell you that the Mandels are not a loving
family." She thought about what she'd said, then added, "I
keep feeling that it's got something to do with animal
activism. The mother was—"

"Message for Sergeant Escobedo," said Beltran's secretary,
stepping into the office. She handed a piece of paper to
Manny.

After he'd glanced at it, he said, "Mexico claims the
boyfriend's been with his sick *abuela* all this time. Since the
day after Lechuga was arrested."

Beltran shrugged. "So Randall hired someone else. As for
your idea, Elena, you're telling me you think the zoo director
could be behind this? The man's been a pillar of the
community for thirty years. Next you'll be fingering the
llama nut." He grinned.

Manny joined him in a chuckle, which Elena found
depressing. Her sergeant often took her side. Had he checked
her reports on the rabies disaster in Lubbock? If he hadn't,
maybe she shouldn't remind him of that excursion in her
investigation. At least not right now.

"You're not thinking about this clearly, Elena," Beltran
was saying in a kindly voice. "After you're done with the
debriefing on last night and the Shooting Review Team—"
Elena groaned. "—you really ought to take a couple of days
off. Rest up at your friend's house. And while you're there,

maybe you can talk her into dropping her suit against the city."

"No matter who's behind it," said Elena stubbornly, "we have to start with that cat."

"When do you think it was brought in?" asked Manny.

"I left early in the morning, went home for dinner, left again at seven, and didn't get back till eleven. It had to have been there before Mark Futrell arrived, whenever that was. I suppose it could have been there, still tranquilized, when I came home for dinner. I'm assuming you'd have to tranquilize a mountain lion before you could haul it around; I don't even know that for sure."

She thought for a moment. "You know, I smelled something before I took my shower. It wasn't like—" Remembering that overpowering odor of blood and cat when she returned from the jazz session, Elena gagged. "It wasn't like later, but it could have been the mountain lion."

She took a deep breath and pushed the memory from her head. "We can probably get a fix on the times by questioning my neighbors. They're all old and like to sit around looking out windows. And we can question people in the faculty apartment house where Mark lived, maybe find out what time he left. But the cat's the key. We've got to be sure it came from the zoo. Find out how someone would have gone about stealing it. That kind of stuff."

"She's right," Escobedo agreed. "No matter who's behind the killings, we may be able to track them down through the cat. Where it came from, when it was delivered."

"O.K.," said Beltran. "But I know you, Elena. Alope Randall's just the kind of woman you'd take to. Don't let that blind you to—"

"Come on, Lieutenant. That's what you said to me about Sarah Tolland, and now we're getting sued."

The lieutenant's face turned red with anger, and Leo poked Elena. Tactless me, she thought. "We better get to the zoo."

"Right, do it," said Beltran, glaring at her.

"Jeez, Elena," said Leo when they got out into the hall. "Can't you watch your mouth around him? I hear he lost a night's sleep coming out to your place to see if you were O.K."

"Called me '*niña*' about ten times," grumbled Elena, remembering after the fact.

"And now you have to remind him that he screwed up the acid bath case."

"Well, he did!"

46
··

Tuesday, April 11, 9:15 A.M.

Because the detectives called ahead, the veterinarian and the director were waiting for them in the administration building when they arrived at the zoo. "Have you autopsied the cat yet?" Elena asked Tockler.

"I have. The toxicology results will take time, but I can make a good guess as to what we'll find. There were needle marks on the cat's skin. We can assume that tranquilizers were administered so that Leopold could be moved around with some degree of safety."

"How'd you find needle marks?" asked Leo. "Was the cat bald?"

"I shaved the hide," said Dr. Tockler. Darwin winced. "Another interesting thing, beside the broken left foreleg, was that the cat must have been kept hungry before it was delivered to your house, Detective. It had eaten within hours of death, but had nothing else in its stomach."

Elena closed her eyes. Mark had been its last dinner, something she didn't want to think about. "You called the cat by name, so I guess we can assume that it's the one stolen from the zoo."

"It's ours," said Darwin. His face was white, his eyes anxious. "Native to this area. Part of the West Texas Habitat Collection."

"Oh?" Elena stared at him. "In that case, Dr. Mandel, I'll

235

need to know where you were yesterday between seven-thirty in the morning and eleven at night."

"Are you intimating that *I* put Leopold in your house?" asked Darwin.

"Your brother was murdered. Then your sister. Then a detective investigating the murders is attacked. That makes you a suspect, sir," said Leo.

"Aside from the fact that I wouldn't try to kill you, or anyone, Detective Jarvis, I wouldn't do that to Leopold," said Dr. Mandel, his pink-lensed glasses misting with emotion. "I'm aware that police officers carry guns. Do you think I'd endanger my mountain lion?" Then he sighed. "I am sorry about your friend."

"You were going to tell us where you were," Leo prompted.

"Of course." Darwin sighed again, looking defeated. "I was here at the zoo by seven-thirty. With all the demonstrators we've been having, I don't dare spend time away."

"Did anyone see you?" asked Elena.

"The night guard saw me coming in. My secretary saw me from eight on."

Elena was taking notes.

"I left at six-thirty, two hours after the zoo closed to the public, and went straight home. The guard can vouch for the time I left. It took me twenty minutes to reach my house. My wife had dinner on the table. We ate." He scribbled his home telephone number on his business card and handed it to Leo. "We spent a quiet evening watching a very interesting video about South American monkeys in their native rain forests. Then we went to bed. About eleven-thirty."

"Your wife was there the whole evening?" Elena asked.

"She was."

"You were there the whole evening?"

"I was."

"*Someone* must have planted the cat," she muttered.

"I realize that," Darwin agreed. "Although I can't imagine who would do such a thing. Perhaps someone with a vendetta against the zoo. Did you see the letter in the *Times* this morning?"

Elena hadn't and looked toward Leo, who shrugged.

"Now my mother's old friends are turning against me,"

said Darwin. "And why would they? We belong to a species-survival plan. Many of these animals would become extinct if it weren't for zoos. Here, look at this. I couldn't believe Arleen had written it." He opened a drawer and extracted a newspaper clipping.

Elena recalled her interview with an animal activist named Arleen. She took the clipping and began to read:

Dear Sir:

No one who loves animals can approve of a zoo. How would you feel if you were cooped up in a cage and stared at every day by another species? And now we hear that the zoo administration is so inept that animals are being stolen, drugged, and used to kill people. Shame, Darwin Mandel! Your mother would be appalled to see what you've come to. The zoo should be closed.

Arleen Nevinell
President, Los Santos Animal Rights League

Letters to the Editor, Los Santos *Times*, Tuesday, April 11.

There was an animal activist connection, Elena thought. If Mrs. Nevinell's group was responsible for the elephant drugging and the animal abductions, and after that the murders of a man who hunted and a woman who wore the skins of endangered species, as well as the public relations disaster for the zoo, they might consider that they were avenging Cecilia Mandel for the perceived treason of her children to her ideals. But would anyone be that fanatical?

Well, Cecilia had evidently been instrumental in loosing a bunch of rabid dogs ten years ago, and Cecilia was Arleen's hero. Elena passed the clipping to Leo, who read it while she asked Darwin if the snake and the mountain lion were endangered species.

"No," he admitted. "They're part of the local fauna program."

"So these people would resent the caging of animals that

could be running around, or slithering around, as the case may be?"

"Even local habitats are being reduced by the growth of towns and cities," said Darwin defensively.

"What would this letter have to do with the cat at your house last night, Elena?" Leo asked. "You haven't been picking on animals."

"I'm investigating deaths by animals," she replied. "So are you. We're both connected to the deaths of Dr. Mandel's brother and sister. Maybe I asked someone a question that made them nervous." She stared hard at Darwin, but she was thinking about Arleen Nevinell as well.

"I can see why you'd think that," Darwin acknowledged, "but I didn't want Rosalba and Malcolm dead. Why would I?"

"Money," said Leo.

Darwin stared at them helplessly. "That's ridiculous. I don't need more money. Please check out my—my alibi."

"If you were the one who took the cat when it turned up missing, an alibi for yesterday wouldn't do you any good," said Leo. "Maybe you took it home and—"

"Took the cat home!" Darwin looked astounded. "Leticia would never allow me to bring a potentially dangerous animal home. The presence of a motherless monkey sends her into a panic. Talk to her if you don't believe me."

"What about the snake? Have you ever taken a snake home?" Leo asked.

"Of course not," said Darwin.

"We'll want to talk to zoo employees again," said Elena. "Especially people who work with the cats."

"By all means," said Darwin. "Ah—ah—Good Lord, I can't even remember the name of the cat keeper."

"Marcie Rapaport," said Dr. Tockler. "Are you, by any chance, now free to date, Detective?" he asked Elena.

Elena gave the veterinarian an indignant look. How tactless could you get? He evidently thought her boyfriend had been killed last night by Leopold, leaving the field open to him. Maybe she ought to check *his* alibi.

As they were leaving, Leo said to her, "Just because he

didn't have the cat stashed at home, doesn't mean he didn't have it somewhere else."

They talked to everyone they could find at the zoo, including Marcie Rapaport, a young woman with dark hair pulled back in a sort of George Washington club, boots, jodhpurs, and matching waist-length vest. Marcie the Lion Tamer, Elena thought, wondering if the woman used a chair and whip.

Marcie said whoever took the cat had keys. There was no sign of a break-in, and she had *not* left the cat's night quarters unlocked. "Cats are too dangerous for carelessness. Someone stole Leopold. Dr. Mandel said at the time, 'Why would anyone steal a mountain cat? It's not as if they make good house pets.' Which is true. Leopold wasn't bad tempered as cats go, but he wasn't happy to be here. He'd have escaped and headed for the mountains if he could. But he didn't because he couldn't."

"Say you had the keys. How would you go about kidnapping the lion?" Elena asked.

"If you were dumb enough to do it?" Marcie stuck a thumb in the front pocket of her jodhpurs and tilted her head in thought. "Well, you'd lure him into something like an airline carrier. With meat. Or—and this would be faster and surer—you'd zap him with a tranquilizer dart, put him in something—preferably wheeled; he weighs well over a hundred pounds—and haul him off."

"Where would you keep him?"

"Well, not in the house, I wouldn't imagine. Most people think they stink."

Elena agreed. She'd never forget the smell in her house. In fact, she might never get it out of the house.

"You could keep him in a dog run. Wouldn't be too safe, but then someone who'd steal an adult mountain lion can't be very interested in safety."

"You mentioned tranquilizers. Have any disappeared from wherever you keep them?" Elena asked.

Marcie laughed. "If they had, I'd know," she replied. "They're locked up."

"Where?"

"Vet's quarters. And they're dangerous. We have to wear

gloves, masks, the whole protective bit when we use them."

"So if the thief didn't get the stuff here, where could he have bought or stolen it?" Leo asked.

Marcie shrugged. "If you've got the money, you can buy just about anything. Juarez would be my guess. It's easier to get proscribed drugs there than here."

"We'll never run down the buyer across the border," Leo murmured to Elena.

"We could check the Narcotics Squad," she suggested. "They might know who to ask. You can talk to them, Leo."

"Still avoiding Frank?" He grinned.

"If you're through with me, I've got cages to clean," said Marcie.

Elena bought lunch from the refreshment stand, skirted the coin-operated, three-bear merry-go-round with its red-derbied, vested bears ridden by whooping toddlers, and walked back to take a bench across from a monkey cage, where Leo, who had gone out to the car, met her. Crunching potato chips and sipping Coke between bites of hot dog, thinking about the night before and her final conversation with Michael, Elena felt very depressed.

"Maybe you *should* take a few days off," Leo remarked, once he'd started on his second hot dog. "You haven't said a word in fifteen minutes."

"How would you feel if Concepcion just dumped you?"

"You're talking about that Michael guy? I heard he turned on you because you found his brother dead in your house."

Elena nodded and took another bite.

"No big loss. I never thought Futrell was that great."

"Thanks for the sympathy," Elena snapped.

"Hey, your troubles are nothing compared to mine," said Leo. "I just called home. The obstetrician thinks Concepcion could be carrying five babies. Five! How the hell am I ever going to support five kids on a detective's pay? I'll be poverty-stricken for the rest of my life."

Elena sighed, wondering what it cost to raise five children. He'd probably have to take a second job or give some babies away. "Want another dog?" she asked.

"No. They taste like somebody swept them up off the floor and stuffed them into a plastic hot-dog skin."

"I read an article that said that's exactly how they make frankfurters," said Elena. "How about a Fudgesicle?"

"Yeah, O.K.," said Leo. "Might as well enjoy the good life while I can afford it."

47
..

Tuesday, April 11, 3:05 P.M.

Darwin Mandel's house was a square, two-story brick Colonial with a green yard—birdbath, grass, trees, bushes, symmetrically arranged and faithfully watered. It looked like something a New Englander might hallucinate while dying of thirst in the desert. Leticia Mandel, white hair becomingly curled above a plump face and body, answered the door herself, studied the detective's identification like a sensible citizen, then offered them iced coffee and chairs in her Early American living room.

While their hostess was in her kitchen preparing the refreshments, Elena studied the room, which was inundated by a cozy tide of embroidered samplers with pithy quotations, copper warming pans, fireplace bellows, and other reminders of pre-Revolutionary America. All the room lacked was Betsy Ross in a mob cap stitching up an American flag, Elena decided and gratefully accepted the iced coffee from a silver tray that had probably been made by Paul Revere.

"Thank you, ma'am," said Leo. "First, could you tell us about the animals your husband has brought home in the last few months?"

"What animals?" asked Leticia Mandel. "Obviously I accept Darwin's obsession with them; it's his job." She had an accent reminiscent of the Kennedy family. "But I do draw the line at having animals here. Especially zoo animals. They

242

have no respect for upholstery, and they are not housebroken. We tried having a kitten once. A Persian does look nice curled up on a braided rug in front of the fireplace, but we had to get rid of it. Too much untidy shedding. Now, what did we do with it?" Mrs. Mandel frowned, trying to remember. "I believe we gave it to Darwin's brother, whose snake ate it. Poor cat. I haven't been to J.J.'s since."

Interesting, thought Elena. Did J.J. still keep snakes? What kind of snake ate cats? "Then your husband has never brought animals home?" Elena asked.

"Never."

"O.K.," said Leo, glancing at his partner. "Tell us what you and your husband were doing yesterday—times, activities, and so forth."

Leticia looked both intrigued and tickled, her blue eyes twinkling merrily. "Are you asking me for an alibi, Detective?"

Leo cleared his throat and tried to look forceful. Elena happened to know that, aside from the accent, Leticia Mandel reminded him of his grandmother, who came to town every year and stuffed him with homemade cookies. He took a sip of his iced coffee. "If you don't mind, ma'am."

"Not at all," said the lady. "Darwin left the house about seven after a breakfast of oatmeal and prunes. He went to work. I spent the day vacuuming the attic, piecing a quilt, and preparing the soil in my sweet-William bed, not to mention preparing our evening meal. Darwin arrived home at a little before seven, and I served him a New England boiled dinner—corned beef, cabbage, boiled potatoes. I'm sure you're familiar with the dish."

Elena wasn't and thought it sounded awful.

"Monday is New England boiled dinner night. Friday is fish night—not that I am Roman Catholic, but the fish man came on Friday at home, so we always had fresh fish. It's not as easy to get here—no fish man." Leticia laughed cheerfully. "Saturday is Boston baked beans and brown bread. It makes me feel more at home, here in this unlikely place, to follow family customs. Sunday we often have roast lamb, mint jelly, English peas, and—"

"What happened after dinner?" Leo interrupted.

Mrs. Mandel looked at him as if he'd spilled his drink on her braided rug or committed some comparable *faux pas*. "We watched a videotape about monkeys. Small monkeys with white ruffs—quite Elizabethan. Or was that Sunday night? At any rate we watched an animal tape. I believe I dozed off."

"Did your husband leave at any time that evening?" Elena asked. "Perhaps while you were napping?"

"Of course not. Darwin was quite enraptured with the film. And I am a light napper. Then Darwin discussed the social interactions of the monkeys in question. After that we both read for an hour. Darwin is a great reader." She waved toward a floor-to-ceiling wall of books. "Animal studies, of course. I'm quite accustomed to his book buying, and as long as he confines himself to that wall, I don't mind. In fact I think the bookcase adds to the coziness of the room. Don't you?"

Leo and Elena nodded dutifully.

"Of course, when he buys a new book, an old one has to go—into storage, off to the zoo, whichever he prefers. One can't have the books taking over the house, can one? No indeed. Limits must be set. Order maintained."

"And after your hour of reading?" Elena asked, beginning to feel sorry for poor Darwin, who only got enough book space to foster the cozy decor.

"Why, we went to bed. And before you ask, neither Darwin nor I left the house or even the room until we rose this morning. I fixed kidneys and eggs for breakfast—my great-grandmother's recipe—"

Kidneys? Elena gagged discreetly. Leo was staring at the woman as if she'd served barbecued dog.

"Darwin cleaned his plate. He eats everything I put in front of him, although I do think he could be a bit more vocally appreciative. However, one can't have everything, can one?"

"What time did he leave?" Elena asked. Leticia's answer matched Darwin's. Nothing there unless he'd rehearsed his wife by telephone, but if a lie was involved, Leticia would probably have refused.

"Do you remember the day when the elephant trampled Mr. Zubarate?" Leo asked.

"Indeed I do," said Leticia. "Darwin was distraught. As

were the Zubarates, I would imagine. There are a good many of them. Too many for the man's income. I highly disapprove of people who breed children they can't afford to raise."

Leo turned pale, thinking of his multiple offspring, no doubt.

"And what are the Zubarates to do now?" Leticia asked. "When their breadwinner is gone? They'll have to go on welfare. I disapprove of welfare. Families should be self-sufficient."

The woman must be a Republican, Elena thought. Real sympathetic to the poor and unfortunate.

"Was Mr. Mandel home the night before the elephant attack?" Leo asked.

"Not after dinner."

Elena gripped her pencil.

"We went to a meeting of the Los Santos Historical Society. Darwin provides material on animal life in the nineteenth century. You'd be amazed to know that there was tall grass in the Los Santos area then and herds of cattle grazing on it. It must have been very pleasant to see greenery that thrived on its own."

Elena had known about the grass but doubted that it had been all that green, certainly not for any sizable portion of the year. "And after the meeting?" she asked.

"We came home, read for an hour, and went to bed."

"Do you remember the night the mountain lion and snake were taken from the zoo?" Leo asked.

"Certainly. Darwin was in Cleveland at a conference of zoo directors. He was so upset when I called to tell him that he took the first plane home. I remember quite clearly because there was a financial penalty for changing the airline tickets, and the hotel would not refund the two days lodging he had prepaid. Nor, because of budgetary problems, was the city paying for the trip." She leaned forward to straighten a crocheted runner on the coffee table.

"However, I have written to Ombudsman at the *Conde Nast Traveler* in the hope that they can assist in getting our money back. A wonderful magazine, incidentally. It allows you to read about exotic places without having to actually visit them and endure the dreadful problems the readers write in about. Are there any other questions I can answer?"

There weren't. Elena thought glumly that Leticia Mandel would make a very credible witness for the defense if the D.A. should ever charge Darwin.

"We'd better cover my neighborhood," said Elena once they had left. "See if we can find anyone who saw the cat being delivered. I don't know how he got past my security system. It's set to keep Frank out, so it should have—"

"We'll do it tomorrow," Leo interrupted. "I have to get home."

She couldn't very well argue with a man whose prime concern was his pregnant wife, but Elena herself couldn't let the case go. Back at headquarters, she retrieved her truck and headed for her neighborhood. Avoiding her own house, which she couldn't bear to look at, she concentrated on houses close enough that the occupants might have seen something.

However, the only unusual occurrence Monday, other than the arrival of so many police cars late at night, was a power outage in the morning. The outage lasted forty minutes and explained why her VCR hadn't recorded the national news; it had interrupted washday in several households, not to mention television viewing, application of heating pads, running of sewing machines, and electric lawn mowing. Otherwise, nothing had been noticed by Elena's elderly neighbors, no strange vehicles or people, no deliveries to Elena's empty house, no security alarms going off.

Had the murderer delivered the cat during the outage? By way of the alley? She hadn't noticed that her clocks were off when she came home for dinner, but then most of them ran on batteries. Had he caused the outage? If the answer was yes, the cat had been in the house while she fixed and ate that steak dinner, while she talked on the telephone to Rafer and Michael, while she dressed for the jam session. A wave of shivering swept over her, and she leaned her head on the steering wheel of her truck until it passed. Then she headed for the Westside, grateful that she had somewhere to go, somewhere that had never housed a mountain lion.

48
..

Sarah's usual practice was to microwave some frozen lump from her freezer or eat out. Feeling unable to face either prospect, Elena had stopped at a supermarket before going to the university apartment house where Sarah lived, then cooked dinner when she got there. She had even planned a meal that didn't include Mexican food, out of deference to Sarah's belief that anything spicy gave her indigestion and caused cancer.

When they had finished their pork chops and vegetables, Elena stared morosely at her empty plate and wondered what she was going to do. On the off-chance that the murderer had another vicious animal and still wished to kill the detective who was chasing him, Elena's continued presence in the apartment put Sarah in danger. On the other hand, she couldn't afford to rent a place while making payments on her own house. That meant she'd have to move back. The thought engendered a shudder.

Nonetheless, she said to her hostess, "Tomorrow I'll be going back to my house, Sarah, and I want to thank you for taking me in." She smiled tremulously. "It was really so kind of you, coming out in the middle of the night and—"

"Nonsense," said Sarah briskly. "You are not returning to a house where your lover's brother was torn apart by a mountain lion."

247

Elena could have done without the explicit description. However, she persisted. "Whoever tried to kill me last night may try again, and I don't want you in the vicinity if—"

"That's not a problem," said Sarah. "I've already alerted Chief Clabb, who has put a guard on the apartment building. The man will check the IDs of everyone who comes and goes."

"No one checked my ID," said Elena.

"That's because I gave them your picture. I thought it would be tactless to remind you that you're in danger."

Trust Sarah to put an act of friendship in terms of tact and good manners. "Well, look," said Elena, "I should get back to my own house; it needs to be mopped up."

"I called a cleaning service and had them send a crew. Now, do you have any other objections to staying with me? I think you should plan to be here at least two months; longer would be better. Perhaps you could rent out your house."

"Fat chance of that," Elena muttered.

"Well, you don't have to tell the potential tenant what happened, but *you* certainly can't live there until you've recovered from the trauma of last night's events. Are the police providing you with psychological support?"

Elena gave her a weak smile. "Beltran thinks I should take a few days off."

"An excellent idea."

"But I'm not going to."

"I don't suppose you'll go to a psychologist either."

Elena shook her head.

"In that case, when you're bothered by things, you can talk to me."

Elena put her head into her hands, embarrassed. She was crying again. She'd made an ass of herself last night with all those tears, and now she was doing it in front of Sarah. Sarah handed her a tissue, and Elena blew her nose.

"Start talking," said Sarah. "That's why you got me into the divorced woman's support group—to talk about problems. Unfortunately, I don't know of any group that supports women who have experienced mountain-lion attacks, so I'll have to do. What's bothering you?"

"What isn't?" said Elena morosely. "Michael's dumped

me, his brother's dead, Leo's turned mean because Concepcion is going to have five babies."

"Five?" Sarah looked horrified.

"She was taking a fertility drug."

"Couldn't they just adopt a baby?"

"She wanted her own."

"Well, she certainly accomplished that. *Five babies*! It's not as if the world needs more children. What else?"

"Well." Elena sniffed and mopped her eyes. "The wrong person may have been arrested in the case."

"That doesn't surprise me," said Sarah. "I suppose it was your lieutenant's idea."

"Yes, actually it was, and of course, he's on the warpath. No, that's not fair. He was nice to me the night of the mountain-lion attack."

"Anything else?" asked Sarah.

"Isn't that enough?" said Elena, mopping up more tears.

"Well, then, we need to take action where it's possible. We can't do anything about Mark, except go to his funeral. As for Michael, I consider his conduct reprehensible. You're well rid of him."

"I liked him."

"I know you did," said Sarah, "but your taste in men is dubious. He was jealous and possessive."

"I know he had his faults, but—"

"And his conduct last night demonstrated the worst of them," said Sarah.

"His brother had just died—horribly."

"I realize that, Elena, but you'll get over Michael. You're just feeling vulnerable. Now, what else was there? Ah, the arrestee. Since I couldn't protect myself last spring, I can hardly help the young woman who's supposed to have shot an arrow into Arnold Mandel, and I can't do anything about your lieutenant, beyond suing him, so that leaves your partner, Leo, and his five offspring."

"Well, you can't do anything about that," said Elena. "She's certainly not going to abort five babies, or even one. They're Catholic. Anyway, she's six months along."

"No doubt he's upset at the prospect of five squalling,

quarreling children in the house, whose upbringing he can't afford."

"Exactly," said Elena, wadding up the tissue and stuffing it away in her pocket.

Sarah looked thoughtful, then walked into the living room.

"What are you going to do?" Elena called after her, beginning to get worried.

"I'm going to see what I can do about your partner's financial problems." Elena listened with astonishment while Sarah talked on the telephone to Dr. Christian Erlingson, chairman of the Psychology Department, Maggie Daguerre's lover, Maggie being the computer guru of the police department. Sarah was suggesting to Dr. Erlingson that someone in his department might like the opportunity to do psychological research on the rearing of quintuplets.

Elena hurried into the living room. "We're not sure it's five."

"One moment, Dr. Erlingson," said Sarah and put her hand over the receiver. "How many are there, then?"

"Well, it might be four," said Elena. "For all I know, it's six."

Sarah nodded, removed her hand from the receiver, and said, "Dr. Erlingson, it might be four or six. We can't be sure at this time. But my thought is that, in return for the opportunity to carry out such an interesting and long-term research project, the Psychology Department would support the children financially, in which case you will undoubtedly want to begin the search for funding." There was a long pause while Sarah listened to what Dr. Erlingson had to say.

Elena thought he was probably telling Sarah that it was a dumb idea, and he didn't want to have anything to do with it, and he didn't have the money, because for Pete's sake, it would cost a fortune to raise five children, or four, or six, whatever the number turned out to be.

"Very good," said Sarah. "I'll expect to hear from you." She hung up. "He's going to start the funding search immediately. And he has a young professor who should be delighted to take on the project. Of course, he doesn't really need to look very far for funding. The university has tons of money. So I think your partner's problem is solved. That ought to cheer him up."

"It certainly cheers me up," said Elena. "How intrusive will the research be?"

"I have no idea," said Sarah. "Probably they'll want to visit the home once a week or something like that."

"Well, that doesn't sound too bad," said Elena.

"Shall we watch the news?" Sarah suggested, glancing at her watch. By then it was ten o'clock, the discussion of Elena's woes having taken some time. When Sarah turned on the television, the news anchor was commenting on the continuing disruption of the local golf tournament by Los Santoans Against Rampant Immorality. The picture showed them parading in front of the country club.

A roving reporter interviewed Father Bratslowski, who said his parishioners had been horrified to receive word of public llama copulation. Ora Mae Spotwood said she disapproved of all copulation, public or private, when the parties were not married. J.J. Audubon Mandel pushed his way through the crowd of spectators, who were waving to the cameras and snickering at the interviews, to say that he considered the two llamas in question married, that they had been a couple for several years. Father Bratslowski said that marriage was a sacrament of the Church, and any arrangement between llamas was obviously of the despicable common-law variety. J.J. suggested sarcastically that the priest might like to perform the rites for his llamas. Father Bratslowski informed J.J. that he had been a Golden Gloves boxer in his youth and was quite prepared to deal with those who denigrated the Church. Ora Mae said that, married or not, such sexual behavior undermined public morals. J.J. had the last televised word when he said he'd like to see her try to train a male llama not to take advantage of the opportunity when the female was in season, and J.J.'s female, unbeknownst to him, must have come into season at the beginning of the tournament.

The TV interviewer, who couldn't get a question in edgewise, walked away, trailed by the camera, and said, "And that's what's been going on here at the country club, Larry, during the big last day of the tournament."

"Never a dull moment in Los Santos," said Sarah, laughing. "You won't see anything like that on the local news in Chicago or New York." She thumbed the remote to turn the set off. "Didn't you find that Mandel man rather peculiar? If his llamas have been banned from the tournament, what was he doing there?"

"Defending them, I suppose," said Elena. She looked at her friend fondly, probably the only friend she had left, and she didn't deserve Sarah, who was so kind and supportive. "Did I ever apologize for arresting you last spring?"

"Yes," Sarah replied, "repeatedly," and handed her another tissue. "Elena, you really must see a psychologist. All this weeping isn't like you. If you don't want to go to someone in the police department, there are several professors at the university who do clinical work."

"No, thanks," said Elena. "I just need a good night's sleep."

"Well, I'd give you a sleeping pill if I had one, but I don't believe in them. Would you care for some hot milk?"

"You're such a good person, Sarah." Elena blinked back more tears.

"Thank you," said Sarah. "How about a nice cup of cocoa?"

"I don't think you have any. In fact, there's hardly anything in your cupboards. I'll have to go shopping again tomorrow."

49
••

At four-thirty in the morning, Elena had awakened in a cold sweat, unable to get back to sleep, the dead hazel eye in the mangled head still staring at her. When she arrived at headquarters at eight, Leo told her that Beltran had assigned him to work with Beto on the labor aspect of the case. "We're going after Alope Randall—her bank accounts, her associates, her movements during the times of the murders and before. If she paid someone to—"

"What about me?" Elena interrupted.

"You're off the case." Elena flushed angrily, but Leo said, "Hey, Beltran doesn't want you to get killed."

Furious, Elena slipped back to her desk without signing in. Beltran might think she was off the case, but she wasn't. Thumbing through her notes, looking for something she had missed, she found her interview with Rosalba Mondragon, who had said that if Elena wanted to know more about J.J. Audubon, she should talk to Bernie Golden. Elena also decided to revisit Arleen Nevinell. After that letter to the editor, Arleen looked like a suspect, she or someone in the Los Santos Animal Protection League. Elena wondered how many people she'd have to check out to follow that lead.

Her telephone rang, and she debated answering. Officially she wasn't here. Curiosity won, and she picked up. "There's a memorial service for Mark at eleven this morning," Sarah told her. "The chapel here at the university."

Elena didn't want to go, to see Michael or endure the stares of people wondering why Mark had been at her house. "I'll be at your office at ten forty-five," she said.

Then she stuffed her notebook into her purse and headed for the reception area. "Carmen," she said as she passed through, "will you report me sick? I don't feel too great."

"I'm not surprised," said Carmen. "Even your hair looks bad."

As she left, Elena smoothed her hands over her head, trying to pat down the loose ends. She hadn't taken much trouble with her braid this morning. But who the hell cared?

She left, climbed into her Ford pickup, and headed for the country club, where she found Bernie Golden sulking in his office because his tournament had been a disaster. "Have you and J.J. been friends a long time?" she asked without preamble.

"About a month too long," said Bernie angrily. "I'll be lucky if I don't get fired." He was staring morosely at a newspaper photo of llamas on his golf course. "I should have known better than to let him talk me into using those evil-tempered creatures. J.J. thinks he's so great with animals. Ha!" Bernie sneered. "When he was sixteen, he had this big snake he claimed would do anything he told it to. J.J. took it out to his grandfather's place—his mom owned the property by then—and the snake ate four chickens while J.J. was saying, 'Now Samson, don't do that.' After the snake got through and the lumps were traveling down its body—I mean to tell you, that was a disgusting sight—J.J. said that it was just doing what it was born to do and animals shouldn't be frustrated by having their true natures subverted. The damn snake ate a cat too; I think it was Darwin's."

How did the chicken story relate to her case? Elena wondered. She'd have to think about it. "You know I'm investigating the murder of his sister. I'd like you to tell me more about him."

"You think J.J. killed her?" Bernie looked astounded. Then he said, a vengeful light in his eye, "What do you want to know?"

"Anything you can tell me. About him. About the family. About his mother."

"O.K." Bernie unwrapped an oatmeal bar. "Want a piece?" he asked. "Good for the cholesterol." Elena declined.

"J.J. was crazy about their mom. I guess he was under the impression that she was crazy about him too, but I doubt it. Cecilia was much more interested in animals than people. She left him her money though, and she had a lot. She came from one of these old New Mexico families—Hispanic on her mother's side. They had land grants along the Rio Grande. Raised cotton, chiles, and pecans."

Bernie took aim and shot his oatmeal wrapper into the wastebasket. "Her father was a horse breeder. His horses ran on tracks all over the country, but especially in New Mexico. He got killed. Really weird thing. He managed to get caught by one of those machines that shake the nuts out of a pecan tree. After his death, Cecilia's mother went into a convent, and Cecilia got everything. This was, of course, long after she married Jacob."

Caught in a pecan shaker? Elena scribbled notes as he talked.

"Then shortly before Cecilia died, she changed her will and left everything to J.J. Snuck a lawyer into the house when the old man was at work. The original will left her husband fifty percent, and the kids were to split the rest. But of course, Jacob had disinherited J.J. by then. I guess that was her way of taking care of her baby. Maybe she did like him. I don't know."

"How did Jacob react?"

"He filed suit to have her declared incompetent and the will set aside. And actually, she may have been. I heard she was out of her mind the last week or so before she died."

"Did they go to court?"

"It never came to that. J.J.—he told me this himself—he said he threatened his father. Said he'd tell the newspapers what his mother died of. He never told *me*, and I don't know why Jacob would have been afraid of people knowing how she died. It was some kind of a fever." Bernie grinned. "Maybe it was a venereal disease. You think?"

Elena knew how Cecilia had died and that, had it become public, Jacob would have been exposed to expensive litigation.

"So anyway, the old man backed off, but he made J.J. promise that he'd never say a word."

Elena paused in her note-taking. So that's why J.J. had been so upset the first day of the tournament—when he accused her of telling his father that he'd been talking about Cecilia's death. Why he'd insisted that she call Jacob. Had the old man threatened to refile the suit contesting the will?

And J.J. had missed the first part of the tournament. Where had he been? Putting a mountain lion in Elena's house? Getting even? Was she supposed to make the call, then die before she could pursue the case any further?

"So J.J. promised," said Bernie. "He wanted the money. But he hated his father more than ever after that. I guess somehow he thought he'd failed his mother by knuckling under. Wish I knew what that was all about."

"How did J.J. feel about his brothers and sisters?"

"He didn't like them either. Especially Arnold and Rosalba. Maybe he did kill them." Bernie looked surprised at his own reasoning. "Doesn't seem like J.J., though. He's always screwing up. Doesn't figure he'd actually manage to kill anyone even if he wanted to."

It occurred to Elena that if J.J. was the killer, he'd only managed to kill two out of his four intended victims. She and Darwin had survived. There was no reason to think he'd have wanted to kill Virgilio Zubarate or Mark Futrell.

"But who knows? Maybe he pulled it off," said Bernie. "You'd think he'd go after his father if he was going to kill anyone."

"Why did he hate his brother and sister?"

"Because they were his father's favorites. He was jealous. And because he thought they had gone against everything his mother stood for—all that loving and protecting animals stuff."

"How did he feel about Darwin?"

Bernie shrugged. "I don't know. Maybe he liked Darwin. Mostly J.J. focused on himself. But Darwin had him painting animal pictures for the zoo. J.J. probably needed the money. He's screwed up a lot of stuff. His father's horse-breeding operation for one. Then he evidently didn't pay enough attention to the chile and cotton fields. Insects got in and ruined the crops. After that, all the other growers in the valley wouldn't talk to him. His pecan groves are getting old, production's off, and he hasn't planted new trees."

"What happened with the horses?"

"Two things. In the first place, J.J. made some bad breeding decisions. Didn't pay enough attention to blood-lines. Went with his intuition. So his horses weren't as good. Then the Tiguas opened their casino out on the reservation, and attendance fell off at the track, so the local market for horses isn't as good anymore. Result—he's losing money."

"So he went into llamas?"

"Right. He had his heart set on this llama venture turning into a moneymaker, but after the way they performed here at the club, that's never going to happen. His life hasn't been what you'd call a big success even if his mama did leave him everything she'd inherited. Is any of that helpful?"

"Yes," said Elena. He'd given her a lot to think about. J.J. might well be the person with the strongest motive for murder after all. Good old-fashioned hatred and jealousy. Especially because of the conspiracy of silence about his mother's death and the fact that he'd acquiesced to it. Maybe he even hoped to inherit from Jacob when there were no other heirs left.

But J.J. came off as such a wimp, it was hard to believe that he'd killed four people. She thought about the mountain lion in her house. Would J.J. have the nerve to kidnap a mountain lion from his brother's zoo, keep the lion a week or so, then sneak it into her house? *She* wouldn't have that kind of nerve.

50
##

Wednesday, April 12, 11:30 A.M.

As Elena left the art deco chapel at Herbert Hobart University after the memorial service for Mark Futrell, it occurred to her that this was the third such service she had attended in less than a year. There had been the memorial for Angus McGlenlevie, Sarah's ex-husband, after bones had been found in his bathtub; the service for Analee Ribbon, the student felled by the Charleston Dancer statue in the library; and now Mark, killed by a mountain lion in Elena's bedroom.

As with any public gathering led by the university president, Dr. Sunnydale, the ceremony had had its peculiarities. He obviously had no idea who Mark Futrell was and had delivered the eulogy from notes given to him by Vice-President for Academic Affairs Harley Stanley. Therefore, when Dr. Sunnydale mentioned "the untimely death of our young physical education professor, killed in an attack by a—" he had stopped speaking, aghast, reread his notes, and exclaimed, "Mountain lion?"

He then turned to the vice-president and said, "There must be some mistake. Am I to understand that there are lions running loose in the Franklin Mountains? Perhaps upon our campus? Was this poor fellow attacked on his way to the gymnasium? Have our police taken measures to protect the students? This is terrible!"

The panic igniting in the evangelistic university president

was doused when Harley Stanley murmured, "Actually, sir, he was in a lady's bedroom."

Dr. Sunnydale, looking even more astonished, asked, "And she kept a lion in her boudoir?"

At that point Elena's face was burning. Once Dr. Sunnydale stumbled to the end of his remarks, various faculty members from the Phys Ed Department, all young and fit and looking extremely chastened, had reminisced about Mark's talents as a golfer—Elena wondered whether Mark had been at the tournament where the llamas misbehaved—and as a bicycle-racer, recalling that he had come in third in the race last fall on the High Road to Taos. Elena remembered that, having met Michael for the first time while she was guarding a murder suspect who had participated in the race. One professor said, if you had to die young, the best place to do it was in a pretty lady's bedroom. At that point, Sarah grabbed Elena's wrist to keep her from stalking out.

When it was over, Sarah asked if Elena had seen anyone suspicious there, anyone who might be guilty of "murder by predator." "No," Elena told her, "but I'm beginning to think I know who's doing this stuff. Maybe I'll close the case this afternoon."

"Good," said Sarah. "Then you can put it behind you. Mark's death was not, after all, your fault."

"Tell that to Michael," said Elena bitterly. She'd stopped feeling hurt and was now furious with her former lover. She and Sarah were in the Sacred Vestibule outside the chapel where waiters offered mimosas, a mixture of orange juice and champagne, or Bloody Marys, which the university evidently considered proper for a cocktail party held before high noon. Since she wasn't really on duty—officially she was home sick—Elena went for the champagne and orange juice, thinking that she might as well enjoy herself. She bolted half the glass, sneezed because she'd got champagne bubbles up her nose, and popped into her mouth a piece of melba toast plastered with an exotic egg-salad mixture. "Might as well live it up while we're here," she murmured to Sarah.

"I suppose," Sarah replied, "although I was planning to begin a journal article this afternoon, and I've never found that alcohol improves my prose style."

"Fine," said Elena. "I'll take your drink." When she reached for Sarah's Bloody Mary, Sarah snatched it away.

"Elena, alcohol is a depressant. I don't think that's what you need."

"I'm not depressed. I'm mad."

"Could I have a word with you, Elena?"

She turned her head, shocked because it was Michael who had spoken. "I don't see that there's much else to say, Michael," she replied. "You have my condolences over the death of your brother, and I intend to get his killer, but it was *not* me." She looked him straight in the eye.

Michael flushed uncomfortably. "I know I did you an injustice the other night, but I was upset. Elena, I—"

"I was upset too, Michael. I'm the one who faced a mountain lion under my dining room table and then discovered a body that I thought was *you*. So why don't we just—"

"I want to apologize," said Michael. "I've found out what Mark was doing at your house."

"Well, that's more than I know. Did you find out how he got in?"

Michael nodded miserably. "He took my key and had a copy made."

"That's what I told you. So what was he doing there? And don't tell me he thought I was crazy about him. I didn't like him. I made it perfectly clear. I'm sorry, Michael. I know he was your brother, but—"

"Elena, you'd better let me tell you what happened."

"I'd be interested to hear this too," said Sarah. "After your abominable conduct the other night, I can't imagine—"

Michael snapped, "This is a private conversation."

"Anything you have to say to me, you can say in front of Sarah," said Elena.

He looked at both of them resentfully. "Very well. It seems that he had a bet with his colleagues in the Physical Education Department."

"What kind of bet?"

"That he could take you away from me."

"I see," said Elena angrily. "A bet. Jock behavior? Is that it? And every time I told you he was bothering me, you just ignored it because 'jock behavior' is acceptable among males?"

"Well, how was I to know what he was up to?"

"Because I *told* you!" Elena took a deep breath to get her anger in check. "You've known him all your life. He's never done anything like that before?" Michael looked sulky, and she snapped, "Well, look at it this way, Michael. He won the bet. You're probably his heir, so you can collect from his colleagues."

"Really, Elena, they're feeling terrible about this. They feel responsible for his death."

"So they should," said Sarah. "Isn't that just like a bunch of men in a locker room. Making bets about women. Disgusting. My sympathies on your brother's death, Dr. Futrell. Come along, Elena."

"Wait a minute," said Michael. "Since we know what happened, and I've apologized, couldn't we—I mean—I'd like to think maybe we could—"

"If you mean we should continue dating, I don't think so," said Elena. She'd had plenty of time to go over the situation in her mind, and every time she remembered the things Michael had said to her, she became angrier. It might not be Michael's fault that his brother had been unkind and unprincipled, but Michael had been quite willing to lay all the blame at her door, and that at a time when they should have been consoling each other, not indulging in recriminations.

She walked off with Sarah, who said, "You haven't had too much alcohol, have you? Why don't you go back to the apartment and take a nap?"

"I'm going to headquarters," said Elena.

"But you've been drinking, Elena."

"Don't worry, Mama," said Elena dryly. "The fit of fury I just experienced burned off all the alcohol."

51

Elena slipped into the department unnoticed. Except for Leo, the other detectives were on the street or having lunch. "How's your investigation of the garment-industry angle going?" she asked. "You and Beto find anything?"

"We've been going over Alope Randall's bank accounts. If she paid anyone to steal the animals and set up those attacks, it doesn't show in her accounts. That's a woman who spends very little, although she's got it to spend."

"I suppose someone could have done it for the principle of the thing, to wreck Los Santos Apparel and then screw up the investigation and cover his ass," said Elena, although she didn't believe it.

"Or for hatred. Like Angela Lechuga," said Leo. "It's gonna be hell to find out who."

As it would be if she went after the Los Santos Animal Protection League, Elena thought. "One of the things I did this morning was talk to a guy at the country club named Bernie Golden. He's a long-time friend of J.J. Mandel."

"You still following that trail?" Leo shook his head. "Beltran—"

"No, listen to me," she interrupted. "It was an interesting conversation. J.J. hates the whole family. I mean he *really* hates them. Especially his father. The only person he loved was his mother." Elena went on to tell Leo the story of

Cecilia's death, the cover-up, the fact that Jacob was going to contest the will but had to back off because J.J. blackmailed him.

Leo frowned. "Do you make this J.J. as someone who'd go around killing people?"

"It took guts to stand up to Jacob about the will, but then I suppose J.J. was desperate. He needed that money his mother left him, and he blamed his father for her death. Although after a certain point, there's nothing you can do about rabies."

"Jeez. Imagine dying of *that*!"

Elena nodded. "You've got to admit, using animals to kill people is a twisted thing to do. It's not the kind of murder you'd expect of labor advocates or seamstresses. But maybe, just maybe, an animal activist would think it was poetic justice, a perfect revenge for the cover-up of his mother's death, which J.J. probably saw as her martyrdom to the cause."

"What are you talking about?" Leo asked dubiously.

"Death by predator," she replied. "It's a sort of reverse hunting. A sick game, but—"

"I'll say," Leo agreed. "That's crazy."

"Maybe *he's* crazy. Who knows what's in his head? He *could* be the one, Leo. Anyway, I want to go out there this afternoon. Can you break free and go with me?" She tapped a finger nervously on her desk, not looking at Leo, and admitted, "I don't want to go alone. For all I know he's got another mountain lion stashed out there."

Leo, who had been leaning against the partition that separated his cubicle from the next one on Homicide Row, straightened and began to tap dance.

"Oh, come on, Leo," Elena pleaded. "This is no time to practice your routines."

"I'm thinking," he replied and went dancing off down the aisle, then came tapping back. "O.K.," he said. "I'll go. But we gotta tell Manny what we're doing."

"What if he says no?" Elena complained. "This needs to be followed up."

"If he says no, we drop it."

Elena didn't buy that. If Manny said no, she'd have to go

by herself, no matter how many wild animals J.J. might have out on that ranch. Hell, he might sic a llama on her. Could llama bile cause injuries? It sure had done a job on her jacket. Sarah had given her a button that said Computerize the World to put over the bleached spot. Although Elena didn't really hold with the sentiment, she didn't want to buy a new jacket or wear one with a llama-bile stain.

In five minutes Leo had joined her in the parking lot. "We're cleared, but Manny's not too happy about it."

They checked out an unmarked car and headed toward the interstate to circle the mountain and cut over to the back roads that would take them to J.J.'s ranch. A mile or two past the Schuster exit, when they were even with the towering chimneys of the smelter, a message came over the police radio band: "Detective Leo Weizell, your wife's gone into labor."

"Oh, my God," said Leo. "It's too early." He shot off onto Executive Center and turned back toward town. Elena wanted to protest, but of course, she couldn't. "Now listen," he said, "don't go out there without me. O.K.?"

She nodded, but didn't promise. Slapping the light on the roof, hitting the siren, Leo tore up North Mesa, then through Kern Place and across the mountain.

"You want me to go to the hospital with you?" Elena asked.

"No. Why don't you go home and get some sleep? You look awful."

"Thanks a lot," she replied.

After that they fell silent until he pulled into the police lot. "We'll visit Mandel as soon as I get free," he promised, heading for his car.

Elena trudged dispiritedly back to her desk, where she found a message from Sarah saying that the Psychology Department had arranged full support for the children Leo and Concepcion were going to have. But if Concepcion delivered this early, not all of the children would survive, maybe not any. Elena had been waiting to tell Leo the good news until she was sure the project would be funded; now she was glad she hadn't said anything.

The telephone interrupted her thoughts, and the caller gave her a surprise when she answered.

"Hi. This is Jo Priego. Guess where I am?"

Elena had no idea.

"I'm at Ceci's *abuelo's* house. An' guess who's sittin' in his lap?" Jo giggled.

Good lord! Surely, Jacob hadn't taken up with his son's mistress.

Jo squelched that bizarre idea by saying, "The blood tests came through, an' we got invited to lunch. They're crazy about each other." Jo sounded pathetically happy. "Ceci dumped her milk on his carpet, an' he laughed. I nearly fainted. Then she climbed up in his lap, an' he gave her a kiss. She's callin' him Granpa. How about that?"

"I'm glad for you, Jo," said Elena, hoping the new development meant that Jacob would take care of them.

"Yeah, me too," said Jo, sniffling. "He's been real sweet. Only yelled at me once. Anyway, I gotta get back, but I wanted to tell someone, an' I thought of you."

That was pretty sad, Elena decided after she'd hung up, when the only person you had to call about good news was a police detective you'd met once. Jo Priego needed some family. Maybe she'd found it.

Elena stared at her blank computer screen, thinking about J.J., about the possibility that he'd killed his own brother with a bow and arrow, that he'd tried to have Darwin trampled by an elephant, that he'd locked Rosalba in a bathroom with a rattlesnake, and finally that he'd been perfectly willing to let Leopold, the hungry mountain lion, tear Elena into bits to keep her from pursuing him—if he was the murderer, if he was the man who was loosing hunters on unsuspecting victims. She had to know one way or the other. Before he took another shot at Darwin. Or killed Jacob. Or found out that two-year-old Cecilia Priego had just joined the Mandel family. Especially before he, or whoever it was, targeted the child.

Elena left a note on Leo's desk telling him that she'd decided to go to the llama ranch after all. Manny already thought she was on her way, so she didn't have to tell him and get into an argument. Although there wasn't another detective free to go with her, she couldn't afford to wait. Accordingly, she went out to the lot, climbed into her own pickup, and

headed for the interstate again. It would be two-thirty or so
before she got to J.J.'s, and the sky was already overcast and
gloomy. Unusual for a place that called itself sun city and
claimed to have 365 days of sunshine every year.

She took a farm road through Canutillo toward Anthony,
bouncing mentally between the thought that she was a fool to
go by herself and the thought that if J.J. was the murderer, he
might even now be out trying to kill Darwin or his father,
thinking that he'd inherit everything because there wouldn't
be anyone left. It was sad. Four children, and Jacob had only
two left, one of whom he'd no longer acknowledge. Well,
now there was Ceci, his only grandchild.

Along the river the land was flat with mountains and mesas
rising in the distance. Later in the year the fields would be
green with chiles, later than that with white cotton bolls. The
pecan groves would flower, leaf out, and become heavy with
nuts, marching in neat rows with bare ground between each
tree. Fields would be flooded when the sluice gates were
opened in the irrigation canals. Had the old Spaniards farmed
that way in the valley, using irrigation? Chimayo and the
other villages in the Sangre de Cristos had *acequias* that were
old, old. And men were still elected by the communities to
police the irrigation ditches and see that they were cleaned
out.

She wondered what J.J.'s Hispanic ancestors on his mother's side would have thought of llamas as a cash crop. Not
much, she imagined. Her relatives in Chimayo and Truchas
would laugh at the idea of raising South American pack
animals to pull golf carts.

J.J. seemed to screw everything up. Even murder—if he
was the murderer. She turned left off the two-lane country
highway onto a dirt road that led toward his ranch, glancing
up at the sky. If it rained, the road would turn to mud. Good
thing she'd brought her truck, which had four-wheel drive.

As she drove into the large dirt clearing outside the walls
of the hacienda, she saw something that she hadn't seen the
last time she was here, something that turned her blood cold.
A brown pickup truck. After turning off her engine, she
climbed down and walked over to look. The truck had a white
logo that said "Mandel Farms." She and Leo had looked at

Alope Randall's brown pickup with "Border Legal Clinic" printed on the side and suspected her of murder. But this was the truck that had been in Arnold's driveway the first time Cyclops Security drove by. Angela Lechuga in Alope's truck would have been there later, after Arnold was dead, just as Alope and Angela had said.

Elena walked up to the gates of the hacienda, pushed one open, and went through the pretty courtyard, thinking the bastard had everything—this beautiful house, all kinds of rich land, a mother who had loved him enough to leave it to him, and still he hadn't been satisfied.

She slid her hand into the sling bag on her right shoulder and closed her fingers around her 9-millimeter handgun. If she had to, she'd shoot J.J. He deserved it. Putting that mountain lion in her house. A shiver ran up her spine when she thought about it. One way or another, she'd get him. She took a deep breath, letting the rage seep away. Then she lifted her left hand, with the right one still in her handbag, and banged the knocker on the carved doors.

52

Before Elena could knock a second time, J.J. himself opened the door and gave her a friendly smile, saying, "Come in, Detective. How nice of you to call. Have you come to say you've found out who murdered my brother and sister?"

"And Mr. Zubarate," she added. "And Mark Futrell."

"Futrell?"

"He was the man who was killed in my house by the mountain lion."

"Ah. How terrible for you, Detective. Do you think these killings are connected? Was Mr. Futrell a close friend?"

"No," said Elena. "He was uninvited." They were walking down the hall toward the great room. "Who do you think killed them, Mr. Mandel?"

"I thought we'd agreed that you'd call me J.J.," he said pleasantly. "I couldn't imagine. Darwin would probably be better able to answer your question than I. I understand that the mountain lion and snake came from his zoo."

"So they did," said Elena. "But Darwin can account for his time on the night when the animals were abducted. Also for the day or evening when someone put the cat in my house."

"I see. Well, perhaps someone else from the zoo," said J.J. "That seems to be the connection, doesn't it?"

"I'd have said the Mandel family was the connection, and there are only three of you left." She gave him a searching

268

look. "It's not likely that your father's responsible, since he's pretty much immobilized by the stroke. And he'd be unlikely to kill the son who was running the company for him."

"Ah, yes, the company," said J.J.

Elena thought she caught a note of bitterness in that echo. "And we know it's not Darwin, because his time is accounted for. That leaves you, J.J."

"Fortunately for me, I'm prepared to stave off accusations." He pulled a pistol from under his *guayabera*.

"A gun?" Elena asked, surprised but unworried since her own gun in the handbag was pointed at him. "I wouldn't have thought that was your style. You're a much more imaginative killer than that, J.J. And then everyone knows I've come here to talk to you. It'll be kind of hard to get out of this one."

"Actually, I'm not planning to shoot you, Detective. I do have more imaginative plans. And it won't matter that people know you've come here, because you'll meet with an accident in my house while I'm away."

"I see," said Elena. "What kind of accident?"

"An accident involving an animal, of course."

"Well, before you feed me to one of them, maybe you wouldn't mind satisfying my curiosity, telling me why you did all these things. Do you think your father is going to leave Los Santos Apparel to you once the others are dead?"

"I doubt it," said J.J. "And it wouldn't matter if he did. You truly don't understand my motivation, do you, Detective Jarvis?" He looked disappointed. "However, I am willing to enlighten you. I almost wish you could survive this visit to explain my actions to others."

"Explain what?"

"It's so simple." J.J. smiled. "I did it for Mother. She's so disappointed in all of them. Not one of her children has been true to her principles—except me. Arnold had to die because he's an animal killer. I thought it a nice touch to end his life with a bow." Elena was tempted to shoot J.J. on the spot, but curiosity got the better of her.

"Did you know that Arnold murdered six deer with his bow? Six lovely, graceful creatures who might have lived happily to the end of their lives if Arnold hadn't stalked them. So I stalked him." J.J. smiled, each smile less twinkly, more cold. "He laughed when I took his bow off the wall. Reminded me that Grandfather always said I couldn't hit an elephant at six yards. But Arnold miscalculated. I'd practiced. And I think I proved Grandfather wrong. I hit a much smaller target at six yards—my brother. Right in the heart. And then that young woman, Arnold's idea of human game, came along and did me one better by loosing the falcon on him. A lovely touch. Ahab must have been delighted. Falcons love eyes, you know. I'd have done it myself, but I had to get out before the security patrol came back."

"Oh, they saw you."

"They may have seen my truck. They didn't see me."

"And what did Rosalba do?" asked Elena, thinking she knew, thinking J.J. was crazy, killing people for the way they treated animals.

"Rosalba was responsible for many, many animal deaths with her furs and her boots and her leather. She didn't need to cause the deaths of God's creatures so that she could adorn her person. But she did. Did you notice that she wore furs to my opening? Flaunted them in my face, knowing how I felt. Her death was appropriate too. Rosalba once had a rattlesnake belt. She showed it off to me. Shook the rattles at me. She said the only good rattlesnake was one you ate or wore. My sister actually ordered and ate rattlesnake at a restaurant in Washington, D.C. I was appalled. So that lovely albino rattlesnake got revenge for its whole species."

"And Darwin? Darwin's not cruel to animals."

"Of course he is," snapped J.J. "Do you think incarcerating a wild animal in a zoo is the action of a kind man? Making spectacles of creatures who are yearning to be free? Don't you realize that Darwin treated Pansy, a magnificent animal, as if she were some sort of lap-dog. Pansy would have been delighted to trample him. It's just unfortunate that he wasn't there that morning."

"You're saying Pansy enjoyed being given amphetamines?"

"I rather imagine she did," said J.J., eyes twinkling again. "People do. And she loved the fruit they came in. She did her pathetic little tricks for me when I threw her pears and apples."

Elena shook her head. "It was a cruel thing to do, J.J. You

didn't see her flapping her ears, flinging trees, lumbering around that enclosure."

J.J. went pale. "It wasn't cruel. I gave her a moment of great satisfaction. The venting of rage is healthy," he insisted. "I'm a case in point. I'm enjoying catharsis every time I avenge my mother and all the animals who are so cruelly treated by humans. You can be sure that Pansy enjoyed trampling that zoo keeper more than he enjoyed being trampled." J.J. was speaking calmly again, smiling.

"I think Mother would have been proud, don't you? Of course, I couldn't free Pansy. There was nowhere for her to go. But I would have come back for White Fang, if you hadn't returned him to the zoo. That was cruel, Detective. You shouldn't have done that.

"And I would have returned to free Leopold," J. J. went on. "He could have been loose in the Franklins right now if you hadn't shot him. That wasn't supposed to happen. That was worse than Leopold pouncing on that man instead of you. Not that Leopold would have cared. No doubt Mr. Futrell tasted as good to him as you would have." J.J. sighed and added, "At least, Leopold died happy. Mother would like that."

"I think she'd be appalled," said Elena, "that one of her children would try to kill the other three."

"Oh no, that wouldn't have bothered Mother. She didn't really care that much about us. Mother loved animals, and I've made the animals happy."

"The mountain lion is dead," said Elena.

"But soon you'll be dead, and Leopold will be avenged." He smiled. "Mother will finally love me. As much as she should have loved me when I was a child."

Elena's hand was in her purse on the gun. All she had to do was pull the trigger, shoot through the purse, and J.J. was history. He might shoot at the same time, but he'd probably miss. Perhaps he realized that. He was backing away.

"How did you get the rattlesnake and the mountain lion out of the zoo?" she asked.

He laughed. "I had copies of Darwin's keys. With the keys it was easy—for someone like me who knows how to handle animals."

"Where did you get the tranquilizer for the cat?" She was watching him closely to see what his next move would be.

"Across the border. I have contacts. I speak Spanish. You'd never have traced me through the tranquilizers. Or the amphetamines."

He looked so pleased with himself that Elena was again tempted to shoot him. After all, he was holding a gun on her. He'd said he was going to kill her. She'd be exonerated by the grand jury.

"In a way—" began J.J. thoughtfully. He was reaching behind him. Elena couldn't see exactly what he was up to. "—in a way it's a blessing Pansy didn't get Darwin. The elephant attack, coupled with the missing snake and cat, caused him no end of anxiety. I was quite pleased about that. For a while, I thought he might be indicted for my actions. Wouldn't that have been ironic?"

Elena realized that he was fiddling, one-handed, with the lock on a large cage, opening the door.

"You have a security system in your house, Detective. I had to sabotage the lines into your neighborhood to circumvent it before I could bring Leopold in. Well, I have one in my house that doesn't depend on electricity. Nature's security system."

Elena watched in horror as a great boa constrictor began to slither out of the cage. "This is Samson," said J.J. He pulled a perfume atomizer from his pocket and, stepping forward, sprayed it at her. She felt the droplets hit her arm and neck, and she moved backward nervously.

"*Eau de Lapin,*" explained J.J. "You'll notice that Samson is heading toward you. He thinks you're a big, tasty rabbit. And believe me, Detective, if you have a gun clutched in that purse, it would take a very special shot to kill Samson. And you, unfortunately, don't know where to put such a shot. I rather imagine he'll get you before you can do anything about it.

"And of course, I'm standing here with a gun as well, although I'd prefer not to use it. I want it to look as if you entered my unlocked house while I was gone and fell victim to my security system."

"You'll never get away with this, J.J.," she retorted, casting an uneasy eye at the snake, who was writhing in her direction at a leisurely pace. She longed to wipe the rabbit essence off her chin and clothing but didn't dare take her attention off the snake and J.J.

"Perhaps not," he replied, "but as I said, it really doesn't matter as long as I can get Darwin. Samson here will provide me with the time. Since I failed with Pansy, I've decided to go to the other extreme. I have a lovely little bee. One sting, and Darwin will die of anaphylactic shock. Because, you see, I'll be there to make sure that he doesn't get his medication." J.J. glowed with pleasure. "My brother is allergic to bees, so he'll die. Very quickly. While I'm watching."

"So will you," said Elena. "Of a lethal injection. You can't kill six people and not expect to get the death penalty."

"A death penalty has already been imposed on me, Detective." With his free hand he reached up and pulled off his luxuriant hair, revealing a completely bald head. Without the expensive wig, he was even balder than his brothers. "I'm dying of cancer, Detective. They've given me chemotherapy—that's obvious—but it's failed. Catharsis through murder has improved my mental health, but nothing, it seems, can be done for my body."

Jesus, thought Elena. The snake was taking its time but still heading in her direction. One bullet for J.J. and the rest for the snake. Would that do it? Her gun hand was starting to sweat.

"A lovely little bee," J.J. crooned. "Tiny but lethal. Poor Darwin. He'll be the last game I'll have time to hunt. But will live long enough to explain my revenge to my father."

"What do you mean?" asked Elena.

"He never liked me. And then he threw me out. He said I was no longer his son, but losing one son didn't matter to him because he had three other children. Now he'll have none. Not even me. Again I'm exacting a suitable revenge, making the punishment fit the crime, as the Lord High Executioner said in the *Mikado*." He hummed a few bars. "Maybe my father will have another stroke when I tell him. Mother will be delighted. He let her die, you know."

"She had rabies."

"I didn't tell you that," he hissed, slipping back into the lifelong fear of his father. He took a deep breath, waggled his gun playfully, then continued his explanation. "He wouldn't even send her to the hospital. He wouldn't let anyone know that she had died freeing those poor dogs. Then he wanted to overturn her will. When she'd finally done something to show her love for me, he wanted to nullify it.

"But I'll win in the end, Detective. When I get through with my father, he'll have nothing left. Nothing but his own miserable life. I'd kill him too, but I don't think he's afraid to die. So I'll let him live. In misery. I'm hoping for a stroke that will paralyze him on the other side. Leaving him alive but trapped in a dead body.

"And what about you, Detective? Are you afraid of death? Samson here will crush the life out of you." He glanced fondly at the snake. "Too bad you insisted on investigating the family instead of the garment workers. Even when that woman was arrested for Arnold's death, it wasn't good enough for you. You had to keep nosing around. Too bad, too bad. Now you have to die as well."

God, she hoped J.J. was wrong in thinking you couldn't put a bullet in Samson that would stop him.

"I'm very fond of Samson," said J.J. "I shall enjoy watching him crush you because I know he'll be taking so much pleasure in it."

Sadistic bastard, Elena thought and raised her purse. No time for any more revelations from J.J.; the snake was too close. She tensed her trigger finger, and there was an earsplitting blast.

53
:.

The blast wasn't from Elena's gun, or from J.J.'s, because the snake had been blown in two. Only a shotgun could cut a snake that size in half, or so Elena reasoned. "Don't do it," she said when J.J. tried to pick up the pistol he'd dropped. She leveled hers at him in a two-handed grip, then glanced to the side toward the sound of breaking glass. Having shot the snake through the window, Leo was now using the shotgun to break out the rest of the glass so that he could climb in.

"I thought I told you not to come out here without me," he grumbled.

"I thought Concepcion had gone into labor," she retorted.

"Turned out to be indigestion." Leo climbed through the long window.

Moving toward J.J., Elena kicked his gun away. "Turn around," she ordered.

"You've killed Samson," said J.J. Tears were running down his face.

"Hold your hands in back of you."

"Why?" he sniffled.

"Because I'm going to handcuff you."

"I'll do it," said Leo, laying down the shotgun.

"You've ruined everything," J.J. cried. "Now I won't get another chance at Darwin, or to confront my father."

Leo cuffed him.

"It was going to be the high point of my life," J.J. whimpered.

"Oh, shut up," said Leo and shoved him toward the door.

"To please Mother. To make her proud of me."

"We'll have to leave your truck here and go back in the unmarked," said Leo. "Did he confess?"

"Well, he wouldn't have thought of it as a confession. More like bragging," said Elena. "But evidently he killed his brother and sister because they were unkind to animals. He didn't mention hating Arnold and Rosalba, but I'm sure that had something to do with it. And as he said, he wanted to please his mother, not to mention spiting his father."

"I thought his mother was dead."

"She is."

Hustling J.J. through the courtyard, Leo looked back to exchange a glance with Elena. "I sure hope they don't let him get away with an insanity plea."

"I am not insane," said J.J. with dignity. "Could you turn off the sprinklers, please? I don't want the courtyard over-watered."

They ignored him. "He wanted to get even with Jacob. Leave him without any heirs," Elena concluded.

"Or leave himself as the only heir," said Leo, putting his hand on J.J.'s head and pushing him into the back seat of the police car.

"That wasn't my intention at all," said J.J. "I'm not a money grubber like the rest of them."

Leo slammed the door. "Like I believe that," he retorted.

"According to him," Elena said, "he's dying of cancer."

"Good. Save the state the cost of a trial," said Leo.

"You're a heartless person," said J.J. from the back seat. "Cancer is not a pleasant death."

Leo started the car. "You think being squashed by an elephant is? Or any of the other stuff you did? You've killed four people."

"I guess he wanted to take everyone with him before he went," said Elena. "Including me. You were supposed to think I walked into J.J.'s house when he was away and the snake got me." She fastened her seat belt and turned to their prisoner. "Of course you forgot Arnold's daughter, J.J."

"Arnold doesn't have a child. There are no grandchildren," said J.J. "No heirs."

"Except Ceci, Arnold's daughter by his mistress."

"Ceci?" He'd turned pale.

"Cecilia. Arnold named her after your mother."

"You're lying!" cried J.J.

"Just before I left headquarters, Ceci's mother called to say her daughter was sitting on Jacob's lap."

"That's a lie!" J.J. leaned forward, face flushed and desperate. "None of us got to sit on his lap."

"Guess he's mellowed," said Elena. "Anyway, you failed, J.J. Your father's got a son and a granddaughter."

J.J. began to sob.

"Knock it off," snapped Leo. Then he turned to Elena and said, "How could you just stand there with that monster snake heading in your direction?"

"I guess I trusted that you'd come along and blow it away," said Elena, grinning. She could smile now; then she'd been close to panic.

"Yeah, right," said Leo. "You owe me big, Jarvis." They left the estate road and turned right on the two-lane highway.

"No," said Elena. "You owe me, because I've got financing for all those children you're going to have."

"What's that supposed to mean?"

"Well, if you'll let a psychology professor from H.H.U. observe Concepcion and the children every so often, the university will support them. Sarah called me this noon to tell me."

"You're kidding." Leo looked stunned. "They're going to pay for everything?"

"That's what they say."

"How did you manage that?"

"I need to blow my nose," said J.J.

"Wipe it on your sleeve," Leo advised. "If you'd stop crying, you wouldn't have that problem."

"I told Sarah, and she fixed it," said Elena.

"Good old Sarah. I always knew she didn't kill Angus McGlenlevie."

"Oh, sure you did," said Elena.

"Maybe we ought to stop by the university on our way to

the jail and get a written contract before they change their minds," said Leo. "What do you think, babe?"

"I think calling me 'babe' constitutes sexual harassment."

"Picky, picky," said Leo exuberantly.

"Also I think you're on shift, even if I'm not, and we're bringing in a murderer."

"So J.J.," said Leo, "you're really the guy who drugged the elephant and stole those animals from the zoo to kill your sister and make a try at Elena?"

"Certainly," said J.J., sniffling. "I'm very good with animals. Much better than my brother. I should think that's obvious; look at the disarray the zoo is in."

"Well, you're the one who caused it, J.J.," said Elena.

"I believe I'd prefer to be called Audubon Mandel," he said stiffly. "I think J.J. lacks the dignity due a man who has successfully killed four people by using natural predators. How many people can say that they've accomplished that feat?"

"Not many," muttered Elena. "But the predator in this case is you."